CW01627996

Wilting Violets

THE SONS OF TEMPLAR MC - NEW MEXICO

BOOK TWO

ANNE MALCOM

Cover: TRC Designs
Editing: Kim BookJunkie
Proofreading: All Encompassing Books

For all the dreamers.

Prologue

ELDEN

MY BROTHER WAS HOLDING a gun to my head.

I'd expected this to happen from the second I laid eyes on her.

The second I touched her.

Tasted her.

She tasted like perfection and my eventual demise.

I knew that this was a ticking time bomb. That *we* were a ticking time bomb. I also knew that it was a matter of *when* he found out I was fucking his stepdaughter. Not if.

I could've avoided this.

If I'd been strong enough to leave her alone. To say no to her. To get the fuck out of this club and as far away from her as I could've.

But that had been beyond my control.

Everything to do with Violet was beyond my control.

And on some level, I'd been willing to die for her. If it was a choice between a bullet and never knowing what it felt like to be inside of her, I'd choose the bullet.

Every fucking day.

"I should blow your brains out right here, right now," Swiss seethed.

I didn't argue with him, though I did disagree.

Violently.

I knew my brother was hanging by a thread right now and that there was a reason no one had stepped forward to try to do anything. Even though he was a husband and a father, he was still fucked-up, impulsive and unpredictable when he was mad. He was still very fucking dangerous.

And he'd just found out I'd been involved with his step-daughter for years.

So, he was mad.

Therefore, his piece was pointed in my face.

"There was a time in my life when I probably wouldn't have fought you," I told him. "A time when I might've just let what happened happen. When I didn't care much if I was living or dying. Because I didn't have anything to live for."

I didn't stare at him. Nor the barrel of the gun he was pointing in my face.

No, I stared at the indigo eyes of the woman I loved. The mother of my child, tears streaming down her face.

"Now I've got somethin' to live for," I said, not to Swiss but to her. "I've got everything to live for. Not gonna argue with you that this got fucked-up. That I made some bad fuckin' choices in the midst of this. But you're never gonna get me to wish away what I did. Because if I did, I wouldn't be standin' right here."

I kept my eyes on her as I tensed, waiting. I wouldn't go down without a fight. Fuck no. But if he was that far gone and was going to pull the trigger, she was going to be the last thing I saw before I left this world.

CHAPTER
One

TWO YEARS EARLIER

VIOLET

I WAS SITTING on a roof with a bottle of Jack Daniels in my left hand, a joint in my right.

The roof of an outlaw biker compound, it's important to point out.

It was three in the morning.

The witching hour… when the veil between worlds was thin, when demons were more capable of sinking their talons into you, scorching your skin right to the bone… If you believed in such things.

I did, as it happened, believe in such things.

I was somewhat of a cliché for my generation. I liked crystals, astrology—I was a Scorpio rising, Sun in Sagittarius—and loved to read spicy fantasy novels with a strong female lead. I believed in magic, angels, demons, sprites and the Fae.

But my demons were not of the metaphysical variety. They

didn't come from the underworld or from mystical realms either. They were much too common, much more cliché. Uninteresting. Which made everything worse. If I was going to be battling demons, at least life could make them interesting, worthy of a chapter in my autobiography.

Violet Edwards, demon killer… It had a nice ring to it.

As opposed to Violet Edwards, just another fucked-up, rich kid with daddy issues.

I didn't normally hang out in outlaw biker compounds. Nor did I drink Jack Daniels or any other dark kind of whisky. While in France, I had developed a taste for Pinot Noir, a crisp Rosé from the South when it was hot out.

But when in Rome and all that.

And my particular situation called for Jack… A crisp rosé wouldn't do shit to dull the edges.

The night was unusually quiet. Even though I'd only been at the compound a few days, I'd come to understand that silence, even in the middle of the night—especially in the middle of the night—was hard to come by at an outlaw biker compound. All of the married members, my mother's good friends, lived in houses of their own. Which meant that it was all of the single men who lived at the clubhouse. And they liked to party. Party freaking *hard*. They also liked to do a lot of other stuff that shocked even my not so naïve eyes.

No one seemed worried about sexual acts being performed in public after certain hours. To the contrary, it seemed some of them liked being watched. When that started, I took that as a sign to put myself to bed—especially considering my current condition. But something had also awakened inside of me, a want to stay. A need. And every time, my eyes had always found aquamarine ones, my body pulsating as we made eye contact, as it became clear he had been watching me too. The weight of that stare and my current condition had me scuttling back to my room, heart beating fast and shame covering me like sweat.

I found I liked the rhythm of the clubhouse, the men who lived there. I enjoyed the club life, learning about a different way of existing. I might've enjoyed it a lot more if my world hadn't been rocked once again in the bathroom of my mother's little house she shared with Swiss.

The one I had to get out of, for a multitude of reasons, not the least of which being what I found out in that bathroom.

I convinced my mom I did not need to be under the same roof as her and her new fiancé where even the thickest of walls couldn't contain the evidence that my mother was happy. And satisfied.

It didn't give me the *ick* that most might've had hearing their mother having great sex. Well, it gave me the *ick*, but just a little. Mostly, it made me happy. Amongst some other very complicated feelings.

I had never heard my mother and father have sex. Then again, we'd lived in a large, sprawling house.

I'd never heard him beat her either.

But that had happened.

My entire fucking life, my father had beat my mother.

And she'd taken the opportunity of me going to study abroad as a window to escape. To drive across the country, find herself at a biker compound and fall for an outlaw biker. Then my father had also driven her across the country to try to beat her to death.

I'd learned all of this… less than two weeks ago.

And I was still processing the shattering of my entire childhood. Of everything I thought my mother was.

In addition to what I'd carried with me across an ocean. The weight of which was almost impossible to carry but a weight I could not transfer to my mother. Not now, not when she was finally happy for the first time in her life.

I had never seen my mother happy. Not truly free. Not once in my entire life. Until right then. So yeah, I would not be the reason that happiness was shattered.

Hence the Jack and the joint.

I wasn't a habitual smoker. Sure, I'd tried it a bunch in high school along with the plethora of drugs available at all the rich kid parties our parents didn't know we threw or attended.

I'd enjoyed drugs. Still did enjoy them. A little truth that my mother thankfully didn't know, even though I told her almost everything.

But recently, I'd come to realize how much we'd been hiding from each other.

My casual drug use being the least of it.

I realized that there were going to be many things I kept from my mother. Not because I didn't want to tell or because she wouldn't want to know. I knew she'd want to know, to be there for me, to give me all she could give. Which was the problem. My mom had already done that. My mom was her own complete person with her own traumas, with her own set of battles. I couldn't expect her to always fight mine.

She'd spent her whole life protecting me from a truth that would shatter my world. It was my turn now.

She was opening her own restaurant. We'd had a party celebrating a few days ago. She'd been glowing with excitement, happiness. A purpose. Something of her own. I'd been struck with inspiration of what to create for her and had been spending a lot of time on my computer, planning out the space. It had been a very welcome distraction, focusing all of my energy on creating something for my mother, being a part of this new life she'd created. But there was only so much time I could spend in front of my computer. The second I closed the screen, reality rushed back in.

Movement in the corner of my eye jolted me out of my thoughts. But because my thoughts were so thick and thorny, because my mind was cloudy from the booze and weed, the man had been able to come close to me without me noticing.

Which was no mean feat since you had to climb up a ladder on the edge of the building in order to get up to the flat space on the roof cluttered with patio chairs and a side table with an overflowing ashtray. I was not the only one who sought out this place. Because of that, the ladder, while sturdy, creaked a little when you ascended it.

I didn't hear the creak.

Or the thump of motorcycle boots on the concrete as he walked toward me.

None of my survival instincts kicked in to let me know this man was near. And they should've. Because one look at him and you'd know… you'd know that he was dangerous. Something would prickle at the back of your neck. Your leg muscles would tense as if preparing to run, but your feet would grow roots to keep you in place. Your heart would beat so wildly in your chest that the bones would rattle. Your thighs would press together; you skin would turn damp.

As would your panties.

Okay, so maybe not *everyone* would be turned on by standing in front of a six-foot-something biker with muscles and a thousand-yard stare from icy blue eyes. A man two decades older. With a carob-colored beard that I wanted to scratch the insides of my thighs.

Yeah, I had all of those feelings the second I laid eyes on Elden.

I had all of those feelings despite everything going on in my life at the time I met him. And I had *a lot* of things going on when I met him.

He didn't say anything when his boots landed in front of the chair I was sitting in. That didn't surprise me. Elden was a man of few words. Very few. In the short amount of time I'd known him, I'd only heard his low, gravelly voice a handful of times, uttering only the bare minimum words needed to get his point across.

None of them had been directed at me. He'd seemed to have made a concerted effort not to make any kind of conversation with me, yet he was always close by, always somewhere, always unnerving me with his nearness and his forced disinterest in me. And it was forced. I may not have known the man, but for whatever reason, I knew that he wanted me. And I wanted him. Despite everything.

And *everything* was a word that encompassed a fuck of a lot.

I was disgusted that I could be so… wanton in desiring a man so forbidden while my body was not entirely my own.

I didn't know why he came to the roof tonight. Maybe he didn't even know I was there. Maybe that was where he went to get some peace when the craziness of the club parties became too much. But that wasn't likely. Though Elden was older than most of the men who engaged in the craziness, he wasn't *that* much older. The club had varied shapes and sizes of men patched into the Sons of Templar, all from different backgrounds but all searching for the kind of freedom the cut offered.

The cut. The leather vest they all wore at all times that signified them belonging to this club.

The one that had become my mother's family at some point while I was across an ocean, ruining my life.

He was standing in front of my chair, looking down at me. His figure was imposing, all-encompassing. He blocked out the moon and stars, took over my vision. Though I didn't have measuring tape on hand, he had to be over six foot. If I stood, I'd come up to his shoulder, maybe his chin.

And he wasn't just tall, he was wide. All muscle.

His shoulders were broad, biceps stretching the fabric of the tee he was wearing. I had the urge, a very strong urge to lick the sinewy muscle of his forearms. His dark hair was pulled back into a low bun, and not in a hipster man bun, but a bad ass biker man bun. Silver threaded through that dark chocolate hair, and the goatee that should've, would've looked insane on anyone else—well, apart from Jeff Bridges of course—but made him look rugged and chiseled at the same time. There were creases in his forehead, the kind of creases that made a man looked weathered, wise and impossibly handsome. Creases that communicated he frowned often, and not many lines on the edge of his eyes that hinted that he rarely smiled.

And I had real life knowledge to back those claims up. In the time I'd spent here, I had yet to see him smile, his default expression seemed to be a glower that should've scared the pants off me. Instead, it melted my panties.

Those eyes. That was what drew you to him. Okay, the height, the muscles, the impossibly sexy man bun and goatee drew you to him. But the eyes held you captive. Mediterranean blue, endless pools of intensity, of a masculinity that I should've bristled against. Eyes that rooted you in your spot.

I had to do something about the way Elden was looking at me. Either to stop him from wanting me or to stop him from thinking I was some perfect, pure thing he couldn't touch… I wasn't sure which.

"I had an abortion this week," I said, looking straight at him.

I needed to say the words out loud. Needed to stare into his icy irises as I said them. And though it didn't make a whole lot of sense, I needed to tell him. Needed this one stranger to know the thing I hadn't said out loud. Not even to my closest friends.

Not even to my *mother.*

My first instinct, that morning in her bathroom when seeing those two lines, was to go running to her.

As much as I liked to think of myself as grown up, as a woman who had been living and existing in Europe with her older French boyfriend, traveling across the world, digesting all sorts of life altering information and not breaking down—it was in that moment, realizing I was pregnant, that I was confronted with how much of a child I still was.

I'd wanted my mother.

It was that simple.

Then there was the other thing. The thing that I'd done very well at repressing. Not healthy. Not in the slightest. But in order to live with myself, I had to force myself not to think of it. Otherwise, it would all crumble down.

When I got here, to Garnett, New Mexico, even after hearing that my parents were divorced and my mother was engaged to another man without even knowing my parents were having trouble, I'd planned on telling her. Not about the pregnancy. I didn't know about that yet, or maybe I did and was ignoring all of the signs my body was giving me because I couldn't handle it. Because I needed those margaritas, those glasses of red wine to get me through.

Still, I planned on telling my mother the *other thing*. Spewing its nastiness all over the idyllic life she'd created. Selfish, maybe. But maybe it was a little vindictive too. Maybe I'd been pushed to tell her when I heard she'd gone and created a whole new life in less than a year without telling me.

Maybe I'd wanted to punish her a little for that.

In the past year, I'd learned that there were a lot of things I didn't like about myself.

And maybe I wanted to see what it sounded like, delivering that news out loud. If it made me different, changed the way Elden looked at me. Everyone thought I was so pure, so innocent, perfect. That I needed to be protected from the harshness of the world, unaware that I already bore scrapes and bruises I hid from everyone.

I didn't want to hide those from Elden, though. Because I didn't want him to see me as pure or innocent. As a girl. I wanted him to see me as a woman. One who did things like got abortions and told people about it, out loud without shame or guilt.

He blinked only once, staring at me without shock or judgment. But something else awakened in those icy eyes, something that blazed like flames.

Fury.

I knew enough about the men of this club to understand that

they were crazy protective, alpha males, so that fury was likely on my behalf.

I couldn't help but roll my eyes. "Before you Hulk out, the sex itself was entirely consensual, and I was very *involved* in the process... I am not some innocent girl who got taken advantage of," I took a swig of the Jack. "I'm just a young woman who drank too much and let an asshole with a good jawline and an accent convince me we didn't need a condom."

It was likely the booze or the weed that made me so forthcoming with all of the details. And it was likely the booze or the weed that made me forget that offering this information to a protective alpha male would only make him madder.

There was a tic in Elden's jaw to communicate this fact, his hands now fisted at his sides.

"Who took you?" he uttered, the words coming out like stone grinding against stone, turning to dust. Flickering through the air, absolutely covering me.

I blinked at the question. It wasn't a ridiculous question to ask, it was quite practical, really. But it was not, in a million years, the kind of question I expected Elden to ask. Not that I had any reason to expect anything from Elden. I didn't know him well enough to have created a set of expectations for the man.

Yet I did. Expect things from him.

"Colby," I replied, on reflex more than anything else.

He stared at me. Unblinking. It was unnerving. Even through the haze of booze and weed it was unnerving. It might've been downright terrifying if I'd been sober.

"Colby," he repeated.

It was not a question. Or a clarification. It was a threat. A single word coated in violence, suggesting some kind of reckoning.

Not directed at me. No, at the man who took me to and from my abortion. Who fulfilled a deed that was not required nor expected of him.

No good deed goes unpunished, it seemed.

I nodded slowly, my body thrumming with something that cut through my inebriation.

Not quite fear. But something close.

"Why in the fuck did *Colby* take you?" he ground out.

His anger, like my expectations of him, didn't make sense. We barely knew each other. We hadn't engaged in any meaningful conversation—or any conversation for that matter until I blurted out about my abortion a few minutes ago. There was no ownership or intimacy here.

Or at least there shouldn't have been.

But there was.

Inexplicably.

"Because he's my friend," I answered honestly.

Colby was the closest man in age to me here who wore a patch. Not counting the Prospects who everyone treated like they were pledges in a fraternity. Not that the Sons of Templar were like any kind of fraternity.

Colby, like a large majority of the Sons of Templar, was hot as fuck. Muscles, tattoos, that air of alpha male badassery that cut through all of my deep-seated feminism. His dark hair was on the longer side, and it brushed over his face in a way that made it so he was always running his hands through it. He was tall, quick to smile with a grin that made women melt. His family was from South Korea, and he confided in me they weren't happy that their only son patched into a biker club.

Arguably, I should've had some kind of reaction to Colby. He was the most appropriate of all the outlaws for me to have a reaction toward. Well, him and Lucas, who was lankier than the rest, wore skinny jeans, Dr. Martens and thick glasses that made him look like a hipster badass. Not many people could pull that off. I liked Lucas too, but Colby and I hit it off. As friends.

I didn't have a reaction toward him because he was far too appropriate. Despite him wearing the patch and having a weapon strapped to him at all times.

But still, Colby was closest in age to me, and we immediately connected. Of course, he tried to flirt his way into sleeping with me, but he didn't go feral and cruel when I gently told him I needed a friend who wasn't trying to sleep with me, and who didn't think I would sleep with him if he pretended to be my friend long enough.

He took it completely in stride, and we hung out. Like an outlaw and a previously sheltered 'good girl' might. He taught me how to shoot, and we had started riding lessons. Because up until now, it was only the men who rode Harleys. The women were all on the backs of their bikes. Colby had tried to explain to me how important that was in this life. I'd pushed back about how fucking archaic it was, in addition to only men being allowed to patch in. He'd chuckled good naturedly and hadn't tried to argue with me further.

If I had the choice, I probably wouldn't have told even him about my pregnancy, but I'd needed a ride home from the clinic. I'd needed someone to walk in with me because I wasn't strong enough to walk in alone.

Not because I doubted my choice. I was one hundred percent certain it was the correct one to make at this juncture in my life.

There are women, many women who are strong enough to go through that entire process alone. Who have no choice. Who, in my opinion, are fucking superheroes.

I was not one of those women. So, I made the choice. I blurted it out to Colby who, to his credit, didn't blink at the information. He had tactfully tried to ask about the father, with that familiar alpha fury in his eyes. Then later, when he'd walked me through the line of protesters—who immediately stepped back from us when he turned his glare in their direction—he'd asked less tactfully about the father. Sure, he could guess. I'd just come back from France, from a man who I'd been certain I was in love with.

Colby had fussed over me like a mother hen once we got back to the clubhouse, arranging a soft blanket over me on the sofa, bringing a plethora of snacks, and then curling up beside me for a *Vampire Diaries* marathon.

He was Team Damon. Obviously.

He was gentle and safe, comforting, protective. He was hot, a hint of a boyish rogue still remaining even though I figured that all the things he'd done to wear that patch had taken boyhood right out of him. But still, a glint of mischief, of softness remained.

To me, he was like a brother. One I'd never had.

It was not Colby who I dreamed about. It was the man standing in front of me, looking like the most handsome nightmare.

"He's your *friend*," Elden repeated through gritted teeth.

It occurred to me that Elden had glared at Colby a lot whenever we were together. I figured that was just because Elden was a broody type of guy. Maybe not.

I titled my chin up at him in defiance. I got it. He felt possessive over me for the same reason I felt possessive over him. There was something between us. Something we both tried to ignore and clutch at the same time.

But now wasn't really the moment for him to throw his weight around. Not when I was wearing a pad the size of a diaper and fighting my way through cramps that were like having PMS on steroids.

"Yes," I snapped. "Colby is my *friend*. The kind of friend who drives me to an abortion clinic without asking questions, without glowering with alpha male fury, who takes me to get a milkshake afterward and doesn't force his company on me when I want to be alone."

Elden folded his arms across his chest, shifting his weight as if he were cementing his feet to the floor, eyes narrowing ever so slightly, communicating that he was not going to let me be alone. He was going to force his company on me.

And I was glad.

The thought of being alone right now was utterly fucking wretched.

But Elden's presence was something else entirely. It made me... ashamed that I wasn't overcome with thoughts of what I'd done this week.

Of what my mother had been going through my entire life. Of my mother nearly fucking dying.

Those remained in the back of my mind, but at the forefront was Elden.

I stood on unsteady legs, uncomfortable with the large pad between my legs... for the bleeding. Because the decision, the procedure and the walk through all those fucking protesters was not enough. I had to bleed heavily for days—it could be weeks, depending on the woman, they said—and not use a tampon or DivaCup because they increased my chance of infections.

That discomfort between my legs should've been enough to stop me.

It wasn't.

Because of Elden's stare. Because of the electricity between us that shouldn't have existed under the current circumstances. Because of the booze and the weed divesting me of my inhibitions.

I stepped forward, and he froze. My hands clutched the sides of his cut, and I reveled in the worn leather of the vest.

He went stock still, but he didn't push me away.

"Kiss me," I demanded, my mouth inches from his. "I need to taste something other than cheap whisky and regret."

His eyes flared in surprise and something else... the attraction that had been crackling between us since the moment we met.

The attraction he'd been fighting for a number of reasons. Because he was in an outlaw biker club where they took honor and brotherhood very seriously. And his 'brother' was going to be my stepdad. My very protective, over the top, stepdad. Technically, my *only* dad since my biological father was a man who had beat my mother my entire life, without me knowing, and had recently almost killed her.

He was dead to me now.

Which was neither here nor there, but I supposed it could've been one of the reasons why Elden was fighting the very obvious attraction to me. Or since he was *chronologically* old enough to be my father—only because my father had been a teenager when my mother had me.

I didn't think I was so predictable as to be into the bad boy, but there I was, on a roof at a biker compound, smoking a joint, dangling a bottle of Jack between my fingers and asking a man almost twice my age to kiss me.

Elden—who had made it his mission to not be alone with me but who also lingered, presumably to make sure no other member was alone with me—didn't move. It seemed like he didn't breathe for a handful of moments. His eyes were glued to mine, and I watched thoughts rush through his mind.

It was reasonable that he was weighing how responsible it was to kiss the eighteen—almost nineteen—year old who was almost the stepdaughter of one of his best friends/brothers who would likely kill him if he found out about aforementioned kiss.

Worry and dread clutched my stomach then, at the thought that he might deny me—which of course, he was well within his rights to do—and I'd have to sit here on the roof feeling rejected on top of everything else.

I should've taken the words back, blamed them on the booze, my emotions, whatever.

But I didn't.

I stared at him and waited for him to make the decision that would change both of our lives.

CHAPTER Two

I DIDN'T BREATHE until he grabbed the back of my neck, roughly, with all of the hunger and primal need he was communicating with his eyes. He yanked me so our mouths meshed together, both of us desperate, ravenous to make it last longer, make it deeper. It marked me, that kiss. In ways I wouldn't understand until much, much later.

Because it wasn't just the best kiss of my life—although it was that too—but it was both of us knowing that giving in to this attraction would be disastrous, yet we did it anyway. It was both of us giving in to the most carnal parts of ourselves, knowing we couldn't go back, regardless of whatever happened from here.

The kiss lasted a lifetime, yet also felt like it was over in a second. Over much too quickly for my liking. It was proof that whatever it was between us was something chemical, something outside of our control, and something even someone as badass as Elden couldn't fight against.

"I've never been kissed like that before," I murmured breathlessly, swaying on my feet.

Elden's hands found my hips, steadying me, tethering me to this earth.

He didn't say anything. He hadn't said anything except barking about Colby. Maybe I should've taken note of his silence and mimicked it with silence of my own.

But I was never good at being silent. Especially not in that moment.

"If only I'd met you before I went to France," I said, still floating on a cloud, my troubles thousands of feet below me. "If I'd met you, I wouldn't have been distracted by some smooth skinned, manicured, tanned, snobby Frenchman who got me pregnant and then punched me," I rambled. Then I screwed up my nose. "Or maybe he punched me *then* got me pregnant, but I don't think so because I left pretty much the morning after he punched me."

My joint was smoldering on the ashtray, and I realized I was still holding the whisky, which turned out to be delightful because I wanted to continue the kiss, turn it into something more. Though I obviously couldn't turn it into something more because of what was happening with my body. Then, despite the high of the kiss and the actual high of drugs and alcohol, the self-hatred returned.

Because I was so caught up in my own shit, I barely noticed that Elden had turned into a statue, his hand no longer gentle on my hip. Actually, his grip was tight enough to hurt, but I enjoyed that. I'd been feeling numb for so long, the pain was good.

"It's funny," I whispered, staring into eyes that had been liquid moments ago yet were now gemstones of glittering fury. "They say that the cycle of abuse can repeat. That more often than not, it does repeat. A young woman who sees her father beat on her mother, no matter how despicable, terrifying and heartbreaking she might find it, will somehow find herself in a similar situation as a grown woman."

I took a long pull of the whisky.

"I didn't *see* any abuse," I continued. "None. I didn't have any inclination that it was there. I knew my father was a misogynist. An elitist, sure. Although I was a daddy's girl, I was well aware of my father's flaws." I shook my head in disgust. "I just thought he was *human*... not a monster."

My heart thrummed, speaking of my father, and my throat burned with fury. Fury that I'd been trying my hardest to swallow since I found out. Fury that had been giving me excruciating heartburn. I was chewing antacids daily, even though I knew that treating the symptoms and not the root cause wasn't going to do shit. Plus, I was probably ruining my kidneys, liver and whatever else drug companies were doing to people.

Treating the root cause would be confronting my father. Speaking to him. Looking at him in the face. And I refused to do that.

So, I'd continue to eat twice the recommended dose of antacids and engage in self-destructive behavior.

"But still, even oblivious, I was able to repeat the cycle," I scoffed, looking up at Elden, who was hanging on my every word. Literally hanging on my every word. My hip was radiating pain under his grip. I fed off that.

"In theory, Jacques was nothing like my father," I told him, working off adrenaline and the mixture off weed and liquor. "He was French. Liberal. Romantic. Exciting. Passionate." I rattled off the adjectives, thinking about the rush of lust I'd felt when I first saw him. When he spoke to me in perfect, accented English, his dirty brown hair shadowing half of his face.

His long and thin fingers had continually brushed it out of his face in a smooth and graceful movement.

Those long, thin fingers had balled into a fist and punched me in that same smooth and graceful movement too.

"But it turned out, he was exactly like my dad in all the ways that mattered," I muttered, shaking my head at my own stupidity.

Still, Elden hadn't moved. It didn't seem like he'd even breathed. But I was too far gone to understand what that meant, how dangerous he was in that moment. I hadn't told anyone this. Not even my closest friends... although I didn't really have those. I had girls I went to school with. Some of whom I enjoyed the company of but had nothing in common with—they were happy to live off their parents, adopt their religions, their political parties, hold whatever beliefs they needed to in order to keep their trust funds. And that was fine, for them. For me, I wanted to travel, I wanted to change the world, I wanted to bring down oppressive systems, bring about change. Anything but live the life my friends' mothers lived.

Live the life my mother lived.

I'd already lost touch with my friends from high school anyway, and all of my friends in France were Jacques's friends. I hadn't been to campus yet and didn't know anyone there… I'd signed up to be part of a house share with a bunch of girls I didn't even know.

My best friend was my mother.

And I couldn't tell her *this*.

So, I was telling Elden. Right after he gave me the best kiss anyone ever had and likely making sure he wasn't ever going to kiss me again.

"Knowing I sought after a man who beat me, without any kind of knowledge of what my mother went through, is next level fucked-up," I finished with a sigh.

There was no way for me to forget Elden's presence, but I'd gotten so tangled up in my narrative that I hadn't realized what I was saying. The impact it might have. I had forgotten the breed of men who wore the Sons of Templar cuts.

Ultra-hot. Ultra-alpha. Badass and violent to the core. Intense as all hell. Elden even more so because he'd just kissed the shit out of me.

There was a stillness, a quiet, so charged, so dangerous that I forgot to breathe. I was sucked up into his orbit.

"What did you just say?" he murmured, his voice a blade cutting through the night.

Goosebumps raised on my arms with the knowledge of a danger, a deadliness emanating from him.

I couldn't speak. Not when confronted with the raw violence that was seeping from him.

He stepped forward, and I scuttled back, not realizing I was standing on a roof without railings. Elden's hand darted out to circle my upper arm, yanking me back in just as my left heel tried to step on empty air.

The result of this was our bodies landing flush together, Elden's hand settling on my hip, strong and purposeful. To keep me from plummeting to the ground and perhaps from trying to escape him.

He smelled of leather and musk. And the faint aroma of cigarettes, which should've turned me off but only added more layers. Spicy aftershave that sank into my pores. He smelled like a fucking *man.*

"Violet." My name was a warning. His grip tightened, and he yanked me closer.

My name was so sweet from his mouth.

"You made me taste you, and then you told me that," he uttered, eyes wild.

I blinked rapidly at his tone, the pure violence in it. Considering what I'd just told him, considering everything happening with men in my life, I should've been afraid. Terrified. The man was exuding violence.

But I wasn't. I was comforted. Though I didn't have evidence to back up the thought, something told me he was a violent man. A deadly man. A man who would burn the earth to cinders if he had the occasion to. That he wasn't afraid to inflict hurt.

But not on me. No. Never me.

"He's going to regret ever thinking he was worthy of you," he uttered. "He's going to regret being fucking born."

And on that, he purposefully pulled me far away from the roof's edge with one hand then pulled his phone from his cut with the other. He stared down at it as he pressed the screen then held it up to his ear.

"Colby," he grunted. "Need you on the roof now. Violet's here, needs to be taken down safely and put to bed without you layin' an untoward hand on her. Unless you want me to feed you your fingers one by one."

I blinked at him as he didn't wait for a response, putting the phone back in his cut.

Again, he pulled me, sitting me down on the chair I had previously been ruminating in.

"Stay there," he commanded. His voice was rough, but then he brushed the hair from my face with a gentleness that didn't seem possible coming from a man overcome with such primal fury.

"No one will ever hurt you again, Violet," he murmured, laying a kiss on my forehead before walking off.

Walking the fuck off.

I didn't even get the chance to follow him before Colby ascended the ladder, strutting over to snatch the bottle from my hands with a raised brow.

"Now, I'm not your babysitter, but if you're going to mix weed, whisky and the pills they gave you at the clinic, at least do it in a place where you can't stumble off the side of a building," he requested dryly, his brows pinched in concern.

It took me a second to figure out the root of his concern, what with the kiss, the beans I'd spilled and the intense proclamation from a man I was low-key obsessed with.

I looked from Colby to the edge of the roof, frowning. "What? You seriously thought I was going to jump?"

His attractive face relaxed, a gentle expression on it. "I mean, you're a strong ass bitch, but you've also been through a lot the past few weeks. And though regularly, Jack and weed make great dates, not so much when they're the only ones at the party. It can make things seem dark and inescapable."

I regarded him and his tone. It seemed knowing. Sad.

Though Colby was younger than most of the members, he had his shit together. Still had that air they all possessed, like bullets could bounce off them.

I forgot that sometimes the people who looked the most bulletproof were the ones nursing the most wounds. Ones who might bleed out quietly without asking for help.

"Now I'm going to paraphrase Albus Dumbledore," he continued, voice peppier now, or as peppy as a man like Colby could get. "Finding our way through those dark times can be as simple as remembering to turn on the light," he grinned. "Or you know, by finishing the rest of *The Vampire Diaries,*" he winked. "Then we've got all the spinoffs."

I couldn't help but smile as he held out his hand in invitation.

I didn't take it straight away, though. Something inside of me was almost desperate to stay up on this roof, where reality couldn't find me. Where I could relive Elden's lips against mine. Where I could hope that he would find his way back up here and carry me down.

But that wasn't how life worked. And even if it did, that wasn't who I was. I knew that, even though I currently only had a tenuous grasp on my identity.

So, I took Colby's hand.

And I climbed down the ladder on my own, if under the watchful eye of a friend.

A few days later, I was nursing a coffee and a hangover in the kitchen. The kitchen that my mom loved. Where she'd spent the first mornings of her time at the Sons of Templar compound. For good reason. When I arrived, I had expected some kind of ancient, stained, whiteware situation. But everything was gleaming stainless steel, clean and full of produce and various nut milks.

Lucas, the muscled, tattooed biker, was a vegan.

A biker vegan who wore a large knife on his belt and a visible gun strapped to him. Though I couldn't be sure, and I didn't have any evidence to prove this, I was relatively certain that being a biker in this particular club meant violence was a part of life.

I wasn't exactly versed in urban life, having grown up in pastel suburbia, but I also guessed murder was a part of life here too.

Again, these were all educated guesses. But I didn't think you wore two deadly weapons on your body unless you planned on using them.

I enjoyed the freedom of the clubhouse. There was always someone somewhere, even at two in the morning. And I wasn't the only woman in residence. There was a rotation of 'club girls' who I soon learned were there to service the members of the club in… whatever way they needed. At first, like most of the tenets here, I'd been disgusted. These men were using women as sexual objects. But the more time I spent here, the more I got to know the women, got to understand what the connection to the club meant to them. They came from different backgrounds, yet they all felt like society didn't fit them, had failed them, didn't make them happy. They found what they needed here, they found a place to belong, and they were empowered. In charge of their own sexuality and unafraid to show it.

Who the fuck was I to judge?

They were all kind to me, taking me under their wings in some way.

Kiera, one of the more recent club girls, impossibly tall and elegant with flawless ebony skin and curves to die for, had become a friend. Not close enough to tell her much, but enough so I was able to subtly ask her about who Elden slept with. The pinch of her lips told me that I wasn't being at all subtle, but she didn't call me out on it. She'd simply told me that Elden didn't sleep with any of the club girls. Each of them had tried, since he was a man who looked like he could fuck, but he'd respectfully rebuffed them. He was an enigma to everyone.

Yet he'd kissed me.

My lips still felt swollen, seared with his brand. My mind was racing with what that kiss meant, wondering where he was and trying to pretend that everything was normal.

If living at a biker clubhouse and having Swiss show me the house he was buying for my mother could be considered normal. My body, at least, was returning back to normal, the bleeding already stopping, the cramps gone. We'd caught it early enough, the doctor said, that it wouldn't be as physically traumatic as it might've been. But she'd warned me about the emotional trauma, had given me pamphlets and urged me to talk to someone. I was sure for women in different situations than mine, this would be traumatic. It would be something they'd never forget. Something they carried with them always.

But I didn't feel that. I'd made the right decision. I knew that. And it was over. I didn't lose sleep over it. Didn't feel like I'd done anything wrong. Because I hadn't.

"Elden's more of a grumpy bastard than normal," Colby commented, biting into an apple, leaning against the breakfast bar. His eyes darted to me as he spoke. He had not mentioned me being up on the roof with Elden, and I was thankful for it.

"Well he fucked off for three days… I thought he was finally getting laid or torturing his victims, so he should've come back cheery as all hell," Lucas put in, sipping on his oat milk latte.

My fork paused midair, and my heart stopped. "Elden's back?" I asked as casually as I could.

I had been on somewhat of a bender these past few days because these guys liked to party, and it was hard to stay here and not join in. Then there were the more obvious reasons I wanted to use alcohol as an unhealthy coping mechanism.

When I looked up, Colby was watching me closely. He was still the only one who knew about the abortion. Well, him and the man who had disappeared since that night on the roof.

The man who was apparently now back.

If the looks the two men were giving me were any indication, my casual tone left a lot to be desired.

"Just got in," Colby offered with a shrug.

My fork clanged onto my bowl as I dumped the contents of it, rinsing it with a forced air of nonchalance. I could feel the eyes of the two men on me, ignoring that the best I could.

"I've got, uh, forms I forgot to send for… college," I lied, not looking at either of the men.

"Uh-huh," Colby replied.

I all but ran out of there, not too worried about how bad I was at lying. Let them think what they wanted.

My heart was a thorn in my throat as I walked down the hallway to Elden's room. I'd never been inside it, but I knew where it was.

Fourth door on the right. Almost at the end of the hall. The hall itself was long and narrow with dark brown doors evenly spaced on either side. It reminded me of a dorm room setup; each member was allocated their own room with an adjoining bathroom… something that even college dorms didn't have.

Each room was roughly the same size… enough room for a double bed, nightstands, set of drawers and maybe some kind of chair or desk situation. Some of the residents used this merely as a crash pad for when they drank too much and had their own homes outside of the compound—almost all of those being the men who were married—while the majority of the patched members lived here exclusively.

It made sense with a lot of the members, especially the ones closer to my age. You weren't supposed to have a home, grow roots… They were meant to have a place to store their shit and lay their heads. Even the handful of graying, older members with beer bellies seemed to give off a vibe that they belonged in this kind of environment.

Elden did not give off that vibe. There was something almost… regal about him. He was silent, stoic, always dressed neatly—albeit like a total badass outlaw—without a wrinkle or stain to be found, all of his clothes expensive and good quality. You looked at him and you saw—beyond the fact that he was hot as balls—that he was someone. Something. He was important. Powerful.

You imagined some log cabin in the middle of the woods that he built by hand. Or even a sleek apartment in a high-rise somewhere. You expected him to reside somewhere that was entirely his own. His domain. His castle.

You did not stare at Elden and expect him to be living in a dorm situation with a dozen other bikers who partied, fucked and lived loud and messy. Yes, the clubhouse itself was always clean, smelling of lemon products mixed with whisky, but that was only because there were prospects and hired help to make sure it stayed that way. Well, and because Macy, Freya, Caroline and now my mom spent a lot of time here, and you could see their touches everywhere.

I didn't knock. Though I probably should've. I just walked in. His room was neat. Painstakingly so. The steel gray comforter was pressed and smoothed to perfection, and I knew that if I lifted it, I would see the sheets folded with military corners. Not that I knew if Elden had been in the military.

It smelled of him. His aftershave and a minty cleaning product that was not the same as the one they used in the main areas. It made me think that he didn't let anyone in here to clean his space. That made sense to me because he was quiet, private, reserved. Except when he kissed me. When he found out someone had hit me.

I was desperate to find out everything there was to know about him. But for now, I had one pressing question.

Elden's eyes flared with what might've been surprise when I first walked in, but I could've imagined it. His face was a cold mask, giving nothing away. Yet with his eyes on me, I felt like I was burning up.

If only I'd known I was going to see him today. I would've

worn something different. Then again, I didn't look bad. I was wearing a matching workout set, burnt copper leggings and a matching crop top that did wonders for my small bust and showed off my midriff. My hair was piled onto my head in a messy bun, with rebellious tendrils escaping to frame my face. I wasn't wearing makeup, so there was nothing to hide the blush that crept up my cheeks, likely reddening my alabaster skin with his gaze. It felt exciting. Uncomfortable, but in an almost… addicting way. I didn't know how I'd gotten through all of these days without his eyes on me.

Elden's hair was loose, brushing his shoulders. My fingers twitched as I had the overwhelming urge to run my hands through it. The tee he was wearing underneath his cut again struggled to contain those arm muscles I could drool over.

"Where have you been?" I demanded, hand on my hip, trying my level best not to look at the bed in the corner.

I had been alone with Elden on exactly one occasion—the rooftop three days ago. When he'd kissed me.

When he'd taken me off the face of the earth and placed me somewhere completely different. Then left. Left me to question everything. To think about him nonstop and wonder what was wrong with me. I'd never thought about a boy like this. Never let one rattle me so.

But this wasn't a boy.

This was a *man*.

And he made me feel like more of a woman than I ever had in my life.

"A trip."

The air vibrated as I waited for more, his eyes gluing me in place, his gaze shaking my resolve.

But nothing more came. No explanation. I figured I wasn't really entitled to one, but was I? I was just the teenage girl who was staying with the club because of my family connection. I was just a kid to him. Except, I wasn't. Not since the second we'd laid eyes on each other.

"A trip where?" I asked, losing whatever battle was raging between us in our silence.

He stared at me without answering.

"A trip *where,* Elden?" I repeated, my voice sharper this time.

His gaze didn't leave mine. "I've got shit to do," he clipped, trying to dismiss me.

Except, if he were trying to dismiss me, he would've broken his gaze, turned his back on me, walked me out of the room and slammed the door in my face. He did none of those things. He just kept staring at me.

My knees quivered. My breath shallowed. For a brief moment, I totally forgot my reason for being here; I totally forgot every other reason for being on this earth except for being able to meet his stare. For that moment, I existed solely for Elden, for this second, where we stared at each other without saying a word. I lingered in the moment because it made me feel like I was his. Because that's how he was looking at me. Like he was claiming me in some way.

I realized, in that moment, that no one had ever really *looked* at me before. No one had seen me like this man did.

Yes, my friends, my family may know me better, but no one had looked at me like *this.*

I broke out of the moment like I was reaching the surface after flailing underwater for an almost terminal amount of time.

"Elden." His name simultaneously tasted sweet and sour. I hated that I didn't have an ownership over it, yet something carnal told me he was mine. "Where were you?"

Silence reigned for a few moments longer. "Taking care of business."

I put my hands on my hips, irritated at his placid demeanor, his vague answers. Again, I ached for a kind of kinship with this man so that those answers were mine. I wished that I had a valid reason to be stomping in here demanding answers without feeling like a child.

"Club business?" I clarified.

He shook his head once.

Something fluttered in my stomach. "Did this business take you out of the country?" I asked.

His jaw was hard as he crossed his arms across his impressive chest. My gaze slid to the way his considerable biceps flexed with the movement.

Something decidedly below my stomach pulsated. Desire that I rightly shouldn't have felt so soon after my procedure bloomed between my legs.

Then again, this man had awakened something inside of me just days after my procedure. It said more about me than it did anything else.

My eyes went to his knuckles… They were bruised, red and scabbed.

My heart beat faster.

"Don't make me lie to you, Violet," Elden finally replied.

The ground swayed underneath me. My name out of his mouth was unlike anything I'd ever heard. It made my skin tingle, every single one of my nerve endings crying out for something. For him.

When I stepped forward, his body tensed, but he didn't move.

"Then don't lie to me, Elden," I whispered.

He didn't speak. Just stared at me in that blank but somehow not empty way.

The silence was too uncomfortable, and I rushed to find pieces of myself to give him so we weren't just strangers staring at each other with an intimacy that shouldn't exist.

"I don't like to drive in the rain," I blurted, unaware as to why. "I don't tell anyone that. Because it seems so trivial, pathetic and weak. Because it doesn't align with the story I tell myself about how strong I am, how independent, how I will be able to live my entire adult life without needing a man." I sucked in an unsteady breath underneath Elden's gaze.

"But I hate it," I whispered. "I get anxiety so strong I feel like I'm having a heart attack. I can't breathe. But I won't stop, even though it's likely even more dangerous to drive in the rain while feeling like I'm having a heart attack. I can't give in. Won't. So I do it."

I swallowed roughly. He didn't say anything, barely moved.

"I used to steal things," I continued, my cheeks hot with shame. "Nothing important. Lip-gloss. Batteries. Whatever I could get away with. I've felt this pressure to be perfect my entire life. Because my mother was so perfect." My eyes went downward. "Of course, now I understand she felt like she had to be in order to keep herself safe." My voice was small now.

"I resented her," I continued, still looking at the ground. "For being so buttoned up, so obedient, for not challenging the conventional gender roles my father pushed her into. Knowing what I know now, I feel ashamed for that. But I also still resent her a little. For not leaving sooner. For letting him hurt her for years. For letting me live in that house with him. Love him." My voice shook as I fought back tears.

There it was, my deepest, darkest secret, out in the light with him.

I didn't know he was right in front of me until I saw his motorcycle boots on the carpet where I had been looking. His fingers found my chin, lifting it upward.

His eyes were liquid aquamarine, and his features were no longer hard and empty. They weren't completely soft either. But this was an expression I hadn't seen him use, not with anyone, and I'd been watching him pretty damn closely.

This expression was mine.

"I flew to France," he murmured, searching my face.

Although I had suspected it, I hadn't let myself fully believe it. Just another scenario I'd created in my head… the hot, older biker feeling so intensely for me after just one kiss, he flies across an ocean to punish the man who put his hands on me.

But it happened.

He did it.

"Found the fuck who hurt you," he continued, brushing his fingers across my jawline.

My heart was a roar in my ears.

There were a lot of questions to ask at this juncture. Like how he found Jacques when all he knew was his first name. Like why he flew to another country for a girl who shouldn't matter to him.

"Did you kill him?" I asked, my voice thin.

"No. But I made him wish I did."

My stomach plummeted. I was against violence. After everything in my past, I should for sure be against violence.

In principle, I was.

But right here, right now, I couldn't find myself to feel bad for Jacques, feel anger toward Elden for avenging me in that ancient way.

The air seemed to shimmer around us. He smelled of home. Of safety. Warmth.

Elden's eyes searched my face, lingering on my lips.

My breath caught.

I was certain he was going to kiss me again.

"You're going to leave this room right now," he murmured, eyes finding mine once more. "Because if you don't, I'm gonna lose control. Gonna want to claim you in a way that you're not ready for, in a way that will make things infinitely more complicated for you." He paused, gripping my chin tighter as if he were changing his mind. And I would be totally on board with that.

But a split second later, he stepped back, rubbing the back of his neck.

I swayed on my feet but managed to stay upright.

"Walk away, Violet," he ordered.

Prickles of desire swept through me, not just at the authority in his voice, but the slight waver in his tone. His hands were fisted at his sides, posture rigid, as if he were battling with control.

"Now," he barked.

And despite all the things I wanted from him, namely to be claimed, I walked away.

CHAPTER Three

TWO WEEKS LATER

NO ONE SAW me walk to the hall. And if they did, they must've assumed I was going to my room in the compound, maybe to collect something I'd forgotten. It was still empty, even though I'd moved out of it and into Mom and Swiss's after the wedding.

There were no more excuses now. My stepfather had bought a huge house, one with a primary bedroom a whole wing away from the rest of the house. The walls were thick, he informed me. Sound didn't carry. He'd assured me of this with a grin while my mother had blushed and smacked him on the arm. She'd been glowing with happiness as he'd pulled her into his body and murmured something in her ear that made her blush even more.

My mom was still on a high from the wedding.

The day itself was amazing. Swiss had surprised my mother with the house he'd already shown me, having asked for my approval. It was perfect. Absolutely perfect. Warm. Bathed in light. There was a garden, wild and bursting with color. The desert sprawled around them a gorgeous backdrop. An oasis for them both.

The night before the wedding and my birthday, we'd spent one last night in the little cottage I adored, Mom not knowing it was her last night. She didn't know she was getting married the next day either. She thought I was staying because it was my birthday the next day. That was only part of the reason. When we woke up, Swiss gave me a leather jacket and a ride on his motorcycle. Mom gave me a necklace I planned to wear daily.

The burn remained at the back of my throat. Memories of past birthdays. Ones where Mom's smile was genuine but tight. There were no leather jackets. No motorcycle rides in pajamas. There were my father's gifts. Expensive. Appropriate. Evidence that he only knew who he wanted me to be, not who I actually was.

But I still missed him.

I hated that. Hated the small part of myself that longed for a sign he cared. That he really wasn't the complete monster it appeared he was.

Luckily, the day was not intended for such intrusive thoughts. The day was for my mother getting a new home. A new husband. A new beginning.

The entire club had shown up to celebrate her and Swiss. Elden was there too, of course. I didn't look at him. I couldn't. I was afraid my poker face was not that good. So, I focused on Mom. On celebrating.

I'd been planning on seeing him once I got back to the club that night. But once I got there, he was nowhere to be found. By design, I guessed. He'd spoken about control, about claiming me the last time I saw him. When things were raw. When we couldn't deny the chemistry between us. Now that there had been distance, he was probably thinking about the age gap. My connection to Swiss.

So, I didn't see him the night of the wedding.

Didn't see him in the weeks after that, weeks that were a whirlwind of working at the coffee shop my mom had worked in previously, designing her restaurant, babysitting for Freya, Caroline and Macy. Immersing myself in my mother's new life.

It should've felt odder, but I realized that my whole life, my mother didn't fit as my father's wife, even though she played the part expertly. Her clothes always fit perfectly, never a hair out of place, but it was the skin she wore around my father that didn't fit her. The smile that was too wide, too forced, that didn't meet her eyes. Even the way she'd moved was careful, purposeful.

With her and Swiss, it was different. She smiled with her whole face. With her whole body. She moved without thinking, naturally. He followed her with his eyes whenever she was in the room. He called her 'Countess'.

We had Christmas morning, just the three of us. Again, I battled against the feeling of family, of warmth, happiness that came with the holiday. I wondered what my father was doing. What my grandparents were doing.

I figured the club did some kind of big Christmas thing, but my mom insisted it be just the three of us, watchful over me the whole day as if she sensed my unease. I didn't show it. Wasn't honest with her about my feelings.

The new year came and went with a huge New Year's Eve party my mom and Swiss threw at the new house. I was helping her organize that, still working on the design for her restaurant while battling with my feelings about college. I was leaving a little earlier than I needed to, a week before my second semester actually started. It was something I'd scheduled before I even got back from France, and now I regretted it, wanting to stay longer now that I knew what life was like here.

Especially since Elden had made a brief appearance at the New Year's Eve party and left before midnight. Before I could make good on any of the plans I'd had for midnight. Which meant I got very drunk with Colby, Lucas and Javier, a newer patch who was closer to my age and who tried his best to kiss me at midnight.

The days after that were filled with work at the café, hanging out with Colby—because I liked his company and also because I was trying to catch a glimpse of Elden.

He was definitely avoiding me.

And I wasn't going to let that happen. I needed to see him before I left.

Those kinds of thoughts, beer, my upcoming departure and my overwhelming need were what brought me to the door at the end of the hall that night.

We'd been having a going away party for me. Mom and Swiss were long gone.

The party was in full swing as it approached midnight. I'd already texted my mother to let her know I'd be crashing at the club. She'd reminded me about the time we had remaining and demanded I be back for shopping bright and early. There were a lot of exclamation marks.

I'd promised, then made my decision to walk down the hall. He was there. I'd seen him walk into the room when I was playing pool with Colby and Lucas. His eyes had locked with mine for a split second before he strode directly in the direction of his room.

The party in the common room was still going on, as it would be until the wee hours of the morning, I guessed. No one would notice me slipping in, and hopefully slipping out in the early hours of the morning.

My hand shook as it fastened around the doorknob, but I didn't falter. This was the right decision, come what may.

I felt completely back to normal… physically, at least. I wasn't sure how long I was supposed to wait before having sex after having an abortion. I guessed probably longer than it had been. Maybe it made me a bad person, for wanting him so soon after what I did. But maybe it made me human. Plus, I had three condoms in my purse that I was going to make sure he put on. No 'I'm taking you raw' crap. Not when men made a choice that they didn't have to face the consequences for.

The door opened with a creak.

I figured he might be asleep. In truth, I'd imagined, in great detail, how I'd crawl into bed with him, naked, and where things would go from there. It was one of my talents, imagining complex, romantic scenarios in my head in which the ideal outcome would be me being the heroine, the love interest, and on more than one occasion, the queen of some Scandinavian country.

But as it was with all of these scenarios, it never turned out as I imagined. Although unlike the rest of the occasions, I was not disappointed.

Elden was fully dressed, awake and… reading.

He was lying on top of his expertly made bed, ankles crossed, reading. Complete with reading glasses. That he really, really pulled off.

I tried to spy the title of the book he was reading, but he moved too quickly the second the door opened, dog earing it and placing it on the nightstand along with his glasses. He was on his feet in an impressive amount of time.

"You move like a panther," I informed him. "And you look great in glasses."

Elden did not look pleased with my compliments. He looked very pissed off.

"What are you doing?" he growled as I closed the door behind me.

"It was my birthday a few weeks ago. You didn't get me a gift." I stepped forward, my feet sinking into the carpet of his bedroom as I slipped off my heeled mules. "It's a new year. I didn't get to kiss anyone at midnight."

I had dressed with a purpose tonight. My dress was black, made from silk with red flowers all over it. It contrasted with my pale skin, skimmed over every one of my curves and finished mid-calf. My black hair was curled so it tumbled past my shoulders, framing my face. I'd gone for minimal makeup, only a sharp cat eye to emphasize my eyes, which I thought were my best feature.

There was no chill in the room, but my nipples pressed through the thin silk of my dress. Elden found them as his eyes skimmed my entire body.

His gaze was hungry. Unadorned.

Not the same way he'd looked at me on my mother's wedding day.

His eyes had always met mine, every time, shocking me like I'd just put my hand on a live wire, but they always darted away quickly. And that gaze never went south of my eyes.

Which was a good thing. He couldn't very well be checking me out… I was now officially Swiss's teenage stepdaughter. It didn't matter that I was a legal adult and had been for one year now. Not to Swiss, at least.

Not to my mother who still thought of me as a little girl.

Elden didn't.

Of that I was sure.

So that's why I came to his room at five minutes to midnight, after enough beers to get rid of my nerves but not enough to fully impair my judgment.

"Stop, Violet," Elden rumbled as I advanced on him. He rubbed his hand over his mouth, eyes moving slowly over me. They left fire in their wake.

I stopped, even though I didn't want to. Even though I wanted to defy him. To keep on walking, going after what I knew we both wanted. But I was powerless against him.

"You need to leave," he ground out.

I tilted my head at him. "Do you want me?"

I'd never been so brazen in my life, but it felt good. Powerful.

His body twitched. "Of course, I fuckin' want you. I want you so bad I can barely fuckin' think straight. But—"

"But I've had an abortion, I've been abused by a man, found out my mother was beaten my entire life and my father almost killed her. Therefore, I couldn't possibly be in my right mind, and therefore, it's a villainous act to fuck me?" I finished for him.

His jaw turned hard. "Amongst other things."

"What other things?" I slipped the strap of my dress off my shoulder.

Elden's eyes followed it. "Like me being old enough to be your fuckin' father."

I rolled my eyes. "If you were fifteen," I conceded.

His gaze was stony. "I'm too old for you. I'm a bad fuckin' guy." His eyes swam over me like liquid flames. "And you're a good girl."

I struggled to maintain my composure, to find the bravado I walked in here with.

"I am a good girl," I agreed softly. "But I want you to make me your bad girl."

I could tell that was the exact fucking right thing to say when something changed in the air, something changed in Elden. My whole body quivered.

I wasn't sure what I expected when I came in here.

Well, I expected sex. I wanted sex. With every fiber of my being. I knew it would likely be good. Be the best I've ever had if that kiss was anything to go by. Elden emanated a surety in his gait, of his masculinity, that made it clear he was all man. And that he was great at sex.

Sure, appearances could and likely often were deceiving.

But not with him.

The sex would be good.

And I wasn't shy regarding my sexuality. I'd been very confident about it. It had made the boys I'd dated nervous. They were taught women were meant to be shy, timid, awaiting their instruction and ignorant enough not to be disappointed if they came in less than a minute and didn't care about the female orgasm.

A women's ineptitude in the bedroom was fetishized because men could get away with being selfish. A woman who knew what she wanted, what she deserved was a dangerous creature.

That was something I was proud of… my confidence. But it had all but petered to nothing now that I was there. In Elden's bedroom, where he called me a 'good girl' yet looked at me like I was everything he craved. Like I was a woman. His fucking woman.

My knees were shaking, and my palms were damp.

The moment hung in suspense. My future split in two. Something told me this was a pivotal moment. And it all hinged on him.

If Elden rejected me here and now, the shame would burn hot and deep. I'd take it with me, bury it and my feelings for this man away. I would avoid him. Wouldn't try something so bold and brazen again. Likely I'd find some college boy. Maybe a few. More than a few because I'd always be searching for this feeling. The one I knew was rare, that couldn't be replicated and was unlikely to occur twice in a lifetime.

If he didn't reject me… I had no fucking clue what my future would entail. It would be messy, no doubt. Full of pain and heartbreak. Because there was no way this story ended without heartbreak. Yet I was here anyway, biting my lip with anxiety at the prospect of the former future.

"Take off your dress," Elden demanded, his voice low and husky.

My teeth sank deeper into my lip, drawing blood now.

Elden's eyes flared as he focused on my lips.

I just stared at him, unable to move.

"Don't make me repeat myself," he murmured.

My body spasmed as his tenor caressed my most precious of places.

My hands shook as I fumbled with the zip on the side of my body, shimmying out of my dress.

Elden's swift intake of breath was the only reaction he had to me standing there, barefoot, wearing only a thin, cotton G-string that could barely be considered underwear. My nipples stood at attention, aching for his touch.

His hands were fisted at his sides, his entire body rigid, his muscles contracted, the sinew of them looking like they'd been carved from granite. My eyes gravitated down to his jeans, and I gasped when I saw the very large outline of his erect cock.

Yeah, he liked what he saw.

My nipples throbbed harder as I rubbed my thighs together, already desperate for friction.

"Panties." The single word barely sounded human.

I flinched in delight.

Then I gingerly stepped out of my panties.

Elden's eyes moved with devastating slowness down my naked body. Though we were three feet away from each other, it felt like his hands were moving across my tender skin, driving me crazy.

Never in my life had I had an experience like this. Not with a man fully dressed and me completely naked. Not with a stare full of pure hunger and… worship. Not with a slowness that indicated he had control, total control over his baser instincts. Before, men had been in a hurry, ripping off my clothes, eager to get the act done, to obtain the orgasm they were chasing.

Elden looked like he had all the time in the world. Like he was preparing for a feast.

"Sit down on the bed and spread your legs," he ordered in a cold voice that drove me wild.

My feet moved of their own accord, my body moving on instinct, knowing that obeying him would lead me to the most devastating orgasm of my life. I could feel it building now, and he hadn't even touched me.

The comforter was cool and smooth against my bare skin, the mattress firm. I was thankful for it, to not have to rely on my legs to hold me up.

Elden had moved so that he was standing closer to me now, still fully clothed.

"Wider," he grunted.

Wordlessly, breathlessly, I obeyed him.

I'd never exposed myself this way to anyone that wasn't a medical professional. Unbidden, the rustle of a paper gown sounded in my mind. My feet were cold from the stirrups. The room smelled strongly of disinfectant, and the nurse spoke in calm, comforting tones. I didn't feel conflicted over the decision, I felt relieved… which made me feel guilty, heartless.

"Violet." The voice was urgent now.

I blinked.

Elden was closer now.

He was on his knees in front of me, hands resting firmly on my thighs.

"Stay with me," he demanded.

His hands flexed, harder this time.

I hoped that I'd be left with a bruise.

"You're in this room, with me," he said softly even though his eyes were pits of desire.

His hands, not gently, pushed my thighs farther apart, then his gaze went downward.

"If we're gonna do this, I'm gonna taste that pretty pussy before we do anything else," he murmured. "I'm gonna make you break apart so I'm the only one who can put you back together."

All thoughts of the gown, the cold stirrups went up in smoke.

I didn't have time to breathe, to recover, because he did exactly what he promised. He tasted my pussy.

He didn't just taste it, he devoured it. I fisted the sheets of his bed because otherwise, I feared I might float right off. Elden worked relentlessly, mouth moving expertly, finding parts of me that no man had ever been able to locate.

And he was right, I thoroughly broke apart when his tongue worked me to an exquisite climax, hands still gripping my thighs tightly.

By the time I regained my sight without seeing stars, I realized that Elden was no longer kneeling before me. He was standing, staring at me with wild eyes, in utter worship. The mere look itself almost sent me over the edge again. It was a physical thing, the weight of his gaze caressing me while pulling back all of my layers and settling into my soul at the same time.

"You sure you're ready for me to fuck you?" he asked in a rough voice. "'Cause as much as I want my cock inside you, I'm gonna carry this image of you naked on my bed, your sweet pussy on my tongue to the fuckin' grave. That is all I need, Violet. We don't need to do more. I don't need more from you. This can be it. But you have to tell me right now. 'Cause I'm not gonna do something you're not ready for. And I'm not gonna be able to control myself once I'm inside."

I blinked rapidly, digesting the words that were doing strange things to me. "Elden," I rasped. "I don't want you to control yourself. I want you. I'm ready. And if you don't fuck me right now, I think I might go insane." That was not a hyperbole. It felt like I was dancing with sanity, that Elden was the one holding on to it all.

His eyes flared, then he immediately started working on his belt.

A rap at the door made him freeze.

Both of our heads turned in that direction.

"Brother," Swiss's voice filtered through the door. "Got a situation. We're out in five."

My eyes zeroed in on the doorknob, my blood instantly cold, thinking about what would've happened if my stepfather had decided to walk into the room and saw me naked in Elden's bed.

He would've killed him.

Elden was standing stock still.

"Yep," he grunted, voice tight.

The doorknob didn't rattle.

"You got company?" Swiss teased through the door.

"Fuck off," Elden ground out. "I'll be out in three."

Swiss chuckled. "Whatever, bro. If you're that quick, I feel bad for the poor bitch."

My spine was frozen solid, and it seemed as if every molecule of oxygen in the room had been sucked out.

Elden hadn't moved, and he didn't reply to Swiss now, he just stared at the door, body slightly in front of mine as if to protect me if Swiss walked in. But it wasn't me who would need to be protected if he walked in.

A bitter taste filled my mouth.

There was a long pause followed by another chuckle before the sound of motorcycle boots thumped against the floor.

Neither of us moved for a while, we were still frozen in the moment.

I wished Elden had stayed frozen forever when his head finally moved, and his eyes landed on mine. They were no longer full of hunger, worship, ownership. His face was devoid of emotion.

His boots thumped on the carpet as he retrieved my dress and panties, tossing them on the bed beside me.

"Get dressed," he barked.

I winced at his tone, my body still sensitive from his touch that now felt like something I'd imagined.

He didn't look at me as he took a gun out of his bedside table, slipping it into his cut. I didn't even react to seeing that, despite it being the first time I'd seen a weapon up close in my life.

"Lock the door behind me," he said to the carpet. "Drive back to your mother's place." Finally, he looked at me. A thousand tiny daggers pierced my skin. "Don't come back here."

And then he walked out.

ELDEN

I had fucked-up.

Majorly.

I did not fuck-up. I had ironclad control over my life, over every single decision I made. I knew the consequences of losing that control. Could feel that cold in my every pore, the scent of metal and sweat. Never fucking again would I lose control. It was not just a promise I'd made myself but a vow necessary for my survival. I knew I'd die before I'd go back to that memory.

It wasn't difficult. Not overly. Especially not when I found the Sons of Templar, found comfort in the structure, even though it looked like chaos from the outside. There was a hierarchy, certain rules—ones that looked nothing like the bullshit laws citizens followed—the main one being to never betray the club. I excelled at following the rules, at wearing the cut. And I'd almost, fucking almost, felt at home.

Until her.

The second she walked in, with her midnight hair, her flushed cheeks, her perfect fucking alabaster skin, the violet eyes that seemed to fucking glow. Something inside of me shifted. Something inside of me snapped. And I fucking hated it. Hated her. Hated myself. Refused to believe I could become obsessed with a woman—one who was barely a woman—the second I laid eyes on her.

I was a piece of shit, I knew that. She was still a fucking *teenager*. One of my brothers was about to be her stepfather. She had gone through fucking hell. And there I was, thinking about what it would feel like to have her pussy clench around my dick.

I'd never been so disgusted with myself. Never battled for control so damn hard or failed so consummately. I was unable to stop watching her, to not be near her. My eyes focused on my brothers, the younger ones who hovered around her. I'd been preparing myself to rip their fuckin' arms off if they laid a hand on her.

I wasn't sleeping. Barely eating. I was going fucking insane.

And that's what had me going onto that rooftop. Because I had no other choice. Because I would go crazy without breathing her in. Without touching her skin. Just once. Just fucking once.

Because I was a piece of shit who couldn't make the decision a good man would make, and that would've been to leave town.

That was my plan, initially. Follow her up to the roof, give me something to take with me, go Nomad to try to escape her memory, find control in another club.

But then I saw her. The sadness etched into her beautiful face. She'd told me what she'd gone through. Then she'd asked me to fucking kiss her. And even after what she told me, I did it. Because I was selfish. And because I wanted to give her what she wanted. I wanted to give her the fucking world.

The second I tasted her lips, I knew I couldn't leave. Knew I couldn't have her either but knew that I wouldn't be able to live if I didn't know she was safe, protected. It was fucking insane, didn't make any sense, but I wasn't a slave to reason with her. Only instinct.

And the second she told me what that French fuck did, my fury burned bright, and I was thankful to have a goal. Something to focus on. Someone to hurt.

The distance from her didn't clear my head, though. Didn't give me even a tenuous grip on control. Not when the second I got back, she was in my room looking like something the Devil was sending me to ensure I'd be damned forever. Tight, little fucking yoga pants that showed all of her curves. A top that didn't cover her fucking bellybutton… All I could think about was running my tongue over that skin.

I'd almost lost it right there and then. But I'd managed, somehow, to keep my shit locked down.

These past few weeks were hell, watching her. Seeing her at that fucking wedding, in that dress. Then at the New Year's Eve party, wearing something sparkly and much too short with that new patch drooling all over her. I'd had to leave before my control splintered completely. I'd been holding on to it with a death grip, thinking I might actually survive until she went to college, when I'd get a respite, when I'd be able to get my shit together.

But then she came into my room.

Even God himself wouldn't have been able to deny her. You know, if God existed, which He didn't, and if God was a he, which She most definitely wasn't.

And I failed. Whatever kind of test that was. I failed.

I tasted her pussy, examined every inch of her delicate, creamy skin… it was seared into my memory. And I couldn't give a fuck if I burned in hell for eternity, it was fucking worth it.

Until Swiss knocked at my door, and I realized how fucking close I was to ruining it all.

"You're quiet," the man himself observed at the warehouse. A shipment came in a day earlier than we'd expected. It wasn't unusual for shipments to arrive in the middle of the night, less likely to get shit from the new sheriff that way. We were there to make sure no shit went awry.

My arms were crossed over my chest as I kept my eyes on the truck and the men unloading it.

"Bitch you were fuckin' that good, was she?" he prodded, grinning.

"I'm a good girl. But I want you to make me your bad girl." Her perfume took over my senses. Sweet, but with an edge. Her nipples were perfect peaks underneath her dress.

I tasted bile. If only he fucking knew.

He'd kill me, probably.

Tell me I was fucking around with something priceless, something pure, something I had no business corrupting. And he'd be right.

I fucked-up. It was that simple.

Swiss nudged me, and all of my limbs turned taut.

"Jesus, bro, lighten up," he joked. "You're wound tight, even for you."

The fucker was not exactly a ray of sunshine himself. That was what we'd bonded over when I first patched in, that we were fucked-up. Everyone who took the patch was fucked-up in one way or another.

I knew people had been curious about me, prospecting so late in life with a bunch of fucking teenagers. No one had known it was that or death. Sure, it had taken a hit to my ego, having to prove myself with a bunch of kids. But it also meant something to me. Earning my place here.

Hansen was the only one who knew about my past, what brought me here. There was no judgment, and he didn't tell anyone. That was my choice.

And over a lot of whisky, I'd eventually shared my history with Swiss. Because I trusted him. And he trusted me. He'd considered me a friend. Part of his family.

Yet I'd gone and fucked that up in a way that couldn't be forgiven.

Self-hatred burned in my throat, bitter and familiar.

"Just don't want these fuckers trying anything," I nodded at the soldiers working for the Russian mafia, our connection for the weapons coming out of the old Soviet Union. They were an old and dangerous organization. They were unpredictable and not completely trustworthy.

Swiss's head turned to the truck. "Yeah, well, it'd be their funeral if they did," he muttered.

War with the Russian fucking mob was the last thing we needed right now, but it did sound tempting if it meant I could be distracted.

"Wanted to ask you..." Swiss returned his attention back to me. "No one has tried anything with Violet at the club, have they?"

My throat constricted, making it hard to breathe, and it took everything in me not to react. "No," I forced the lie out, still tasting her pussy on my lips. "No one is that stupid."

Swiss nodded once, cracking his knuckles. "Yeah, suppose you're right." He clapped me on the back. "Plus, if they were, I could trust you to put them in their place, if I wasn't there to look out for her."

I grimaced, unable to speak, only managing to nod my head.

"After everything she's been through, last thing she needs is another man ruining her life," he finished, twisting the knife even further.

The worst thing was, he was fucking right.

And I somehow had to figure out how to undo what I'd done.

CHAPTER
Four

VIOLET

IT HAD BEEN days since he left me naked in his room at the club. After he'd simultaneously rocked my world and ruined it.

I hadn't found the time to seek him out before now. Mom had been obsessed with getting me ready to go back to school, with me helping her furnish her new home. And despite the need I felt, I wanted to help her. She was starting over, literally. She was building something. She was happy. I wanted to be part of that so desperately. It was like I was getting to know a new person. I was knowing my mother as the real her instead of the woman my father had molded her into.

He'd called me. My father. Spoke to him long enough for me to smash my phone and tell my mom I dropped it. I got a new number then buried all my rage and sadness deep down.

The shopping was a distraction, taking care of the last-minute plans for my first semester on campus. I was nervous. The first semester in France had been an adventure for me. Almost removed from reality. I'd been caught up in perfecting my grasp on the language, experiencing my new identity as an adult, falling in love

—or *thinking* I was falling in love. Then I hit the earth with a thud that came as a punch to the face. Everything else had happened quickly, and I'd barely been able to catch my breath since.

It felt unreal that I was going to college now, somehow fitting into the normal, expected path for me.

All through my last year of high school, I had been restless, anxious to start college, to experience that lifestyle. To escape the small, stuffy town I grew up in.

Now I didn't want to leave. I wanted to stay and work at the café, I wanted to bask in the New Mexico air… And yes, be close to Elden.

I imagined what that might be like.

We could move into the small house Mom and Swiss used to live in. I'd work at the café part-time, maybe finish my degree online or at the local college thirty minutes away. We'd go riding on the weekends. We'd party, me nestled in his lap, his arm around me, claiming me.

Life would be simple and easy.

Of course, this was just a fantasy but one I wanted desperately, even though a few months ago I had much bigger plans for my future. I'd wanted to change the world. Wanted to experience new cultures, new cities. I'd wanted success. But those were my father's dreams merged with my own.

College had always been my father's dream. I didn't even like the idea of elitist institutions that turned teenagers into rabid creatures, focused on grades, extracurriculars, and whatever was needed to gain them entrance into a school that made millions off them.

I just had to figure out a way to tell my mom I did not want to go to the Ivy League college she'd been so proud of me for getting into. I wouldn't be living the life she literally went through hell to give me.

Then there was the news that I wanted to be with Elden. A man the same age as her. Yeah, that would not go down well. At all. I'd have to talk Swiss down. He would go crazy protective. But I'd convince them. Somehow.

But I needed to see Elden first. Needed to remind myself that this thing between us was real, that it wasn't just a fantasy.

I'd finally found the time to go to him. It was early in the morning, before my shift at Oliver's. Julian had finally decreed I could be trusted with the espresso machine, high praise coming from a man who took coffee as seriously as he did. I had never had a job before. My father had forbidden such a thing.

The work was hard, but I'd enjoyed it. Julian had already planned on me working whenever I was home from college.

Everything was moving much too fast, my life returning to its regularly scheduled programming as if my life, my family and my entire world view hadn't been dumped on its head.

And all I could think of was Elden.

Hence me walking toward his closed door. But I didn't make it there. Because the door opened.

I stared at the woman as she walked out of Elden's room. Her mascara was smudged under her eyes, hair mussed. She smiled shyly at me as she pulled down her skirt, walking down the hall. Her heels dangled from her hands.

She wasn't familiar. Not a club girl. Someone who had obviously attended a party last night while I had a quiet dinner with Mom and Swiss, listening to my mother make plans for the trip they were taking to drop me off at Brown.

My hands fisted at my sides as she walked past me, her shy smile dying as it became clear I wasn't going to smile back.

I wanted to. I tried to make it a habit to smile at every woman I made eye contact with. Society had brainwashed us into thinking we instinctively must perceive every woman as a threat, as competition... so that we wouldn't see each other as allies. We wouldn't work together to topple the systems created to oppress us.

It was my main goal to topple the patriarchy. And even in this moment, I knew that scowling at this woman was me projecting my own anger and insecurity. That anger was best directed at Elden, and even then, I wasn't completely entitled to it. We weren't a couple. He could fuck whomever he wanted.

Still, I scowled at the woman walking past me. Still, fury simmered within me, strong enough to pump my legs and stomp all the way toward the door she just closed.

I didn't feel like myself as the door slammed open. As it bounced off the wall, puncturing the drywall as it did so. All of this happened outside of me, as if I were possessed. I supposed I was. Possessed with jealousy. With a fury, a hurt I couldn't breathe around.

Elden was shrugging on his cut when I walked in. I glared at the Sons of Templar insignia, even though it symbolized my mother getting everything she wanted, being protected for life. Even though without it, I wouldn't be here.

Which was probably why I hated it so much. Because without the Sons of Templar, I would never have known Elden existed, and I never would've felt a pain, an obsession like I did with him.

He turned and stared at me with a measured coldness that sank somewhere deep, pulled out parts of me.

"You need to leave," he commented, staring straight into my eyes.

I looked away because I couldn't handle that expression, devoid of anything. My gaze landed on the bed, mussed and messy. My throat burned. They had just gotten out of it.

"No, I don't," I replied, my voice uneven and too wild for my liking. But I couldn't control it. Not as I looked back at Elden. "This is obviously some kind of warped, fucked-up, alpha male move… You are trying to push me away because you think it's what's best for me. Because you don't want to admit what's between us."

"There's nothing between us," he said flatly.

I flinched.

"That's not true, and you know it," I replied in a small voice.

His expression didn't waver, but he flexed his fist at his side. I held on to that small reaction as proof of what I was saying.

"I know you're a sheltered little girl who wanted to take a walk on the wild side," he commented, voice cold. "Who wanted a rebellion, a distraction."

Again, I flinched, but I jutted my chin upward in defiance.

"You're what I want," I argued, stepping forward.

Elden's jaw turned hard, and he held out his hand, pushing me backward. Not roughly. Not using an ounce of the real force I knew he could exert.

But the motion cracked something inside me.

"You don't know what you want," he spat, voice devoid of emotion. "You're just a kid."

I didn't flinch that time, which I was proud of. I was also proud I continued to stay upright as pain splintered everything, including my last remnants of hope.

"You don't mean that," I said defiantly, not ready to back down yet.

"Yes, I fuckin' do," he shot back. "You're a kid I'm forced to be polite to. You're a hot piece, and I was givin' way to my baser instincts. Nothin' more, nothin' less. You don't mean shit to me."

My stomach heaved, and I tasted bile. But I was still standing.

"Don't embarrass yourself any further," he added, lighting up a cigarette and blowing the smoke in my face. I winced at the bitter and acrid smell. "Fuck off back to college, find yourself some fuckin' boy who will be impressed by you."

Then without a second glance, he pushed past me and left me standing in his room, with the damaged drywall and my shattered heart.

"Sweetie, you left without even saying goodbye."

I clenched my teeth against the hurt in my mother's voice. I punished myself for that. For taking that goodbye away from her.

"We were going to go together; I had it all planned," she continued, her voice soft but disappointment ringing in her tone.

I sank down to the floor of the hotel room I was staying in after driving ten hours straight.

"I know, Mom," I said, trying to force my voice to sound even, normal. Whatever the fuck that was. "I just… needed the drive to clear my head." It wasn't a lie. Not entirely.

"I understand," Mom said after a beat of silence. "I can't imagine what these past few weeks have been like for you, and I'm so sorry—"

"No," I interrupted, pain splintering my fingertips as I gripped my phone, cringing at the blame in my mother's voice. "Don't you dare apologize, Mom," I stated firmly. "You have nothing to be sorry for. I'm so happy for you. There are no words for it." A single tear ran down my cheek. I took a deep breath. "Your life is wonderful," I whispered.

"Only because you're my daughter," Mom returned.

I smiled even though that wasn't entirely true. Her life had been hell because I was her daughter, because she wanted me safe, wanted me to have a nice life. Her life was only wonderful because I'd left home, giving her the opportunity to escape my father.

My heart bled. "I'm sorry," I murmured. "I didn't want to hurt you or worry you." I also knew there was no way I could pretend to be okay in front of my mother. She'd instantly see that something was wrong, and everything would come tumbling out. Swiss would definitely hurt Elden for breaking my heart like this.

And despite the cold, angry part of me that wanted Elden to hurt, I couldn't do it. So I'd called Julian, told him a lie about my college housing, gone back to my mom's house, thrown things into a suitcase and left in the car Mom had bought me the week before. Mom and Swiss hadn't been there, some kind of sign that the universe was looking out for me.

"How about you change your flights to…" I trailed off, trying to figure out when I'd be whole enough to pretend I was okay in front of my mother.

It felt like I'd never be okay.

"A month from now?" I decided. "My schedule is still up in the air, but I know I don't have class on Fridays, so we could make a long weekend of it?"

"A month?" my mother repeated in what could almost be described as a shriek. "Honey, Violet wants me to wait a *month* before we visit."

"Baby, she probably just wants to party her ass off for the first month," Swiss offered, and I almost smiled.

"That is not helpful," Mom muttered.

"Just to let you know, you're in deep shit for takin' off like that," Swiss grumbled, addressing me now.

My heart clenched again.

"I'm sorry," I apologized again.

"We're gonna be there in a month," Swiss informed me. "To the hour. Prepare yourself, kid."

"Don't you dare do too much decorating before I get there," my mother ordered. "And how are you going to put that bed frame and dresser together? They arrive in a couple of days. I'll research those Task Bunny people, but how do we know they're not serial killers or sex predators?" she fretted.

I did smile now. "Mom, I can put a bed and a dresser together."

"I love the confidence you have in yourself, sweetie, and I do believe you can do anything you put your mind to, except putting together flat pack furniture," my mother argued.

"Your faith in me is astounding," I replied dryly.

"She can do it, baby," Swiss said confidently.

My heart warmed. My father had never had that kind of confidence in me.

"And don't you dare invite any man into your home that you don't know," Swiss addressed me once more. "You have any trouble, I'll make some calls, get some of the Rhode Island chapter to come and do the heavy lifting."

I hadn't been aware that there was a Rhode Island chapter of the club. Then again, it was a national club, so it made sense. "Swiss, I cannot have a bunch of hot, muscled bikers doing the heavy lifting for me," I scoffed. "That totally goes against everything I stand for. I'm a capable female."

"Of course, you are," he agreed immediately.

My mind moved quickly, weighing the pros and cons of his suggestion. Something wicked inside of me formed a plan. "Actually… I do have a lot of furniture, and there a lot of stairs. If you could call them, that would be great."

"Good to see your principles are unwavering," Swiss teased.

I smiled wide. "Hey, a girl also has to recognize that fighting the patriarchy *is* making them do all the heavy lifting."

"Amen, sista," he replied.

Some of the ice around my heart began to melt.

"Okay, honey, I'm not happy about this, but I'll agree to it," Mom jumped in. "But you have to text me photos of every room in the house, and don't leave your drinks unattended, don't walk home alone, and I read about this app you can install on your phone—"

"She'll be fine, baby," Swiss interrupted for me, his voice warm.

I settled on the floor. My mom would be fine too. More than fine. And that warmth in Swiss's tone only reinforced that I'd made the right decision in keeping my mom in the dark. She'd protected me all my life in order for me to stay happy and clueless. It was time for me to do the same.

"I promise I will stay in constant contact," I began to choke up.

"You will, or I won't need a scary biker to do any of the menacing stuff. I'm pretty good at it too." Mom's voice was thick with tears.

"I love you, Mom," I whispered.

"To the stars, sweet girl."

I paused, biting my lip. "You too, Swiss," I added quietly.

It was true. It had been a whirlwind getting to Garnett and learning how completely my life had changed, but it had also been impossible not to love the man who treated my mother like she was the most precious thing on this earth. Who asked for my permission before marrying her. Who bought her a home. Who gave her room to be herself. Who gave her a true family. And he made me feel all the things my biological father never had.

He made me feel respected. Heard. Protected. Like an adult with my own unique ideas.

A hole opened up inside of me. One that had maybe been there all along, but I'd just ignored because I wasn't brave enough to face the reality of what my father had been. What I was losing.

"Love you, kiddo," he replied, his strong voice not quite as solid as it had been moments ago.

Once I hung up, I sat on the floor of the hotel bathroom for a long while.

ELDEN

"Someone has to take care of Violet."

I looked around the table as multiple brothers sat up a little straighter, their eyes lighting up.

It was a good thing that Swiss wasn't here or else there would be some men missing their eyes for looking like that at the mention of his stepdaughter.

"She left for college earlier than Swiss and her mom expected," Hansen explained.

I gripped my fists underneath the table as I remembered the way she'd looked at me. Remembered her crashing into my room then watching her crumble as I broke her down.

And she'd left. That day.

It was for the best, I told myself.

"Got the Rhode Island charter keepin' an eye on her," Hansen continued. "They're close, which is good, but if shit ever goes down with her, want someone from this chapter willing to drop everything to make sure she's a'ight." Hansen let out a sigh. "And I have a feeling, from what I've come to know of Violet, there is a high probability of shit goin' down."

There were smirks around the table. She'd already made quite an impression on everyone.

I fucking hated that.

"I'll do it," Javier, one of the newer patches, volunteered. Young. Handsome. A fucking player. He'd make sure no harm would come to her—fucker may've been handsome, but he was also a Son. That meant he would not hesitate to kill a man or woman if they threatened this club or those connected to it.

He was also twenty-fucking-five, fucked anything that moved … therefore he liked to fuck women. And he did not want them on the back of his bike. He wanted them in his bed, wanted to brand them—the fucker actually did that—then sent them packing once the sun rose.

Now, most men in the club operated in a fashion similar to this, without the branding portion of it, but they swapped that out with whatever depravity had been born out of their fucked-up lives.

We were all fucked-up in one way or another. You didn't patch into the Sons of Templar MC because you were well adjusted and came from a happy home.

My eyes drifted to one of the few men whose eyes had not lit up at the suggestion… blond haired, square jawed, all-American Anderson. He had come from a happy home. White picket fence and that kinda shit. And he was married to a nice girl, had a kid, another on the way.

Yet here he was, sitting at the table with outlaws and murderers.

He was the exception. Not the rule.

The rule was, you put this cut on because a piece of you was missing. A vital piece that made it impossible for you to operate in society. A piece that thirsted for blood, violence and pussy. Or dick if you were inclined that way.

Javier was one of our youngest patches. And most recent. Which meant he did not have enough self-preservation to know that he was essentially signing his own death warrant by even thinking about fucking Violet.

Swiss, her stepfather, considered that girl to be his blood, and he was the most fucked-up, ruthless and vengeful of us all… which was really saying something.

Just the thought of Violet's creamy skin being marked by Javier —even with her consent, especially with her consent—had me grinding my teeth tightly, red slowly creeping over my vision.

Fuck.

I took in a deep breath.

"No, you fuckin' won't," I clipped out, taking great pains to keep from growling. I didn't look at Javier, didn't trust myself to. Instead, I focused on my president, Hansen, whose eyes were on me. I didn't like the small uptick of his mouth, the knowing glint in his eye. He saw too fucking much.

"I'll take care of it," I grumbled.

The uptick grew, and I clenched my fists harder.

Colby was also smiling. He was Violet's best friend in the club. I hated that friendship too. But he didn't look at her like he wanted to fuck her. Hadn't made a move. So, he was breathing.

"It's settled," Hansen declared. "You're on deck for Violet if needed."

I nodded once. She'd hate it. Hate me. But that was fine. That was good. That was how it was meant to be.

VIOLET

I was walking around angry.

Although angry seemed too light of a word for how I felt. Too thin. Too pedestrian. You're angry that you missed your flight.

Angry that a friend of yours told a secret she promised to keep. Angry that they killed off your favorite character in that show you're binging.

Anger is a fleeting emotion that burns hot and quick. It promises to be temporary. But this… thing inside me was not temporary. It was living, pulsating inside me. Leeched onto my insides like a parasite. Except, as much as I wanted to tell myself this anger was something foreign, the worst part was, it was me.

An ugly, unknown, impatient, intolerant, toxic part of me. The part that had resulted in a constant, painful ache on the left side of my head from grinding my teeth so hard in my sleep. I could barely eat due to the agony that came with the simple motion of chewing. The part of me that laid awake at night, staring at the images of whatever show I was using to try to lull me into unconsciousness, my body fighting sleep until the early hours. Then my mind battled wakefulness when I did manage to lapse into a thin slumber full of turmoil and too graphic dreams.

It seemed so fucking stupid to be walking around a college campus of people who were my age, laughing, walking in groups, already friends. I felt very alone. More alone than I ever had in France, an unfamiliar city in a country where I didn't know a soul. But maybe that's why I felt so alone here. There were many people who cared about me, but few who truly knew what was going on in my life. And the one person who knew everything had made it clear he wanted nothing to do with me.

I'd walked aimlessly around the campus, trying to find the feeling I was supposed to have here. Then I'd followed directions off campus and down tree-lined streets, barely paying attention, turning only when the robotic voice on my phone told me to, stopping when it said I'd arrived.

"You Violet?" a masculine voice asked me as I lingered in front of the charming Victorian that would serve as my home for the next year. We had the option to extend the lease through our undergrad studies, if we chose. But I didn't know the girls I'd be living with. I didn't even know if I wanted to be here to finish my degree. Except I had nowhere else to go. Garnett was too dangerous now. Full of pain. I didn't fit in there. This was it. The place I was meant to be.

I jerked, turning around to see four motorcycles parked on the curb as well as a moving truck. I had not heard any of them pull up.

The man was older with a long, gray beard, faded tattoos and a beer belly. But he still had the certain… *jen ne sais quoi* everyone wearing a Sons of Templar cut seemed to have.

The men behind him were younger, one wearing a 'Prospect' cut, who looked closest to my age, lanky and moody. The other two were a little older, both with muscles, tattoos and strong jawlines.

There were a bunch of sorority girls across the street gaping at them. I wasn't sure if it was in disapproval or appreciation. I didn't much care.

"I am Violet," I said to him, holding out a hand.

"Bill," he replied gruffly, shaking my hand.

I raised my brow at the name. Most of the men I'd met had badass nicknames or just badass names that they were born with. I'd not yet met a biker named Bill.

He grinned at my brow quirk. "I know, I know," he muttered good-naturedly. "It's the name my Momma gave me, so it's the name I'm gonna keep."

I smiled at him. "As you should."

"Your shit in there?" he tilted his head toward the moving truck.

I nodded. "I really appreciate you guys coming out to do this. I figure it's not in the usual job description."

"No such thing as a job description when you wear this cut," he smiled widely, his handlebar mustache curling toward his cobalt eyes. "We were in the area, don't mind helpin' out. Plus, it's always fun scaring the piss out of Ivy Leaguers," he winked. "Come on boys," he turned, whistling at the other men.

Each of them got off their bikes, one of the middle-aged bikers lifting his sunglasses to give me a meaningful look that rightly should've done something.

But it didn't.

Nonetheless, I smiled slyly.

"Holy fuck!" a female voice commented from beside me.

I turned to regard the owner of the voice.

A petite, dark-haired girl stood beside me in bright purple platforms that gave her an extra six inches. Her skirt was also purple, tight and short, a sheer purple shirt haphazardly buttoned, showing a black bra underneath. She had on multiple gold necklaces. All of them looked expensive, as did the purse in the crook of her arm. It was silk and had Saint Laurent printed all over it.

She pushed white vintage sunglasses to the top of her dark brown hair which had butterfly clips throughout it.

Her eyes were expertly rimmed with liner, long lashes framing her burnt copper gaze. Her skin was porcelain and flawless, her nose larger than the rest of her delicate features but only made her more uniquely attractive.

I was instantly jealous of how put together she seemed. How confident.

"You know them?" she jerked her head to the men she was staring at who were carrying furniture into the house.

I nodded. "Well, my stepfather knows them. They're… friends. Here to help out."

"Well, I owe your stepfather and you a really big fucking thank you," she chirped. "I haven't been laid in a hot minute, and that one in the middle looks like he knows how to please a woman."

Her eyes were on the Latino man who had hair brushing his shoulders, bulging muscles and an air of mischief.

"He does," I agreed.

"I'm Sariah," she held out a hand stacked with rings. "Not

Sarah. I've been fighting it all my life. I have a Jewish mother and a Mormon father who wanted me to emulate the 'princess of the Lord,'" she said in air quotes. Her tongue darted out to trace her shiny pink lips as she followed the men with her gaze. "Needless to say, that kind of backfired."

I couldn't help but grin. "Violet," I offered.

Her eyes raked over me. Though the gaze wasn't judgmental in the least, I suddenly felt self-conscious. I hadn't washed my hair in a couple of days, and it was piled messily on top of my head. Nor had I had the energy to wear makeup, the dark circles under my eyes unmistakable. I was wearing jeans that fit low on my hips because of the weight I'd lost over the past few days, a tight tank and Converse. Not my usual style, but I didn't feel like my usual self.

"Violet, my new roommate and effortlessly beautiful, stone-cold hottie with outlaw biker connections," she snickered, meeting my eyes. "Love you already." She reached out to squeeze my hand.

I didn't expect the contact, but it was nice. I hadn't had human contact since Elden pushed me away in his bedroom at the club.

My throat burned with the memory. I'd used all my antacids on the drive.

"Now, I've got booze in here," she held up her large and expensive purse that indeed had a bottle sticking out of it. "Let's order pizza, drink and watch the men work."

She didn't give me the opportunity to answer, just gripped my hand harder and dragged me inside.

I didn't say it out loud, but I found myself endlessly glad that she was my new roommate too.

CHAPTER *Five*

I DIDN'T, as a rule, answer the phone when unknown numbers called me. Actually, I did not answer the phone at all. No one in my generation did.

Except when it was my mother or my grandparents. Those numbers were programmed into my phone. My father's number was blocked.

This number was not saved.

But this number also had a New Mexico area code. It was probably spam. And even if it wasn't, even if it was who I thought it was, I shouldn't answer.

Shouldn't.

Not *didn't.*

"What the fuck?" a voice demanded in greeting.

Everything inside of me froze. The voice sent shivers down my spine. For a moment, I lost my breath. But then I remembered... I remembered the smell of the smoke he blew in my face, the shy smile of the girl with the messy hair. His words, biting and cruel.

My back straightened, and I pushed past the pain that was thankfully numbed because of the bottle of tequila in Sariah's purse that was now half empty in our kitchen.

"Who is this?" I asked sweetly.

"Violet," Elden warned. "You know who the fuck this is, and you better tell me right now that not a single one of those fuckers laid a hand on you."

"Forgive me, but I have no idea what you're talking about," I told him in a stiff tone.

"I know the Rhode Island chapter was called in to help you fucking move," he seethed.

My hand was shaking as I toyed with my hair in the mirror. "They were," I agreed. "But I still fail to understand what it has to do with you, nor is it any of your business whether or not any of them touched me." I let my hair fall down my back, regarding my outfit.

I had showered. Washed and blow-dried my hair. I'd put on makeup.

Sariah had inspired me to get back to myself again. I loved fashion, and looking good helped you feel good, my grandmother always said.

I'd promised myself I wouldn't let a man be the reason I stopped taking care of myself.

I had on high-waisted pants that cinched in my waist, and the wide legs skimmed over the spiked heels I was wearing. My cropped tee showed off a fair amount of skin but still looked chic. I wore the necklace my mom got me around my neck, and the leather jacket Swiss gave me was sitting on top of my shoulders. It gave my classic outfit an edge. I had an edge now. It was best to lean into it, I figured.

"The last time I saw you, you'd just got done fucking some other woman," I told Elden, the memory sharpening that edge of mine. "Don't think I'll put up with your bullshit, misogynistic double standards."

"If a single one of them touched you, they're dead," he growled, not even addressing the comment about the other woman. Of course, he wouldn't. He was entitled to fuck whomever he wanted while I was required to remain pure and unsullied just in case he decided he wanted me again.

I sighed dramatically, hating that I was having such a reaction inwardly, but outwardly, I was very proud of my composure.

"No, they're not," I replied flatly. "You don't get to call me and growl like a fucking caveman, threaten to hurt people for touching me. Because it's none of your business. I'm none of your business, *remember*? And I really don't appreciate you projecting your bullshit views on me. I'm in college. I'm allowed to experiment however much I want and with whomever I want. Kindly lose my number."

Then I hung up.

My heart thundered in my ears. The urge to immediately call him back was so overwhelming I felt sick. Literally sick.

I almost did it, and maybe I would've, had Sariah not chosen that moment to walk into my room.

"Bitch, you look great," she declared, eyes flitting over me. "I need a pair of shoes to go with this outfit." She gestured to the hot pink, silk shirt she was wearing, unbuttoned to show the lacy bra that was also pink. She wore jeans that were ripped and fit her like a glove. She looked effortlessly glam, expensive and grown up.

"I had my eye on..." she trailed off as she peered into my neatly organized closet. "These!" she held up a pair of pink heels that I'd worn to some charity function or another.

She didn't ask if she could borrow them, just sat on my bed and slipped them on her feet.

It filled me up, the way in which she made herself at home in here. The way she was completely comfortable with me, acting like we'd been friends our entire lives, like we hadn't just met earlier today.

There was a connection there, one that I didn't think I could ever have with a friend. Similar to the connection I felt with Elden, but not in a way that could destroy my world. In a way that made me feel I wasn't quite as alone as I once was. I instantly felt like I could tell her anything.

"That was just a biker twice my age threatening to kill anyone who laid hands on me, even though he pushed me away after giving me one of the most intense orgasms of my life. That was after he flew to France to beat up the guy who hit me and also got me pregnant. I got an abortion. I feel guilty for not feeling guilty about it. Also, my mother is married to the best friend of the guy who just called. She met him after leaving my father, not telling me that she'd left him or that my father beat her my whole life and almost killed her," I blurted it all out in one breath.

Sariah, who had been halfway through fastening my heels on her feet when I began, blinked a couple of times with wide eyes.

Oh, fuck. I'd already pushed away the one person I felt connected to here.

"Okay," she said mildly. "Well, we're gonna need more booze. A lot of it," she declared. "And then you're gonna go into a lot more detail." She finished fastening the shoe then got up. "Tomorrow, we'll go and buy a fuck lot of crystals. And sage. Plus shoes."

She walked over to me and pulled me into a hug.

She smelled of Tom Ford and expensive shampoo.

I sank into the embrace, not realizing that's exactly what I needed.

"I hadn't told anyone that," I whispered into her hair.

She held me at arm's length, regarding me. "Holy fuck. I have no idea how you haven't exploded or like, gone deep into a Taylor Swift hole, listening to Red—her version—on repeat," she slowly shook her head. "You're very fucking impressive, Violet."

"I don't feel it." Tears built in my eyes. "I feel like a fucking mess."

"Well, you are," she agreed with a smile, linking her arm in mine. "But a hot fucking mess. And, honey, everyone's a mess on the inside. That's why cocktails were invented. And we're going to have many." She winked.

She walked me into the kitchen where we did have many cocktails with our other roommates—who were also here early and who I liked a lot, but I didn't share my story about Elden with—and I thought, maybe, just maybe, I was going to be okay.

The first few weeks in my new house passed in somewhat of a blur. Even though I'd arrived a week before classes technically started, there was a lot of unpacking, organizing, shopping and partying to do.

I'd chosen to load up on classes so I wouldn't have time to think about things.

Though I wasn't at all religious, I found myself truly believing that Sariah was a gift from a higher power. It was legitimately impossible to wallow around her.

She knew the gory details of everything that had happened in France and when I got back. She hated Elden in solidarity with me.

Except I didn't hate him. Not one bit. But I got good at pretending I did.

Our other two roommates were great. Henri was Korean and a double major. Her hair was cut in a severe bob that made her look much older than she was. She came from a hideously rich family and was constantly put together in monochromatic outfits and holding a stack of textbooks. She also loved to party and was in a polyamorous relationship.

Ollie always wore a beanie and had a smattering of freckles across her face. She was a tech major who spent a lot of time in her room on her computer but also baked kickass muffins, which she did for us every morning. Mostly because she was wired from the energy drinks she'd been chugging all night while she was doing… whatever it was she did on that computer.

Our house was an eclectic mix of all of our styles… bohemian, glam, eccentric, classic. We had a chore chart, and everyone seemed to get along harmoniously even though we were all pretty different.

Sure, I was still feeling a little sorry for myself and unsure in my own skin because it still burned with the ghost of Elden's touch. I didn't sleep much, which was fine because there wasn't much time for sleeping. Not with all the campus parties we had to attend because I needed to be 'introduced' to our year, according to Sariah, who seemed to know everyone there was to know and whom I had yet to see wear the same outfit twice.

All of her clothes, accessories and her car hinted that she, too, like Henri, had seriously loaded parents. But since mentioning them in regard to the origin of her name, she hadn't spoken of them once. I understood that, considering I'd rather donate a kidney than speak about my father.

I hadn't heard from him. There was no way for me to hear from him since there was no way for him to get my new number, and his was blocked. My grandmother would never give it to him. I wrote her a long letter about… well, everything. Because I wasn't sure how to say it on the phone and because I couldn't be sure how she'd react. I adored my grandmother. She was warm, kind and had a wicked sense of humor. My grandfather was a little more stuffy, serious, but he was one of my favorite people in the world.

Still, my father was their only son. I couldn't imagine what it would be like to hear what a monster he truly was. I also couldn't imagine what he was telling them in my mother's absence.

It hurt my heart not to be in contact with them, not to share my new home with them, not to send my grandmother photos of the outfit I wore to the first day of classes—she had wonderful style and followed fashion week like it was the Super Bowl.

I hoped with everything in my heart that my grandmother would believe my mother. That I wouldn't be forced to lose almost all of my family in one fell swoop.

Again, the ache of that prospect, my inner turmoil over Elden and everything that happened in France was swirling inside of me as I partied and commenced my first weeks of classes.

They were tough. I shouldn't have expected much else considering I was taking the maximum number of courses and majoring in architecture at an Ivy League school, but I'd been a little spoiled with the European approach to learning and life in general. Everything was slower there. There wasn't that frenzied urgency to be the best, the idea that there was only a certain amount of places at the top, and if you paused, if you made time for rest, then you'd forsake that spot to someone who wanted it more, someone who hustled harder.

Again, it was a good thing because the less time I had to think, the better.

I had not heard from Elden since I told him to lose my number, and him not calling meant he was respecting my wishes. But still, when I went to sleep, it was to fantasizing about him turning up at my door—in the rain because it made it more dramatic—while declaring that he couldn't think without me then carrying me into my room and claiming me.

That did not happen.

But the rain did.

A torrential downpour—apparently, a record amount for the area in one hundred years—began just as I was driving home.

The anxiety began the second the first rain drop hit the windshield, and I was an absolute wreck by the time the downpour was in full effect. It was hard to breathe, my fingertips numb from my ironclad grip on the steering wheel. My vision blurred.

It was one of the worst attacks I'd had, most likely made worse by all of the emotions I'd been ignoring the past weeks. Had it really only been… eight weeks since my life changed so completely? Though a therapist might not agree with me, I was proud that this was my first mental breakdown.

From somewhere far away, my phone buzzed, and on autopilot, I pressed answer on the car's screen.

"Are you driving?" the voice rumbled through my car, battling against the hammering sound of the rain and my sobs.

I could suddenly feel my fingers again, and I could breathe underneath the weight on my chest, his voice floating into all those chaotic places and creating a state of calm.

"Elden?" I hiccupped. Even in my current state, it felt nice saying his name. I hadn't even let myself think it. I'd been trying something different.

It hadn't been working.

"Yeah, baby, it's me," he said, his voice gentler than I'd ever heard it.

"Why are you calling me?" I asked, my heart rate slowing further as the road came into more stark detail, though I still couldn't see more than the distortion of taillights.

"Are you driving, Violet?" he repeated, voice still gentle.

I nodded, focusing on the road but also on the tenor of his voice. Things got slower. The world no longer seemed like it was going to implode.

Then I realized he couldn't see me nodding. "Yes, I'm driving," I told him. "I had a full day of classes and I forgot to eat, and my roommate said she really felt like burritos from the good Mexican place," I babbled, letting my grip loosen a tad on the steering wheel.

"You see, there's a Mexican place that's fifteen minutes closer to our house where we go to in a pinch, but if we're really stressed or just super hungry, one of us always goes to the good Mexican place." I took a deep breath. "We have a rotation," I continued. "It was my turn today."

At some point during this tirade, my heart rate had almost completely returned to normal, and I didn't feel like I was about to die.

"How far from home are you, baby?"

Again, his tone was even, deep, moving through the air like honey, smoothing itself over all of my ragged edges.

It was only then that I realized he was calling me 'baby'. He had no reason to call me 'baby'.

I was not his baby. He told me that I was nothing to him the last time I saw him.

But he was calling me. It was raining.

I blinked away my tears as realization dawned. He had been watching the weather forecast, so he knew it was going to rain today. And he called me. Because he remembered what I'd said about the rain.

My vision cleared completely.

"Why are you calling me?" I whispered.

"Why haven't you eaten all day, Violet?"

I frowned at the road in front of me. "How do you know that?"

"You told me, before explaining the difference between the Mexican places."

I let out a sigh. "I've been busy."

"You shouldn't be too busy to fuckin' eat, baby," he grunted.

"You shouldn't care," I snapped. "Don't even get me started on the things you shouldn't be doing. Riding a motorcycle without a helmet… recipe for a brain injury if you don't die immediately. And smoking. Like, who smokes anymore? Yes, it may look cool, and you pull it off like a bearded, biker James Dean, but the lung cancer is not cool or sexy." I sucked in a deep breath. "And don't call me baby," I added as an afterthought.

There was a long silence on the phone, and I feared for a moment that he'd hung up. Anxiety crept up my throat.

"How far are you from home?" he asked, obviously choosing not to argue with me at this point.

I let out a dramatic sigh.

"Ten minutes, maybe less if I go a little faster."

"Don't drive any fuckin' faster," he ordered.

Something skipped inside of me at the firmness of his words, remembering when he'd demanded I take off my dress.

Though I liked to think I was in the driver's seat of my own life

—and right now I was literally in the driver's seat—something inside me relaxed when Elden took control.

I let off the gas just a little.

"Are you going to hang up now?" I asked in a small voice, terrified that I'd lose him.

"No, Violet," he replied firmly. "I'm gonna be right here until you pull up to your house."

Something inside of me relaxed. No, everything inside of me relaxed.

The rain battering the windshield was the only sound for a long time. "Are you afraid of anything?" I finally asked.

There was a small pause before he answered. "Besides somethin' happenin' to you?"

My heart skipped, and I did my best not to latch on to that.

"I'm afraid of small spaces," he admitted in a low voice. "Of being locked in somewhere. Trapped somewhere. My room at the clubhouse is barely big enough to keep me sane."

I digested that information, my body rebelling at the thought of him fighting against panic by just living in his room at the club. I held on to that information tightly, wanting to tattoo it somewhere so it could be mine forever.

"Why don't you live somewhere else, then?" I asked him. "Somewhere bigger."

"Because there's nowhere else for me to go. The club is my home."

My heart spasmed at this admission, at the vulnerability in his tone. The club, for whatever reason, whatever was in his past that I wasn't brave enough to ask about, was all he had. And I was jeopardizing that. Me wanting him could take that all away. Swiss was a more established member of the club, he had more rights. That's what I assumed at least.

"How old are you?" I asked the question that would make things all the more difficult between us. I knew he was older. The lines in his weathered skin told me that, the silver in his chocolate hair told me that. But 'too old for me' was a vague concept and I needed to know numbers. Not that it would make any difference.

"Thirty-five," he said without hesitation, his tone hard.

I sucked my teeth. There it was. The number. Sixteen years between us. My mom had had me by that age.

Not that it mattered to me. If anything, the stretch of time, how it made this all the more forbidden, made me want to sink my nails deeper into this. Into us. Yes, that was fucked up, but I didn't give a shit.

We didn't speak for the rest of the drive, but he was there. I could hear him breathing against the sound of the rain.

"Elden," I whispered, putting the car in park. "Why did you call me?"

The rain poured on the roof of my car as I waited for his answer.

"Because, baby, you don't like to drive in the rain," he murmured. Then he was gone.

I sat in the car for a long time after that. Maybe even would have all day if Sariah hadn't come up with a leopard print umbrella, knocking on my window.

"Bitch!" she called through the glass. "You better not be letting those burritos get cold, or they will never find your body."

So, then there were burritos. Henri made margaritas. We watched movies and got drunk. I fell asleep on the sofa. Ollie woke me up at three in the morning on one of her trips to the fridge.

I stumbled to my own room, collapsing on the bed, only then remembering Elden's last words to me with the patter of rain on the roof.

I had not heard from Elden since the day it rained. My Mom and Swiss came to visit exactly one month, to the hour, since I called them.

Mom took me shopping, and Swiss fixed things around the house while Sariah followed him around asking about brothers and cousins.

My roommates were vaguely obsessed with my mother and stepfather, which made sense because my mom was amazing as was Swiss. Together, they were something else entirely.

It was our final night, out for dinner, just the three of us when Mom shared the news.

I had suspected since she was constantly nursing a glass of wine, slyly handing it off to Swiss when she thought I wasn't looking. Then there was Swiss being extra protective of my mom, which was saying something. He threw a fit when she walked in with her arms full of shopping bags.

But I'd wanted Mom to have her moment.

So, I let her take us out for a nice dinner and watched her shift nervously in her seat as she worked up the courage to tell me. She was likely rehearsing some kind of script in her head.

But by the time the waiter came with iced waters, she just blurted, "I'm pregnant."

I didn't visibly react.

Swiss tried his absolute hardest not to chuckle.

He failed.

Mom hit him in the bicep, which likely did more damage to her hand than his arm.

"Don't laugh at me," she snapped.

His eyes twinkled. "I've got an eternity with you, can't make that promise, Countess," he said. "Plus, you're fucking funny."

"I have to agree with Swiss on that," I chimed in. "Though sometimes not on purpose."

Mom scowled at me before her brows quickly pinched in worry. "Are you mad?"

I blinked at her. "Mad?"

"That I'm pregnant," she explained. Swiss tucked her into his shoulder, obviously unable to see my mother in even a little bit of turmoil without touching her.

"Mom!" I half yelled at her. "I am not mad. I'm so, so happy for you. I cannot wait to have a little brother or sister." I was telling the truth. My heart did swell with happiness, not just at the prospect of a baby sibling, but for my mother getting the chance to have a different kind of life. The kind she deserved.

"You're really happy?" Mom asked.

"Are *you* happy?" I countered.

Her eyes swelled with tears, and she didn't speak, only nodded.

Swiss's face was soft, his own eyes alight with something that could not be described as simple happiness.

"The restaurant is going to be ready to open in a couple of months," she told me, wiping away tears.

My jaw dropped at both the change in subject and the news. I'd finished off my designs for the space, sent them to an actual architecture firm and contractor.

"I didn't think contractors moved that fast." I took a long sip of my wine, attempting to regain my composure

Mom looked at Swiss. "They do when my husband is around," she muttered with a grin. "We're having the grand opening," she looked back at me. "You have to be there."

I did have to be there. To support my mother.

In just under two months. That was enough time. To get myself strong enough to see him again. Maybe I wouldn't even see him.

"Of course, I'll be there," I promised my mother.

Maybe those months would change everything.

Maybe I wouldn't feel this way.

Or maybe I'd feel exactly the same. It didn't matter. I had to go back eventually. Had to face him some time.

CHAPTER
Six

TWO MONTHS LATER

"SWEETHEART, YOU OUTDID YOURSELF," my mom hiccupped from beside me.

We were standing in the middle of 'Violet's'.

It was the day of the grand opening.

I'd had the week off for mid-semester break and arrived a few days ago. Though I was full of complex feelings about Elden, though I hadn't been able to sleep the week leading up to this visit, everything in me relaxed once I made it through town limits. I opened the window of the car and leaned out, smelling the crisp, desert air that was welcoming in warmer weather.

Most of my time was spent doing last minute stuff with mom for the restaurant, working on assignments and helping Julian out at the coffee shop. I made time to hang out with Colby at the club, and when I was there, I jumped every time a man in leather walked through the door.

"He's off on a run," Colby offered when I almost gave myself whiplash trying to see who had entered the room this time.

"Who?" I replied when I saw it was just Javier, who had yet to understand I was never going to sleep with him.

"No one," Colby grinned. "Because I know you don't have anything going on with anyone wearin' a patch. But you know, if you did, that particular person would be out on a run. Not due back until next week."

My body sagged with disappointment and relief as I took a long pull of my beer. "I don't know who you're talking about."

"Uh-huh," he muttered. Luckily, he didn't push it further.

He was gone. The week I was back from college. It had to be by design. Maybe it had nothing to do with me. Maybe I was nothing to him.

Except he called me when it rained.

"I can't believe you designed this!" Mom yelled, looking around the room.

I jumped out of my thoughts and back into the room with my mother. My mother who was beaming, wearing a burnt orange dress that showed off her tiny baby bump.

"Mom, I didn't design all of this," I argued. "There were things the contractors had to change because I'm not actually a qualified architect."

"I don't give a shit," Caroline put in from her spot beside me. "You're designing our house when we renovate."

"You just renovated," Macy snapped, walking from the bar area with a glass of champagne.

Her, Caroline and Freya were all here to help Mom out since she couldn't do any heavy lifting. Except every man in the club was doing the heavy lifting, and we were just moving chairs around and gossiping.

"I want you to do my place," Macy said.

"I really am not qualified," I told them all.

"Bullshit," she replied. Yep, my mom cursed now. "You did all of this, and you know it." Her eyes watered. "You're so talented, Violet. I can't wait to see what you do with your life."

Caroline, Freya and Macy all exchanged looks then made their way back toward the kitchen, whispering about sneaking some appetizers to give Mom her moment.

Though it was a wonderful thing for my mother to say, the words scraped against my skin. She said things like that whenever I spoke to her. How excited she was about my future. All the great things I would do. Like there were still plans for me. Like I should keep going down the road my father had forced us down.

I shook those thoughts off and regarded the space.

I'd wanted warmth. Wanted it to compliment the New Mexico landscape. The walls were rough plaster, full of texture and painted a warm beige. There was a huge arch separating the bar area and the dining area. The tables were round, reclaimed wood, the chairs plush and comfortable. There was greenery everywhere including hanging plants. The light fixtures were vintage chandeliers, mismatched to give the space a unique look. I'd kept the exposed beams of the roof, the windows looking out toward the desert.

"Okay, it looks great. And I could use this for my final project," I agreed.

Mom pulled me into a hug. "I'm so proud of you."

I leaned into the hug, seconds away from falling apart in my mother's arms.

"Countess," a gruff voice barked from the entrance.

Mom let me go, and we both looked to Swiss who was examining us with his arms folded across his chest.

"Uh-oh," my mom murmured. "I obviously lifted something I shouldn't." She grinned and kissed me on the cheek before walking toward her husband.

"I'm pregnant, not an invalid," she snapped at him with faux annoyance.

I watched them bicker until Swiss yanked her in for a kiss I probably shouldn't have witnessed.

That was when I started thinking about things I shouldn't. Like Elden. Like why my father was so evil.

That was also when I made my way over to the bar and poured myself a glass of champagne that Freya had already opened. Though drinking myself into oblivion was a bad plan, at least it was a plan.

The opening was a huge success.

The food was amazing, the company was better only because the company was my new family, and the wine was great. I may have been overserved. Or overserved myself.

The booze helped at first, making it easier to smile, laugh, play the part of the resilient, talented daughter home from college, taking everything in stride and not longing for the man who was as old as her mother.

Well, it worked until it didn't.

Until dinner was over and no one noticed me slip out.

It was cold outside the restaurant, and I wasn't wearing a coat. A booze blanket sufficed, though.

"Why aren't you here?" I demanded, holding the phone up to my ear after dialing the number I probably shouldn't have.

"You're drunk," Elden observed.

I scowled as I teetered on the curb, looking at everyone inside Violet's. They were laughing. Drinking. Eating.

"Whether or not I've had a cocktail to celebrate my mother's restaurant opening is beyond the point," I slurred, slipping off the curb and catching myself. "The point is you're not here."

"Where are you, Violet?" Elden asked.

"I asked you a question first," I hissed, frowning at the car idling way down the street. The lights were off, but I could swear I saw a shadow in it.

"I'm on a run," he replied tightly. "Now, I'm asking you

where you are because it's late, you're fucking drunk, and it's too damn quiet wherever the fuck you are. If you're outside alone—"

"What?" I demanded. "You're gonna spank me, *Daddy*?"

There was a dangerous silence on the other end of the phone.

"Don't you ever fuckin' call me that again," he demanded, his voice colder than the early spring air.

We were silent for a long time. I continued to stare at the car that hadn't moved. Elden didn't hang up.

"Go back inside, Violet," Elden sighed quietly, sounding tired.

"Why aren't you here, Elden?" I whined.

"Because you're there, baby," he murmured. "And we're playin' with fire right now. I don't want you getting burned."

My breath caught in my chest. "What if I want to be burned by you?"

"I'm doing the right thing here, Violet."

"For whom?" I demanded, thinking of all those ugly words he said to me the last time I saw him.

Elden didn't answer.

"Yeah, I thought so," I muttered.

"Go back inside, baby," he said, softer this time.

I stayed on the line for a long time.

He didn't hang up.

Not until the door to the restaurant opened and Colby poked his head out.

"Violet!" he barked. "What the fuck are you doing out here alone?"

"Just a second!" I called to him, but Elden had already hung up.

I went back to school after Mom's opening. She promised to send me any and all baby updates. I was designing her nursery, and even though it was more décor than any kind of design, I enjoyed it.

Sariah was happy to have her partner in crime back and made me tell her everything about Garnett and the Sons of Templar.

Elden called when it rained.

If I was driving, we spoke for however long it took to get to my next destination. I drove extra slowly and lingered in my car for as long as I could. We didn't venture into the more dangerous topics… like what the calls meant or if he was seeing anyone else, though I tortured myself with the memory of that woman coming out of his room.

He asked about my classes. His tone got deep and tight if I mentioned lack of sleeping and eating. I didn't even mention the partying, which there was a lot of. I asked him precious little about his life in Garnett because those questions were much too dangerous. I asked him about what he was reading, and then the second I got off the phone with him, I bought that exact book so we could talk about it the next time he called. Once, there was a barking in the background of one of our calls.

"Did the club get a puppy?" I asked, no longer focusing on the rain or the tightness in my chest. In fact, the only tightness I got in my chest when it rained was caused by the excitement I felt hearing Elden's voice.

"No," Elden answered. He was a man of few words, but it was rare that he answered using only one.

"There's a dog in the background," I pointed out.

Elden sighed audibly. "You're not gonna stop askin' about the dog, are you?"

"Nope. I love dogs. I always wanted one, but my father never allowed them." My breath caught as I realized I'd mentioned him. I never did that. Not even in passing.

"Local shelter calls me," Elden began, filling the silence. His voice was deep, smooth. It calmed me. "If they get a dog in that they can't get adopted here and need someone to transport it to a family outside of the city or state. They don't have enough funding for that. So, I do it."

I digested that information. "So, you rescue puppies?" I asked on a whisper.

"I transport dogs across state lines when I have the time," he corrected.

I grinned. "You rescue puppies," I sang, my fondness for this man growing with every passing second.

"You should have a home," I decided. "One that isn't a room in a clubhouse. One that has space. Land. For dogs." I thought about the space I'd been designing for him in my head. "Open plan," I continued. "Lots of windows. Nothing closed in. So you feel free."

Elden didn't say anything for a long time. All I heard was the barking.

"Are you there?" I asked, concerned.

"Yeah, baby, I'm here," he said, his low tone wrapping around me.

It had changed something, me talking about a home. Me talking about his future. I didn't know what exactly it was... But we didn't speak for the rest of the drive.

I found myself praying, hoping for rain, scouring the weather forecast just so I could go out driving in circles when rain was predicted. Sure, it was a little crazy, but Elden made me abandon sanity. I might've been living a college life and even enjoying it, but I only felt partially whole there. Whatever free time I had was spent imagining what life would be like if I was with Elden.

I was getting to know that. In small slices. On rainy days.

My need for him hadn't dimmed. Not even a little.

I couldn't bring myself to even drunkenly make out with the many frat boys Sariah had pushed into my arms. I wished I could because that would be some juvenile way of punishing him. But the whole point was to have him *stop* seeing me as a child.

Those thoughts were swirling in my mind, along with a mild hangover and stress about an assignment due at midnight tonight, as I walked across campus.

I didn't even notice him until he was standing in my path. I almost bumped into him. I didn't recognize him at first, and I reacted on instinct, my hackles going up, alarm bells ringing in my head to get away from this man. He didn't fit in with even the scruffiest of the hipsters. He was out of place here, everyone giving him a wide berth, but I'd been too caught up in my own head.

"Sorry," I muttered, glancing up, intending on walking quickly away.

But then I focused a little more on him.

"Dad?" I stuttered. The word came out on instinct, even though I'd sworn black and blue to anyone who would listen that he wasn't that to me anymore. Well, I didn't talk about my father, so I didn't swear to everyone, but I reassured my mother every time she brought him up that I was done with him, and I didn't want to talk about it. I knew it bothered her. Knew that she carried a lot of guilt for something that wasn't hers to carry. I knew she worried about me endlessly, which was why I was still playing the part. I was still Violet, her sensible, well-mannered daughter with radical ideas to be sure, but not to be worried about.

Certainly not the Violet who did drugs, got abortions and became infatuated with bikers almost twice her age. It saddened me, the lies I told my mother to protect her. That the reality of experiencing adult type things—the things I had been so anxious to experience—had created a distance I never could've imagined having with my mother.

But the biggest lies I told her were when I spoke about my father.

When I said my biological father was dead to me.

All talk. Big talk. Confident talk. Talk that I had believed, to the very core of me, was the truth.

My father was a monster.

But he was also my father.

He was the man who'd cheered me on from the sidelines at soccer games. Who had pulled me into his arms every night when he came home from work, smelling of expensive cologne. He had read me bedtime stories. Put Band-Aids on scraped knees.

That couldn't be erased. No matter how much I wanted it to be.

Especially seeing the man he was now.

He didn't *look* like my father.

My entire life, my dad was always put together. In expensive suits, ties, loafers. And when he wasn't in those, it was pressed polos, shorts, immaculate sneakers. Not a hair out of place. Not a wrinkle or stain to be seen.

But he was in a T-shirt. A wrinkled T-shirt. There was a red splotch below the collar that looked like ketchup. His chin was covered in stubble. His eyes were bloodshot, hair mussed and much too long.

His sneakers were scuffed and dirty. And he'd lost at least twenty pounds. His arms were scrawny and pale.

The effect of seeing my father like that hit me square in the chest. Seeing him at all would've rocked my world, but seeing him like this filled me with concern. Pity. He looked so small and weak. Except he wasn't weak. Not when he'd used his power, influence and strength against my mother. Hate bubbled up in my throat, battling with love, regret, horror, disgust, pity, heartbreak.

"Vi," he greeted, his voice raspier than normal. Something about it was lacking. Cold.

I stepped backward when he moved as if he was going to embrace me. Even from the distance I'd created, I could discern that he didn't smell like expensive cologne. He smelled of sweat and cigarettes.

"What are you doing here?" I demanded.

He winced at my tone and the way I recoiled from him.

It hit me somewhere deep. Someplace inside me that hadn't been hardened by the truth of who my father was. Something inside of me that was soft, innocent… a little girl who missed her Daddy.

He rubbed the back of his neck, looking downward in shame. "I-uh, I just wanted to see my precious Violet." His voice was uncertain as he looked up at me.

Rage burned hot and low in my belly. I folded my arms. "Oh, how sweet of you," I replied with a bite. "What would you like to do? See my house? Meet my roommates? Go out for dinner? Catch up on old times?" Sarcasm dripped from my tone. "And by 'old times' I mean my entire childhood that my mother spent hiding bruises and injuries from the piece of shit husband who *beat her*!" I shouted.

People walking past stared. I was making a scene in the middle of the quad, but I couldn't bring myself to care. Suddenly, that little girl inside of me didn't want her daddy. She wanted to scream, stomp her foot, throw a tantrum in a way that only a toddler can… having not been conditioned to deftly hide their feelings beneath a veneer of lies.

My father opened his mouth.

"Don't," I stepped forward. "Don't utter one single excuse or self-pitying explanation." My eyes trailed up and down his body. "Not that you can sink lower in my estimation." I blew out an angry breath. "You tried to kill my mother. You spent years torturing her, controlling her, beating her." I realized that I had been waving my hands and had begun jabbing my finger into his chest. I felt the real and sudden urge to attempt to rip him apart with my bare hands, and a smaller, mortifying urge to fall into his arms.

Instead of doing either, I intended to push past him, find the nearest bar that didn't card and drink myself silly.

But my father grabbed on to my wrist. His hand was both cold and clammy, and his grip was too hard.

The scent of his body odor had me scrunching up my nose.

"Violet," he pled, squeezing my wrist enough to hurt. "You need to listen to me."

My heart stopped pumping so quickly, and my fury was deflating fast, running out of me and giving way to those more complicated feelings of loss and longing.

"You need to let her go before I kill you with my bare hands and traumatize all of these privileged, young coeds," a voice boomed from right beside me.

I jumped, my hand still held captive by my father. Obviously, I was not expecting my father to show up to my college campus, but I most definitely was not expecting Elden, complete in a Sons of Templar cut—it later occurred to me I'd never seen him out of it—standing in the quad, staring daggers at my father while literally threatening to kill him.

My father's eyes flared at the sight of Elden, his hand squeezing tighter so I let out a little whimper of pain.

Elden's fury turned palpable, and he stepped forward, looming over my father, making him look impossibly small and pathetic.

"Let. Her. Go." Elden commanded, the air seeming to shimmer around him.

People were staring as they walked past, practically tripping over each other as they did so. It was not every day they saw an outlaw biker—who was hot in a way that college boys couldn't be—looking like he was about to rip the arms off someone.

For a second, I worried this would turn into more of a scene, and I would actually witness my father being beaten to death then have to see Elden carted away and taken to prison for murder.

Something shifted in my father's eyes, something cold, foreign, evil. Something that made me taste blood as my teeth sank into my lip.

He gave my wrist one last squeeze before letting me go. It was cruel, that squeeze. Born out of a need to inflict pain, prove a point. Exert some kind of power.

My stomach lurched, and I was thankful I hadn't eaten today.

"Your mother did this," he hissed. "Brought you down to the gutter with her, made you associate with trash." He was obviously talking about Elden but not brave enough to look him in the eye as he did. "You're going to ruin your life—you being around those criminals that whore has obviously forced you to associate with."

I recoiled as if he'd hit me. My mother, I assumed, was the whore.

Elden tensed further, and I got the impression he was going to do something, so I stepped in front of him, which likely pissed him off to no end, but I didn't really care at that point.

He was going to protect my honor, or whatever the fuck. Except I could protect my own.

"My mother associated with trash for eighteen years of her life," I countered coldly. "She's finally living the life she deserves. With a real man, not some…" I looked him up and down with disgust. "Coward. If I ever see you again, I'm getting a restraining order. Leave now, before I decide to let Elden do what he's yearning to do and beat you to a pulp just like you did to my mother for fucking years."

I didn't give my father a chance to spew anything else. I turned my back on him and walked away.

Elden followed me.

CHAPTER Seven

FOR ONCE, no one was at the house.

It was quiet, smelled of some expensive candle Sariah had left burning—she did this quite often, so it really was a miracle that the house hadn't burned down yet—and the sage she'd burned just yesterday to protect us from negative energy.

That hadn't worked.

It was quiet, too quiet, the only sound being Elden's motorcycle boots on the hardwood floor.

It felt impossibly odd to have him in this space. He was a juxtaposition to every piece of our décor which was varying degrees of girly. Although this renovated Victorian had high ceilings and a large, open plan living room, he made it all look impossibly small. He seemed to take up every inch of space.

Even though I'd been imagining him being here for months, I found myself incredibly nervous in his presence.

He was looking around carefully, as if he was cataloguing every vase shaped like the female form, every framed print of various feminist heroes, every plant hanging from the ceiling or nestled on a bookshelf.

"How did you know?" I asked in a small voice.

We hadn't spoken.

Not once during the walk home.

He'd just strutted beside me, keeping pace, ignoring every stare from men and women on the way. Even in the midst of my turmoil, I'd noted the looks and hated them. Hated that I couldn't put his hand in mine. Claim him.

When his eyes finally met mine, electricity crackled in the air. My body sparked with the unique feeling that only he could awaken inside me.

"How did you know that my father was going to be there?" I clarified when he didn't answer the question straight away.

"We keep tabs on him," he answered matter-of-factly, eyes never leaving mine. "Got the notification he'd left Carver Springs and was heading this way. I got on the next plane. Obviously not soon enough." There was an undertone of fury in his voice. "He shouldn't have set foot on campus," he bit out, raking a hand through his hair. "He sure as fuck shouldn't have been able to get close enough to lay his hands on you."

I looked down to my wrist. It had been throbbing, but I'd ignored it. I blinked at the discolored skin around it, an angry red ring that would eventually turn into a bruise. Though I'd never once doubted what my mother told me about his violence, it was something completely different to see evidence of it on my skin.

A lump formed in my throat, and my eyes burned. I fought against the tears he didn't deserve.

A large hand cradled my wrist with exquisite gentleness.

I stared numbly at it as Elden raised my wrist to his mouth, laying a featherlight kiss on the inflamed skin.

The lump disappeared. My eyes stopped burning.

My eyes found his.

We stayed there an impossibly long amount of time, staring at each other, not saying a word.

I wasn't sure what to say. There was too much to say. I worried that whatever I said would ruin this moment, would bring reality hurtling in.

"I have an assignment due at midnight," I blurted.

Oh my god.

Of all the fucking things I could've said, *that* was what I chose.

I could've told him I hadn't stopped thinking about him. About the way he'd kissed me on the rooftop. How I made myself come thinking of his mouth on me. How I dreamed of him.

But no.

I talked about an assignment. Something that would remind him of my age, that I was in college. That I was just a kid. Just a kid who was his responsibility to save because my stepfather's club did that kind of thing.

His thumb stroked my wrist. It was no longer throbbing.

"Okay, baby," he murmured against my skin, inhaling for a second before letting it go.

My heart fell.

He was going to leave.

And when he left, I'd have nothing to think about but my throbbing wrist, my growing bruise, my father's tone, that alien look in his eye.

Unable to move, I watched him walk away, willing myself to find the courage to ask him to stay, beg him if need be.

But he didn't walk toward the front door. Instead, he moved into the kitchen.

I watched him open the fridge, inspect the contents… which was likely a lot of booze, condiments, an assortment of nut milks, kombucha and not much else. Sariah did a detailed grocery shop and organized the fridge—she called it 'cultivating'—meticulously, but she was also on a deadline for an assignment, so she had been living at the library.

I stood rooted in my spot and watched Elden close the door with one hand, the other holding a carton of eggs, cheese and some vegetables.

"What are you doing?" I managed to ask.

He looked up. "Gonna make you somethin' to eat, gonna make sure you eat it, then I'll find somethin' to read," he nodded to our color-coded bookshelves, "while you finish your assignment."

I just stood there, digesting the information. "You're not going to leave me," I surmised.

Something shone in his eyes that I couldn't decipher. "No, Violet," he rumbled. "I'm not going to leave you."

My entire body relaxed. I was able to take a deep breath.

He watched me for a few more moments. "Baby, your assignment," he said softly.

I jerked back into reality. "Right," I whispered. "My assignment."

It was an important assignment too. Worth twenty percent of my final grade. And my teacher was a hardass. I respected her, though, because she was almost impossible to please.

Still, I didn't move.

"Violet," Elden gritted out, cracking his neck. "You keep standin' there lookin' at me like that, you're not gonna get that assignment done."

My whole body quivered at his tone. For a second, I was ready to abandon the assignment and college all together if that meant he was going to make good on what his tone communicated.

But reason won out.

Barely.

So, I went to start on my assignment.

Elden cooked us omelets that were out of this world. He could cook. I filed that away in that special place I'd kept all the slivers of information I'd gathered about Elden. He read the classics, he rescued puppies, he could cook.

We ate in silence, me with one hand, the other on my computer.

I didn't even realize I'd finished until he took my plate from me and commenced doing the dishes.

Once that was done, he did as promised, perusing our bookshelf and positioning himself in the armchair that faced the breakfast bar I was working at.

I'd look in his direction every now and then, and our eyes would meet. My stomach would flip, and I'd battle everything inside of me to focus back on the task at hand.

The hours flew by, and I submitted the assignment at 11:59.

No one had arrived home either, obviously partying, staying with whomever they were sleeping with or also overloaded with work.

"Done," I breathed, exhausted and barely able to keep my eyes open.

Elden closed his book.

Panic curled in my chest as I stumbled off the stool, my ass and legs numb. Elden was there to steady me.

My hips sizzled beneath his touch.

I gazed at him with heavy lids, trying to commit each of his features to memory, cement in that soft yet intense expression pointed in my direction.

"Do you want to watch a movie?" I asked, slurring my words from exhaustion.

The corner of his mouth turned up. "Violet, you're about to fall asleep standing."

I blinked rapidly, trying to appear much more awake than I was. "No," I protested. "I can't go straight to sleep after doing all that anyway. I've got to wind down." It was a half lie. I usually couldn't sleep after cramming for a test or an assignment. There was science that proved how detrimental bright light right before bed was, and I always forced myself into my room with a book to help my nervous system wind down.

But Elden was here. I wouldn't stay up thinking about him, wondering what he was doing, who he was with, if he was thinking about me. Because he was here. With me. Thinking about me.

He considered my words, measuring them. I was shocked

awake with worry that he'd refuse, say he'd have to leave now, go back to the life that didn't include me.

But he lifted his hand, running the back of it along my jaw. "Okay, baby," he said, voice velvet.

He walked me to the sofa, placing me down on the soft cushions before reaching for the remote. "You choose," I yawned. "My brain is no longer working."

He smiled. I tried to catalog that too since I was pretty sure I hadn't seen Elden smile in my life, but my faculties were shutting down.

Elden sat close to me, and on instinct, I tapped his arm.

He lifted it immediately, and I didn't think twice about burrowing into his chest. I inhaled the leather smell, the scent of him, my nervous system settling. But there was a scent absent. My eyes found his bicep and the small patch on it. I reached out and circled it with my finger.

Elden's body stiffened. "What's that?" I asked sleepily.

"Nicotine patch," he answered, voice tight.

My body jerked, and I tilted my head to regard his face. He was only inches away. "You quit smoking?" I whispered.

He nodded once.

It could be a coincidence. Had to be. I'd mentioned the smoking thing once. In passing. A coincidence. I stared at him a while longer until my eyelids fluttered, and the effort to keep my head tilted upward was too much. I laid it back down on his chest.

"I missed you," I whispered, already half asleep.

He brushed my hair. "I've missed you too."

Or maybe I dreamed that. Because I was asleep before the movie even started.

And I woke up in my bed, alone the next morning.

Elden was gone.

ELDEN

It was one of the hardest things I'd ever done, leaving her. I sat there for a long fucking time, on that sofa, with her sleeping against my chest. She'd passed out in seconds. She was exhausted. And not just from working for hours on some assignment that I guessed was complicated as fuck. Not just from an interaction with her piece of shit father that had crushed her.

No, from *months* of squashing all that shit down. Pretending she was okay, that her world hadn't completely crumbled in the space of a few months.

She was protecting her mother, I knew that. Because that's the kind of person Violet was. Because she didn't want to taint the happiness her mother had finally gotten. Which was why she never told her about the abortion, about that French fuck hitting her. Why she pretended that cutting her father out of her life after learning what a monster he was wasn't a big deal.

Swiss was keeping close fucking tabs on her. Because he, like everyone else, was waiting. For all of this to come to a head. For her to break down.

But it hadn't come. Yeah, she was partying a lot—something I fucking hated, especially since she was every frat fuck's wet dream—and she wasn't sleeping or eating enough, but her grades were excellent. She designed her mother's fucking restaurant on top of everything else she was already doing.

The house she lived in was clean but bursting with items belonging to each of the women who lived there. She spoke fondly of them all, Sariah being the one she was closest to. I could see Violet in the house. In the prints on the walls. In the fucking sage, the crystals, all that new age shit she believed in.

Her room was flooded with her scent, with her personality.

A room that was equally cluttered and neat, overflowing with the dichotomies of her personality. Framed prints of Ruth Bader Ginsburg, books on feminism, on alternative therapies, herbal remedies, countless hardbacks of fantasy books. There were also piles of textbooks on architecture and a large drawing board in the corner with plans for her mother's restaurant still sitting on it.

Like her room, Violet was so multifaceted, I figured it would take a lifetime to know her completely. I was greedy, wanting to know it all in one night, skulking around her bedroom after I placed her in her bed. I knew I didn't have a lifetime. That even this night was stolen.

But I was ravenous to take whatever I could of her. There were only so many times I would get lucky to be the one around when we got the call about Preston. She would only be in college a while longer before she went out into the world and some smart motherfucker found her, made her his.

It burned my throat to think about, filling me with so much fucking fury I had to go to her, watch the steady rise and fall of her chest to find control again.

She was it. She quieted everything for me. Staring at her perfect rosebud lips, her alabaster skin, the midnight strands of her hair splaying out on the pillowcase like she was fucking Snow White.

Here was a woman who deserved the hero.

And that definitely wasn't me.

The hero would've denied her that night on the roof. The hero wouldn't have even been there. Wouldn't have gone crazy over a fucking teenage girl.

Yeah, that was villain shit.

I was the villain. And I needed to leave before I corrupted her further.

CHAPTER

Eight

VIOLET

I DIDN'T TELL anyone about the altercation with my father.

Not even Sariah.

It felt wrong keeping something from my best friend, but it had rattled me. As had waking up the next morning to the scent of Elden on my pillow but the man himself nowhere to be found.

He'd done his job. He'd protected me from my father, made sure I was safe then left me. The club was keeping tabs on my father, he said.

Because he was violent. Because he was dangerous.

And they'd been alerted that he was coming here, so someone had to come to make sure he didn't hurt me.

Elden had been doing his duty to the Sons of Templar.

Nothing else.

That's what I told myself, at least. I tried not to think about him, tried not to pine for him. The weather was getting better. It didn't rain. And when it did, I wasn't driving. I ignored his calls, though it killed me to do so.

Sariah and I both decided to sign up for summer school, even though my mom complained about not having me home, and I felt guilty about not being there for her during her pregnancy. Not that she needed me. She had Swiss. He'd take good care of her. And I wouldn't be able to pretend with my mother. Wouldn't be able to lie to her about how I was, what was going on in my life. She definitely did not need to know about my father's visit.

But I promised I'd visit. And I would. When I felt stronger.

Things were going along… until they weren't.

Until Sariah came home one morning with red-rimmed eyes and smudged eyeliner. Until everything happened after that.

ELDEN

"We got a situation with Violet."

Every cell in my body tensed. Before this moment, I had been relatively calm. We were sitting in church, going over business, discussing strategies for dealing with the new sheriff who was not as agreeable toward donations to his retirement fund as the previous sheriff had been.

Fucker had a stick up his ass and ethics. He also had some plan to rid the town of us. Good luck to him on that one.

Everything else was running smoothly. As smoothly as things could go in this life.

I thought of her every day.

Every fucking day.

Multiple times a day.

I had to remind myself, hourly, of what would happen if I got on my bike, rode to her and made her mine.

There would be blood.

The club would suffer.

More importantly, *she* would suffer.

And I would do a lot of things for her. Would gladly bleed. Even though I'd never thought I'd be willing to cause shit with the club—the only thing that had mattered to me in a long time—I was willing to do that… For her. To make her mine.

But one thing I'd never do was cause her pain. Not even for a second. And I knew that me acting on instincts that kept me up at night, instincts I battled with daily, would ruin the rest of her life. And no way was I willing to do that. I'd suffer through every fucking second I had left on this earth to protect her.

So, I'd hide my feelings for her from my brothers, my only family. Which is what I was trying to do after Hansen had said her name.

Swiss was right fucking across from me. Swiss who loved that girl like she was his own. Because of that, we had her monitored every day, to make sure she was safe.

Swiss, who had a pregnant wife at home, who he was protecting from all the shit that was going on with Violet.

He'd been on me the second I got back from Rhode Island, dealing with her father. I'd spent a couple of days in Carver Springs, sitting on my bike outside the shitty condo he was now living in, watching him, making a point.

I assured Swiss Violet was fine, which was true. Except she was too fucking skinny, those curves of hers fading fast. She had shadows under her eyes from lack of sleep. She was not fine.

But there was nothing any of us could do to save her from herself.

So, we waited.

Until we got this call.

"She's been arrested," Hansen added, eyes flying to Swiss whose fists were balled on top of the table. He was pissed but obviously not surprised. Hansen had obviously filled him in first before we sat down at the table.

As he should've. That was his right, as her stepfather. No one else should've been entitled to that information.

Except I found myself angry, fucking furious that it wasn't

mine. I didn't have ownership over her like every cell in my body was convinced I deserved.

"Don't want Kate to know," Swiss bit out. "And if she finds out I hid this from her, she'll have my balls." His eyes went around the table. I restrained a flinch when they skimmed over me. "So, I'll be cutting things off the motherfucker who doesn't keep this shit locked down."

I didn't doubt him. Despite Swiss being one of the most depraved motherfuckers in the club—tied with Hades—he loved his wife more than anything, and would move heaven and earth to make sure her life didn't hold any more discomfort than was humanly possible.

"What's the charge?" Lucas asked, concern in his tone. No doubt he and Colby were both pissed and worried, both of them close with Violet, something I fucking hated. Colby closer of the two.

They were just friends, which was why they were both still breathing, but I hated that he knew her, hated the protective rage in his voice.

"She was involved in a bar fight," Hansen sighed, rubbing his temples. "Don't know much else since they haven't processed it into the system. We've got a lawyer en route, and hopefully, she'll be out by the time someone from this charter gets there. But we also want to get the details of this incident, make sure the proper party faces consequences."

"I'll leave now," Lucas said without hesitation.

My fists clenched, and it took all of me to stay stationary.

"No," Hansen said. "Need you here. Also need someone who will be able to keep his shit locked down."

His eyes found mine. I was known to be the most controlled in the group.

"You good with this job, brother?"

I kept my face blank and searched his own for any kind of inclination that there was something beyond my even temperament as to why he was choosing me.

Surely, he didn't know shit. Hansen wasn't someone to find out shit and hold on to it. He would share it, and he sure as fuck would've talked to me about it. Because his main job was keeping this club together and destroying things that would tear it apart.

So yeah, he couldn't know shit.

"I'll go too," Colby volunteered, looking to our president.

Though the last thing I wanted was someone else with me, especially him, it would be good. Someone to keep me from giving in to baser instincts.

"All right, take Elden's lead, though," Hansen said.

Colby had a phone to his ear. "I'll organize us bikes and pieces for when we land," he said.

My chair screeched as I stood. I did my best to keep my movements smooth, purposeful but unhurried. No one needed to see I was about jumping out of my skin to get to her.

I raised my chin to Hansen before walking out. There was no fucking way I could face Swiss, but he didn't give me a choice. He followed me out, clapping me on the shoulder.

"Appreciate you doin' this, brother," he said.

I nodded in response.

"Fuckin' kills me not to go, but I'm not lettin' Kate get tangled up with this. And I'm sure as shit not leaving her when she's fuckin' pregnant."

I nodded again. Swiss had a dark past with his last family, so he wasn't going to lose this one.

"Ain't no one else I trust to take care of her, brother," he continued, squeezing my shoulder. "So, thank you. And make sure you fuck up anyone who needs to be punished."

That I could do.

VIOLET

After what happened, Sariah did not want to talk. And I tried. Henri tried. Ollie tried. She did not want to talk. She did not want to address what happened. Not since the cops nor the fucking dean didn't want to do anything. We'd been determined. We'd been ready to write to news stations, to write petitions. Ollie had offered to, "ruin his life and his credit," and fuck with his trust fund and stock options. Although I worried about what kind of crimes would be committed in order to do that, I'd been all for it.

But Sariah banned us all from doing anything. It was the one time since that morning, since that horrible morning, that she'd broken down.

We were all scared. None of us knew what the right thing to do was, but we knew the wrong thing was forcing her to talk, to take action when she wasn't ready. We had meetings about it. We agreed to watch her, be there for her and wait.

Then when it became clear she was going to deal with this by acting like nothing happened and party harder than normal—and normal was already a lot, even for college—each of us made sure we were available to go to these parties with her and not leave her alone for a moment.

Henri and Ollie weren't staying for summer classes, so it was just her and me in the house. I was trying my best to keep up with her and still keep up with my classes.

She was partying away her problems. And even though I was slightly more aware of it, I was too.

I had not spoken to my father since his visit. Had not heard the even, deep cadence of Elden's voice. It left me feeling untethered, fearful as ever about my place in the world.

So, I partied.

Until the day of the costume party that migrated to a bar we had become regulars at. Everything had been fine. We were going to do shots and order cheeseburgers.

Then Sariah went pale. Even the rouge she was wearing as part of her costume seemed to melt away. She shrunk. All the way down. Which seemed impossible in the platform heels she was wearing. But she did it.

And I did not think. Not about anything. Except the way my friend shrunk. The way that her smile had been forced lately. That she hadn't been sleeping. That the clothes she loved, that communicated her personality, had been a lot more conservative. Covered more of her. Like she was trying to disappear under them.

All I thought was that my friend was shrinking, and the fucking asshole responsible for it was leaning against the bar, laughing and acting like he didn't have a care in the world.

Then I wasn't thinking about anything. I was punching him in his stupid face.

I didn't expect things to escalate as far as they did. Though I was mighty proud of all the licks I got in. I wasn't entirely sure how I got hold of the pool cue that I was beating him with, but I was happy it found its way into my hands.

I probably wouldn't have stopped beating him until people finally pulled me off him. I was still very pissed. By the time the police got there, I was even more pissed. And I may've made them aware of that fact. With my fists. Which pissed them off and got me arrested. Which caused me to do a lot more yelling about how they were arresting me and not the pussy crying about a broken nose and a couple of cracked ribs. Maybe I threatened to hunt someone down and kill them. I couldn't be sure.

So yeah, that's how I spent the night in jail.

I used my phone call to call Sariah to make sure she was okay. She was. She was very upset, though. Blamed herself.

She was in the lobby of the police station, so I could actually hear her through the hall as she became more hysterical on the phone. Time was spent trying to convince her that none of it was her fault. More time was spent convincing her to go home and get some sleep before she got arrested too. It was almost impossible to convince her, but I did... Only after threatening to harm her new Chanel purse.

That had done it. I'd also ordered her to call one of our friends, Keelie, who was also doing summer classes to come and sit with her at home.

Then some uppity asshole told me I'd taken too long. I probably should've asked her to get me a lawyer or whatever you were meant to do when you got arrested, but I was sure it would get worked out in the morning. They couldn't hold me forever.

I quietly seethed in the cell for the rest of the night, thinking about all the ways I was going to expose these asshole cops and make sure they got what they deserved.

Those thoughts were so intricate that I didn't even notice the officer unlocking the door of the cell until it creaked open.

"You made bail," he glared at me.

"Nice shiner," I flashed him a cynical smile.

His entire form stiffened, and he moved to stand in the doorway so I couldn't pass. I didn't flinch, even though I felt a flutter of fear. It was still early morning, there was no one else around. This fuck already made it clear he didn't respect women, but I didn't think even he was brazen enough to lay a hand on me. You never knew, though. I'd humiliated him.

Humiliated misogynists were dangerous.

"What are you gonna do, buddy?" I asked sweetly, leaning forward. "I fucking dare you to lay a hand on me. It would make my case a cake walk, and once my lawyers are done with you, you won't even be able to work as a mall cop."

And I would. I had my father's money. I had a trust fund that I didn't want to rely on, but I was happy to use it to hire a ridiculously expensive lawyer to do exactly as I promised.

The cop glared at me a beat longer before stepping aside.

But then he grabbed my upper arm much harder than he was supposed to. I wasn't even sure he was supposed to grab me. I gritted my teeth and didn't so much as wince in pain. I let him drag me down the hall out to the main area of the police station.

I figured Sariah would be waiting for me outside, having gone home to change since she was the only one who knew I'd been arrested, therefore, she was the only one who could pay my bail.

I did not expect a very tall, very pissed off, bearded biker with iceberg eyes to be standing right by the door with his arms crossed against his chest and murder in his eyes.

Those eyes were focused on the officer… More accurately, the officer's grip on my upper arm.

He surged forward, so close that his body pressed into mine. I sucked in a ragged inhale, my body having a carnal reaction to him despite the inappropriate circumstances.

"Get your hand off her, now."

The officer straightened his back as he took Elden in. Again, it was very early in the morning, and there weren't many people in the office, but there were enough to witness an officer who thought way too much of himself get ordered around by an outlaw.

"You can't tell me what to do," he scowled, squeezing my arm tighter.

I didn't show any pain on my face because I was genuinely worried that Elden might very well murder the officer right then and there. And I did believe in his ability to get away with murder, but I figured it would be really hard if said murder was committed in a police station.

Elden's eyes glittered with a fury I'd never seen, not once in my life. "Let her go," he repeated.

Apparently, even the puffed-up officer could sense how far his illusion of authority would go with Elden.

He let go of my arm.

Elden did not hesitate to yank me behind him while he leaned forward and had a very intense, scary stare-off with the officer. He didn't say anything. Again, he didn't need to.

The officer went pale then hastily turned his back.

I swallowed my smile.

But then it was time for Elden to turn his intense and pissed off stare in my direction. Those eyes roamed up and down my body.

The stare was not the kind of stare that made desire pool between my legs. Or at least it wasn't supposed to be. The desire pooled there, nonetheless.

Even scary and murderous, Elden was sexy. *Especially* scary and murderous he was sexy.

Well, until he opened his mouth, at least.

"What the fuck are you wearing?" he growled.

"What do you mean, what am I wearing?" I asked, not at all liking his tone.

"I mean you're almost fucking naked," he seethed.

"It was a costume party," I replied, scowling at him. "I went as Elle Woods going as a Playboy bunny," I explained although the bunny ears and tail kind of needed no explanation.

"*Legally Blonde*?" I offered when he didn't get the reference. My fingers combed through my knotted hair. "I lost my wig at some point too, a shame since I do look good as a blonde. Maybe I'll go blonde," I pondered.

"You are not changing a hair on your head," Elden snapped. His jaw was tight as he glanced around the station. Every single male in the vicinity quickly looked away.

Well, everyone except one.

"Watch where you put your fuckin' eyes," he barked at an officer walking past.

The officer in question did not give him any kind of retort about watching the way he spoke to an officer of the law. No, he just averted his eyes like a good little boy.

It was jointly comical and hot.

Elden shrugged off his cut and the flannel shirt he wore underneath which was a shame since he looked exceptional in a flannel. A delightful cross between a lumberjack and an outlaw.

He wore a black tank underneath his flannel, one that molded over his torso in a very nice way. His arms were muscled, corded, not smooth. They were peppered with scars that were all the more noticeable in the harsh fluorescent lights, unhidden since he didn't have tattoos like almost every other outlaw.

I wondered about his scars.

Wondered about what else was underneath his tank. Wondered how agreeable he'd be to me finding out.

Until he spoke with the flannel outstretched.

"Put this on," he ordered.

I frowned at the flannel. "I'm not cold," I told him. Although that was kind of a lie. I had sobered up during my time in the cell, and the air was turned way down in here.

"This is not about you bein' cold, which you fuckin' are," Elden grunted, eyes on the gooseflesh on my arms. "This is about you wearin' that," his eyes skimmed my body once more, "in public, around a bunch of men who are thinkin' things about what's mine."

"Oh, no he didn't," a girl murmured from the booking bench.

I put my hands on my hips. "I think he just did," I told her then focused on Elden. "It looks like you've made it through your whole life without being educated on this fact, so it's my utter delight to enlighten you. I am not responsible for what men think. It is not my duty to cover up in order to not tempt men into thinking or doing things that they shouldn't be fucking thinking or doing."

Elden was glowering in fury. "They shouldn't be fuckin' thinking or doin' shit. But they will. So put the fuckin' shirt on."

"Shit, he ain't hearing you, babe," the girl muttered.

"He is not," I agreed, hands still on my hips. "So, boys will be boys, huh?" I tilted my head. "Men are not going to change nor stop acting like animals, so the responsibility remains on the woman to change what she wears, how she acts in order to make sure she doesn't *invite* those looks or sexual assault."

"You tell him, girlfriend," my new bestie encouraged.

Elden's nostrils flared… he was pissed, which was fine since I was absolutely furious.

"Men shouldn't rape women, but they still will because, you know, boys will be boys," I continued, almost shouting now. "So, women should do everything in their power to make sure they're not raped. Even though there is no such thing as doing everything in your power to *not get raped*."

I angrily swiped away the tears running down my cheeks.

"And even if they get caught, these fucking good old boys won't do shit." I gestured at the various officers around who had stopped to watch the show.

I guessed it could be considered funny to watch a playboy bunny shout at a biker.

But nothing, *nothing* about this was funny.

"You can do everything right, and still, one night you're having fun, like you should be allowed to do, and then some fucker with a powerful father and enough connections can do what he wants, and no one fucking punishes him," I screamed. "And then when I see him at the bar and decide to do what these assholes didn't, I'm the one who gets arrested!" I threw my hands up in the air, returning my gaze to Elden. "But sure, blame it all on me for putting on some fucking bunny ears."

"Someone touched you, baby?" he asked delicately. Quietly. With a calm that was a lot more terrifying than any shout or growl could've been.

It took me a second to realize he'd understood how personal that little speech had been. And he thought it was me. Thought that something had happened to me.

I shook my head rapidly. "Not me," I choked out.

The fury dissipated from his face, his features relaxing. But only a little.

"Who?" he demanded.

"Sariah," I whispered. "She didn't want me to tell anyone. She was… embarrassed." The single word sent spears through the center of me. The image of my tear-stained best friend, who always seemed so big, so full of light, embarrassed about something that had not at all been her fault almost brought me to my knees.

"He got her drunk. Way, way too drunk. She was not in the state to consent to shit. But he did it anyway." I sucked in a ragged breath. "I convinced her to go to the police. And they didn't do shit." I glared around the room again. "Because it was her word against his. And he has powerful parents. A good reputation. Sariah has a reputation for being a party girl, and she had the audacity to wear a fucking short skirt. So, of course, it was her fault."

I'd been holding it together for this long—well, as much as I could—but having something this horrible happen to my best friend had shaken me to my core. Men all around me were violent. Dangerous. I was angry about it. So fucking angry.

Not as angry as Elden was, though. He was clutching the flannel so tightly that his knuckles turned white.

"Who," he spat the single word out.

"The asshole who I got arrested for trying to fight tonight," I scoffed. "Not that it was much of a fight; he was too much of a pussy to do much of anything."

Elden's eyes flickered upward to the ceiling before returning to me. "Why didn't you call me?"

I frowned. "Well, calling you when you're across the country and he was only a few steps away wouldn't really work," I looked down at my nails. "Plus, I was acting on instinct."

"Not tonight," he huffed out. "Why the fuck didn't you call me the second this happened to Sariah?"

He was asking me like this was a rhetorical question, as though calling him was the obvious thing to do. Of course, I had entertained the idea of calling Swiss and letting him know what happened and let the protective bikers do what protective bikers did to men who raped women.

But Sariah had been violently against us doing anything behind her back. Even though I figured I'd be doing her and the world a favor by letting the bikers do what they did, I would not betray her that way.

"Why would I call you?" I asked him.

"Because you're mine," he informed me.

I folded my arms in front of me. "I am not yours."

He sighed. "You fuckin' are."

"You told me that I was nothing to you," I countered.

"Jesus Christ, Violet, we're not talking about this now."

"Yes, we are," I snapped.

"No. We're gonna talk about that and you trying to go up against a sexual predator without callin' me later. For now, you're gonna tell me where he lives."

My body jolted.

He was not kidding. I looked around the room again. The only one really listening to our conversation at this point was the drunk girl on the bench, and one quick glance at her told me she'd fallen asleep, which was a testament to how drunk she was because this was an entertaining show.

I leaned forward, speaking quietly. "Tell me you are not planning a murder in a *police station.*"

Elden's body went stiff.

I'd gone up on my tiptoes in order to make sure no one but Elden heard what I said, placing my hands on his chest to steady myself. My lips had grazed his ear as I spoke.

Now, the current circumstances did not warrant any kind of sexual chemistry. And the closeness, the touch wasn't even sexual. It was just us. Our bodies reacting after so long apart.

I lingered there because I needed to linger in the safety he offered. Everything had been spinning out of control. I'd been scared, genuinely terrified of what was happening to my friend. Terrified about what we still had to live with.

But Elden's presence meant that everything was going to be okay.

We stayed suspended in the moment for a beat until Elden's hand gripped my hip.

"We're going to get you home and talk there," he murmured.

I nodded once, not allowing myself to speak.

His hand went to the small of my back after he opened the door for me, and I got a little thrill from the intimacy of it.

I was surprised to see Colby leaning against a bike in the parking lot. It couldn't have been his bike since they got here so quickly. Then I recognized Bill, who had helped us move that one time. He lifted his chin, making sure to keep his eyes on my face.

I gave him a little wave.

My hand throbbed as I did. I remembered the punching and that my fist was now red and swollen. It had stopped bleeding, at least.

Colby did not respectfully keep his gaze on my face; it trekked all the way up and down my body, a wide grin lifting his lips. "You need to be in a robe, not a cut, Hef," he said to Elden.

Elden did not find that funny if the way he pinched the bridge of his nose was anything to go by.

"You're officially one of us, darlin'," Colby's gaze returned to me, unperturbed by Elden's murderous glare. "You punched a cop, spent a night in the slammer, and I will say, none of us have ever done it with as much style."

I did a little curtsey. "See how much more interesting things would be if you let a woman patch into the Sons of Templar?" I planted my hand on my hip.

Colby tilted his head, regarding me.

"I think it would be better if I got photographic evidence of the whole effect," he waved his hand up and down my body.

"Okay, that's enough," Elden stepped in front of me. "Violet, get on the bike."

I stared at the bike on the curb.

The only time I'd ridden on a motorcycle was the time Swiss took me for a ride on my birthday.

My mother was involved in a motorcycle club. It was pretty much their main mode of transportation. Mom had forbidden me from riding on the back of a motorcycle, except on my birthday when an exception was made.

But she spent a good amount of time on the back of Swiss's, so her argument was kind of moot. I'd pointed this out to her, and she had said that the Sons of Templar were not your run-of-the-mill men who owned motorcycles.

Certainly not your run-of-the-mill boys who rode motorcycles to impress girls, she'd added. They did not care about the safety of those girls. They put females on the back of their motorcycles on a whim.

The Sons of Templar did not just let any woman on the back of their bike. From what I understood, only Old Ladies went on the backs of bikes. And the Sons of Templar themselves seemed so in control of everything they did, so aware of the power of things that could be used as weapons, they were more cautious, less likely to get in a motorcycle accident. Especially not with their women on the back.

I'd argued with my mother that the Sons of Templar did not have superpowers, but now I wasn't so sure.

All I was sure about was Elden ordering me on the back of his bike. In front of two of his own brothers.

Granted, Bill wasn't a member of the New Mexico charter, so he probably didn't understand how or why our relationship might cause some waves. Colby had known something was going on pretty much since the beginning, but his mouth remained shut on the topic. I trusted him. And despite Elden being very mad at him at this current moment, it seemed he trusted him too.

Interesting. He'd always been very weird about my friendship with Colby. From the start. Even though it was very clear that we were only friends. Yet Colby was here with him.

"I'm in a bunny suit as you so aptly pointed out," I informed Elden. "I will look insane on the back of your bike in this."

Elden didn't look at me. "I tried to give you my shirt," he pointed out. "And I think there was a long speech about that gesture. You had your chance. Now get on the bike."

I gaped at him. But he was still staring at Colby, who was now doing his best not to burst out laughing.

The police station wasn't that far from our house. I could walk. But I'd been in fuzzy heels for hours now, and they were not designed to be worn for hours on end. They were designed to look cute with the outfit. Ideally only to be worn inside as a tool of seduction or around a costume party. But not from a costume party to a bar, then in a bar fight, then from the bar fight to a jail cell. And I didn't want to take them off in the jail cell because… gross.

So, the pain was pretty fucking intense right now, and the walk might damage my toes permanently. And despite my protest, I didn't much care about what I'd look like dressed as a bunny on the back of Elden's bike.

All I cared about was that I was on the back of Elden's bike.

So, I climbed on.

I was pressed up against his back, my arms around him, the bike vibrating underneath us. The world melted away during the short trip. It was just me and him. It felt right.

Me trying to forget about him was a fool's errand. It was clear, very clear, that we were always going to be in each other's lives. He'd come for me, like he'd promised he would. He'd saved me. Always would.

Whether I was his or pretending I wasn't.

And I was sick of pretending.

I didn't want to get off the bike when it roared to a stop outside our place. But I was mindful of Sariah, of the blame she was likely feeling. The very misplaced blame.

So I got off. Elden stayed where he was.

"What are you going to do?" I asked him, rubbing my arms against the chill I suddenly felt seeing him sitting there, knowing he was going to do something I shouldn't believe in.

I was against capital punishment.

Or at least I thought I was.

"You really want to know?" Elden asked me.

I regarded him. Was he protecting me because he thought I couldn't handle the truth? Because he didn't want me connected in any way? Didn't want to taint me?

"Yes," I told him.

"We're going to kill him," he replied without hesitation.

There it was.

I knew that the club was about violence. Though I was sheltered, I understood that. Had seen that. But I'd always seen these men as fathers, husbands, friends. And finally, the man in front of me as… mine.

Knowing that they engaged in violence in an abstract way was one thing. Having him say it straight to my face was another.

Maybe Elden expected me to recoil from him. Run. Beg him not to do that. Yell.

I knew for a fact that he didn't expect me to lean forward and kiss him tenderly on the lips. He went stiff for a split second before he grabbed the back of my neck and kissed me back, not tenderly.

"Be careful," I said against his lips. "Come back to me."

His eyes burned with emotion. With everything. "Always," he vowed.

Then they roared off.

CHAPTER
Nine

ELDEN

WE'D GONE BACK to the Rhode Island clubhouse to catch some sleep, a shower and to make some plans.

I'd filled Colby in on everything that went on as soon as we made it in.

His face had tightened with anger when I told him what happened to her roommate, but his eyes danced once I got to what Violet did.

"Okay, let me get this straight," Colby snickered. "Violet tried to fight a rapist. Alone. In a bar. Dressed as a Playboy Bunny." He waved his hands. "No, excuse me, dressed as Elle Woods dressed as a Playboy Bunny," he corrected like that meant anything.

I nodded.

"And she got a few good licks in?" he asked.

I nodded again, unable to speak through my fury as I thought of the bruises on her knuckles.

"She's badass," he grinned.

I wasn't going to disagree with him on that one. But I couldn't stop thinking about her, not hesitating to go up against some lacrosse player twice her size without a thought because he'd hurt her friend.

Couldn't stop thinking about her in that fucking outfit, my reaction to her despite the circumstances. The feel of her on the back of my bike. The way she'd kissed me before I left.

She was mine. I'd told her that in the police station. I was fucking sick of fighting it. Even though I knew I had to.

I put my phone to my ear.

"Elden," she breathed my name.

My cock twitched, remembering the way her pussy tasted. How her mouth had tasted a few hours ago.

"You good, baby?" I asked.

"Sariah's good," she answered. "Or better, I think. I didn't tell her the specifics, but I told her that she's never going to see him again."

I walked outside, out of earshot of anyone else. "That's good, Violet. But I didn't ask how she was. Asked how you are."

She paused as if confused. As if how she was wasn't important. Because that was Violet. Her focus was on her friend, and rightfully so. But last night had opened some shit up for her. I saw it. Heard it. It cut me to the fucking core.

"I'm fine," she said in a frail voice.

"You don't have to be fine," I told her.

Her breath remained even on the other end of the phone. When I went to sleep at night, I thought of that sound. Of the rain pounding against the outside of the car when I called her. Of that steady breath. I used to think of metallic clangs.

But now I thought of her breathing.

"I know," she whispered. "But I'm… okay. I feel good knowing he'll get what's coming to him." She cleared her throat. "Does that make me a bad person?" she asked shyly.

"Fuck no, it doesn't," I barked at her. "It's impossible for you to be a bad person, Violet." I forced my voice to be softer this time.

"You're not a bad person either, Elden."

My cock twitched again at my name coming out of her mouth. At her soft tone, her gentle words. The way she spoke to me like she believed I was something. Someone. Worth her time.

"You don't know that," I argued.

"Yes, I do," she retorted in a whisper.

Colby came outside, giving me a chin lift.

"I've got to go, baby," I told her. I fucking hated getting off the phone, but I was hungry to feel the death of the man who'd hurt her. Hurt her friend.

"Okay. Will I see you? Before you go?" Her tone was hopeful. Vulnerable.

Fuck. I'd been cruel to her. Said shit I didn't mean, shit that still haunted me, yet she continued to speak to me with that soft tone.

I looked to Colby. He knew shit was happening between us, yet he hadn't said shit. I didn't think he'd say shit. Though he was loyal as fuck to the club, Violet was his friend. Saying anything to anyone would hurt her, and he knew that.

"Maybe," I said, not wanting to make a promise to her I couldn't keep.

"Okay," she mumbled, unable to hide the disappointment in her voice.

It hit me square in the chest.

"Ice your hand, baby," I told her, remembering how red and angry it was.

"I will. Bye."

"Bye."

I shoved the phone in my cut.

"Ready?" I asked Colby.

"Ready," he bobbed his head.

Wire in the Amber chapter got us all the details on the fuck who hurt her friend. We watched the place for the rest of the night, waiting for the right moment to go in.

It wasn't hard to break into the fancy apartment he was stayin' in. The place was a mess of booze bottles and pills. He did the job for us, really.

As much as I itched to make his death long, painful and bloody, we had to be smart about it. There couldn't be any questions about the cause of death. No reason to look outward, especially after Violet getting in a fight with him the night before.

Wire fucked with the security cameras in the apartment complex so no one saw us come in. No one saw us leave either. Cause of death would be ruled an overdose. No one would question it. No fingers would point to Violet. Especially since the club's lawyer had already managed to get charges brought against him, and the cops who didn't take Sariah's statement in the first place.

Tragic story of a rich boy who knew he was facing time in prison and took the coward's way out.

"Wish we could've made it last longer," Colby complained as we got in the SUV we'd parked down the street. Bikes were much too loud. We weren't wearing our cuts either. I trusted Wire to make sure we weren't caught on any cameras, but it was always better to make sure no nosy citizen could identify us.

"Yeah," I agreed, getting in the car.

We didn't speak until I made a turn that took us the opposite way rather than back to the Rhode Island clubhouse.

"We're making another stop," I informed him.

"Yeah?" Colby asked, checking his clip.

"Cop who brought Violet out," I said. "Had his hand on her. In a way that was personal. Didn't like the way he looked at her."

Colby's jaw was clenched. "He the one she punched?"

I nodded. Because Violet did not only attack a rapist, she punched the cop who apparently didn't take her friend's report seriously.

Colby grinned. "She's very vocal about how the club needs to open the patch up to women… She'd make a good first member."

Violet had not hidden how despicable she found it that the club's only roles for women were club girls or Old Ladies. She did not understand the power both sets of those women held. But it also amused the fuck out of me to watch her duke it out with Hansen about the long-established rules of the club, rendering him speechless once she was done with him.

"She'd make a good Old Lady too," Colby added, looking at me.

My hand tightened on the steering wheel. "No more fucking talking."

Colby didn't say another word. He didn't have to. The damage was already done. He'd said out loud what I'd been thinking since I tasted her lips.

My gun at his temple woke him up.

I smiled at the terror in his eyes. "You've got two choices," I informed him. "I kill you right now, and trust me, that would be my choice." My trigger finger itched. "Or you can live by packing whatever shit you can pack in the next five minutes, and never come back here. You try to do anything stupid, we'll know."

Wire had already hacked into every account this fucker had. Already had him under surveillance. It was not an idle threat. They never were.

I pressed the gun in harder. "I know you owe a lot of people money. Know you like to gamble. Know you like your girls young. Barely legal." My teeth grinded at that little gem Wire had unearthed from his search history.

He was a cop in a college town. He like fucked-up porn. He had power here. If we'd found any evidence that he'd done anything with that power—beyond not listening to a woman who was assaulted, which was crime enough—he wouldn't be getting any other fucking choices.

As it was, I was still eager to kill the fucker. But it would be messy. Killing a cop would bring a lot of bullshit. Bullshit I was more than willing to deal with for Violet, but I also had a club to think about.

"We'll be watching you, so if you try to come back here, try to tell anyone about this little visit or try to wear a badge somewhere else, it'll be back to choice number one," I hissed. "My personal favorite."

The bitter stench of piss was overpowering as the coward's bladder let go.

He did as we asked, so unfortunately, I had no reason to kill him. But it meant that I would be going back to Violet without blood on my hands.

In the literal sense, at least.

I was covered in it, if you wanted to get metaphorical. Which was why, among many other reasons, I had no business touching her, claiming her.

But I did it anyway.

Because, despite what she said, I was not a good man.

VIOLET

I had been a wreck since the second Elden had roared off on the bike.

Of course, I hid it from Sariah. She didn't need that from me. She needed a friend who gave her the space to be a wreck. To break down. And she did. She cried. Cursed. Let out all of the feelings she'd been holding on to so tightly.

She agreed to see a therapist after I'd gently suggested it.

And when I'd told her about Elden and Colby's appearance, and that they intended to make sure that he was never heard from again, her eyes had lit up with bloodlust I hadn't expected from her.

"If only I could do it myself," she muttered. "I've binged *How to Get Away with Murder* because Queen Shonda wrote it, and because it's a fucking great show, but I don't think I'd be able to put it to practice," she sighed. "And I don't think I have the heart for it."

I squeezed her hand. "You have the biggest heart I know," I told her truthfully. "This does not define you."

Her eyes welled as she looked at me. "I know," she whispered back. "I have great tits and an even better personal style… That defines me."

We both burst out laughing, and I came to understand that friends, real ones, found reasons to laugh in even the darkest of times.

The rest of the day was spent in sweatpants, watching Nora Ephron movies and eating copious amounts of snacks we didn't normally keep in the house.

I hid my unease from her, even as the night crept on and Sariah fell asleep on the sofa.

There was no way I was going to be able to sleep, so I drank way too much coffee—even for me—and tried to work on my assignments. I failed at that, trying to write a paper on the art and architecture of the Roman Empire was not something to do after three cups of espresso while worrying about the man you had a thing for who was murdering the man who'd raped your best friend.

I settled for a particularly spicy fantasy trilogy, but even that felt wrong. So, I just settled for staring at *Real Housewives* yelling at each other, my phone right beside me and the volume turned way down low so I could hear the rumble of a motorcycle.

Except there were no motorcycles. There was a gentle tap at our front door, though. I jumped up so quickly, I sent my empty coffee cup flying. It made a clatter, yet fortunately, Sariah did not stir. She hadn't when I'd been using an espresso machine at three in the morning either. She was deep in a sleep that she'd needed for weeks.

I smoothed my hair and did my best to wipe crumbs off my

sweats, cursing myself for not changing, or at the very least washing my face. But it was too late.

The sun was teasing the horizon, and it served as the perfect backdrop for Elden standing at my front door.

He looked good.

Beyond good. I could only assume he'd also been up all night, although not a hint of that showed on his face. I did a quick scan of his body. There were no obvious wounds. No blood. No signs indicating that he was hurt.

My body sagged in relief. "I was worried about you," I told him, meeting his eyes once more. They were glittering with something I couldn't quite place.

"You don't need to worry about me, Violet," he murmured softly.

I stepped forward, desperate to be closer to him, to feel the heat of his body. He stiffened as I did so, but he didn't move backward.

"I'll always worry about you," I whispered, grabbing on to the sides of his cut.

When Elden reached up to stroke my face, I closed my eyes, leaning into his hand.

We didn't talk for a while. The birds greeting the morning took over the silence.

"I need to go," Elden said finally.

I squeezed my eyes shut tighter. I had known this was coming. It wasn't like he could come in and everything would change. Sariah was on the sofa having just gone through a harrowing ordeal. That did not stop me from wanting to pounce on him. But me having sex with the man I was falling for was not really appropriate.

When I was brave enough to open my eyes, he was staring at me. He likely had been the entire time.

There was nothing else to say now. We both knew this wasn't the right time for us. Maybe there was no right time for us.

His hand fell back to his side. I missed the weight of it right away.

"Have a safe flight," I said weakly.

Elden didn't speak for a long time. "You're strong, Violet," he finally said. "But you don't have to be. You're not alone." His eyes burned with intensity. "I'll always be here for you."

And then, in direct opposition to what he'd just said, he turned his back on me. I watched the patch on his back move as he got into the SUV idling at the curb, then it drove off.

I stood there for a long time.

Things were going well.

Which, of course, was when everything went to shit.

Sariah and I finished summer school and took a trip to Nantucket for a few days in a beach house I'd rented, reading, relaxing and pretending the rest of the world didn't exist. Elden didn't call.

It hadn't rained.

I hadn't gotten arrested again.

There was no reason for him to call.

The fall semester started, and I again loaded up on classes, taking meetings with advisors to see if I could finish even a semester early. My grades were good, great even. It was possible for me to graduate earlier, but the advisors didn't seem to understand why since to be fully qualified as an architect I'd need three more years of further study, at least. I wasn't thinking about that, though. It made my heart race. All I was thinking about was my birthday, the end of my teenage years, and graduating college.

I'd been so anxious to do everything my entire life. To finish junior high so I could go to high school. To graduate so I could see the world, to leave France and the French asshole to get into a college routine.

Now I couldn't wait to get out of college so I could feel more like an adult. And yes, most of the reason for that had to do with Elden.

It meant, in my many fantasies at least, that we could become something. That we could share more than a few stolen moments, intense looks, proclamations of ownerships. Phone calls in the rain.

And me rushing college was in a way rushing toward the secret coming out, one way or another.

Because after I graduated, I'd have to make choices. Even if I didn't study at Brown for another three years. The plan had always been New York, maybe even London, to start interning at an architecture firm, work my way up. Travel. Get an apartment, live a fast-paced life, lightyears away from the kind of life I'd grown up in.

That plan had always been firm. I'd fantasized about it millions of times to the point I knew the color of my sofa in my small but chic apartment. Either in a Brownstone in New York or some old brick house in Notting Hill.

I hadn't accounted for life getting in the way. For my feelings to change. Goals to change. Hadn't accounted for my fantasies to change into a quieter, warmer vision of life that felt more like me.

I was struggling between two different futures. One that I'd wanted before I could remember—one I wasn't sure I wanted for the right reasons because I'd just wanted anything that hadn't been my mother's life. And one that had changed because of a man. Something I promised myself I'd never do was warp my future so it fit around a man. Cut away pieces of myself so I was smaller, more malleable. Even though I know Elden didn't want that for me. He was keeping away partly because Swiss might very well kill him but also because he believed I deserved better.

In short, I was a mess.

I was also operating off far too much caffeine and nowhere near enough sleep. At least that problem was not unique to me.

Everyone at this school and everyone in our household was dealing with that.

When my phone rang, my stomach dipped. It wasn't raining, so it still could be him. Although he could've been calling to declare that he couldn't live without me, that he was abandoning all of his noble intentions. That we'd ride off into the sunset.

But it wasn't Elden, it was my mother. I wasn't disappointed, or at least I shouldn't have been. I *liked* talking to my mother. She was animated, passionate about her life. She was funny... I hadn't known that my mother was funny. Hadn't known my mother was not a Stepford robot. I was getting to know her as a complete person. Beyond that, she was due soon. Her life was blooming.

"Mom," I greeted warmly. "How are you? Is Swiss still sitting at the bar of the restaurant, glaring at everyone so they don't come in and make you cook?"

My stepfather was somewhat protective over my mom. Now that she was pregnant, it was an entirely new level. Mom was determined to work in the kitchen of the restaurant right up until her due date. Swiss was determined to make sure that there were no patrons in the restaurant for her to cook for.

I almost spoke again to see if she was still on the line when she didn't respond for several long moments.

"Sweetie, I think you should come home," my mother said in a gentle tone that chilled my blood. One I'd only heard once before. When she was preparing to tell me my father was an abusive piece of shit who almost killed her. It was a tone used before bad news. Before earth-shattering news.

My back straightened. "What happened? Is it the baby? Did Swiss get into an accident?" My mind ran through all the possible terrible things that could've happened, which were many when your stepfather was a member of an outlaw motorcycle club who likely broke the law and put himself in danger on a daily basis.

But I'd never worried about such things until that very

moment, until I was confronted with the perils of that life encompassed in my mother's tone.

I'd never worried, not once, because I'd seen the way Swiss looked at my mother. With a love that seemed to soften the air around her. But also with a ferocity that made me believe that he would defeat anything and anyone who dared try to take him from the things he loved.

It hit me just then that I'd truly believed my stepfather could and would defeat death… law enforcement, natural disasters and everything in between.

But no one, not even someone as badass as Swiss, was immune to reality.

My body started to vibrate with fear that I'd never experienced in my life. I felt as if I'd been walking happily, and this phone call had hurtled me off a cliff I didn't even know was right beside me all along.

"No, we're all fine, Violet," Mom's words were warped, as though she spoke from underwater, muffled and low.

It took me a second to process them.

"You're fine," I repeated.

"Yes," she said firmly. But that gentle, ominous edge to her voice lingered.

My mind ran quickly through all the possibilities, stuttering on gray eyes and the man they belonged to.

"Is El—everyone at the club okay?" I demanded to know, an edge of panic leaking from my heart into my tone. My mother was still unaware of any connection I had to the biker old enough to be my father. Yet in the midst of my panic, I was still protecting that secret.

"Everyone at the club is fine," Mom reassured me.

I let out a long breath, my limbs still taut.

"It's your father, honey," she sighed.

My heart thumped against my chest. My fingertips numb. "Did he hurt you again?"

Fire crawled up my throat.

"No!" she yelled through the phone. "I'm really not good at this," she muttered. "He was found this morning… He's gone, honey."

I gasped at the news, processing it. *Gone.* A euphemism for death, I deduced.

Dead.

I chewed at my lip.

My father was dead.

My breathing returned to normal soon after my heartbeat did. My limbs relaxed.

"Violet?" Mom's voice was saturated in concern and louder than normal. I got the impression it was not the first time she'd said it, trying to get my attention.

"I'm getting on a plane," she declared. "I'm coming to get you."

My body jerked. "Mom, you are not getting on a plane. You're about to give birth to your baby."

"I have two babies," she corrected. "And one of them just lost her father."

Lost. Like I wanted to find him in the first place. Like he was something precious to me.

Maybe he had been.

Or maybe the idea of him was.

"He wasn't my father," I stated bluntly, my voice colder than I'd intended.

"Sweetie… Yes, he was," Mom's voice was thick with hurt and grief. Not for herself, surely. My father had beat her for years, tortured her and almost killed her. My mother was a good person with a great heart, but even she would not be grieving that man.

The hurt was for me.

"No," I told her, staring at myself in the mirror of my room. My cheekbones were high, sharper than normal because I was overloaded on classes that were getting harder and harder. I was existing on processed snacks and black coffee. Hence the dark circles under my eyes which, contrasting against my ivory skin, made them seem an off-purple hue, similar to my irises.

"We'll get you on a plane, sweetheart," Mom pressed on. "You can come home. I know your grandparents will be having a service—"

"I'm not going," I blew out a heavy breath. "I want to be there for grandma and grandpa. And I will be. I just won't be *there*."

I didn't know what kind of service my father would even have. Before I left for France, there would've been hundreds of people there. Important people. People he'd spent years sucking up to, throwing parties for, making sure his family looked perfect for... better than theirs for.

But my father's fall from grace had been swift. He'd lost everything. My grandparents cut him off. And I understood how fickle and false the circles he'd been running in were. Once he wasn't a member of the country club, he no longer existed to those men he'd golfed with for years.

He'd died alone.

I thought of the man who had gripped my wrist months ago. How desperate he was. How pathetic.

Then, without wanting to, I thought of him kissing my head when I'd woken up from a nightmare. He'd promised monsters weren't real. That I was safe.

The man who read all of my school papers before I submitted them, concentrating on every word I wrote, smiling with pride.

It was one thing to hate a father who was pure evil—who had tortured my mother for years. It was quite another to hate a man who had been both evil *and* my father.

"Violet?" my mom asked with concern.

I realized she must've said something, and I hadn't replied. "Sorry, Mom, what did you say?" I rubbed my eyes. There was a wetness there that made me angry. I scrubbed it away.

"You're not betraying me by honoring the memories you have

of your father, sweetheart. He *was* your father. You don't have to choose a side in this. You don't have to hold on to your anger. You can be sad about losing him."

My heart stung at her words and all of the pain bubbling up. "I already lost him, Mom," I choked out.

"Sweetheart—"

"Mom," I cleared my throat. "I promise I'm okay. And I'll be home soon, okay? For the baby. I've got assignments. They're important."

"I'm sure your professors will understand," she tried. "I can call them."

"No," I replied more firmly this time. "Mom, I… can't. I just need to get my work done. Okay?"

Her extended pause told me that she was considering pushing it. That she heard how close I was to breaking. I prayed she didn't. I didn't need to be prodding at things I'd buried. I especially didn't need to be doing it right now.

I'd push all of these problems down until I graduated, and maybe a while after that. I'd manifest them in unhealthy ways and spend thousands on therapists when I was in my thirties.

Like a normal person.

"Okay," Mom relented, and I let out a breath of relief. "But I want you to call me," she added. "Every morning. And if it gets to be too much, I can send someone up to get you."

I stifled a groan. "Mom, I'm an adult. If it gets to be too much, I'll just drink myself into a stupor."

"Not funny, Violet," she snapped.

"Okay, okay," I sighed. "I promise that I will change my flight if need be. But I really need to get these papers done."

I stared at the books surrounding me, the words now nothing but a mess of shapes.

"I'm here, if you need me, darling," Mom whispered, her voice cracking.

It took everything in me not to break down. "I know, Mom," I murmured. "I love you. I've got to go."

"Love you!" she called, and I hung up the phone.

I stared, blinking at myself in the mirror for a while. Who knew how long I would've sat there, all day maybe. But luckily, I had roommates who were not worried about protecting my personal space.

"Oh my god, I just did a hot yoga class… hungover. I've never been closer to death in my life," Sariah exclaimed the second she walked through my door, collapsing on my bed dramatically… as she did everything dramatically.

I quickly turned, staring at where she had sunken onto my throw pillows, arranged neatly on my bed as they were every morning after I woke up. My life may have been a mess, but my space couldn't be.

"Messy house, messy mind," my mother used to say. I'd only recently come to understand that our home was always immaculate not because my mother didn't want a messy mind, but because she didn't want my father to beat the shit out of her.

My *dead* father.

Sariah frowned at me. "What happened? Is it your mom? Is she in labor?" she sat up in excitement. Sariah thought it was amazing that my mother was pregnant, that I was going to have a baby brother when I was almost twenty years old. She'd already been shopping up a storm. She'd met her and Swiss when they came to visit and instantly fell in love with them.

Mom had also instantly loved Sariah because it was impossible not to.

"No," I replied, preoccupied with worries about this news and what it might do to Mom. Her due date was in a week and a half. I was leaving in a week to go and be with her.

"It's my dad," I said, voice faraway. "He's dead."

Sariah's mouth opened, yet she didn't speak, lost for words. I'd never seen her lost for words. "Holy fuck," she eventually whispered. "And I just came in here talking about hot yoga. I'm such an insensitive asshole. I'm so sorry, babe."

I knew she probably wanted to hug me right then, comfort me because that was the kind of person Sariah was. But she also knew me really well by now and was incredibly good at reading people and their body language, therefore, she understood being hugged was the last thing I needed.

Being hugged meant this was real. That I was grieving for my father. And that wasn't true. You didn't grieve for monsters.

"What do you want to do?" she literally jumped off my bed, moving into action. I knew she was not going to leave me alone, no matter what I said.

And I also knew, no matter what I said to my mother, there was no way in hell that I was going to concentrate on assignments.

Likely the healthiest way to deal with this was to go on a walk, get fresh air, sunshine, perspective.

Talk it out with Sariah, who would listen without judgment. Maybe then come home, drink tea, make something healthy to eat, take a long bath and feel better. Fresher. More able to handle this situation.

Yes, that was the healthiest way to deal.

"I would like to get very, very drunk," I said.

Sariah clapped her hands. "I'll get the tequila."

CHAPTER *Ten*

IT HAD BEEN HOURS.

We'd started in the living room.

Then we'd gone to a dive bar that had cheap drinks, great wings and didn't card. We'd hustled a couple of douchebags in a game of pool.

They'd left after trying to stiff us the fifty bucks we'd won fair and square. Sariah had stood up to them, ready to choose violence if need be, but Stan, our bartender with a handlebar mustache and a 'take no shit' attitude, had rounded the bar and said something like, "you want to pay these two girls, or you want to try your luck picking on someone your own size?" Stan technically wasn't their own size. Well, he was the size of both of them put together, so that worked.

Both men had handed over the money and left after that.

Sariah had kissed Stan on the cheek in a thank you, and he'd blushed before murmuring that we'd both have to eat a cheeseburger before he served us any more booze.

We had finished the cheeseburgers happily. Sariah had murmured something about calling some 'contacts' to get us the good weed. Then she'd gone outside to call them since there was interestingly no cell service in our little dive bar.

It was nice. It was dark and cool in there, and there was no possible way for the outside world to sneak in.

I was chewing on a cold fry, thinking of exactly nothing when a man walked up to my table.

"Someone like you shouldn't be sitting alone," he drawled.

The man who spoke was wearing an Affliction tee, had on designer jeans, was about ten years too old to be a student on campus, and likely came here to try to pick up drunk college girls. There was a whole breed of these assholes, trying to act younger than they were, trying to impress younger women with their flashy, tacky shit.

He probably had a wife at home.

"Someone like me—a woman—should be able to sit alone and not be bothered by assholes," I countered, slurring some of my words, resting my elbow on the table and cradling my chin in my hand.

His face contorted in irritation. "You don't have to be such a bitch."

I rolled my eyes. "Yes, because a woman who rejects you, must be a bitch instead of, you know, sane and reasonable to not want to catch a venereal disease."

His cheeks reddened, and he stepped forward, to do what, I didn't know.

The bar had become more crowded in the time we'd been here. More students had come here to blow off steam, so Stan was busy at the bar.

But the man did not make it any closer to me. Someone grabbed him by the back of that Affliction shirt and snarled, "Walk the fuck away."

A very familiar voice.

The sleazy guy quickly scuttled off, not even trying to face off against the man who could snap him in two without hesitation.

Now it was just me and him.

I wiped my dry eyes to bring him into focus. It took a couple of tries. There were three of him. Then two. Then Elden materialized in much too stark detail for my liking. Wasn't that why I was drinking so much? To make the edges of everything softer, blurry so the edges wouldn't cut me quite so much.

"What are you doing here?" I asked. I had intended on making the question biting, accusing, loud. But it came out quiet and flat. The effort it took to speak and stare at him drained me.

"What do you think I'm doin' here?" he growled, rounding the table and pulling me from my chair.

I expected him to drag me out of the bar. To curse me for drinking, for being alone in a bar, for whatever else I'd done wrong in his eyes.

But to my surprise, he didn't do any of those things. He cupped my face in his hands, so gently, and stared into my eyes.

Suddenly, I was devastatingly sober, and all of the feelings I'd been drowning in booze came surging forward.

"Kiss me," I whispered. "I need to taste something other than tequila and sadness."

His searing gaze dropped to my lips at my plea, my words so similar to the ones uttered on a rooftop when we were strangers. But he didn't hesitate like he did then. Not for a moment.

His lips found mine. Not the same way they did on that rooftop, but softer. More knowing. This was not a frantic, desperate kiss.

I didn't quite know what it was.

His face hovered in front of mine. Music thumped from somewhere faraway. People were laughing, talking on another planet.

We were the only ones there.

"You can't keep on saving me," I rasped, breathless.

"Can't I?" His gaze pinned me, brushing hair from my face. "Because I will. Long after this is over, when you've found yourself a different life, a better life… a better man. When I'm nothing but a memory for you, I'll still be there. Happy that you've found what you deserve and watching to make sure no fucker takes that from you. Taints it. Hurts what's mine."

My hackles went up, even while my heart grew to an aching size in my chest upon hearing his words. "You mean this future—this ridiculous future that I apparently have no say in—when I'm with another man..." I couldn't even finish the sentence, sickened by the mere prospect. "When I'm with another man," I repeated, just because I wanted those sour words, that bitter thought to poison him too, "you think I'll still be yours?"

His expression didn't waver, no fury danced in his eyes. "Yes, Violet, you'll always be mine."

"I leave you for five minutes, and this is what I find?" a voice cut into the moment.

Both of our heads turned to regard Sariah, looking at us with her hands on her hips. She did not look surprised.

"Took you long enough." It took me a second to realize she was talking to Elden.

I looked between the two of them.

"You called him?" I asked Sariah, trying to move out of Elden's grasp. That only served to have him tuck me into his side.

I leaned into him on instinct, comforted by the softness of his cut, the scent that was unique to him.

"Of course, I called him," she said as if it was obvious. "Now, I know a girl needs her best friend throughout the tough times in her life, and I'll always be here for you. But I know that there are also jobs better suited for a tall, very attractive biker who looks like he might just burn down this bar if you told him you were cold." She winked before her eyes went to Elden. "You got this?" she asked.

His response was a quick dip of his chin.

"Good," she walked forward, kissing my cheek. "I'm here for you, babe. Whenever. Wherever. Just like Shakira said." Her eyes turned more serious. Sadder. "But right now you need to go home."

Home. She didn't mean to the house we shared together.

She meant Garnett, New Mexico.

Not Carver Springs.

Maybe that had been my home when I believed the lies that had made up my childhood.

But Garnett was my home.

"What about you?" I asked with concern.

"Well, I've got a date with a hot blond," she grinned wickedly, motioning to a pretty girl sitting with her friends two tables over. She was staring at Sariah.

"As long as you'll be safe," I told her, already worried about my friend who was finally beginning to heal. To date.

Something sparked in her eyes, but it was gone as quickly as it arrived. "Of course, I will. Call me when you get home."

And then she was gone.

Once again, it was just me and Elden.

I didn't say anything more about that future, the one where I was with another man. I didn't say anything; I just let him walk me out of the bar. Despite how drunk people were, the crowds parted for him effortlessly. It was impressive.

"Don't want you to freak out," he said when we made it outside. I had been expecting it to be bright, but night had long fallen. We'd been in that bar for hours.

I was a mix between drunk and hungover. My head was throbbing. "I'm already freaking out by you telling me not to freak out."

"Your Mom went into labor not long after you got off the phone with her," he told me calmly.

"What!" I shrieked.

"Told you not to freak out," he commented.

I scowled, fumbling for my phone which was buzzing with notifications. I had a bunch of missed calls from Mom, Swiss, Freya, Macy, Caroline… pretty much everyone at the club.

"Are they okay?" I demanded, thinking of all of the things that could've gone wrong. Thinking of Swiss losing his first little baby.

"They're fine," Elden replied firmly. "Both your mom and your brother."

I sagged in relief. But that only lasted a moment.

"We've got to go," I snapped. "Like, right now."

Elden put his hands on my shoulders to stop me running off into the night. "No," he said gently. "You're gonna go back to your place. Have a shower. Some coffee. Sleep. Then we'll take the first flight out in the morning."

I gaped at him. "Are you crazy? I have to be there for my mom."

He nodded. "First, you need to be there for yourself."

I froze at his words, sat with the knowledge of what they meant. I was only half sober. Which meant I was half drunk. I'd barely slept eight hours in the past five days. I was a mess. And I did not want to meet my baby brother smelling like a dive bar and looking a mess.

Nor did I want my mom to be worrying about me on the day she gave birth and was likely exhausted and ecstatic. Surely, she was already worrying about me since no one had been able to get ahold of me.

Shit.

"Okay," I conceded.

Elden waited while I showered, waiting with a strong cup of coffee and some toast when I emerged, hair dripping on my shoulders while clutching the towel tight around me.

He was so large in my bedroom, sitting on my bed. Everything about the moment felt incredibly surreal, right down to the arrival of my baby brother and the departure of the man who was supposed to be my father.

I felt joy. Sadness. Anger. Resentment. Worry. All of those things came rushing at me with the hot shower, the coffee and the food. There was a reason that I'd decided to drink myself into oblivion, because oblivion was wonderful.

Now I had to deal with all of these feelings in addition to a hangover. And Elden seeing me like that… Not exactly what I'd wanted.

I also felt oddly self-conscious being naked around him. He'd seen me naked before. He'd seen the most intimate parts of me. Tasted them. The mere memory sent desire shooting to the base of my spine.

But that was a lifetime ago. When I was infatuated with him, held captive by nothing but need. Since then, he hadn't touched me beyond a few kisses. There was more than infatuation between us now. The stakes were much higher.

"Are you staying here?" I asked meekly, still clutching the towel to my body.

Elden's eyes stayed on mine. "You think I'd leave you?"

My knees knocked together as I shook my head slowly.

"Can sleep there." He gestured his head to the armchair in the corner that was stacked with textbooks and vetoed outfits.

I raised a brow. "Do you want to sleep there?" I asked.

"Fuck no," he replied instantly, eyes still not moving downward.

The air crackled between us.

Though I had previously been overcome by everything happening in my life, by everything that needed to be handled outside this room, it suddenly became very clear that it was just us in the room.

Until morning, at least.

And I did not intend to waste that time.

My towel dropped to the floor.

Elden let out a hiss.

I didn't move. Nor did he.

He just stared at me, gaze skimming from my head to my toes.

"Come here, Violet." he ordered, voice smooth and rich.

I didn't hesitate to go to him.

He opened his legs, and I walked in between them, his hands landing on my hips, pulling me to him so his head rested on my naked belly.

My hands found his hair, running through it. Every nerve ending in my body was awake, aware, hungry.

But we stayed like that for a long time.

Until Elden lifted his head and looked up at me.

His gaze stole the air from my lungs.

"Get on your back, Violet."

My spine tingled. My knees shook. I didn't move. Because I couldn't. Which was fine since I had a very capable, very powerful biker holding on to me.

I was on my back in seconds.

Elden stood there, staring down at me, cataloging every piece of my skin with hungry, wild eyes.

Then his hands found the backs of my legs and he, not gently, pulled me so I was at the edge of the bed, he was kneeling, and my legs were over his shoulders.

Then his mouth was on me. Then he split me apart. Repeatedly.

At some point, when I must've had a break from reality, Elden had taken off his boots, his cut and his shirt.

He kept his jeans on, though.

I blinked my way back into existence, staring at his hard cock through his jeans.

I sat up, licking my lips.

"Violet," he growled. "Don't fuckin' look at me like that. I'm holdin' it together. But barely."

I frowned up at him. "Why do you need to hold it together? I want you."

His eyes glittered. "I want you more than anything on this fuckin' planet right now," he admitted, voice rough.

My insides did a somersault.

"But," he continued, "I'm not takin' you now. Not like this. You may not think it's true, may piss you off for me to say this, but you're vulnerable right now." He trailed a finger lazily down my neck. "But I wanted to give you something. I'm also a greedy fuck and needed to taste your cunt again."

My body shook from the force of his words.

"But I'm not taking you," he repeated firmly. "Not now."

I bit my lip in frustration. I wanted to argue. Very fucking badly. But he had made up his mind. I saw it with the hardness of his jaw, the cords in his neck that were carved from marble. Plus, Elden may not have complete control around me, but he would never do anything that he thought would hurt me.

It wasn't the right time.

"Okay," I agreed slowly. "But let me give you something." I leaned forward, my hands on his belt.

Elden grasped my wrist, stopping me. "Violet," he warned, but his voice was thick. Wild.

I gazed up at him, sinking down to my knees. "I want to do this, Elden."

His hands stayed around my wrist for several moments, his body strained, his lips thinning.

But he finally let my hand go.

I smiled wickedly, making quick work of his belt and freeing him.

He was big. Which was no surprise. My hand scaled down his length softly, reveling in the way his body jerked at my contact, the hiss of breath I heard from above me.

I may have been on my knees, but I had all the power right then.

"I'm going to suck you," I whispered, looking up at him. "All of you. You're going to give me all of you."

Elden's face was contorted with hunger, need. He was mine.

So I didn't hesitate to take all of him in my mouth. He let out a strangled growl as I took him in farther, his hands going to the back of my head, tangling in my hair, yanking at the strands.

He was teetering off the edge. He was going wild. This man who held so tightly on to control. Everywhere but with me. With everyone but me.

That's what had me sucking him hungrily, what sent one hand between my legs as my desire crawled up again with this act. I moved faster with my mouth, in tandem with me working myself between my legs.

His breathing got heavier, his strong thighs trembling as I worked him and myself relentlessly. I trailed my tongue along his length, languishing in the power I had, in the way his entire body was shaking.

Elden let out a low growl that sent shivers down my spine.

As I reached the apex of my own pleasure, he emptied himself into me, and I took all of it, all of him, greedily.

The second he was done, Elden didn't hesitate to lift me off my knees, walking us both to my bed.

I promptly curled up against him, almost completely on top of him.

"Fuck, Violet," he rasped, stroking my hair. "You're my bad little girl, aren't you?"

"Yes," I breathed against his chest. "Yours."

We fell asleep like that, tangled in each other, exhausted from what we'd done. What we'd started again.

What would never end between us.

CHAPTER Eleven

"HE IS the most precious thing I've ever held in my hands," I whispered, looking at the closed eyelids of my sleeping brother.

He was still gripping my finger, even in the middle of his slumber.

He had slept everywhere but the bassinet the hospital provided. Most of the time he was in his father's large, comfortable arms.

Swiss was in love with his son. His eyes gleamed with a fierce kind of love that showed me that my brother was protected, adored.

Swiss had the family he deserved.

My mom, propped up in her hospital bed, barely looking tired and glowing with happiness, had the family she deserved.

She had been relieved to see me arrive at the hospital in the late afternoon—Elden and I had been up at dawn to catch our flight, not speaking as we got ready in the morning—and the trip itself had been quiet.

It was strange to do something as benign as travel with him through an airport. Everyone stared at him. Because of the cut, maybe. But also because he was something to stare at. He was imposing in a way that had nothing to do with his muscles, the topaz gaze, strong jaw or even his badass goatee—one that had marked the inside of my thighs last night—and had eyes that anyone would ache to have land on them.

I'd scowled at the women shamelessly checking him out in the security line, and I'd felt an irrational amount of anger that I couldn't shout out that he was mine.

So, fueled by jealousy, I'd slipped my hand into his after we'd retrieved our bags from the x-ray belt. He didn't have anything but a small duffle, and he refused to let me even roll my compact suitcase.

He'd frozen when my small hand slipped into his large one. My stomach twisted, preparing for his rejection. But instead of letting me go, he held me tight, pulling me in for a quick but firm kiss on the lips.

It was a thrill, like a rebellion to walk through that airport without our secrets, without pretending we weren't something to each other. It felt right. No one stared at us… well, beyond the people who stared at Elden. When I passed a mirror, I saw a bearded man with icy eyes and a Sons of Templar cut with a shorter woman, her eyes bright, hair pulled off her face. Though I wasn't wearing any makeup, I didn't look young, didn't look like it was ridiculous for us to be together.

We fit.

Until we didn't.

Until Elden subtly but purposefully created distance when we landed in New Mexico.

It stung. Burned. Even though I knew it was the right choice.

I pushed it to the back of my mind when I made it to the hospital, when I told everyone half truths about where I'd been, what I'd been doing. I had been studying. Then I had been drinking at a bar without cell service. Then I went home to sleep before flying here.

I told my mother all of this, not having to make eye contact because I was too busy falling in love with my brother. Neither my mother nor Swiss had any inkling I was lying because they were both tired and distracted by their world growing bigger and more beautiful.

"I want to hold him forever," I whispered, rocking him gently.

"You can hold him for however long you want, though you may have to fight me and his dad," Mom countered with a tired smile. "But you also can change his diapers and deal with sleepless nights so you don't get any ideas."

I scoffed at the mere idea. "Mom, a woman can say she loves a baby without her womb and ancient procreation instincts taking over all rational thought."

"Well, just in case," she muttered. "I'm too young to be a grandmother. Plus, I don't want to be on Jerry *Springer* when I have a grandson the same age as my actual son."

I stared at her. "Considering I haven't just given birth and am not planning to, I think you're good."

"She's just tired, aren't you, Countess?" Swiss murmured, kissing her head. "You just created a whole world today."

The moment felt precious, soft, stolen.

I gently placed my brother down in his cradle—where he wouldn't likely be for long—and quietly left the room.

I leaned against the wall outside the hospital room, closing my eyes. Everything felt very unreal. My brother was here. My father was dead.

I had to call my grandparents. I was overcome with guilt that I hadn't done that already. They had lost their son. Even though they'd cut him off the second I sent a letter to my grandmother, telling them everything. My grandmother had come to visit my mother in Garnett not long after that. Then she'd stopped by Brown to see me, informing me that they would never speak to my father again. They'd chosen me and my mom over him. Without any hesitation.

A choice that couldn't have been easy. They were good people.

They loved their son. They could not understand how he'd turned into what he was.

They'd accepted the whole new life that my mother had created. They came for Christmas. Got along with Swiss.

But they lost their son.

So, I had to call them. Once I figured out what to say. How to speak to them. How to say I was sorry he was dead when I didn't know if I was.

Maybe I was. Maybe I had been harboring yet another fantasy of him having some kind of wakeup call after losing everything. Him redeeming himself, changing, turning into a good man.

But even I knew that there was no redemption after what he'd done for years. There was no story where he changed completely and became the father I deserved, the son my grandparents deserved. This ending, though painful, was the best we could've hoped for.

The door closed gently, then Swiss leaned against the wall beside me.

"He's lucky," I whispered. "My brother. To have you as a dad."

"I'm lucky," he countered. "To have him. Your mom." His head turned toward me. "You," he added.

"I know you're protectin' your mom," he continued. "Know that you're hurting, even if you don't want to be. Even if it pisses you the fuck off. You lost something. Even if it wasn't him, it was the idea of what he could've been. The memories of what he was before all this shit came out."

"You're allowed to hurt, darlin'." Like his words, his stare was soft and unyielding. "And I know that no matter what I tell you, you're not gonna stop protectin' your mother. But I don't know if you've noticed, I'm kind of a badass," he grinned. "You don't have to protect me from shit. You can hurt, Violet. It's okay."

Maybe it was his steady and understanding voice, maybe it

was the creeping exhaustion of the past few months, maybe it was just because I couldn't pretend anymore, but the second Swiss put his arms around me, I buried my face in his chest and sobbed.

For a long time.

I did not attend my father's funeral.

My grandparents did not mention it when they arrived in Garnett a few days after Declan's birth. They looked tired. My grandmother didn't look as flawless as she usually did; her eyes were red, the creases in her face deeper somehow.

But she still fussed endlessly over Declan, still arranged all the gifts she bought him around the adorable nursery.

My grandfather was quiet. He, like everyone else, doted on the new member of the family, but his smiles were sad, his eyes looking at his grandson but also seeing the son he had lost. I know both of them felt uncertain about their connection to him, worried that they had no claim. I also knew Swiss had some kind of talk with them that changed the atmosphere. Made them surer of their roles.

He was a good person. The best.

My mother and brother were safe with him. I was safe with him.

As long as I kept my secrets, my truth, far from him. It was at some point during the time spent at home after Declan's birth that I realized how bad things would get if he ever found out about me and Elden.

It would break apart the idyllic family they'd worked so hard to create. So even though it hurt me, even though it killed me, I did not seek Elden out again while I was back in Garnett.

He didn't seek me out either.

It hurt. Even though I was a woman, was capable of making

the first move, going out and getting what I wanted. I couldn't make that choice. Couldn't decide to go and ruin both of our lives.

And as horrible as it was for me, I resented him for not making that choice either.

It hadn't rained in two months.

Which was why I didn't hear from him.

The bitter cold brought biting wind, dreary days and the threatening prospect of snow. But it never did.

And it didn't rain.

So Elden didn't call.

Even though I'd been faced with hard truths in Garnett, after Declan's birth, I'd had some kind of warped idea that that night might've changed something. Might've shifted things between us.

But of course, Elden was still beholden to the club, though he never said it out loud. I knew I'd never be his. Not with my stepfather being his brother in everything but blood. I may not have had a huge amount of experience with outlaw motorcycle clubs, but I was quickly understanding the dynamics, and it was easy to see how seriously they took their commitment to the club.

It sent me into a spiraling depression. Probably not entirely because of Elden. I assumed at least part of it was about my father's death and everyone tiptoeing around me, waiting for me to have some kind of reaction. Any kind of reaction. Sariah was worried. She'd gently suggested I go to see her therapist—it had helped her greatly. It was a good idea, I knew that. It was healthy. And it was irresponsible for me to shove things down. Still, I'd refused just as gently as she'd offered.

She also didn't leave me alone, dragging me to and from every party she went to—which was a lot—even though we were both bogged down with work due before the Christmas break.

There was barely a moment to pause, to suck down coffee and

scarf some muffins that Ollie made before I was out the door, back only to shower and change into whatever outfit suited the theme of whatever party we were going to.

One of the many parties was where I met him.

When I was vulnerable, angry and vicious enough not to gently rebut his advances. Because as much as I wanted to tell every guy who hit on me to go and fuck himself, I couldn't since once a man was rejected, he was unpredictable. He could've spiked my drink, followed me home to try to rape me... That kind of thing.

Or maybe I was just sick of rejecting them. Maybe I was sick of looking down my nose at college boys, measuring them up against a man I would never have.

The reason didn't matter much. All that mattered was that I met him, let him flirt with me, let him take me out on dates. When he mentioned his parents were in Europe for Christmas and he didn't have the time to go because of his winter internship—I didn't even know those were a thing—I invited him back to Garnett with me.

I don't know why I brought him. No, that was a lie. I knew *exactly* why I brought the nice, square-jawed lacrosse player home for the holidays. To the Sons of Templar clubhouse where there was a Christmas Eve party happening.

This time of year was tense for the club, I'd come to learn. It was the anniversary of the massacre that happened when some rivals—I was sketchy on the details since no one told me them because I was too young, too sheltered, whatever the fuck—had come in and killed almost everyone in the entire club.

It felt faraway yet much too close at the same time. Faraway because, up until the time I found myself in Garnett, New Mexico, I had lived a sheltered life.

My father's death had been the only time I'd been touched by death. And even that I had forced away, hadn't let myself think it affected me.

Death hung heavy over the club, the loss they'd endured. I

hadn't experienced it fully last year, not with my mom being adamant to keep me away from the club this time of year.

Now they were her family. Now, although she was worried about me, we were fully immersed in the club.

Not that there weren't smiles, happiness, and gleeful children running around with candy canes in their little fists. There was all of that. But I didn't miss the sadness tinged in the eyes of Macy, one of the only survivors of the massacre. Her, Hansen and Jagger. They didn't make it *feel* sad… yet that sadness silently seeped from each of them, just as it invisibly did from the paint on the walls.

A chaotic Christmas, bursting with family. I'd never experienced anything like it. All of our Christmases had been decorated, curated to perfection. Although I'd only truly seen this with the gift of hindsight. As a child, I hadn't known any better. I'd been excited for Santa, for the gifts, the food, the special kind of magic that only came in December. It was only now that I realized the way my mother, already tightly wound, was tenser than usual, skittish, obsessed with the decorations, the cookies, the Christmas party we threw every year. It was only now that I understood my mother was doing everything in her power to avoid getting the shit beaten out of her by my father.

But even then, even being as naïve as I was, I understood there were rules. That I wasn't supposed to rip my presents open with abandon; I was to carefully pull them apart, not to make a mess. There was no screaming, no acting out in front of my father's guests at the Christmas party. There was a specific way to act. It went unsaid, but the silent words were spoken loud enough for even a five-year-old to hear.

It was never as stark, what I hadn't had, what my father had taken from us, as it was the first Christmas we had with the Sons of Templar. The first Christmas I saw my mother with a man who respected her. Adored her. Worshiped the ground she walked on. Who was completely hands-on with my brand-new brother. Who didn't expect my mother to take care of everything while his life remained the same. No, he changed diapers, he got up at night. He did whatever he could to make my mother's life easier.

She moved differently. Floated around the kitchen of the house he bought her, not worrying if a gingerbread man had wonky legs or was fatter than his counterpart. There was a lightness to her eyes that I didn't know existed.

Of course, these things brought about feelings of joy, but it wasn't that simple. There was the guilt. The overarching and near crippling guilt that I'd been too preoccupied with the latest makeup set, doll or pair of sneakers to see the sheer terror underneath my mother's false smiles. That I had lived an entire lifetime not noticing what she was going through. Then there was the sadness that came along with that. Sadness that my mother had gone through that. Then the more shameful anger, the constantly simmering fury that my mother went through that. For years. Resentment that she didn't leave, didn't take me away so I wouldn't have to carry around this burden for the rest of my life. I knew that was a selfish and disgusting way to think, but I couldn't help it.

I hated myself for it. But it didn't stop the way I felt.

That anger and resentment receded with each moment I got to spend with my mom, Swiss and my little brother. You couldn't be around them without your heart filling with hope. That maybe real love—that fairy-tale, Hallmark, Disney type of love—existed after all.

I'd never seen my mother truly alive.

Especially at Christmas.

So there I was, sabotaging it by playing games. By making my mom's eyes light up when I turned up at her door with a boy in tow.

He was everything most parents wanted their daughter to bring home.... Clean cut. Neatly pressed shirt. Blue eyes. Impeccable manners. He wouldn't let me carry a bag, insisted on addressing my mom and Swiss as Mr. and Mrs. Carter. He didn't even blink at Swiss, the muscled, menacing outlaw biker. He took it in stride, not showing an ounce of the breeding that would've urged him to look down on people in motorcycle clubs.

He played with my brother, held him with experience—explaining that his sister had two kids he adored—and all in all acted like the perfect guy.

My mother lapped him up like I knew she would.

Swiss was a little more hesitant. Not just because he was crazy protective—which he was—but because he was an outlaw biker who wasn't impressed with square jaws, pleases and thank yous and pressed shirts. I presumed there was some kind of alpha male test he was conducting on Bennett. A test that he invariably failed. Because Bennett, although he opened doors for me, pulled out chairs for me and treated me with the utmost respect, was not a badass alpha. He was a rich kid from a respectable family who summered in the Hamptons and interned on Wall Street during the winter break.

Swiss had got all this out of him like he was conducting an investigation. Bennett had offered all of the information freely, the ultimate parental pleaser. Unfortunately, Swiss was not that kind of parent.

And that was just the beginning.

My mom and Swiss's nice house in the New Mexico desert was kind to him. Albeit it with Swiss's steely glares and harder than necessary handshakes.

It was when I took him to the Sons of Templar compound for Christmas dinner that I baptized him by fire.

He did not deserve it. He may have been from a wealthy, WASPY family who didn't believe in global warming and reminded me too much of my own upbringing, and he may have been in a rich frat and had friends named Chad who I wouldn't leave my drink alone with, but he was a disturbingly decent guy.

We'd been on three dates. Actual dates where he'd picked me up from our house and everything. My roommates had legitimately thought we were being robbed when he rang the doorbell and no one had ordered food or was waiting on a package.

He took me out for dinner and paid each time, making it clear that it was because he picked the restaurant and arranged the date, so it was his responsibility, not because he believed I wasn't capable of providing for myself. He asked my fucking *permission* to kiss me. After the second date.

He was an odd mix of the conservative first son belonging to the rich frat at an Ivy League, but he was also liberal when it came to dating and things like consent.

I appreciated it. And it might've even worked for me, *he* might've even worked for me, if I hadn't met Elden. If I hadn't been kissed fiercely by a man who didn't ask for permission or forgiveness. Who didn't give a fuck about the new rules of dating. All he cared about was claiming.

Except he didn't.

Claim me.

Not physically.

And that should've made the progressive, liberal, feminist in me happy. It should've made me even more grateful to have found what passed for a decent guy in college. Especially after everything I'd been through thus far. He was the safe, comfortable route. I figured I deserved the safe and comfortable route.

Yet I was bringing Bennett home. For Christmas. Knowing we were having Christmas dinner at the club. Knowing that Elden would be there. I was using this nice boy who genuinely liked me, who genuinely thought I was a nice girl, and I was throwing him to the wolves.

I felt sick over it. Guilty. I had lain awake in my bedroom, tossing and turning, trying to convince myself to pull the plug on things before it got ugly.

I'd lain awake, tossing and turning… alone, because Bennett was staying in the guest room. Mom had been *so* happy to let me know that after a long fight with Swiss which she ended by using her, and I quote, "womanly wiles," Bennett would be staying in my bedroom.

I'd been horrified yet tried to hide it. As mentioned, Bennett was a gentleman, so I needn't have worried. He'd barely gotten to second base. He'd made it clear he was happy to go further... if I wanted. But I didn't. It felt vaguely like I was kissing a cousin. His lips were too soft, too moist, too hesitant. I'd barely been able to respond to the bumbling affection that did nothing to turn me on. I should've stopped it right there, knowing my body and needs well enough to understand he was the opposite of what I wanted.

But I'd kept pretending I was interested, just "not ready" for the "next step." He'd been respectful, patient and so sweet my teeth hurt.

Not because I had some master plan to bring him home and use him as a pawn in the twisted game I was playing with Elden... That happened organically, after I'd continued dating him because I was trying to force myself into a more acceptable role.

Luckily, Bennett was such a respectable guy that he gently declined my mother's offer of him putting his stuff in my room, saying he'd be more comfortable in the guest room, as his own mother wouldn't have heard of such a thing.

This response should've made Swiss gloriously happy, but I swore I heard him mutter "pussy" under his breath.

Both Mom and I had stared daggers at him, but Bennett either hadn't heard or was polite enough to pretend he didn't.

"You okay, sweetheart?" Bennett murmured in my ear as we walked into the clubhouse for Christmas dinner.

He hadn't so much as raised his brows as we pulled up to the biker compound with barbed wire on top of the gates, security cameras and a parking lot full of Harleys.

"I'm fine," I squeaked, his hand warm and dry in my own.

My heart was thundering in my chest, and my own palm was not dry at all.

Mom looked around from where she and Swiss were walking,

heading into the building first. My brother was strapped to Swiss's chest. Yes, he walked around with a baby strapped to him without shame. He really pulled it off.

My mother's brows furrowed. "Did you just squeak?" she asked with a grin.

I poked my tongue out at her and focused on Bennett. I looked at his kind blue eyes, the softness of his smile, the clear affection and concern in his gaze. He liked me. And I did not deserve him.

This was a big fucking mistake. It was too late to call it off. But I could recommit to making it work with a decent boy who wouldn't fuck me up and cause huge drama with the family I'd come to love.

We stopped just inside to sounds of laughter, muted rock music, the clang of glasses and the low rumble of alpha male conversations.

I made sure not to look around the room and instead focused on Bennett.

I reached up to straighten the collar of his shirt. Yeah, he wore a collared shirt to Christmas dinner at an outlaw motorcycle club. I'd had to tell him to take off the salmon-colored tie he'd paired with his sensible, expensive shirt, slacks and loafers.

"Are you sure you want to do this?" I asked, smoothing imaginary wrinkles on his shirt. "We can just go back to Mom's house, watch Christmas movies and raid the liquor cabinet?" I asked hopefully.

Bennett grasped gently—so gently it infuriated me—onto my wrists, pulling them upward so he could kiss them.

I forced my body not to stiffen under his touch.

"Sweetheart," he murmured.

Ugh, I fucking hated that endearment.

"Although this definitely isn't like any Christmas dinner I've attended," he continued, thankfully unaware of the vague disgust I was feeling at the prospect of being his girlfriend and having those lips on me for a prolonged amount of time.

His eyes skimmed the room behind me, the one I was too cowardly to look at yet. "*Definitely* not like any Christmas dinner," he repeated with a grin. "But I'm so glad to be here. Even if your stepfather does scare the shit out of me," he joked.

I forced out a weak smile. "He's all bark and no bite," I reassured him.

He sagged with relief. "Really?"

I bit my lip. "Really," I lied. "Same with all the guys here. They're all teddy bears really. Just overprotective."

Another lie. A big one. If I really wanted him to leave, I could've just told him that every man here would happily bury him where he'd never be found if he hurt me in any way.

Bennett leaned in to kiss my head. I restrained a wince. "Well, I'm glad that you've got people looking out for you."

My eyes squeezed shut and I breathed through his overpowering cologne, wishing to have a more positive response to him.

But when I forced my eyes open, I found the response I'd been chasing. My entire body caught fire. My heart stuttered. Breathing shallow. White hot desire burned through my clothes.

Elden was not in the main room with everyone else, toasting, snacking, talking. No. He'd just walked in the door. The door we were basically blocking with this cringeworthy embrace.

And he was pissed.

Really fucking pissed.

His cheeks turned red with fury, his eyes darkened with a kind of rage that seemed to shadow the entire room.

His eyes left mine for a millisecond, scanning the room behind me… for what, I didn't know. But seconds later, I figured out he'd been looking to see if Swiss was paying attention to this part of the room. Otherwise, Elden wouldn't have been able to do what he did.

And what he did was stride forward and wrench me out of Bennett's arms. Not gently, but not enough to hurt either. Bennett hadn't been holding me *that* tightly.

"Hey!" Bennett said, not loudly enough to carry over the music or children screaming and laughing.

Elden had a tight grip on my upper arm.

"Let me go," I snapped, not trying to pull my arm back. I was too busy savoring the way my entire body came alive at his presence, his touch, his scent.

I was glaring up at him, and he was glowering at Bennett who had puffed up his chest and stepped forward to do who knew what.

"You let her go," he demanded, showing a side of him that was perhaps a bit possessive. But there was a hesitancy there, as most people would feel when faced with a fully pissed off Elden.

"Not doin' that," Elden replied quietly. "And you're not gonna make a scene. You're gonna take your ass back to whatever country club spat you out, and I'm gonna have a word with Violet."

Elden did not wait for Bennett to argue like it looked like he was going to. No, he just commenced in dragging me down the hall.

Although the clubhouse was crowded with members, families, and whomever else was connected to the club, somehow no one but Bennett noticed Elden dragging me down the hall. Well, Colby noticed, his eyes flaring with surprise when they landed on me. Or more accurately, Elden's arm on me. But instead of raising the alarm, stepping in or being chivalrous, he grinned wickedly at me.

Traitor.

Bennett had not followed us.

He had just let me be dragged off by a dangerous and seriously pissed off biker. Granted, the biker in question was two times bigger and infinitely more menacing than him, and armed, but still. As much as I believed that I was capable of looking out for myself and my disgust for the trope of women being damsels in distress, only existing to be saved by men and to bolster up their sense of strength and glory, a girl wanted to be saved once in a while.

"You cannot just rip me out of another man's arms," I hissed at Elden as he pulled me down the hall.

"He's no fucking man," he snarled. Yeah, *snarled*. "Any man holdin' on to you is on guard, prepared for some other fuck to try to take her from them, and is holding tight to make sure that never happens." He kept dragging me—not rough enough to make a point—while maintaining icy, furious, maddening eye contact. "Any man lucky enough to be holdin' on to you will fight to the fuckin' death to make sure you are theirs and only theirs."

I pursed my lips as an ache formed between my legs. I was unsure of what to say to that since there really was no rational argument. Well, sure, there were a lot of rational arguments regarding the misogynist undertones in everything he'd just said. I could've pointed out that I was a human being with agency, autonomy, not someone to be owned, claimed. I was complicated, full of multitudes and complex thoughts. I wasn't an object to be owned by any man.

But when it came to Elden, there was nothing complicated about me. I was his. He owned me. For better or for worse.

And when he opened the door to his bedroom with an energy of fury simmering around him, I knew it was for the worse.

My blood sang with fear, my panties already damp in tandem with that fear. It excited me. Made me feel alive.

Elden didn't look the least bit excited, his entire body was tense, his face etched into a glower, his whole body was trembling with fury. The door slammed shut behind us, and he pushed the center of my chest so I slammed into the wall.

Not hard enough to hurt, but hard enough to make a point. To dwarf me with his strength. Make it known I was helpless around him.

My knees were knocking together, and my pussy throbbed.

"The first time I kissed you, I knew I was making a mistake

before I did it," he murmured, brushing hair from my face. "But I did it anyway because I had about as much choice as I did inhaling and exhaling. I told myself it would be once. So I could taste you, so I wasn't driving myself crazy, stayin' up all night wonderin' what your lips feel like."

His eyes scurried up and down my outfit. I was wearing a tight, plum leather skirt, knee-high boots, and a fitted, plum sweater. Elden liked it, it seemed, from the way his eyes flared as they ran over my body.

"Now I stay up all night wonderin' what it would feel like to own every part of you." He coiled a strand of my hair around his finger. "What it would be like to be worthy of you. The later parts of the night are spent hating myself for wanting you."

My heart was beating so fast, my entire body vibrated.

"The last time we were together, your lips were around my cock." His voice was soft and cutting at the same time.

My breath caught in my lungs. Or that's what it seemed. I was still standing, so I must've been breathing.

Elden's eyes turned to pits of fury.

"So, what the *fuck*, Violet?" he leaned forward, palm still on the center of my chest. His fingers brushed against my nipples which were already aching and hard.

Although my body burned hot with desire, I tried with everything inside me to keep my expression placid. "What?" I asked sweetly.

"You know what," he leaned even closer to my mouth. "You brought that boy in here to his fucking death."

I tried to swallow the lump in my throat as I fought to roll my eyes. "Don't be so dramatic," I waved a hand dismissively, not breaking eye contact. "We both know you're not going to hurt him." That was kind of a lie. I'd never seen Elden like this, so… unhinged. I had no idea what he was going to do. "You're far too controlled for that. And if you did anything to him, you'd have to explain yourself. And you'd never do that." It was both a challenge and a statement.

Most of me didn't want Elden to do anything to Bennett, whose only crime was not seeing how messed up and uninterested I truly was. I definitely didn't want the club as a whole to have to deal with any kind of violence or drama on a holiday that was already difficult for them.

But a tiny, ugly, unwelcome part of me wanted him to do it. Fight for me. Tear this fucking place apart for me. Because in this world, that would serve as a declaration that I was his. We wouldn't be some fucked-up secret anymore.

Elden didn't break his furious stare, the air still thick around us. His mouth was inches from mine. My chest tingled under the weight of his palm. My body longed for more.

Elden didn't move. He didn't storm down the hall to make good on his promise.

Which was a good thing. A wonderful thing. An innocent boy wasn't going to get the shit beaten out of him, and this holiday would not be ruined.

Yet that ugly part of me was disappointed, it was hurt, and it wanted to strike out. Draw blood.

"What do you care who I fuck anyway?" I shot out, my words barbed, sharp.

Elden went stock still, but I wasn't done.

"I simply did what you asked the last time I was in this room." I looked around his neat bedroom, remembering those biting wounds and the wounds from them that had refused to heal. "I found someone who is impressed by me," I parroted the hot, poisonous and hurtful words.

"You're fuckin' him?" he murmured, voice soft. Or as soft as a blade could be.

My body froze on instinct, out of some kind of default response when faced with someone deadly.

Though I was scared, turned on and about a million other

things, I was also satisfied. I'd made an impact. Evoked a reaction out of him.

I kept my lips pursed shut.

His eyes seared into me with icy blue fury. "He touched you, Violet?" His hand roamed from the center of my chest, skimming down my stomach and slipping under my sweater.

My breath fractured as his calloused fingers ran over the skin of my stomach.

I didn't answer his question. Couldn't. All of my effort was going toward breathing, standing, keeping eye contact with him as his fingers brushed my nipples.

"If he has laid a hand on this perfect fucking skin, I will bury him so deep that even the worms won't be able to find him," Elden rasped, leaning forward so his lips barely brushed mine.

"Why w-would you?" I stuttered against his mouth. "What does it matter if he fucked me or not? What does it matter if I've fucked ten boys in college? It's my right."

I was baiting him when he was already furious. It was somewhat dangerous and irresponsible, but it also made everything inside me glow brighter.

His hand found my nipple, tweaking just to the point of pain.

My pussy flexed, and I let out a moan that had nothing to do with pain.

Elden's other hand pushed under my skirt, brushing up my thigh until he found the thin lace of my panties.

He let out a low hiss, and his gaze turned feral. "It may be your right," he agreed, fingers slipping in, parting where I was soaking wet for him.

My back pressed against the wall as I struggled against the stars I saw as he found my clit.

"But it will mean I'm gonna have to fuck you for hours to remove any memory of a boy who's been inside what's mine," he growled, fingers plunging inside of me without warning.

His palm found my mouth just as I let out a loud moan.

Though we were at the end of the hall, you could still hear the party going on in the common room, the music, the muffled voices.

Elden's fingers paused inside of me, not moving as I ached for them to do. But maybe it was good because if he'd moved then, I would've exploded and likely lost the ability to stand.

"Tight," he grunted. His erection pressed into me. "You haven't let anyone else in here, have you, my good girl?"

I couldn't form a response.

"You're gonna answer me, Violet," he demanded.

His voice was so rough it grated against my skin, against every exposed nerve. "You haven't let anyone else in here, have you?" His fingers moved once more, but languidly.

I moaned again as I slowly shook my head.

"But I'm not your good girl, remember?" I ground out. "I'm your bad girl."

He exposed his teeth in a sinful grin. Then his fingers moved out of me, and my body tensed in protest.

My pussy pulsated as he took the fingers that had been inside of me and put them in his mouth, tasting me.

His eyes flared.

"Need my cock inside you now." His voice was tight, as if he were doing everything he could to control its tenor. His jaw was wired, taut, his lips pulled back. "If I had my way, I'd be fuckin' you for hours," he continued. "I'd make you scream my name until you couldn't speak anymore. I'd fuck you until you passed out with my cock inside you."

I hung on his words, my own body straining with a desperate, aching need for him to do all of that.

"But…" He shoved a hand up my skirt so it was bunched at my hips before ripping my panties off as he freed himself. "This is all we have." He gripped my chin between his hands. "If I were a good man, I wouldn't be touching you right now," he ran his tongue along his lips. "But I'm not a good man."

There was a crinkle of foil, and I wondered vaguely why he walked around with a condom on his person, then I was overwhelmed by jealousy. Or I would've been if he hadn't done what he did next.

He hitched one of my legs around his hips so he was positioned right at my entrance.

"If I were a better man, I'd at least make sure that the first time I fucked you, we could take our time, that I could give you what you deserve." His eyes never let go of mine. "But I'm not," he hissed. Then he surged in.

His hand covered my mouth once more, a good thing too since I was unable to restrain myself.

I constricted around his cock. His gloriously large cock that filled me up, that was so big it almost hurt. Almost. But it was perfect. As if it were made for me.

"I can't control myself around you," he groaned against my mouth.

I let out something unintelligible in response.

His hand circled around my throat. "You are my bad fuckin' girl, aren't you?"

I nodded, or tried to nod against the onslaught of a climax that would ruin my world.

"You're my fucked-up, bad little girl," he repeated, his thrusts harder, more uncontrolled.

My pussy clenched as I teetered on the edge of climax and spots began to dance in my vision.

"Yeah, my little, bad girl," Elden ground out. "Come for me… And don't you fucking dare close your eyes."

I stared at him. My eyes had been ready to squeeze shut in preparation for what I already knew was going to be the most intense orgasm of my life.

"You look me in the eye," he ordered.

That's what splintered me, sent me hurtling from my body,

tethered only by Elden's intense gaze which went wild as he came seconds after me.

I didn't black out, every second etched into my mind. I scrambled to preserve it all so I could revisit the best, angriest, most primal, world-breaking sex I'd ever had.

I'd fantasized about this endlessly. And with all of my fantasies, whenever something close to the real-life version happened, I was disappointed. Because nothing built up in your head is ever as good.

But my brain wasn't capable of dreaming up what just happened.

It exceeded any and all expectations I could've possibly dreamt up.

My knees shook as Elden lowered my leg, pulling himself out of me. My entire body spasmed at losing him.

Elden's expression was unreadable, but his eyes were still heated. They hadn't shut down, hadn't turned cruel.

"I'm gonna go take care of the condom," he told me. "You're gonna stay right here."

Unable to move, I nodded my head, the sounds of the party filtering in from outside the door. The walls were pretty thick here, so they were muffled, but it was clear that we had just had sex down the hall from my mother, her husband, my baby brother and my whole new family.

Oh, and my kind of boyfriend I'd brought home.

And I didn't feel guilty. Not even a little. It… *excited* me.

I marveled at Elden as he walked back into the room, buttoning his jeans. His muscles, his beard, his gait. The way he held himself. This man had just fucked me. *Fucked*. If you look up the definition of that word in the dictionary, there would be a picture of Elden.

His eyes brushed over me with a look that made me feel like a woman. Not just a woman, but one with power.

There was no going back now. No question as to whether he

considered me too young. He'd made it clear he considered me a woman.

His woman.

And though I'd promised myself I would never be defined by what I was to another man, it felt fantastic.

Elden didn't speak for a while. Nor did I. We just stared at each other.

"You're gonna go back in there." He motioned to the door. "Without your panties, with your pussy drippin', claimed by me. You're gonna sit next to that fuck. You're gonna make sure he doesn't lay a hand on that skin I just made mine."

He put his hand between my legs, cupping the bare, sensitive skin there.

I shivered, already hungry for more, already ready to abandon all reason and beg him to fuck me again.

But his hand skimmed upward, finding my skirt which was still bunched at my hips, then he pulled it down carefully. Gently. In direct dichotomy with how beautifully brutal he'd just been.

"Don't care how you do it," he continued softly. "Just do it. Because you were wrong… I will punish him if he thinks he can touch you. I won't make a scene, 'cause I am too controlled for that. But I'll follow him all the way back to his parents' fuckin' mansion. I'll make him hurt in a way that he won't heal right. No one will know it was me. Except you. You'll be walking around knowing I did that for you."

There was nothing I could say to that. Not one single thing. I could barely breathe.

He would do it. Elden would hurt an innocent boy for merely touching what he didn't know wasn't his to touch.

"Go now," Elden ordered gently.

But my feet stayed rooted in the spot. I had to know something. Something that had kept me up many nights. Something that I shouldn't want to know.

"Did you sleep with her?" I asked.

Elden stiffened. He didn't ask me who I meant. He knew who I meant.

He wouldn't lie to spare my feelings. I knew that.

So, I should not have asked.

Ignorance was bliss and all that.

Except I'd spent my entire life ignorant as to what was going on in my own house. There was no way I was going to spend the rest of my life like that. I wanted the truth, even if it hurt. Even if it was ugly.

Ugly truth was better than polished lies.

"No," he said finally. "I was plannin' on it. But couldn't stand the thought of some other bitch chasin' away the taste of you. Memory of you."

Okay, that was not a polished lie. But somehow it hurt too.

"Go," Elden said, nodding to the door.

I did as he asked.

CHAPTER *Twelve*

SOMEHOW, nobody noticed me walk back into the common room on unsteady legs with mussed hair and red cheeks. Nobody noticed that I'd transformed into an entirely different person than I had been when I walked in.

Bennett was all the way in the corner. Macy and Freya had obviously taken pity on him and were laughing with glasses of wine in their hands, keeping him entertained and comfortable. They were the safest people for him to speak to. They wouldn't challenge him to a fistfight, bomb-making competition or whatever it was that the Sons of Templar did to outsiders to make them prove their worth.

I needed to find a way to pull myself together before I spoke to him or encountered my mother, who thankfully, was sitting on a sofa with Swiss who was whispering something into her ear that made her blush.

I had time.

I also had to figure out what the fuck I was going to say to Bennett to make him leave, not touch me and not humiliate or hurt him all at the same time. I was pretty sure there was no way to do all of that. Many women had tried all kinds of polite, kind, considerate ways to break up with men, yet there were still a lot of angry, dangerous men out there, blaming their 'crazy' exes for all of their problems.

Bennett didn't seem like the type of guy to go crazy, but they never did. My father was much beloved around town and likely to be thought of last on a list of men who might secretly beat their wives.

Then again, if Bennett tried to do anything, he'd have an entire motorcycle club after him, and I knew for certain he was nowhere near that stupid.

"Your hair looks… a little different than it did when you first walked in here," someone commented playfully.

My hands went upward, smoothing the wayward strands manically as Colby grinned at me from ear to ear.

"And your cheeks," he continued. "So rosy. Is your lipstick smudged?"

My other hand went to my mouth.

He chuckled. "Chill, dude. I'm just fucking with you."

I scowled at him.

"Your boyfriend has been mighty concerned about your whereabouts," he jerked his head to the corner of the room.

Bennett finally saw me, his eyes flaring with relief and worry.

There was a twinge of guilt, but barely. There should've been a lot more.

"Fuck," I muttered under my breath. "I need booze."

"Well, it seems you could use a cigarette too," he winked. "But we can't smoke around the kids and those things will kill you." He held up two large shot glasses, full of clear liquid. "This will kill you too, but slower, and it's much more fun."

"I could kiss you."

His eyes darted behind me, focusing on something. "Please don't," he requested. "I enjoy my arms being attached to the rest of me."

I looked to where his attention had strayed to. Elden was

walking back into the room, his expression blank, his cheeks not rosy, his hair neat… Well, neat for him, at least. In short, he looked like the brooding, hot guy he always did. Not the broody hot guy who had just fucked his friend's daughter within an inch of her life.

He didn't even spare me a glance.

"As much as this *delights* me," Colby began, "and it does, for you. Not for the club," he grimaced. "This is fucking horrible for the club and could start a civil war or some shit. So maybe try your best to keep it on the down low, at least until the holiday season is over with. Maybe when your little brother is walking, Swiss will be less homicidal then." He blew out a long exhale through his teeth. "Or maybe more homicidal, who knows with that fucker."

I snatched the tequila shot off him, downing it in one gulp, savoring the burn.

"If he hurts you, I'll kill him," Colby grunted. There was no more playful teasing in his tone. This was him being the big, bad, dangerous biker.

"Even though he would probably beat me in hand-to-hand combat," he added, eyes dancing. "I'd have to get imaginative, a little underhanded, catch him while his back is turned." He reached out to squeeze my hand. "But seriously, babe. He fucks this up, he's the problem. Not you."

"Or the problem is the age difference, my stepfather and whatever kind of tortured backstory he has… You all seem to have one," I countered.

Colby winked. "Makes us more interesting and a fuck of a lot deadlier."

A high-pitched whistle cut through the air.

All heads turned in Hansen's direction. "Grub's up," he announced, motioning to the table. "Get your asses in seats."

Everyone, including some… willful children, took heed of Hansen's order.

I stayed close to Colby like a coward, doing my best to shuffle my body alongside his like I could fucking hide behind him. Like Bennett was going to magically forget that I was the entire reason he was in this environment.

It was a shitty move. A really shitty move.

But I was focusing on being as close to Elden as I could without being obvious, and the farthest I could be from Bennett to save him from any repercussions from innocent displays of affection.

It kind of worked.

Colby sat on one side of me, Lucas on the other. Elden was directly across from me. That wasn't what I was intending since it would then become obvious as fuck that I was making a concerted effort *not* to look at him.

I winced as I sat down, my body sensitive from what had just happened. Elden's gaze found mine for a split second, but that was enough to raise the hair on the back of my neck and make my body re-experience everything he'd just done to me.

I forced my gaze down the table to where Bennett was sitting between my mother—who had obviously taken pity on him—and Hades, of all people, who was tattooed within an inch of his life and literally looked like a really hot personification of the Grim Reaper. Except with his wife and kids. For them, he melted.

For anyone else? He made it clear you only got his full attention if he was about to kill you. Or at least that was the vibe he gave off.

I smiled in apology to Bennett who, apart from looking vaguely pale, seemed to be handling himself okay.

I gave my mother a poignant look that was meant to communicate something like *'make sure he's not traumatized for life and doesn't hate me for bringing him here.'*

She smiled and nodded as if she had heard my telepathic plea, turning to engage Bennett in conversation.

I sagged in my chair slightly. I was not out of the woods. Not even a little. I was sitting at the Christmas table with all of my new family—my grandparents were arriving later today for what would hopefully be a less chaotic dinner—having just been fucked by the object of my infatuation and was no longer wearing panties while my mother entertained the boy who was supposed to be my date.

Hansen distracted me from all of this when he stood up from his position at the head of the table, holding a beer.

All conversation quieted.

"Want to thank you all for being here," he began in his rich, deep voice. "This is a difficult time of year for this chapter." He looked down at his wife who reached up to squeeze his hand, her eyes glassy.

"We've lost a lot," he cleared his throat. "And we will not forget those we lost. But they also would want us to celebrate them, to make the club the best it can be and make sure no one hurts this club again."

Someone clanged their glass on the table in agreement, others nodded in menacing and badass ways that were mighty impressive. Elden's face remained a stoic mask.

"We are a family," Hansen continued. "And we take care of our own. We have each other's backs. I love each and every one of you, and I thank you for being here. I'm so fuckin' proud of how we've rebuilt and what we will continue to do." He held up his beer. "Here's to many more years of prosperity, and most importantly, family."

There were a bunch of "hear hears," and, "cheers!"

I lifted my own glass, not looking at Elden and pretending what we'd just done didn't endanger the peace of the family we were toasting to.

Dinner went off without a hitch. I managed to sink into the warmth of the love around the table, the food and the feeling of belonging I'd never felt before. Whenever we were at the table with my father and his friends or family, I'd always held my silverware—correctly, of course—in a grip tight enough to turn my knuckles white in order not to scream out loud at some of the elitist, misogynist bullshit that came out of their mouths. And when I was old enough to understand that I couldn't, *wouldn't* be silent anymore, my protests were always followed by a moment of tense silence and my mother rushing to change the subject, her concerned gaze darting toward my father.

Sometimes my father would chastise me afterward. My mother would always step in, tell me to go to bed.

I now wondered what happened after I went to bed. What punishments my mother experienced in order to protect me.

The thought clogged my throat.

It even distracted me from Elden's presence across the table and the general reality of my situation... That was until everyone finished eating and Bennett's hand clasped on to my shoulder.

"Can I talk to you for a moment?" he asked quietly in my ear.

I jolted underneath his hand, moving quickly so my shoulder was no longer in his grip. My panicked eyes swiveled quickly to Elden who was watching with an impassive face from his spot by the bar.

My breath hitched, hoping that this wouldn't count as the kind of touch that would get Bennett hurt. He was here because of me and because he was a nice guy; he did not deserve to be punished for that.

"Sure!" I said in a tone that was much too high.

Colby snickered beside me, so I poked my tongue out at him before quickly standing to face Bennett.

His face was blank, not angry but no longer warm and inviting as it had been when we arrived.

Shit, he was mad.

Who wouldn't be?

"Let's go..." I looked around the crowded room, everyone congregating in little groups.

There was no corner to sit and talk privately, plus, all of the men here were worse gossips than the women.

"You can talk in my room if you'd like," Colby offered.

I scowled at him. "We'll go outside, thank you," I snapped at him before refocusing my gaze on Bennett who was looking between Colby and I quizzically.

As we walked through the room silently, I smiled tightly at everyone we passed until we made it outside to the crisp air.

I rubbed my exposed arms, cursing my forgotten coat.

Bennett didn't hesitate in handing me his. I hadn't even realized he'd taken it with him.

Though I shouldn't have accepted such a thoughtful act of chivalry considering what I'd just done, I took the coat gratefully. It didn't warm me as it should've because it smelled of him, reminding me of what an asshole I was.

Luckily, none of the smokers had ventured outside, and the parking lot was desolate. I wished for someone to come and interrupt us so I didn't have to have this conversation.

But no one came to save the respectable boy from the girl with questionable morals and a thing for much older, dangerous men.

Well, just one much older, dangerous man.

I opened my mouth to say what, I didn't know, but Bennett spoke first.

"You and him, you're a thing, aren't you?" Bennett nodded to the door leading back into the clubhouse.

I froze. If Bennett saw that, barely knowing me, then other people definitely saw it. Or it was only a matter of time before they saw it.

"I-I, um." I was unable to lie when I was this shocked but unwilling to tell the truth.

He smiled sadly, without the malice I might've expected. "It's okay, I get it. This life..." He looked up at the Sons of Templar insignia painted on the building without distaste, just curiosity and wonder.

"I didn't really know a life like this existed," he shrugged, looking back at me. "Or at least I was conditioned to think the reality was much different than what it really is." He sighed, putting his hands in his pockets. "I understand why you want him. This life is nothing like what I could ever give you, and I think you'd be deeply unhappy with whatever life you'd have with me."

I gaped at him, unable to fathom just how clearly he'd seen me. Just how calm he was. No resentment or anger toward me.

"He seems… nice," he offered, gesturing toward inside.

I continued gaping. He'd had a very intense altercation with Elden. He may have been polite, but no way would anyone be able to describe him as *nice* with a straight face.

"And you seem at ease around him, playful," he continued.

I screwed up my nose in confusion. I was a lot of things around Elden... Unnerved. Alive. Passionate. Nervous and confident at the same time. But not *playful*.

"With me, I now see that you've been forcing it." He smiled sadly. "I would never want you to do that, no matter how much I want you. I want you to do tequila shots with him, joke with him. Be happy. And protected. He will definitely be able to do that better than me."

Tequila shots.

It clicked. He was talking about Colby. He thought *Colby* was the man I had a thing with.

I opened my mouth to correct him then quickly closed it again. If I denied it, then I'd have to tell him the truth, or come up with some convincing lie. No. That wouldn't work. There was no harm in letting him believe a little white lie that would spare his feelings and make my life a little easier.

"Although I'm surprised he wasn't more mad at that other guy pulling you away like that," he frowned. "Though he came up and explained that it had to do with your mother's restaurant, something about a party to celebrate her feature in *Food & Wine*… I wouldn't think a biker would be overly concerned with that, but it's nice to see."

I swallowed a hysterical laugh that hovered in my throat at the thought of Elden being concerned with party planning. And then I silently thanked my friend for having my back.

I nodded somberly, trying to gather myself. "I really am sorry, Bennett," I said sincerely. "I never wanted to hurt you. And I really do like you."

He smiled at me, reaching to tuck my hair behind my ear. I forced myself not to recoil, hoping Elden wasn't looking from a secret perch somewhere.

"I know," he stepped back. "But not in the right way. And that's fine. We can be friends… If you want?"

"I really do want that," I replied honestly. "You really are a really good guy, and you will find a girl who deserves you."

"Let's hope so. I'll make sure to ask my next date whether they have a connection to a motorcycle club because I now know I cannot compete with bikers."

I flashed him a genuine smile. "Please stay," I nodded to where music had started to thump. "We're having a more… reserved dinner at my mom's house, and I'd like you to be there."

Bennett looked past me to where a car was loitering outside the gates. The Prospect guarding had his hand on the inside of his cut looking a little too trigger happy for my liking.

"That's my ride," Bennett told me, eyes narrowing at the Prospect. "And I should probably go rescue them."

"No, you don't have to leave," I told him, thinking how incredibly horrible it was that he'd be alone and rejected during the rest of Christmas.

"I do," he refuted with a sad smile. "Plus, I've actually got a friend in the area who is more than happy to have me for their dinner, though I doubt it will be as fun as yours was." His sad smile quickly morphed into a happier one. "I'll see you at school, okay, Violet?"

I nodded. "We'll have lunch," I said firmly.

He bobbed his head in affirmation, gave me one last look, then walked away.

It was only after I got back inside that I realized I was still wearing his coat. And that was only because Elden was staring daggers at me. Or more accurately, at the other man's coat on my body.

I hastily took it off, making a mental reminder to send it back to him with an apology note of some kind. Though I wasn't sure what I could write in an apology note for dragging him all the way out here and ruining his Christmas.

My mother and Swiss were settled on the sofa, so I sank down beside them, leaning into my mother before kissing Declan's little head as he was cradled in her arms.

"Where did Bobart go?" Swiss asked with disinterest, smiling down at his son.

I scowled. "It's Bennett, and you know it. And he went home. It didn't work out."

"We scared him off, did we? Good, he wasn't right for you," Swiss said at the same time my mother said, "Honey, I'm so sorry. Are you okay?"

"You didn't scare him off," I glowered at Swiss. "I just never liked him in the first place. He's too… nice."

Mom quirked a brow at me. "There is no such thing as too nice."

I raised my own brow back. "Yeah, you *really* went for the nice guy."

"I'm nice," Swiss argued.

I stared at him in disbelief.

"I'm nice to *most* people."

"Honey, I love you so, so much, but you yelled at the cart boy in the grocery store two days ago," Mom said.

"The fucker was about to run into my wife and infant son with a shitload of carts," he scowled at her. "He's lucky that's all that happened."

Mom rolled her eyes. "He was nowhere near me," she stage whispered.

I grinned and rested my head against her shoulder.

She kissed my head.

I wished that it felt the same way it did when I was younger. Safe. Natural. Now there were things between us, secrets, my own, hers uncovered.

"I'm sorry about Bennett, sweetie," she whispered.

My eyes didn't go to him, but my mind did. Not to Bennett... To Elden. "Yeah, me too," I lied. What was one more on top of the pile?

CHAPTER *Thirteen*

EVERYTHING CHANGED AFTER CHRISTMAS.

Elden and I were no longer holding back. He'd claimed me. There was no going back, and neither of us wanted to.

We fucked every second we could during my winter break.

I didn't tell anyone. Obviously. Colby hadn't said anything further, thankfully, most likely because he didn't want to be implicated if/when this all came out, not willing to risk being caught in the crossfire between my stepfather and Elden.

Elden seemed to have come to the decision that he didn't give a fuck about the fire, direct or otherwise, because he, like me, was insatiable.

We did it whenever and wherever we could. The more we did it, the more desperate for each other we became. Nothing dissipated or wore off. Our need for each other grew. We became increasingly brazen. He fucked me on the club's kitchen counter in the middle of the day when anyone could've walked in. I didn't know if both of us secretly wanted to get caught or if the danger of it all turned us on more.

I was working at Oliver's almost every day. For the distraction, not so much for the money. I had plenty from my father since the divorce divested him of almost all of his assets. I wasn't sure how I felt about that. My college was paid for, I never had to worry about money. I was incredibly, incredibly lucky. But the money made me feel dirty somehow. Still depending on Daddy for my future, for what I ate, what I wore.

So, it felt good to be making my own money. I worked at Mom's restaurant, Violet's, whenever I could too. She was back to working often since there was a whole village of women around her to help out with Declan and with Swiss taking him everywhere he could.

Truthfully, I was avoiding my mother. Not just because I wanted every spare moment of mine with Elden but because whenever I was with her, the guilt of our secret became harder to bear.

I only had one more day left before I went back to college. I should've been excited. To get back to the life I'd been so looking forward to. The freedom. Independence. The friends I'd made. What I was learning.

But it felt stifling. Foreign. My dreams had shifted. Not just because of Elden but because they'd been based on the desperate desire to never live that cookie cutter, misogynist American Fucking Dream I'd grown up in.

I was seeing things through a new lens now. With the life that my mother had created in the middle of the desert.

College was sacred to people for many reasons, namely because it provided a kind of segue between childhood and adulthood where you could act like an adult without any of those big responsibilities or decisions.

Except I wasn't on that precipice. I would say I'd well and truly crossed the threshold into adulthood when I moved across the world at eighteen. Or when my French boyfriend punched me. Or when I learned about who my father was. Or when I got an abortion. Or when I looked into the ice blue eyes of the man who rocked me to the core.

Yeah, those events meant I was not satisfied in the limbo lifestyle college afforded. I was an adult. One who knew what she wanted. Okay, maybe I didn't know exactly *what* I wanted, but I knew *who* I wanted.

The bell above the door rang, the one that Julian cursed about one hundred times a day but never took down.

"We're closed," I called out, not looking up from where I was counting cash. "And I don't care how much you bribe me, how far you've traveled, the machine is off, cleaned and it's much too late for caffeine anyway. Do you even care about your circadian rhythm?"

The customer was silent, and all I heard was the heavy fall of feet against the floor.

I froze, looking up, recognizing the sound of his fucking boots.

Elden was striding toward me, eyes glittering with anger.

I lost count of the cash as he rounded the counter.

"You in here alone, Violet?" he asked, approaching me.

Even though it made no sense, I retreated, my back hitting the coffee machine.

I nodded, staring at him as he pressed his body against mine.

"You're in here alone while the whole rest of the street is closed up for the day."

I frowned at this, not sure what it had to do with anything nor why it was the cause for his angry tone.

"And you left the door unlocked," he added, tucking a strand of hair behind my ear.

I hitched up my shoulder. "So?"

His eyes flared. "So?" His head jutted toward me. "So, it means any fuckin' one who wanted could come in here and do this."

He didn't give me a moment to react. Instead, he turned me around, yanking up my skirt.

My hands found the flat of the counter on instinct, my heart in my throat and my entire body brimming with sudden, animalistic desire.

He pushed my lower back down so I was completely bent over, so I was facing the large windows at the front of the café, displaying the quickly darkening night. There weren't many lights on in here, and the windows had a slight tint, but if someone walked past and really peered in, they'd see us.

My nipples pebbled at the thought.

His hands went to my panties, ripping them apart.

The clang of his belt and the crinkle of foil was the only warning I got before he surged into me, snatching my hair and yanking my head back.

I let out a strangled cry from the pleasure and pain as he fucked me with abandon.

He was rough, relentless, hadn't even prepared me for this because he knew my body well enough to know I'd been soaking fucking wet the second I heard his boots against the floor.

"My bad fuckin' girl," he grunted, fucking me. "Is this what you wanted?"

My body tensed at his rage, in response to the edge to him that seemed wild… unpredictable. He was always so controlled everywhere else, but lately, with me, his control had been slipping. He was as much of a slave to this as I was.

His grip on my hair tightened, then he yanked my head closer to him.

My orgasm rushed toward me.

"Is this what you wanted, Violet?" He punctuated his question with a brutal thrust.

"Yes," I whimpered in ecstasy, nearly senseless. "You're what I want, Elden. Only you. I'm yours."

My scalp burned under his grip as I met his eyes. "Say it again, Violet," he commanded, neck tight with the restraint he was still showing even now with his own impending climax.

"I'm yours," I moaned dutifully.

"Yeah," he murmured. "That's my girl. Now come for me."

I was already falling before he spoke, but my body exploded at his words, at the roughness of them.

He yanked my hair tighter as I milked his release out of him, sending us both to a sacred place that I didn't think existed for anyone but us.

I was barely breathing by the time I regained coherent thought. My legs quaked, hardly able to hold my weight. I leaned heavily onto the counter, trying to catch my breath, slow my heart rate.

Elden must've gone, taken care of the condom, because when he turned me around, his jeans were buttoned back up. He thoughtfully pulled my skirt down from my hips, but there was still an edge to him. A wildness to his eyes that only grew the more we were together. His control was fraying. It filled me with satisfaction, made me feel more comfortable with parts of myself they were becoming less orderly, more animal.

But as Elden righted my skirt, I found grasp over more rational thoughts.

"Oh my god," I uttered. "There are cameras in here." My head went to the corner of the ceiling where a camera was pointed right at the cash register. Where I'd just been fucked.

"Oh my god," I rubbed my temples. "We made a sex tape. And not in a good way. Like, a sex positive way. Plus, Julian is cool and very open-minded, but I don't think he'd approve of me having sex where we serve food and coffee."

"Violet," Elden's voice was even, void of any concern. "You think I'd fuck you in a place that was recording the act, riskin' anyone else seeing you coming for me?"

I regarded his face. Whenever I looked in his eyes, I felt a palpable and overarching sense of calm. Like I didn't have to worry anymore. Like outside problems didn't exist in his presence.

"No," I chewed on the inside of my cheek. "No, I don't think you'd do that. But I also don't think you have power over all electrical devices."

"I don't yet have that power, no." His mouth ticked upward

ever so slightly. He was losing control more, yes, but I was also getting more of those half smiles that only I got. "But I do have contact with a brother in Amber who happens to be able to hack into security camera systems as easily as someone can update a Facebook status."

"You're so old," I grinned back at him. "No one uses Facebook anymore."

Elden's jaw flexed at my mention of the years between us, but the twinkle didn't completely leave his eyes.

The moment remained… light, if that was possible after being fucked so hard.

But things couldn't and wouldn't stay light for us. That wasn't our story. Not since the start.

"I don't want to say goodbye to you," I whispered. I was breaking whatever unwritten rules we'd created when we started this thing.

There was no mention of how dangerous the thing we were doing was, and there was definitely no mention of the future outside of that moment.

But there was no escape now. I was leaving tomorrow.

Elden was staying here.

There would be no repeat of this. The next time I came home, there would've been time, distance, Elden would've had time to think about his decisions. He'd try to protect me. And he'd do that by hurting me. I could see it already.

Elden's features hardened, and all light left his eyes. He was no longer the man who'd fucked me like he'd never touch me again, whose lips had twitched in a half smile, who gave me parts of himself that no one else knew existed. No, this was the surly, badass biker with rigidly enforced control over his emotions.

"This need you have for me, it's a reaction to all of your trauma."

I glared at him, my stomach dropping at how abruptly things had changed. "So, you think this is purely because I have daddy issues?" I asked with a bite. "You're going to reduce it down to *that*?"

I shook my head, pushing at his chest, communicating my need for him to get the fuck away from me.

He ground his teeth, obviously pissed that I was getting physical with him even though he was not afraid to do the same to me.

Luckily—for him—he moved enough for me to turn my back on him and go back to the cash register, restarting my count. I needed something to do with my hands. Needed something to chase my angry tears from my eyes.

"Okay, yeah, I've been attracted to older, powerful men my entire life, long before I found out what a piece of shit my father was," I shuffled the cash, most likely fucking it all up because my brain was cloudy from the anger and the orgasms.

"Probably because on some level, I *knew* he was a piece of shit," I admitted, thinking of all the little things my father had done, things I'd cataloged and ignored because I was unwilling to face the truth.

The subtle but demeaning way he spoke to my mother. How rude he was to waitresses. The cold glint in his eye when I called him out for it. All of the affection that was only present when other people could be watching.

I abandoned the cash counting, really hoping that it was right. I put it all back in and slammed the register shut, whirling so I could face Elden.

His arms were crossed over his expressive chest, regarding me with intensity. Although he was *always* regarding me with intensity.

I ignored this. "When I first met you, whatever damage done to me impacted my reaction and attraction to you," I confessed, giving him an intense stare of my own. "Just like whatever trauma you've had attracted you to me."

I put my hand on my hip and tilted my head. "Honey, if you're gonna start slinging mud, you better be prepared to get dirty. Both of us are fucked-up in different ways. Which is the reason we sought each other out. It's something in our chemical makeup that explains our initial reactions."

I narrowed my eyes, wishing I could get through to him with my stare. Wishing I could shake some sense into him. "But not now, not after *over a fucking year* are you going to tell me I'm just a little, damaged girl with issues and no real control over her emotions." I shook my head rapidly. "No. I love you because you wear reading glasses, and because you like everyone to think you're scary and damaged, when you rescue fucking puppies. You call me when it rains. You quit smoking the second I let it be known it bothered me."

Inexplicably, tears stung the back of my eyes.

I'd just told him I loved him.

Holy shit.

I wasn't supposed to say that. This was meant to be a winter fling. This was meant to be both of us getting… whatever this was out of our systems so we could get on with our lives.

But there was no getting on with our lives.

Not after this.

There hadn't been since that moment on the roof.

Elden had gone stock still when I'd said the words that I definitely shouldn't have said. Never once had I felt like a child in his presence. Not once. But here, declaring my love, completely by accident, I felt small and young.

I'd never seen Elden at a loss for words before. Then again, this winter, words weren't really a priority.

"Baby," he murmured.

I braced myself for it. For him to do it again. Tell me I was just a kid. For us to repeat the circle once again.

The ringing of a phone made us both jerk.

"Saved by the bell," I muttered.

I ignored Elden, putting the phone to my ear.

"Where are you?" my mother demanded.

"I'm at the café, closing up." It wasn't a lie. It was the narrow line I trod these days. I never lied to her completely about where I was, I just left out some important details.

Mainly the important detail that was glaring at me right then.

"Well, hurry up, or I'm sending someone over to get you."

Dread slithered through me, thinking of who my mother would send and what they would surmise seeing Elden here with me. "I'll be home in five minutes," I told her, staring at Elden.

"We're not at home," she huffed out. "We're at the restaurant. I closed it down for the night. We're having a going away party, remember?" She said the word *remember* much louder than everything else.

I searched my memory. "Mom, you never told me about a party."

Something rustled against the phone. "I know," she whispered. "Swiss thinks I forgot to tell you… after organizing this whole thing. As if a mother would forget her only daughter going back to college."

"Mom, you did forget."

"Shut up," she hissed. "Swiss doesn't need to know that. I am dealing with a baby boy, and he's a lot. A perfect angel, but I'm a new mother and running a business. He needs to give me a break."

"Okay, Mom. Don't worry, I'll be there in five," I reassured her, hearing the hysteria in her voice.

"Okay, good, good," she muttered. "She's coming, she's just… stuck in traffic!" she called out, I guessed to the people she'd gathered for this party.

"Mom, there's no traffic," I pointed out. "It's like a… five-minute walk."

"Whatever," she snapped. "Just get here."

I listened to the dead air, not ready to put the phone down. It was the buffer between the 'I love you' and Elden.

"I know she hung up," Elden decimated that temporary defense, his voice low and throaty.

I pursed my lips, shoving the phone in my pocket. "I need to go."

"The party."

I tilted my head, scrutinizing him. "You know about the party?"

"Everyone knows about the party."

Though I really wanted to, I couldn't even smile in the face of my mother's baby brain. There was something endearing about her forgetfulness. She had never forgotten things in her life with my father. She could not forget things. It would not have ended well for her.

Yet now she was safe enough to wear what she wanted, say what she wanted, argue with Swiss when and if she saw fit, and she was safe to forget.

She was *safe*.

I tore my eyes from Elden. "I've got to go," I repeated, willing myself not to cry.

Elden didn't say anything. Didn't move.

I did a last-minute check to ensure that all of my closing tasks had been done. I was half prepared to lock him inside if he didn't move or speak, but when I tried to move past him to leave, he grabbed my wrist.

The grip was strong, bordering on painful. Exactly what I needed.

"I love you, Violet," he murmured roughly.

All my breath left my body. I was pretty sure that my soul left my body too. I'd lapsed into one of my fantasies. One of my many fantasies that I had about Elden saying those words.

"I fucking shouldn't," he scoffed. "I hate myself for loving you. For you loving me, especially since you don't know anything about me."

My back straightened. "I know enough," I countered.

He tilted his jaw upward, facing off with me. "I went to prison at eighteen for murder," he said flatly, without priming, warning.

It wasn't the information so much as the empty tone it was spoken in that made me gasp. He was trying to scare me. Trying to make me rethink the words he'd just said.

I pulled my wrist from his grasp. "That was, what? Fifty years ago?" I joked weakly. The age joke didn't land, so I continued on. "It doesn't change how I feel about you now." I walked forward, holding on to the sides of his cut, looking up at him. "Tell me more. Because I want to know more. Because no matter what you tell me, nothing will change."

He sighed. I felt tired just from hearing it, feeling the weight that he had been carrying without knowing the specifics of it. He eyed me, maybe measuring whether I could handle the truth. If he could handle telling it.

I waited, staring at him, holding on to him, trying my best to show him with my eyes that I wasn't going anywhere.

His hands found my wrists, and I was afraid he was going to yank my hands away, but he held on to them, gently rubbing the inside of them with his thumbs. "I came from a nice family, probably not unlike the family of that fuck you brought home for Christmas."

Even though Bennett was long gone and never a real romantic interest, there was still clear and radiating fury in Elden's tone.

"My parents were a product of their parents," he continued. "Not bad people, just bred to think a certain way. A certain, narrow way." He grimaced, lifting my hand to kiss the inside of my wrist before stepping away.

I forced my feet to stay where they were, hating the distance but giving it to him anyway.

"Fuck, I didn't even have a problem with it all. I would've been the frat boy who wasn't near worth enough to deserve your attention." He shook his head, rubbing the back of his neck. "I had a girlfriend. One I thought I loved. Some fuck said the wrong thing to her at a bar, I started punching him, couldn't stop." His eyes were faraway. "I have no fuckin' clue where that anger came from.

That rage. All I knew was that I couldn't stop punching. Even with my girlfriend screaming. Even with two guys pulling me off him. Then three." He paused, his fingers curled into his palms. "My parents had connections. Not enough to get me off completely, but enough to get my sentence reduced."

I tried to picture what Elden looked like as an angry, eighteen-year-old boy facing prison time. I tried to picture Elden as the son of some rich family. Underneath the beard, the weathering of his face, the steely hardness in his eyes... I couldn't envision that. Couldn't see him without the power, the quiet strength, the ability he had to make it seem like he was unbreakable.

"All things considered, I got a cushy sentence for beating a man to death for no other reason than I didn't like the way he looked at my girlfriend." He never took his eyes off me. "Five years. One year longer than I would've been away at Harvard. Early admission. My mother had been thrilled to have the bumper sticker, the sweatshirts. To visit me. Not so thrilled to visit me in prison," he scoffed. "It broke her heart in a way that I'm sure contributed to her death," he added quietly.

My lip trembled at the distant sadness in his voice. A wound long scanned over but never fully healed. Like a bone that fused together wrong.

"I was a rich, spoiled piece of shit, and I was put in a maximum-security prison," he continued. "Though I was a stupid shit who didn't know what real struggle was, I'd watched enough movies to understand that I needed to find protection if I wanted to stay alive and didn't want to become someone's bitch."

My heart hurt at the mere thought of it. Of Elden being lost, vulnerable in that way. I didn't think about the man he killed, though I should've. Maybe it should've made me look at him differently, considering my past with a man who couldn't control his violence. But it didn't. He wasn't the same as my father.

"Had to prove myself." His eyes glazed over with a coldness that seized my lungs. "And I did."

I waited for him to explain what that meant.

He didn't.

He didn't need to. I heard it all in his tone, saw it in his frosty, faraway gaze. Whatever he did was something that helped turn an eighteen-year-old boy into the hardened man in front of me now.

"Lotta shit happened between then and now which we don't have time for," he ran a hand along his beard. "Suffice it to say, five years turned into more. My Mom died year five. Dad a decade in. Much too young." He shook his head. "No one in my family was alive by the time I got out. Not that I would've been recognizable to them by them. Or that I would've recognized them. I was a different man. A bad one."

His gaze shifted away from me, as if he couldn't stand to look at me. I bit my lip and kept myself rooted to my spot even though I wanted to go to him. There was an energy around Elden right now that told me he couldn't be touched. Not right now.

"The people who initially protected me were the people I later became in charge of. In prison, at least," Elden swallowed hard, adjusting his stance. "The same people who offered me a place. Money. All that shit. But I was smart enough to know that if I stayed with them, I'd be back in prison or dead before long. Or maybe I wouldn't. Maybe I'd turn into something significantly worse in order to work my way up. But I didn't do that. I left. Drove across the country. Found myself here." He jutted his chin toward the windows, to the darkened streets.

"I knew there was no fucking way I was going to go back to conventional society." He rubbed his chin. "Knew I didn't want to be with the sick fucks who'd kept me alive all those years. And I figured Sons of Templar was the lesser of two evils. I told myself I could control it. Control is very fucking important when you've had someone else making decisions about when and where you eat, when you see the sun, when you sleep, what you can and can't read." His lips formed a hard line.

I thought about the bookshelves in his room at the club. His reading glasses.

"Control is very fucking important since losing it was what landed me in prison in the first place," Elden said softly.

I didn't know how tears weren't running down my cheeks. I felt them. On the inside, at least.

A lot of things clicked into place. That cold distance Elden created with everyone. It was a survival tactic. Him being dour, silent. Because he was holding it together. He was locked down that tight.

Because in his mind, if he didn't, he'd be back there.

He didn't like small spaces. He'd told me that. And now I knew why. Because he'd been locked in a small place, behind bars, for years.

"I've been very fucking successful at maintaining that control, Violet." He took a step forward, erasing the distance between us. I was thankful for his warmth, his scent. He grasped my chin. "Until you."

I groaned when my phone buzzed. I felt naked irritation at the real world for intruding on a sacred moment. I knew that if I didn't leave right then, there would be a biker hammering on the door and finding us here.

"I have to leave," I whispered.

Elden nodded. "I know."

"This doesn't change anything," I told him, meaning every word.

"I know," he echoed, face unreadable.

I reached up on my tiptoes to lay my lips against his. "I mean it," I whispered against his mouth.

"I know," he repeated again, against my lips, cupping my jaw.

Although I wanted to say more, do more, be more for him, my phone buzzed again. I sighed, knowing this was all we had.

We didn't say a thing as he walked me all the way to Mom's

restaurant. Certainly not goodbye. Because we knew we were far from goodbyes.

I tried my best to be present at the goodbye dinner, the one that my mom put so much effort into putting together, even if she forgot to tell me about it. My mom who had rebuilt her life, who had just opened a successful restaurant while pregnant, who had given birth to a gorgeous baby boy, who had survived things I couldn't even imagine. I also tried to be present in front of the very impressive women mom surrounded herself with. The women married to the Sons of Templar.

Caroline Hargrave, for fuck's sake, was married to Jagger. She was one of the most influential and impressive conflict journalists in decades. And a female one at that.

Not that Macy and Freya weren't impressive too. They really were. Macy was the matriarch of this chapter. She had young children. She held this club together, organized everything that the club did. I saw that.

Freya was married to possibly the scariest man I'd seen in real life. Yet she made that man melt. She had killer style. A really famous YouTube channel.

They all treated me like I was their friend, not their friend's daughter. It was a wonderful night.

Or would've been if Elden's voice wasn't ringing in my ears.

His story haunted me. He carried so much guilt. Blame. Not just for the man he murdered but for his parents. He truly thought he was the reason his parents were dead. His whole life had changed because of the one moment he lost control.

And he freely told me that I made him lose control. Yet another reason for him to fight this thing between us. Yet another thing to fight against.

"Penny for your thoughts?"

I glanced to my side. Macy had settled herself on a bar stool beside me. I hadn't had a moment to myself the whole night. Not with my mom, my baby brother, Colby, Lucas, Javier—who still hadn't got the memo I wasn't going to sleep with him—and all of the Sons of Templar Old Ladies keeping me company. But the night was slowing down.

Swiss had already taken Declan home, giving my mom time to enjoy herself and spend time with me. Luckily, my mother was enjoying herself a lot with Freya and Caroline, talking about babies and sex with their biker husbands. I loved that my mother was having great sex. Being taken care of in every way possible while also able to grow into whatever, whoever she wanted. So, it wasn't hearing my mother talking about having sex that had me slipping away to drink at the bar alone.

It was because these women had a kinship, they belonged to the club in a way I longed to but never could. I couldn't talk about being loved by my own biker because no one knew. No one *expected* that from me. I was a visitor here, destined for a different kind of life. In my mother's eyes, at least.

So, I was drinking alone, thinking of everything Elden had told me, looking for a way out of the web of lies I'd created.

Then Macy sat beside me. I glanced over to her, forcing a grin. "My thoughts aren't worth a penny," I joked.

She did not grin back at me, which was unusual for her. Macy was a naturally happy, light, bubbly person. A little insane, but in the best way. She dressed like a bohemian biker queen. She loved *Lord of the Rings*. Adored her children. Her husband. She had welcomed me into the family without hesitation. She was one of my mother's best friends.

I'd never felt like a kid with her. With any of them actually. They all treated me like a woman. Like I was their friend too.

But Macy was ogling me in a way that made our age difference stark and melted away the layers of our friendship.

"I'd say your thoughts are priceless," she refuted, sipping her drink. "And I bet they center around a man with a thousand-yard stare who is noticeably absent tonight."

My heart hammered at her words. Her tone.

I didn't answer. What did I say to that? I could deny it, but that would be a flat out lie. I'd been careful with my omissions. I left out details, to be sure. Important details. But I never lied to the faces of my family. It was my warped code of ethics. How I lived with myself.

Macy glanced back to where my mother was sitting at the long table set up in the middle of the restaurant.

Conversation and laughter mingled with the soft rock coming out of the speakers.

"No one else has noticed," Macy continued, eyes drifting back to me. "Yet."

I clutched my drink tightly in my hand.

"I'm not judging you." Macy ran her finger around the rim of her glass. "Either of you. Sometimes we don't have control over these things."

I took a long sip of my drink, still unable to figure out what to say. I'd imagined a scenario like this dozens of times. Usually it was with my mother, and I was the one doing most of the talking.

"Be careful," Macy eyed me with both concern and warmth. "I know you're new to all of this," she nodded her head to the table. "I also know I already consider you family." She squeezed my hand. "Though you're new to this, you're very smart. Therefore, you understand the dynamics of our special little family."

I nodded once, my mouth dry.

"And you know your stepfather loves your mother so much that he'd jump in front of a train for her without hesitation," Macy continued.

Another nod from me.

"He'd do the same for you. And however warped it is, however archaic, he considers you his to protect. When he finds out, calmer heads will not prevail."

My throat constricted as her tone turned more somber now.

"These men are hopeless romantics, underneath it all," she added. "But hopeless romance will not factor in when this comes out. This will affect the entire club. And I know that you didn't choose this, but be sure, sweetie. Be sure it's worth it. Be sure you're willing to face the fire with him."

She hopped off the stool.

"I'm here for you," she squeezed my shoulder. "If you ever need to talk about this. I won't say anything to anyone. But know this is going to come out. Secrets don't last long here." She searched my face. "You love him, don't you?"

"Yes," I whispered, finding a way to form words now.

She smiled warmly. "Then this will all work out… eventually." She winked at me then walked back to the table.

Her words followed me all the way back to Providence.

CHAPTER Fourteen

BEING BACK at school felt different. I felt different.

Older. More… worldly. And before Elden claimed me, I had literally traveled around the world. Maybe not as much as people who backpacked around Europe or whatever, but enough.

I'd been so anxious, so desperate to experience the world, be changed by it, that I'd left the country as soon as I could, thinking that I'd become something different, better, less ordinary.

Really, all I needed was to be claimed by a biker.

Sariah picked me up from the airport, holding a sign and everything.

It was written in lipstick on an old textbook, but it was still very charming.

Even though I really hadn't wanted to leave Elden, the life in Garnett, my baby brother and parents, I had missed my loud, stylish, dramatic best friend.

"You know this car has a reversing camera," I informed her, referring to the ridiculously large screen as we left the airport parking lot.

She shifted her gaze from behind her, changing gears before

leveling her gaze on me. "Violet, I will *never* trust a machine. Not counting my vibrator," she deadpanned. "If and when computers take over the world, you think it's gonna be some big show?" She shook her head. "Nah, they'll start slow. Lull everyone into a false sense of security by thinking they don't have to look behind them when they reverse. Then BAM! One day people start getting run over left, right and center. Accidents, pandemonium."

I smiled at her, happy to be back with my insane best friend whom I'd missed endlessly but was nervous as all hell to tell her about what happened with Elden.

I had to tell her what happened with Elden, though. Colby knew something was going on, but he did not know the specifics. Macy also knew something was going on, but nodding and a single syllable spoken did not count as talking about it.

Not in the way I would've with Sariah. There was something sacred about sharing with your best friend that you were falling in love. It made it into something solid, real. Something that you believed was permanent. Because you didn't make those proclamations to best friends if you weren't sure, certainly not with best friends like Sariah. Because if something bad happened, if he did something unforgivable, not only would Sariah hunt him down, but she wouldn't let me go running back to someone I didn't deserve.

Even though I did deserve Elden.

He was everything I wanted. Too bad proclaiming that publicly quite possibly meant my stepfather killing him and causing major drama within the club.

So, yeah, I needed to talk to my girlfriend.

The one who had made lists of different poisons we could've slipped into his drink that didn't show up on classic toxicology reports.

I was pretty sure she was joking and only had that knowledge because she was obsessed with true crime podcasts.

"Those are my enemies," she gestured toward the car that had just slammed on its brakes for no obvious reason.

"You have a long list of enemies," I chuckled.

"I do," she agreed. "Because the list of fucking annoying people in this world is long."

"I fucked Elden in his room down the hall from everyone having Christmas dinner, including my parents and Bennett," I blurted.

There wasn't even a single moment of silence before Sariah slammed on her brakes in the middle of traffic.

Horns sounded all around us, but she didn't pay any attention.

"What the actual *fuck*?" she demanded, staring at me.

"Ri, we are currently stationary in the middle of busy traffic," I pointed out the obvious, wishing I could hide from all of the angry drivers behind us.

She leaned her head out the window. "Go around, fuckers! I just found out my girl fucked the older, outlaw biker she's been *obsessed* with for months! Years, actually!" she yelled.

I swallowed a smile even though I was vaguely worried that someone was about to rear-end us or a cop would drive past. And that would get both of us arrested because no way would Sariah go quietly.

The last time I'd been arrested, I'd gotten off thanks to the club's lawyers and the new investigation into the boy who hurt Sariah, who incidentally, was no longer in the picture. He had 'committed suicide,' and the officer who originally took our statements had gone missing entirely. I knew that was Elden's doing. We didn't speak of it, though. Nor had Sariah and I.

She turned back to face me, cupping her chin with her hand as she leaned on the center console. "Now, tell me everything," she demanded.

"I will tell you everything once you start driving, or… at least pull the car out of traffic," I countered.

For a long moment, I thought she was going to stay exactly where she was, playing a game of chicken with me. Luckily, she thought better of it and drove into a McDonalds drive-thru.

"We need fried things for this conversation," she explained before leaning out her window to order.

I couldn't argue with that logic.

We waited for the fries—and milkshakes because it was criminal to have fries without milkshakes according to Sariah—then settled into the parking lot.

Sariah turned her body in her seat. "Now tell me everything, bitch. And if you leave anything out, I will shave your eyebrows in your sleep."

I stared at her. "Wow, you're vicious."

"You have no idea," she cackled.

So, I did what anyone would do, I told her everything, without leaving anything out.

Even Elden's admission about being in prison, though I second-guessed myself when I said it. It was something very private to him, obviously; something he didn't tell most people, and he hadn't even told me everything. Part of me wanted to keep that to myself, respect his confidence, have it just be mine.

But I didn't feel equipped to deal with all of it. With him.

Our fries and milkshakes were long gone by the time I was done.

Sariah had been rapt, listening to every word, not interrupting once. Or she did once, when she made me repeat how we had sex on Christmas at the club three different times.

"So now I have no idea what to do," I sighed.

"Yes, you do," she scrunched up her nose as though the answer was obvious.

I widened my eyes, waiting for clarification.

She sighed. "You finish the semester, partly because you're pretty much done anyway and because I greedily want you close to me. You continue the relationship… long distance." She tilted her head thoughtfully. "Now, normally I am not an advocate for long distance relationships or monogamous relationships in general, but I think this is a definite exception to the rule. So, you do long distance while you're here, once you get your degree, you go back to Garnett and get his name tattooed on your ass or whatever it is that bikers do to solidify their relationships." She sucked the straw of her milkshake, though there wasn't much left. "And you obviously take me with you so I can be the one to shoot the first gun into the air after you say, 'I do.'"

I gaped at her. "First off, where do you think this wedding is taking place, the Wild West?"

She shrugged.

"And secondly, a *wedding*?" My voice was much higher than normal. "I'm too young to get married. I never wanted to get married. My mother would be horrified. Just at the marriage thing. Then there's the marriage to a man years older than me. Oh, and my stepfather would probably kill him." I listed off the things that I'd tried my best to shove out of my mind the past few weeks.

Sariah didn't look at all perturbed. "Babe, you are not too young for anything. You know your own mind. And although I am not one for insta-love or pretty much any conventional relationship created by patriarchal society to keep women enslaved in domestic tasks and childbearing, I don't think this is that. I think this is fate."

She reached over to squeeze my hand.

"I know you're scared. Know your dad fucked you over big time in the trusting men department and gave you a terrible view on marriage and relationships," she smiled sadly. "But this isn't that. Elden isn't that." Her gaze hardened. "And I know you're not one of those self-sabotaging bitches like in any dramatic sitcom where they fuck things up because they're scared. You are a lot of things, Violet, but you're no coward."

I studied her face, digesting her words. As usual, when it came to fashion, food or any kind of general advice, Sariah was right. My father had fucked me up. And unfortunately, my mother had too. Not on purpose. She had only the best of intentions. She'd made the choice to protect me, and who the fuck was I to blame her for that?

I was scared. That everything had changed in such a short span of time.

"What about Swiss?" I sighed. "Even if all of the rest of our shit gets sorted, there's still the overprotective stepfather."

"There's nothing you can do about that," she shrugged again. "They'll probably have some kind of fistfight because they're men and can't seem to solve problems any other way. You just have to trust that Swiss loves you enough not to kill or permanently maim him."

My stomach churned. "Thanks, that makes me feel *so* much better."

She patted my hand. "Babe, Elden sounds like he can more than take care of himself. Everything will be fine."

I chewed on her words for a long time, and even though I trusted her with my life, I couldn't believe that it would be fine. There was a sinking feeling in the pit of my stomach, an impending sense of doom that I couldn't quite shake off.

I didn't know the protocol with Elden now. I'd only been in relationships with boys before. Games were played. They texted me exactly five minutes after I texted them, therefore I would send my message exactly ten minutes after them.

The stakes were never high. My life was not at risk of ending because my relationship with a seventeen-year-old lacrosse player was over.

Jacques was what I thought I'd been waiting for. A man who

had an established life. Was educated. Knew about fine wines. Treated me like a woman.

Or so I'd thought.

I hadn't truly been treated like a woman until I met Elden.

He called me regularly now. Not just when it rained.

Our conversations weren't long or pining, that wasn't exactly Elden's style. But he called. He asked me what I was doing, if I ate that day. What I was wearing.

Before him, I'd truly thought phone sex was tacky and something people only did in the movies.

It turned out it was not at all tacky. And if you had an alpha biker on the other end of the line, it was really fucking hot.

Even with the phone sex, with all of the assignments, the parties, all the things I was doing to keep busy, to burn off the excess need, I was not sated.

He was always at the back of my mind. I slept like shit, knowing he was so far away, worrying about what he was doing, what kind of danger he was putting himself in.

My self-control was rather impressive, though. Every time I woke from a nightmare or was pacing the house at three in the morning, imagining him bleeding, locked up or in some sort of gun fight, I managed to get myself off to sleep with the help of Sariah's stock of edibles or with one of my comfort shows playing in the background.

This particular night, though, my self-control snapped entirely. I hadn't even thought when I grabbed my phone off my nightstand.

He answered after three rings. "Violet," he murmured, voice smooth and rough, causing all my hair to stand on end.

"I need you," I whispered into the phone.

"I'm on my way," he replied instantly. "Who hurt you? I'll fucking kill them."

I smiled at the raw fury in his tone. I shouldn't have liked it. What with my feelings about violence, about male anger left unchecked and the damage it did to society. But I fucking loved it. "No one hurt me," I replied quickly. "I just had a dream about you fucking me, and I woke up alone in bed. And a vibrator is a sad substitute for you. So, I should've said that I want you. But it really feels like a *need*."

There was a loaded pause. I bit my lip worrying I'd been a little too brash, a little too… clingy. Did I seem like some spoiled brat? Had I ruined things now? Were there games being played that I'd been too naïve to see?

"I'll get on my bike right now." Things rustled in the background, and I imagined him getting out of bed.

My jaw dropped. "You can't ride all the way here."

"My woman just talked about dreamin' about us fuckin' then mentioned a vibrator," he countered, voice husky. "I so can fuckin' ride all the way there."

Heat warmed my cheeks. He'd called me *his woman*.

"It's thirty hours, Elden."

"And?"

I didn't know how to respond.

He was willing to drive thirty hours on a motorcycle in the middle of the night because I told him I had a *dream* about him.

I sat up in bed, putting the phone on speaker and squinting as I pulled up maps, tapping furiously. "Okay, there's a motel roughly halfway between us," I said, zooming in. "If I leave now, we should get there at roughly the same time."

"Violet," he grumbled. "You are not driving across the country in the middle of the night on your fuckin' own. Stay where you are. Wait for me."

My lips spread into a huge smile, getting out of bed. "I've never been very patient," I informed him. "I'll text you the details of the motel. See you in fifteen hours."

"Don't you fuckin' dare—"

I didn't wait for the rest of his no doubt very passionate, alpha order. I hung up the phone.

It rang immediately.

I snickered, answering it. "You can call me all you want," I told him, opening my closet. "It's not going to stop or change anything. You can take out all your anger on me when we see each other. I'm bringing the vibrator."

"Vio—"

I hung up.

Then I shoved some things in a bag, put on my clothes and did exactly what Elden told me not to do.

I drove across the country, alone, in the middle of the night to go to him.

He was there before me. Sitting on his bike in the parking lot, looking every bit like the hot, dangerous outlaw he was. The sun was beating down on him, and he was wearing dark shades and a scowl.

The motel itself was in the middle of nowhere, but it had a bunch of great ratings because a brother and sister had inherited it as a crumbling roadside motel and turned it into a social media sensation, a throwback to the seventies, with bright colors, every room styled differently with contrasting prints and colors. An ode to a bygone era when there weren't chains littering the interstate, when people cared more, when family road trips were taken off the beaten track.

I adored it.

Although I didn't get a moment to properly take it in since my door opened the moment I put my car in park.

"You are in so much fucking trouble," Elden growled, leaning over me to turn the car off and snatch the keys before taking me bodily from the car.

He threw me over his shoulder. Literally *threw me over his shoulder*. I let out a little yelp of surprise and delight as he opened the back door to grab the bag I'd thrown in there.

Keys jangled as he stomped us toward a block of rooms. Apparently, he'd already checked in. It was lucky it was the middle of the week in off-season since this place was normally booked out.

"Um, is everything okay here?" an uncertain voice asked.

A man in his mid-twenties wearing a Hawaiian shirt, fluorescent shorts and flip-flops had been exiting his room and encountered a biker throwing a girl over his shoulder. And though he definitely didn't look like he could take Elden on, he had stepped in anyway.

What a sweetheart.

Maybe the world hadn't gone entirely to shit.

"Fuck off," Elden grumbled.

I smacked his shoulder and did my best to smile reassuringly from my spot.

"Everything is fine. He has my full consent to do this, even if it's totally over the top and unnecessary," I added.

Elden didn't want to see if the guy believed me or not. He strode toward a door, unlocked it then slammed it behind us.

I didn't even get a moment to delight in how funky the room was. My bag was dumped at the door then Elden stomped in the direction of the bathroom.

"You're acting like a caveman," I pointed out, not struggling because I didn't exactly hate the caveman routine.

"Shut the fuck up," he growled. "I'm so fuckin' mad at you. Can't decide whether I'm gonna fuck you or punish you."

My whole body reacted to the primal tone, the words. My toes curled in preparation for either.

Elden reached inside the shower stall to turn the water on. He set me on my feet, my legs unsteady as his furious, hungry glare fastened on me.

His hand circled around my neck. Not hard. Not enough to hurt. More than enough to melt my fucking panties, though.

"You're in so much fuckin' trouble," he rasped.

One of his hands went to my shirt, a button-down. Or it was until he ripped it open and buttons went flying everywhere.

He let out a hiss when it revealed my naked torso. I'd forgone a bra, not thinking it was necessary.

Elden pushed me against the wall of the bathroom as it filled with steam.

His finger trailed down the middle of my chest, my stomach tightening with need as he made it to the waistband of my pants.

My hands went to him, trying to aim for the zipper of his pants, but he caught my wrists.

"No," he bit out, staring at me with swirling irises. "I need a fuckin' second, Violet. I'm battling with control right now. I'm so fuckin' mad at you for not listenin' to me, but I want to take every inch of you. Fuck you so hard that all you know is my cock."

Adrenaline surged through me, not just from the words, not just from his gaze, but at the choppy, tight way those words came out. He was on the edge of something. He was battling to keep himself locked down.

This strong, powerful man was coming apart because of *me.*

I met his eyes, my own hunger nearly splitting me apart. "I don't want you to control shit around me," I whispered. "Do it," I challenged. "Take me how you want. I can handle it. Don't you dare be gentle with me."

There was a single moment of consideration, of pause after I stopped speaking. A single moment when I thought Elden would try to be the better man. Try to protect me from himself.

But then the moment passed, and we were on each other. I was slammed against the wall once again, but this time Eden's mouth was plastered to mine, tongues clashing, teeth sinking into lips. The coppery taste of our blood only drove me wilder as we both frantically tore off clothes.

He was still wearing his boots when we made it into the shower. My legs were wrapped around him. The water pounded down on us both, neither of us caring about anything but each other.

"No," I rasped as I heard the telltale crackle of the foil packet. I had no idea how I heard it over the shower, the roar of my own heartbeat. Fuck, I had no idea how he'd managed to get it in the shower in the midst of this craziness.

Elden froze, looking up at me.

"I don't want you to use that." It was a bad decision. In that moment, I knew it was a bad decision. I had some very good, practical experience as to what such a decision could result in.

The protection was essential. For a number of reasons, but primarily because I did not use birth control due to all of the harm it did to women's bodies and minds.

"Violet..." Elden also knew why protection was important to me. He had not once said a word about it. He had religiously used condoms every time we had sex. I had not thought about how the condoms were also for his protection. How him using them might not have been all about me.

"If you want to," I stated quickly. "Use it. Of course, you should. But I just meant that I don't need you to use it. If you don't want to."

"Violet," his eyes briefly lowered to my lips. "You're offerin' me something here. And I want it. I want to take you raw more than I want to fucking inhale and exhale. But I don't want you doin' shit for me. Being inside you is already the best feeling in the fucking world."

"Elden," I raked my fingers through his hair. "I don't want protection from you. I don't want anything between us."

He measured my words for a scant second before he grasped the back of my neck, slammed me against the tile of the shower and surged inside of me.

His growl vibrated my ribs as he filled me up with nothing between us.

"You're so fuckin' tight," he rasped against the water beating down on us, our mouths inches away from each other. "You're heaven, Violet."

I couldn't speak, couldn't reply. It was all I could do to hold on for dear life.

"How many more times will we have to say goodbye to each other?" I whispered into the night.

Crickets sang through the window screen.

Elden didn't answer. Maybe this was one of our forbidden topics. Maybe there were more rules than I'd realized between us. Our togetherness was thin, fragile, dependent on how long both of us could suspend reality, battle against the outside world, hammering at the door.

We were silent for a long while before Elden yanked me so I was straddling him. My hands found his chest on instinct, to steady myself.

"If I had it my way, we'd never be sayin' goodbye," he murmured into the night. "If I had it my way, I'd be waking up with you every morning." His hands gripped my hips. "I'd be fucking you awake and fucking you asleep. You'd be on the back of my bike."

My skin tingled. Back of his bike. That was the biker version of commitment. It wasn't a marriage proposal, but it was a declaration of intention, of commitment, of permanence.

It should've made me happy.

Except it didn't.

Because it shouldn't.

"But…" I said when he'd stopped talking.

His hands clutched my hips harder. He didn't reply.

"But you won't," I expanded for him. My tone was sharp to offset the hurt in my heart.

"I can't," he said through his teeth.

My throat burned again, and I wished for antacids and maybe a different life. One that still contained Elden but without all the complications.

I tried to climb off of him, but his hands tightened at my hips, not letting me go. I was disappointed and happy, taking it as a sign that maybe, just maybe, he would fight for me. Us.

"You can," I argued, my voice low. "*We* can. I'll make sure that Swiss doesn't hurt you."

Elden's hold tightened for a second longer before he flipped us so he was hovering on top of me, his body pressed into mine, caging me in. Our lips were inches apart.

"I don't give a fuck who hurts me," he exhaled heavily. "If this was about what might happen to me, I would've claimed you publicly in a fucking second."

"But you didn't," I shot back.

"I didn't," he agreed in a soft voice.

I stiffened, or at least I tried to. My body betrayed me. Everything softened and relaxed under Elden's touch.

"Want to claim you, Violet," he stroked the side of my face. "More than anything in this fuckin' world. But it's not the time. Not right now."

I pulled my lip between my teeth, eager to argue with him, to scream about how this wasn't fair, that he was making excuses.

Except he wasn't. He was right. Not now with my mother happily married, with a new baby, the club experiencing peace and harmony.

I didn't have time to argue because his lips were on mine.

We didn't speak the rest of the night. Although maybe we should've.

We spent another full day in that motel room.

Elden only left to get food.

I did not put on pants.

We did not speak of anything outside of the room. We got to experience the unexpected pleasure of waking up together. Of eating meals together. Watching movies together. Sharing beers.

I texted Sariah to tell her where I was, and she sent back a plethora of very explicit texts that I gathered was her form of approval.

It was heaven.

Except heaven didn't exist. Both heaven and hell were here on earth. Us humans brought them both upon each other. And that's what it was with Elden and me... Heaven and hell, intermingled, unable to separate one from the other.

"Where does the club think you are?" I asked him in the early hours of the morning we were going to leave.

"They don't think I'm anywhere." He drew lazy patterns on my back. We'd been desperate, feral for each other during the hours we'd spent in this room.

Now we'd lapsed into something different. Something less wild but something precious. Something comfortable. Intimate. A glimpse into a life we might've had.

My hopeful heart still held on to the fantasy that we could possibly have that. Or a different version of that.

"They don't know you're here?" I clarified.

"It's not a prison, Violet."

I bristled at the reference.

"I'd leave it," he continued, still drawing circles. "For you."

My heart stammered. My lungs burned. He was telling me he'd give up everything he knew and loved.

For me.

What every girl wanted to hear.

Except it wasn't.

Elden's world had imploded when he was eighteen. He lost his entire family. Had to become a whole different person.

And if I asked him to, he'd give up the club. Which would mean he'd have to become an entirely new person without the Sons of Templar. And even if he managed that, Swiss would still find him. We would still have to see him. And my mom. And my club.

Because they were family. One you didn't escape. It wasn't a prison. But it was a life that didn't let you go.

Now it was my turn to do the alpha move and reposition us so I was on top of Elden, straddling him, pressing myself against him so we both gasped in pleasure. We should've been satiated. It should've been physically impossible for us to have any more sex. Yet Elden stiffening underneath me, and my body priming itself in preparation for him communicated that it was indeed possible.

My hands landed on either side of his head as I hovered above him. I kept my naked body pressed as close to his naked body as was humanly possible.

"You're not leaving the club," I informed him, my mouth inches away from his.

"Is that an order?" he smiled, hands on my hips, positioning me so he pressed against my entrance.

My body quivered in anticipation.

"Yes, that is an order," I whispered. "You are not to ruin your life for me."

His firm heat rubbed along my sensitive core. "Not possible, baby. My life was in ruins before you."

I didn't have the time to respond in any kind of way to that because he was inside me.

We barely slept the rest of the night.

But eventually, we did sleep. Eventually, we had to wake up.

Eventually, we had to say goodbye.

My back was against my car. Elden's hands were at my neck. His lips were on mine.

We had been like this for quite some time.

If I had my way, we'd be like this forever.

"I have to leave," I complained against his lips.

"Me too," he agreed. Then he kissed me again.

His phone buzzed in his pocket.

It had been doing that. The phone, and my repeated arguments, were the reason he wasn't trailing me on his bike all the way back to Providence.

He had been dead serious about that too.

I was thankful that the club was calling because having him follow me all the way back to Providence would've weakened my resolve.

Actually, it would've shattered entirely.

"We have to go," he pulled back from me, his eyes a storm of emotions. They held untold depths, I knew that. But something was simmering in them. A knowing.

He couldn't be reading my thoughts, of course. But he saw me better than anyone else did, and I was struggling to hide the pain from my expression.

I held my breath, waiting for him to say something, address the tension between us, what was being left unsaid. But he didn't say anything. His eyes just roved over my face as if he were committing it to memory.

"Drive safe," he ordered. "You let me know the second you arrive back in Providence."

I arched a brow. "Don't pretend you don't have someone tracking my phone."

His brow did not quirk, and his mouth did not twitch. "Let me know anyway."

I pursed my lips and fought against tears, nodding.

When I failed, Elden wiped away a tear that escaped.

He lifted his thumb and brought it to his mouth.

In the midst of all of this, my stomach fluttered with desire, seeing him taste my sadness. He'd tasted everything else.

Elden rested his forehead against mine.

I opened my mouth to say it. Say it all. But he knew it all.

So, there was nothing to say.

He kissed me once more, gently, close-mouthed before opening my door for me. I took one last look at him, my bearded, brooding biker in black, staring at me in a way that every woman would give their left tit for.

It took everything I had to drive away from him.

CHAPTER *Fifteen*

I DID NOT SEE or speak to Elden until I came home for the end of Spring semester, before I started Summer school.

He had called.

I stared at the phone, at his name, with tears running down my face. Later, there were no tears, but there was a margarita in my hand.

Sariah was careful not to mention Elden. When I'd arrived home from the motel, she'd shrieked, "Welcome Home! Are you pregnant yet, you kinky bitch?"

I'd stared at her for ten seconds then burst into tears.

Sariah had reacted quickly, yelling at Henri to make the margaritas and for Ollie to whip up some cookie dough.

"And if anyone says shit about salmonella or whatever the fuck, I will cut them!" she screamed as she told Ollie not to put the cookies in the oven.

I didn't tell her the specifics. Didn't tell her that I took the coward's way out by essentially ghosting him.

I was too ashamed to tell my brave, fearless friend that I couldn't show the man I loved the respect of breaking up with him in person. Or even by phone.

Elden got the picture.

He'd called me. Still did. He didn't leave messages. Didn't text. Elden wasn't really a text kind of guy. But he continued to call. Long after he understood what I was doing. Because he was showing me that he wasn't going anywhere. He wasn't giving up on us.

Like I had.

It made me sick. Physically sick not to hear his voice. Sick knowing I'd have to go back to Garnett and pretend. Not just pretend with everyone else, but with him.

But I couldn't *not* go. I needed to see my brother. My family. I needed to see him. Even if it was from a distance. Even if we looked at each other like we were strangers.

So, I went home.

And I stayed away from him. No matter how much it hurt me. And it did. No matter how often my resolve faltered.

He respected that distance.

For a time.

Maybe I was testing things. No, I *knew* I was testing things.

I pushed it to the edge one day, not long before I was set to go back to school.

Colby and I were coming back from the gun range. He had not spoken of Elden nor had I.

Colby invited me back to the clubhouse for a beer. I went, even though I knew the chances of seeing him were high.

I'd already seen him.

He came into the café. Every day. For coffee. We didn't speak. We only stared at each other, our fingers brushing when I handed him his coffee. I lived for those handful of seconds. Those seconds were what kept me up at night. What made me feel alive.

Other than that, he didn't push it. We kept our distance at any kind of club gatherings.

It was torture.

But he didn't push it.

Until I went too far.

Sitting at the bar of his club, drinking a beer and laughing with another man. It didn't matter that the other man was like a brother to me, and Elden knew that. Not when it had been so long. Not when you were talking about a possessive, alpha male.

Colby saw him first, his eyes widening as he took a sip of his beer before slamming it on the bar.

"I've got to go and… do a thing. Break the law or whatever," he looked toward the hall then back at me before walking out.

I swiveled my stool around, but Elden caught the edges of it by the time it made half a rotation.

My beer slipped from my hand at his closeness. He caught it with one hand, without looking, the other still on the edge of my stool. He placed the beer on the bar.

The only sound came from the speakers Colby and I had been playing music from.

No one else was around. Which was insane. There always seemed to be at least a few members out in the garage portion of the compound, working on cars. I knew some guys were out on a 'run,' whatever that meant, and the rest were at home with their families.

All the times I'd yearned for it to just be me and him, now I couldn't handle it. Now my heart hurt.

I wanted to run… I thought about it, my body tensed and ready, wondering how far I'd get.

"Not lettin' you go anywhere, Violet," Elden murmured softly, as if he could read my mind. "You're makin' a smart choice for the right reasons, and I should respect that," he continued, his voice low. "But I fuckin' can't." He reached up to coil my hair around his finger.

I stopped breathing.

"If you tell me you've changed your mind, that this has run its course for you, I'll never touch you again," I watched his lips move as he spoke, avoiding his eyes. "I'll walk away right now."

I frowned, rage burning my throat. "Do you really think I'm that fickle?" I asked, trying to snap, but I only managed a rough whisper.

When I finally looked at his eyes, Elden was studying me. "No, Violet. I know you're not. I know you're doin' this for me. And fuck, does that make me love you more. As if that were fuckin' possible."

His hands went to my knees, spreading them apart. I didn't fight him. Not even a little. My body opened for him with relief.

He lifted me up the second his mouth plastered to mine, my legs wrapping around him instinctively. I cried out as my skirt parted, my panties rubbing against the rough denim of his jeans.

Elden let out a low growl in his throat as he placed me on the bar, the perfect height for him.

He ripped my tank aside, lips landing on my nipple. I cried out, fingers tangling in his hair.

My gaze went to the tinted windows. People were walking across the parking lot and into the garage bays. It was broad daylight.

Elden was frantically undoing his jeans.

"Someone could walk in," I panted, breathless.

"They could," his eyes were wild, "but right now, I don't give a fuck about anything other than getting into your pussy."

He waited for me to argue. Gave me the opportunity to say no. But I didn't. My fingers replaced his, working desperately at his belt.

The second he was free, he pushed my panties to the side and slammed inside of me. We both cried out.

I was holding on to his neck for dear life as he fucked me relentlessly, furiously, with all of the need we'd built up over the months.

My heart beat frantically as the reality of what we were doing merged with my insane need. We were having sex. In the clubhouse. In broad daylight.

That only caused my climax to rush forward quicker, racing through all of my nerve endings.

"Open your eyes, Violet," Elden commanded.

I did as I was told.

"You're mine," he vowed. "Whatever happens after this. You're mine."

"I'm yours," I promised.

Then we crashed into nirvana together.

We were silent as we cleaned up, the reality of what we'd just done rushing in. I didn't regret it. Especially because no one had caught us.

It was our goodbye. It suited what we'd created. It was irresponsible, dangerous and impossibly hot.

He wouldn't end it now. Not for my own good. He'd tried to do that already. Maybe he would, further down the line, when I was closer to graduating, when I had to make the decision between my two warring futures.

He wouldn't end it until this was close to disaster, until someone found out and his life was ruined.

"The Sons are your family," I told him, standing on unsteady legs. "After what you went through for years. After living a life that wasn't your own, without anyone having your back, without a home." Tears flooded my vision. "You've got that here." I looked around the room. "And I want that for you. I want you, but I can't bring myself to ruin your life."

"You won't ruin my life," he argued, echoing the conversation we had in the motel room.

"I'd do this in a minute, do us, if you wouldn't get hurt in the process," I sighed, my heart breaking. "I'd do this in a minute if everyone would be upset at me. But they won't. Everyone will focus their anger on you. The big, bad, older biker who took advantage of me. Fucking double standards," I scoffed. "Sure, my mom may have some choice words for me, but no one would dream of kicking me out of this life. This is your life," I shook my head. "I hadn't fully realized that... That we're playing with your *life*." I took him in, inhaled then exhaled his scent. I lived in the moment, my body still humming from his touch.

"I don't give a fuck about my life, Violet," he retorted fiercely, making it clear he wasn't going to let me do the noble thing without a fight.

He was going to fight for me, for us, and I wasn't going to win that. But I had to.

He stepped forward like he was going to touch me, yet once he touched me, I'd lose this battle, and all my noble intentions would go up in smoke.

But at that moment, someone was looking out for me as the door to the clubhouse opened, and I took a deliberate step back.

Kiera, one of the club girls, walked in with Javier's arms around her. His eyes jumped to the both of us, gaze sharpening and features turning cold.

I plastered on a fake smile, hoping that it convinced at least Javier. He wouldn't hesitate to cause trouble for Elden if he thought he was getting something I wasn't giving him.

I took that as my opportunity to run.

Elden didn't follow me.

Even though I'd secretly hoped he would've.

It was for the best. It was the only way to avoid disaster.

I spent the rest of my time at home reveling in my little brother and his baby smell. And I worked overtime at the café. Elden no longer came in. When there were club gatherings that I attended, he wasn't there either. Macy gave me worried looks, but thankfully, she did not speak to me like she did at Violet's. I could tell my mother knew that there was something going on. But she thought it was something to do with my father. She tread carefully, treated me gently and didn't ask questions. I took advantage of that, thankful for my father being a piece of shit and letting me hide behind his ghost.

Then I went back to school where I went through the motions.

Well, I went through the motions and then some.

I did not mope.

Not in the house, at least. Not with Ollie's baking, with Henri's cocktails and Sariah's social cachet that got us into every and any party we wanted.

Classes were hard. Assignments were hard. But hard was good. Hard meant I couldn't think of Elden.

Except I did.

Constantly.

Sariah had heard every detail of the 'breakup'. She had tried to delicately tell me that I didn't have to save a man who hadn't asked to be saved. "Don't you hate it when men do that to us?" she'd joked.

I'd smiled and sipped my cocktail but had held fast to my decision. I loved Sariah. I'd never had a friend like her before. She was effortlessly cool, kind, warm, smart. She always wanted to have fun but also kept up her grades. I'd never heard her say a bad word about anyone. She loved men and women and dated both.

She loved them, but she had never been *in* love with them.

It was something she'd admitted freely, wearing her lack of love as somewhat of a badge of honor. Most likely it had to do with something her parents did to her to warp what love meant… She still never spoke about them.

Because she had never been in love, she couldn't possibly understand why I was making that decision. I didn't tell her that, though. It would come off as condescending and cruel to a friend who was trying to help me. A friend who, despite never being in love herself, was a hopeless romantic.

Luckily for me, she didn't try to convince me further.

Elden and I were never going to stay apart. I knew that it was far from over between us. Whatever was happening right now was delaying the inevitable. Until I turned twenty-one, until I graduated, until my stepfather softened from being a father and a husband so that he was less likely to kill Elden.

Whatever.

I wasn't sure how long my willpower would've lasted. Not much longer, surely. Definitely not until graduation or until my twenty-first birthday.

Little did I know it would be when two lines appeared on a pregnancy test.

ELDEN

"We've got a shipment coming from the Russians, and we've got the sheriff sniffin' around, so I want everyone minding their Ps and Qs," Hansen sighed, leaning back in his chair. "This fuckin' guy is getting to be a pain in my ass."

"I could take care of him," Hades offered.

Hansen looked at him. "Much as I am tempted, unfortunately, we start killin' cops, we start bringing more heat in our direction."

Hades tapped his fingers on the table. "Might come to that, he keeps tryin' to fuck with us."

There were multiple nods around the table. The new sheriff was indeed a pain in our fucking asses. For years, the club had enjoyed an amiable relationship with the previous sheriff, who didn't get paid near enough and was a throwback to the old days. He didn't give a shit about what laws we broke as long as we didn't bring shit into his jurisdiction.

Those days were gone. This new sheriff wanted change, wanted to move up in the ranks. No better way of doing that than bringing down a chapter of a national criminal enterprise with ties to the Russian mob. Yeah, they'd pin some medal or something onto his puffed-up chest and send him to Washington after he sent us all to prison.

I'd die before I went back.

"Don't think we're at the stage of killing cops just yet," Hansen replied tightly. "We keep our shit tight, he's got no way to bust us."

It was true. To a point. We broke the law. Ran weapons. Committed murder. Did a whole lot of other illegal shit. No matter how tight we kept shit, if someone was looking close enough for long enough, they'd find something. On someone. Someone would talk.

Shit would come to a head eventually. And it would be messy. None of the men at this table would go quietly. Would go at all. Everyone here would die for this club.

It had come to that, years ago.

It would never come to that again.

Maybe it was a good thing that Violet was keeping her distance. If she was close when this shit came to a head, I wouldn't be able to concentrate. If any of this shit blew back on her, I'd do whatever it took to protect her… no matter what. I'd go back into a jail cell without question, even if I'd rather eat worms first. For her, I'd do fucking anything.

Right now, protecting her was keeping her far away from this shit. Even if it felt like it was killing me.

"We need to keep an eye on these murders," Jagger threw in, leaning forward on his elbows.

Everyone tensed. There had been women killed in a handful of towns around us. Brutally. The Sons of Templar did not stand for any kind of violence against women. Now that so many men in this charter had Old Ladies, families that were everything to them, this news was hitting close to home.

"Youngest was nineteen so far," Colby offered with a tight jaw. "Oldest was in her forties. Wire said there aren't any physical attributes that connect them. All of them worked in some area of the sex industry, though. Escorts. Strippers."

"Want extra security at the strip club," Hansen demanded

immediately. "None of those girls walk to their cars alone. None of them walk from their car to their houses alone."

"On it," Hades volunteered. He had a connection to the strip club since that's where he met his Old Lady. She still had a lot of friends who worked there, and if anything happened to them, it would hurt her.

Hades wouldn't have anyone hurting his Old Lady.

"Same with the club girls," Hansen continued. He eyed Javier and Lucas who were two of the single patches who spent the most time with them. "Want you two to make sure they're not walkin' home alone in the dark."

Javier beamed. "They won't be walkin' home at all, or certainly won't be walkin' right when they do."

There were a few chuckles around the table, but not many. Javier was young and considered himself to be a fuckin' Lothario. It was a miracle that I hadn't ripped his fucking head off for the way he looked at Violet. I didn't like it. Didn't like that, despite her many rejections, he kept fucking coming on to her. Left a bad taste in my mouth.

Hansen gave him a stern look. I got the idea that my president wasn't the biggest fan of that little fuck either. But he didn't let the look linger long.

"Okay, that's sorted." He banged down the gavel and everyone began to disperse.

I avoided Swiss the best I could, as was a habit these days. Couldn't ignore him completely, though. He was a friend. A brother. Which made looking him in the eye that much fuckin' worse.

Like now when he sought me out, slapping me on the shoulder. "You better be comin' to Declan's birthday party, you slippery fucker," he grinned.

It was hard to find the man without a grin these days. Before, he'd done it easily, but only because he fed his monster daily.

Because he needed to hurt people to survive. Before, he smiled with the blood of his enemies and his lovers.

Now all he needed was his family.

"Might be," I hedged, knowing that Violet would probably be there for her little brother's first birthday. Already, my body hungered for her. Even if I could just look at her, maybe I'd be able to sleep. Maybe I'd stop feeling like I was inches away from losing control.

"You will be," Swiss flashed me a menacing glare. "Or I'll hunt you fucking down and kill you." Then he winked and clapped me on the shoulder again.

I didn't smile. Because that joke would become true soon enough.

VIOLET

I didn't tell anyone about the positive pregnancy test. Not even Sariah who, luckily, had some big assignments due and couldn't party as much, therefore didn't notice that I wasn't drinking. If she hadn't had those assignments due, she would've figured it out in a second.

The first thing I wanted to do when I saw those two lines was call Elden. Hear his voice. Let him tell me he'd handle it. We'd handle it. Together.

But I stopped, my finger hovering over the call button.

If I told him, he'd be on the next plane here, that was for sure. To do what, I didn't know. We had not talked about the future. Children.

He was old enough to have them if he'd wanted them.

He did not have them.

And I was too young for a child. I still had at least three more semesters left. Likely a lot longer, depending on how well I functioned while pregnant.

Already, my stomach roiled in the mornings, and I could barely keep down dry toast. I was asleep at my laptop before ten when before, I'd be up until the wee hours either partying or working on assignments then up at seven the next morning.

My mood was all over the place, and I constantly had cramps. That scared me until I saw the on-campus doctor who told me that it was perfectly normal for early pregnancy. Basically, I got PMS with the added bonus of morning sickness.

It was too early for an ultrasound, but they did blood tests, and they all came up pregnant as fuck.

Well, my doctor didn't use that term.

I'd walked around campus for hours, my purse full of pamphlets and prenatals, in somewhat of a daze.

There were options, of course. I could deal with this alone and never tell Elden, but just the thought had me vomiting into a trash can. I got a couple of sideways looks, but it wasn't outside the norm to see such things on a college campus.

I sat on a bench, staring at the brick buildings that stood like monoliths. The buildings that people put blood, sweat and tears into to gain acceptance. Parents saved for eighteen years. Students put themselves into a lifetime's worth of debt.

There I was, debt free, without having exerted any of the blood, sweat or tears, with all the privilege in the world and all the opportunities, financial and otherwise, to study here. Yet I was lamenting that fact. Resenting it.

If I wanted to get a job at one of the big firms, I'd need at least another two more years of study. If not more.

That was the plan when I started.

Before I even started. My father and I had sat down and planned it all out. I'd mentioned taking some time after my initial few years to volunteer, travel some more, take a breath. He'd gotten that stern look on his face and told me that there would be time for volunteer work after I got my degree. After I was married. His tone brooked no argument. He told me he would be very disappointed in me if I did that.

And despite my resistance to following what I was 'supposed' to do, I didn't want to disappoint my father.

But my father was dead.

He had been for almost a year to the day.

My brother's birthday was in three days.

The anniversary of my father's death.

My mom said it was a *complicated* day for me. She tried to talk to me multiple times over the phone, multiple times when I'd been home last. Caroline tried to talk to me. Freya tried to talk to me. They were worried, I guessed. Because they saw what they wanted to see. That I was still at college, getting good grades, not lashing out, not wallowing.

They did not see the partying or the arrest, likely because the club shielded my mother from that. Swiss had taken me aside when I got home and spoke to me about the arrest. He did not chastise me nor yell at me. He kissed me on the head and told me he was proud of me.

It occurred to me that my father had never been proud of me. He'd said it, but he was only proud of me when I did the things he expected me to do. When I acted like his daughter should've. He was not proud of the person I was, merely the person he expected me to be. The person he made me into.

So, I'd never felt warm and comforted like I did when Swiss told me he was proud of me. For getting arrested. For standing up for a friend. For being rash, a little irresponsible and violent. For being imperfect but myself.

It felt nice. And complicated. Because of the guilt I was carrying over the secret.

I almost told Swiss then. About me and Elden. Just so I wasn't hiding anything anymore. Also, so I could finally live the life I wanted.

But I held back. Because it would've tainted the moment. Soured it. There would be no more pride. There would only be Swiss's overarching fury.

At Elden.

Not me.

And I didn't want that.

Nor did I want the secret to continue. It had to come out at some point. But now there was a timeline for everything coming out.

Eight months, give or take.

Most likely five, when it became impossible to hide what I was growing inside me. And it would be growing inside of me. I knew that my reaction to the very thought of another abortion had nothing to do with morning sickness.

I cradled my stomach as I stared at the buildings.

Declan's birthday party was this weekend. I would not ruin that. But I would be going home carrying Elden's baby. And I had to figure out a way to tell him that.

CHAPTER
Sixteen

I WAS a wreck from the second I got on the plane, even worse as I walked through the gate to see my mother, brother and stepfather waiting for me. I had not been able to eat since... pretty much the moment I peed on the stick. I hadn't had any symptoms when I'd been pregnant last time.

Then again, I was now growing one half of a brooding badass inside of me, which apparently took everything out of you.

Sariah was worried about me.

"I know that we still live in a society obsessed with image and skinniness, and the media throws diets and plastic surgery at us like footballs, but you are absolutely perfect the way you are," she said as I'd been packing my bag.

"What are you talking about?" I asked, focusing on my clothes since I didn't like looking her in the eye when I was hiding something from her.

"I'm talking about you barely eating anything all week, even though Ollie outdid herself on those blueberry muffins," she scolded me. "And you don't even have a hangover to blame it on."

I concentrated very hard on my jeans, the ones I would only be fitting in for the next few months.

"I'm stressed with classes," I told her. Again, it was one of my patented non-lies. I was indeed stressed with classes, but that wasn't the reason for me not eating.

Sariah's heels clicked against the hardwood floor as she walked in the direction of my dresser. The drawers opened and closed as I contemplated my jeans and whether or not I was going to throw up.

When a mess of lace landed on top of my jeans, I turned my gaze toward Sariah.

"I'm guessing that the not eating and generally acting off and mopey has to do with the trip back home for your baby brother's birthday," she pressed, going back to my dresser, finding more lingerie and depositing it in my suitcase.

We went shopping a lot. My father's money was burning a hole in my proverbial pocket, and I did enjoy spending it on things that he would hate. Clothing that embodied my personal style of classic yet edgy, lingerie that erred on the side of harlot.

"I'm going home for my baby brother's birthday party," I reminded her. "Not going to the Playboy mansion."

Sariah folded her arms. "From what I hear, the Sons of Templar clubhouse is so much better than the Playboy mansion."

I pursed my lips but didn't say anything.

"Now, I know that this is a weird time of year for you," she began in that soft tone I hated. The tone reserved for girls with dead dads.

Sariah, up until this moment, hadn't spoken to me using that tone.

"And I am assuming Elden will be at this birthday party," she said softly. A different kind of tone this time. The kind reserved for girls with broken hearts.

"Now, I understand you're being sensible and protecting him and the club or whatever the fuck," she waved a hand in the air, tone sharper now. "But people only break their own hearts for noble reasons in fiction. So, I'm not letting you do that." Her gaze was tinged with concern as it grazed over me. "I'm not going to let you waste away. You're my hot best friend, and you're staying that way. Which is why you're going to sneak away from your brother's birthday and get yourself good and fucked by that biker you love."

That teased a smile out of me, despite everything else.

"Ah, she's in there!" Sariah announced triumphantly. "Now all I need is to shove a cheeseburger down your gullet."

My stomach churned at the mention of a cheeseburger, but I forced my attention down at my suitcase. "Elden doesn't like lingerie," I told her.

Her mouth hung open. "Elden is a living, breathing, badass man. He likes lingerie. You are one hot bitch. You look great in lingerie."

"I do," I grinned again. "But lingerie doesn't stay on or whole for long enough for Elden to appreciate how great I look in lingerie." My body heated at the memory of his large, calloused hands ripping at delicate lace.

Sariah was gaping once more. "I have no fucking clue how you're strong enough to distance yourself from a man who rips your lingerie off," she quipped. "But you're to stop doing what you've been doing. For your own good. I'm not watching you waste away."

I glanced up at my friend when her voice shook a bit at the end. Her eyes were misty.

"Promise me you're going to get yourself laid this weekend," she demanded. "Promise me you're going to get back together with your man, motorcycle club politics and stepfather be damned. Or I swear to God, I'll fly down there and fight him myself."

I grinned at that image.

Though I didn't feel right about telling Sariah about the pregnancy before telling Elden, that I could promise her.

"I promise, I am going to get back together with my man," I said dutifully.

"And have a cheeseburger," she added.

My stomach heaved at the thought. "I'll try my best."

Though I intended on keeping my promises, I didn't think I'd be able to handle the cheeseburger one since I'd thrown up five times during the plane ride here.

I didn't look good. I looked pale, even more so than normal, I'd lost a couple of pounds I didn't need to lose, my hair was a mess, and my face was dewy with sweat.

My mother clocked it all the second I met them at the gate, but luckily, I had a very small human excitedly waving his fists at me the second I got close enough. And then, he launched himself into my arms, and I got to use him as a buffer between my worried mother and stepfather.

It wasn't until he was strapped in his car seat that my mother got to hit me with the questions.

"You look sick. What's wrong? Are you okay?" My mother had turned so she could look at me in the back seat.

"I'm fine," I told her, looking at my brother, landing kisses on his little cheeks.

"You are not fine," she barked. "Tell her she's not fine," she addressed her husband.

"I'm not saying anything except when women say they're fine, they rarely are." Swiss's eyes met mine in the mirror. They were twinkling. "I also know our girl is pretty darn tough and is also a college student. She's probably hungover as fuck."

"Swiss!" my mother exclaimed, smacking his arm. "Don't swear in front of your son."

"First of all, he's a baby—"

"He's a sponge," my mother cut him off. "And I don't want his first word to be… *fuck,*" she whispered theatrically.

"Second of all," Swiss continued as if my mother hadn't spoken. "He's my son, so he's going to swear eventually. Plus, a baby saying *fuck* would be fuckin' hilarious."

I grinned, or did my best to. I was still reeling over the 'our girl' comment. That and the warmth in Swiss's eyes.

It settled wrong, rubbed against all of the secrets I was keeping.

But luckily, my mother and Swiss bickered pretty much all the way back to Garnett. Bickered with love and tenderness, with humor, warmth. With Swiss calling Mom 'Countess' and him with his hand on her knee before he held her hand up to his mouth.

Declan fell asleep beside me, and eventually, I followed suit, resting my head on my little brother's car seat.

I only woke when Mom gently shook me in the stationary car. I blinked rapidly, taking in the driveway we were parked on, the charming house and the crisp scent of lavender in the air.

"Honey, you want Swiss to carry you in?" Mom asked.

I was too bleary-eyed and groggy to decipher whether that was a joke or not. "I still have use of both of my legs," I muttered, pushing myself out of the car.

Mom lingered close to me, snapping when I attempted to grab my stuff from the trunk.

"That's the entire reason I married a big, muscly biker," she explained, directing me into the house.

It smelled of fresh baked cookies, expensive candles and my mom's perfume, a cocktail of scents that normally made my whole body relax and pretty much all of my troubles melt away. Normally, I wasn't pregnant, so even in my sleep-deprived state, I almost threw up.

Almost.

"Are you hungry, sweetie?" Mom asked. "I can make you something, whatever you want."

"Sleep," I murmured, fighting against my unpredictable stomach.

Mom walked me all the way back to my room where I slumped onto the bed without thinking.

I even let her pull my shoes off for me. She fussed with the blankets until I was all the way under them.

Her hand brushed the hair from my face as I lapsed between

sleepiness and wakefulness.

"You're working too hard at that school," she pouted. "Or partying too hard," she sounded like she was frowning, but my lids were too heavy to see if I was correct.

I smiled sleepily. "I'm fine."

"I have to agree with my husband... No woman is fine when she says she's fine."

"I *will* be fine," I amended, half asleep.

"I know, sweetie." Mom kissed my head. "Love you endlessly."

"Love you," I mumbled.

Then my mom tucked me in for the last time. Though neither of us knew it then.

I was at the club.

With Colby.

Trying not to vomit.

Half of that was because of the pregnancy, half of it was because of my nerves. I'd spent the entire morning under the watchful eye of my mother, and had somehow managed to convince her that I was indeed okay and not carrying an illegitimate biker's child. It was a good thing she had Declan's party to organize along with a restaurant to run.

I had a biker who needed to be told I was in love with him and carrying his illegitimate child. I was nervous. Very fucking nervous. I'd spent two hours deciding what to wear for this meeting. It didn't help that three-quarters of my suitcase was lingerie, thanks to Sariah. And then there were the five pairs of jeans I'd inexplicably packed.

Luckily, I kept a well-stocked closet at Mom's place. Mom and I had done a lot of shopping. Unfortunately, we had not been shopping for this particular scenario.

I decided on a long, silk skirt in a deep shade of red. Knee-high leather, heeled boots in a deeper shade of red. My sweater was tight and almost black but with a tinge of maroon. My hair was dead straight, a dark curtain against my pale skin. Makeup hid the dark circles, and I tried to offset my general paleness with a soft blush and a pink gloss.

Yes, I looked good, or I did when I left Mom and Swiss's house for the club. I stopped three times to vomit, so my lip gloss was ruined by that point. My hair disheveled. My face likely a disturbing shade of green.

Then there were the sweaty palms and the general air of panic that settled over me as I set my booted foot inside.

"Violet!" Colby exclaimed, getting up from the bar and rushing over to give me a hug. It was so tight he lifted me off the floor.

I did my best to steady myself and not vomit all over him when he placed me down.

"College is making you too skinny," he frowned. "We need to get you a cheeseburger."

"Why does everybody keep saying that?" I whined, pouting.

"Because it's fuckin' true," he grunted, dragging me from the door to where he'd been situated at the bar.

I peered around the room, trying to be subtle about it. There was no one else in the vicinity. Music played quietly over the speakers.

"Sit," Colby ordered.

Because of the panic and the nausea, I complied.

Colby rounded the bar to get a beer from the fridge, taking off the top and placing it in front of me. He did the same for himself, though he already had a half full one in front of his seat.

"It's barely noon," I informed him as he walked back around the bar and sat on the stool beside me.

"What are you, a cop?" he scoffed. "And, you're in fucking college… Don't even pretend that drinking before noon isn't part of the curriculum." He finished the rest of his original beer. "Or do they not do that at the fancy colleges?"

I rolled my eyes. "*Of course,* they do it at the fancy colleges. They do it more, for all the future CEOs and billionaires to prepare for their casual alcoholism and drug addictions," I joked.

Colby grinned. "Perfect training for your weekend of partying with me."

I bit my lip, trying to figure out how I was going to get out of this. Colby took a lot of things seriously, partying being one of them. And usually, I was on board with it. Usually, I wasn't pregnant.

Well, except that one time.

"I'm not in the mood for partying right now." Even thinking about beer made my mouth dry.

Colby laughed. "Yeah, good one. Drink up, bitch."

I didn't take the beer he'd picked up and held to me.

He squinted at me. "What are you, pregnant or something?" he joked.

I pressed my lips together. I was unable to lie straight to his face. I really hadn't thought someone would ask me flat out.

Colby's eyes stopped twinkling with humor, and my friend turned into a scary badass once again.

"You're fuckin' pregnant?" he boomed, leaning forward.

"Shut up," I hissed. "I don't think they heard you in the garage."

But it became apparent that someone had heard when Colby's eyes jumped behind me, hardening into a glare as I was lifted off the stool.

Elden's scent enveloped me. I breathed him in. There was one thing that didn't make me feel sick, it seemed.

I didn't have much time to protest as Elden gathered me into his arms—carefully, more carefully than he'd ever touched me—and walked us out of the common room and down the hall.

It was pure luck that no one saw us. We'd had a lot of that, what with all of the times we'd tempted fate by showing what we were to each other for anyone to see. Maybe fate was on our side.

I liked to think that.

He didn't speak as he walked us down the hall in long, purposeful strides. It should've felt ridiculous to be carried like this. It didn't. Elden's arms were around me, strong, firm, safe. I didn't speak either. Simply gazed up at him hungrily, taking in every detail. His beard was streaked with slivers of silver, groomed and smelled like the Tom Ford oil I'd bought him over the Christmas break. I liked it because I smelled him on me for hours after we left each other.

His face was tanned, weathered, every groove in it serving to make him more distinguished and rugged at the same time. His icy eyes were inscrutable, intense, capturing mine every second step.

My heart was slamming against my rib cage as the door to his room closed behind us. Again, I breathed in the scent of the cleaning products he used, mingling with his own smell. My body settled into it… This was my home. He was. I didn't know when the change had happened. Maybe it was when the second line showed up. Maybe it was long before that. But it clicked right then, there in that moment.

He sat me on the bed, kneeling between my knees. Large hands settled on the silk of my skirt.

"I'm pregnant," I uttered, pointing out the obvious.

His hand cradled my chin, his eyes sparkling with something that wasn't rage or disappointment. "I know."

I blinked at him, coming out of my brain fog, getting over the shock of seeing him again, of feeling him again. "You don't sound mad."

"Why in the fuck would I be mad?"

I stared at him, realizing that he was genuinely confused. He was something else too. It looked like… happiness, but I must've been hallucinating. Outlaw bikers didn't tend to be happy in the face of unplanned pregnancies. Or at least that's what I'd thought.

"Um, because of all the things that made you not want to touch me in the first place," I splayed my palms, my voice shaky. I felt unstable under the weight of a gaze I'd never seen from Elden before. "The age difference, my stepfather, all your thoughts about me being too good for you, about me deserving a life bigger than this… different." I listed them off on my fingers. My hand was still shaking.

"Baby, I knew what I was doin' the second I fucked you raw," he told me, eyes never leaving mine, his hand taking my shaking one and lifting it to his lips.

"What does that mean?"

"It means that I was there the night you had to deal with the consequences of a man bein' selfish with his pleasure, not caring about the consequences." His fury seeped into the air. "I would never let you go through that shit again," he vowed. "I would never have taken you raw unless I was ready for this moment right here."

I digested what he was saying. "So you… *expected* me to get pregnant?" I deduced, blindsided.

"Well, up until recently, we'd been fuckin' every chance we got," he shrugged. "Figured it would happen sometime."

"Okay, I must've ventured into a parallel universe." I ripped my hand out of his grasp. "Because the Elden I knew wanted to keep us a secret under the pain of death because of all of the blood and violence that would erupt if someone, namely Swiss, found out we were fucking."

He cracked his neck. "It was never just fucking with us, and you know that."

"I know that," I thrust my hands through my hair. "But there's a big difference between you admitting that and putting a baby in me. For so long, you've been convinced that you needed to do the good thing, push me away, let me live life without you or whatever the fuck. How did everything change so quickly, without me knowing?"

"You knew," he replied evenly. "You're smart, Violet. Don't

pretend you're not. Don't pretend you didn't know exactly what you were doing the second you asked me to take you raw."

He was forcing me to face the thing I'd been hiding from. Because he was right. *I* was the one who'd told him not to use a condom. *I* was the one who wasn't on birth control. *I* was the one who had 'forgotten' to track my cycle.

It was all me.

On some level, not that deep down, I'd known this was going to happen. Fuck, on some level, I'd *wanted* this to happen so the truth would be shoved to the surface. So we'd have to tell everyone. So no one could hurt Elden. He was the father of my baby now. He was not just the older man who took advantage of a member's stepdaughter.

That and I wanted this for Elden. For me.

Even though I'd droned on to anyone who would listen that I wouldn't exist just to be a mother, a housewife... That I had a different life in store for myself.

Yet here I was.

"I can't talk to you right now." I pushed him away so I could stand up. I felt vaguely sick and mad at myself, yet happiness crept up from somewhere deep. Peace threatened to settle at the possibility of getting everything I wanted. A family. A life with Elden. But I pushed it away. Because I was too fucked-up. Scared. Whatever.

"You sure as fuck aren't leaving right now," Elden bit out, moving to stand between me and the door.

I put my hand on my hip. "It is my little brother's first birthday," I huffed in frustration. "What are you going to do, stop me bodily?"

Elden flexed his fists at his sides, and his eyes flared with fury, but he didn't do anything. He wasn't going to physically force me to stay there, though I could see him battling with it.

So, I used that moment to push past him and walk purposefully out of the clubhouse.

CHAPTER Seventeen

I'D PULLED myself together enough so no one noticed what a mess I was at the party. I'd changed out of my sweater because the sun was shining, making it unseasonably warm for the time of year. I chose a white sundress, putting a light cardigan on top. My face was still too pale, my eyes a little red from the tears I'd let escape, but it was easy to miss.

The party itself was lovely chaos, all of the Sons of Templar children running around, laughing, screaming and causing trouble.

Men in cuts were scattered everywhere, my stepfather at the barbeque with Hansen and Hades.

Freya was sitting by the pool wearing a gingham bathing suit and heart shaped glasses. Hades was not even pretending to be grilling, staring directly at her.

Macy was wiping food off one of the boy's faces.

Caroline was sitting on her husband's lap.

Music poured from the speakers, the desert yawning from beyond my mother's garden.

"Violet!" my mother greeted, Declan on her hip. "Where have you been?"

She frowned at me as she stopped in front of me, inspecting my face. "Are you okay?"

"I'm fine, Mom." I didn't look at her, instead focusing my attention on Declan, tickling his stomach.

My mother didn't look convinced, but Swiss yelled, "Countess, where are we putting the burgers?" from across the patio, temporarily distracting her.

"He says he can do anything, yet when it comes to finding a place to put a plate of burgers, he's helpless," she scowled. "Can you take him?" she asked, not waiting for me to answer before handing me Declan.

I took him gratefully, thankful for Swiss's intervention and for my baby brother's existence.

"Happy birthday, sweet boy!" I cooed, lifting up my little brother, kissing his chubby cheek and reveling in his squeal of delight.

Declan Carter was simply the cutest baby on planet Earth. He was thoroughly adored by his parents, by his big sister, his grandparents and everyone in the Sons of Templar. He was curious, cheeky and always smiling.

He brought a light to our lives that I was constantly grateful for. And he potentially may have a… niece or nephew who would be less than two years younger than him.

If I was brave enough to move forward with the life I'd secretly wanted since the second Elden and I became Elden and I.

But holding my brother, basking in the sun of the garden my mother had curated and turned into a paradise, I couldn't even entertain the thought of repeating the other option.

Having the abortion had been the best choice for me.

The *only* choice for me at that time.

I didn't feel any regret, any guilt because that pregnancy was not created from love. It was a result of deception. A product of a terrible moment in my life, and had I not made that decision, it would've defined me in ways I didn't want to be defined.

Those were my reasons for making that choice. Every woman had her own reason that had nothing to do with anyone else.

But I had no reason to make that choice now. Not when we had created something out of love. Even if our situation was complicated beyond words. Even if it would take my life in a direction I couldn't even fathom, it was ours.

Suddenly, I was going to burst into tears.

It didn't help that Elden had entered the party and was staring at me from across the patio.

Fuck.

"Can you take him for a second?" I asked Macy, who was thankfully nearby.

"Sure, sweetie," she frowned, taking Declan from me. "Are you okay?"

But I was already halfway inside by the time she finished speaking.

I'd been planning on locking myself in a bathroom, getting myself together—without the aid of tequila, which would've been really great right about then—and going back to celebrate my brother, pushing my problems away for the day, at least.

But Elden wasn't going to let me do that.

He snatched my wrist just as I walked into the kitchen.

"What's wrong?" His eyes were glittering with fury, and something else when I faced him.

My eyes bugged out as I scanned the kitchen. Luckily, no one was in there, and from our spot slightly off to the side, no one outside could see us either.

"What's *wrong*?" I repeated. "I'm pregnant, and you're not freaked out about it. Which I guess makes sense because it's not you who has to make all the choices. Who has to decide whether to drop out of college or have the baby—"

He yanked me closer. "You're not dropping out of college, and you're definitely having this baby."

"It's *your* choice, is it?" I ripped myself from his grasp. "You're going to force me to have the baby?"

I didn't even know why I was saying that. I was having the baby. That had already been decided. But the way he'd said that, as if I didn't have a choice in the matter triggered me. I wondered if this was how my mother felt twenty years ago. Except then she had been younger, more scared, without any other choices, without a voice of her own.

Nausea churned in my belly at those thoughts.

"There's a lot of shit that needs to be sorted," Elden agreed. "You're scared. I get it." He lifted up his hand to trail it over my cheek. "But we're in this together, baby. You're mine. Both of you."

The words hit me bodily. Settling inside me like a rock sinking to the bottom of a pond. It was exactly what I'd dreamed of hearing. Exactly what I wanted to hear. Except it scared the shit out of me.

"We're not doing this now, though," I hissed at Elden.

He stalked toward me until my back hit the wall. "We sure as fuck are doin' it now, Violet."

I took a deep breath, trying to clear my mind of his effect on me, but that didn't work well since the breath I took was polluted by his intoxicating, infuriating scent.

His palm flattened on the wall beside my head. "You can be scared, baby," he murmured. "You can be mad at me. You can be whatever the fuck you want. But it's not gonna change the fact that you're mine." His eyes dropped down to my stomach. "Both of you. And, Violet, you in that sundress is drivin' me fuckin' mad. So later, we're gonna fuck. You can still be mad. If you want."

Holy. *Shit*.

My cheeks flushed, and my body warmed, desire chasing away the worst of my fury. My breath shallowed.

I leaned in toward Elden, not caring about the party or who could walk into the kitchen.

But he stiffened, taking three large steps back from me without warning. I frowned at him in confusion, but he was focused on something else.

Someone else.

My mother was standing in the kitchen, looking between the both of us in shock.

"Tell me I did not just see what I think I saw." Her voice was eerily calm.

Of all the ways I wanted my mother to find out about me and Elden, I would never have wanted it to be like this.

"Mom—"

She held her finger up to silence me, not looking at me but at Elden whose expression was unreadable.

"You know, if I tell my husband what I just saw… things are not going to go well," she told Elden softly. "I'm going to get blood on my floor. And I don't want to have to mop it up. I've got a one-year-old… I have enough to worry about, you know?"

Her voice was cold, calculated. She was pissed off. That much I could tell. But there was something else in her words. Betrayal. I could feel it even though she wasn't looking at me.

"M-Mom—" I stuttered, close to tears.

Again, she gave me a finger to silence me.

"I'm going to forget I saw all of this," she waved her hand. "Because I don't want my husband killing his brother today."

I tasted bile at her no-nonsense tone, at the fear I had been holding on to about that very scenario.

"And also because I don't want to have to mop up blood," my mother continued. "Then again, Swiss isn't exactly one to force household duties onto me, so he'd probably mop it up."

My mouth was impossibly dry.

Elden didn't speak. He didn't offer explanations or apologies. He was just staring at my mother because it was clear she wasn't done. Her gaze sharpened onto him.

"And I know I'm married to kind of a depraved badass who has somewhat of a reputation, but when it comes to her," she jabbed her finger at me without looking at me, "I can get pretty depraved, buddy. So just remember that."

My mother was being sincere. There was violence behind her words I'd never once heard from her. With my father, she'd always been soft-spoken, timid. With Swiss, she was definitely not soft-spoken nor timid. But she was never openly aggressive. That wasn't who my mother was.

Until now.

When she turned her glare at me, I restrained my flinch. "We are going to speak in my closet," she pointed in the direction of her and Swiss's bedroom. "Now," she added in a tone that left no room for argument.

I took one last panicked gaze at Elden, unsure of what to do. I knew that making a scene in the kitchen would not be the move. Even though I didn't want to leave him, I did what my mother said.

I walked to her and Swiss's wing of the house on autopilot, feeling numb and also kind of… relieved. This was not the way my mother should've found out about me and Elden, but it was too late to change that. It was too late for a lot of things.

Everything she said was true. Swiss considered Elden to be his brother. He trusted him. They *all* trusted each other with their lives. No matter what this was to me and Elden, Swiss would see it as Elden breaking some kind of sacred rule.

I couldn't stop moving as I entered the closet crammed full of clothes that were nothing like the ones in my mom's old, color-coded, immaculate walk-in.

Her and my father's clothes had always been purposefully separated, a not-so-subtle symbol for the way they'd lived their lives. But in this closet, Swiss's things were blended in with my mother's, motorcycle boots and chunky wedges beside each other. It signified how they lived their lives. It showed me what a fucked-up example I'd had of relationships and marriage my entire life.

She was happy with Swiss.

I wanted that. Wanted my clothes mixed with Elden's in a closet of our own. Wanted life to be uncomplicated, easy. But that wasn't going to happen. If I wanted uncomplicated and easy, I would've had to sacrifice passion, excitement. If I wanted uncomplicated, I would've stayed with Bennett. Would've quietly suffocated in a life with him and never known what it was like to be truly loved.

I didn't believe in the happily ever after that Disney peddled, and hadn't believed in *any* version until I encountered the Sons of Templar and their women.

Now I did.

I was greedy for one of my own.

My mother entered the room, her mouth tight, eyes narrowed. "You need to explain," she demanded, closing the door. "Right now."

I stopped pacing to look at my mother, hating that I felt like a little kid right now. How did I explain everything that had happened with Elden? How did I pour the past two years into some kind of explanation that wasn't going to give my mother a heart attack?

"I love him, Mom." It was the most simple, straightforward answer.

I wasn't sure what my mother had expected me to say, maybe that we were just fucking. Maybe that wouldn't have shocked her quite so much, but all the blood drained from her face.

"And I'm pregnant," I added, deciding to say it quickly, before she had the chance to recover.

You could've knocked her over with a feather. For a moment.

"You're finishing college," she declared suddenly.

I frowned at the way her mind was moving. "Of course, I am."

"You are not throwing away your degree, your future because of this," she continued as if I hadn't spoken. "Plenty of women go to college pregnant. In fact, I read a story about a woman who took the bar while she was in labor. And she passed." She threw up her hands, pacing. "Well, of course, she did. A man would say he couldn't take the test if he had a fucking cold sore." She stopped pacing, eyes flickering up and down my body, pausing on my stomach. "How far along are you?"

"Not far. Six weeks at the most."

She nodded. "Six weeks. And you've got… what, three more semesters left? So that means that you'll be able to attend in person for at least this semester." She drummed her fingers on her chin. "Or we could talk to your professors and see if we could do distance. Maybe defer until after you've had the baby." She paused, her lips parted as if she were contemplating her words. "That's if you want to have it." Her eyes seemed to suddenly clear, properly focusing on me. "You don't have to. There is absolutely no shame in making that choice, sweetheart."

"I know," I ran my hands through my hair, annoyed. Again, not at her. At myself. For not telling her that I'd already made that choice. For wrapping myself in secrets so that I didn't know where my lies began.

I pulled in a deep breath, looking at my mother. "I want this baby." The rest was complicated, terrifyingly so, but that was the one easy truth.

Her eyes brimmed with tears. "How long has this been going on?"

I tugged at my lip. Suddenly my mother was not mad or making plans. She was simply hurt. Hurt that the daughter she thought told her everything had been keeping something so big from her.

"Pretty much since I arrived in Garnett." I hated that the truth would hurt her so much, but I was unable to tell another lie.

Her eyes spread wide in shock, and she didn't speak for a couple of moments as she digested this information. "Why didn't you tell me?" She sounded hurt and tired.

"What would you have said if I had told you?" I asked her cautiously.

"I would've told you he was too old for you, too dangerous for you, and I probably would've tried to forbid you from seeing him."

I nodded.

"He is too old for you," she said firmly.

"Is he, Mom? Because all the boys you would've deemed *appropriate* for me chug booze, play video games and date-rape girls."

My mother's hand flew to her throat.

"I don't have to explain to you what's different about these men because you know that already," I continued. "You've been wanting me to talk about Dad for the longest time, so now I will." I shifted my way, pulling in a deep breath. "He fucked me up. First, before I knew anything, just by being him. By making me feel like I had to be perfect, that I wasn't worthy of his love if I didn't act a certain way. He crafted me into someone who both craved validation and attention from an older man while making it so I only got that if I wasn't my authentic self."

My eyes filled with tears. I'd never said any of this out loud before. I'd never even really *thought* any of it. But it was being forced upon me. It had been bubbling up inside of me for so long, there was simply no more room to store it.

"When I found out what my father truly was, I had to face the fact that not only was I seeking validation from a monster, but my mother had lived through hell for almost the entirety of my life," I hiccupped. "I'm not exactly well-adjusted from that, Mom. I'm fucked-up. I'm going to be fucked-up for life. Not all in a bad way, though."

I tried to smile at her reassuringly since the blood had drained from her face from everything I'd said thus far. It didn't really work.

I swatted away my tears. "Every single person connected to this club is fucked-up," I said softly. "Has horrific pasts. Yet they smile. Throw parties. They accept people despite their damage. Elden accepts me. He makes me feel safe. I don't have to be anyone different to earn his love. He gives it to me. He would never lay a hand on me. He would go to the ends of the earth to protect me. Yet I still don't think I deserve him."

Tears were streaming down my face.

"Because Daddy fucked me up," I choked out. "And I can't stand the thought of you only loving me if I make the right choices and love the right person."

My mother was crying now too. "Oh, my little girl," she whispered, pulling me into her arms.

"I love you for exactly who you are," she murmured against my hair. "And who you are is wonderful."

I leaned against her, sinking into her embrace. We didn't speak for a long time, but she gently pulled me back to arm's length, wiping my tears from my face.

"My love for you is unconditional," she stated firmly. "It does not matter what choice you make, ever. Nothing will ever change that." Her voice shook a little that time. "I understand better than anyone that loving these men isn't exactly a choice. And as much as I hate it, I know that what your father did cannot be reversed." Her eyes hardened. "I will forever carry it with me," she whispered. "What he did to you. How he made you feel that you weren't worthy." She squeezed her eyes shut for a moment. "It's a shock, you and Elden," she said once she opened her eyes. "But I understand it. I saw the way he looked at you. I can't believe it's the first time I've seen it. But, honey, he would move mountains for you. He will protect you and love you in a way that you're worthy of."

She cupped my face in her palms. "And that's all a mother wants for her daughter. We'll work out the details later."

I squinted at her through my tears. "I'm scared," I admitted in a meek voice.

She smiled at me. "Of course, you are, sweetie. That means it's all worth it."

And at that point, my mother took me in her arms again, and I sobbed, finally letting out everything I'd been holding in.

ELDEN

It had taken every ounce of control I'd honed over the years to let Violet walk away. To let her face her mother alone.

Ever since I'd found out she was carrying my baby, I'd had a difficult time letting her out of my sight. It had been hard enough before. But now she had our future growing inside of her, she had my fucking redemption growing inside of her. I couldn't stop thinking about how fucking delicate she was. How many things could take her away from me.

There was a fucking sicko killing women in the area. Tearing them apart. The club had enemies from all sides. On top of that, she could get in a fucking car accident, get sick... I could lose her.

Control had been integral to my survival ever since I got out of prison. Now Violet was integral to my survival, and I couldn't control her, couldn't protect her from everything. Although I sure as fuck would try.

Beyond feeling sheer fucking joy—unlike anything I'd felt in decades—at knowing she was pregnant with my kid, I felt relief. This was an indisputable reason for shit to come to light. For me to speak to Swiss. Have her on the back of my bike finally.

I stared at the man in question, standing at the grill. It was his kid's first birthday party. Absolute wrong time to tell him. But the chances of him killing me were slimmer here.

And I couldn't stand one more fucking second of stealing moments with Violet, hiding how I felt about her.

I was about to step forward when Hansen clapped me on the shoulder. I had no fucking idea where he came from.

"You wouldn't be planning on going to tell your brother you're in love with his stepdaughter on his son's first birthday, would you?" he asked lightly.

My eyes flew to my president. His stare was not light. His grip tightened on my shoulder.

"Although there isn't a right time for that conversation, this is the fuckin' wrong one," he added, tone still conversational.

"How the fuck do you know?" I ground out, unable to keep my tone light.

"I'm the president of this charter." He took a leisurely pull of his beer. "It's my job to know shit that threatens the club."

I gripped the back of my neck. "I would never threaten the club."

"Not on purpose," he amended. "And I know you didn't enter into shit with her lightly. Didn't do it 'cause you wanted young pussy."

Red crept along the corners of my gaze. "I'd be really fuckin' careful how you speak about my woman, or I'll forget you're my president." I meant every word.

I respected the fuck out of Hansen. Considered him to be a brother. Would be eternally grateful to him for giving me the club. But I wouldn't hesitate to hurt him if he talked about Violet like that.

Instead of getting pissed at me or readying to fight, the fucker's lips curved into a grin. "Yeah, I thought so," he muttered. "It seems this charter is destined to have the same curse as Amber when it comes to Old Ladies. Courtships are never peaceful. Never boring, and each is more fuckin' dramatic than the last." His gaze wandered over our brothers and their Old Ladies. "This is gonna be messy, gonna cause shit in the club. I might've told you to end it, if I'd caught it early enough. But I doubt there was a time when it would've been early enough," he sighed.

He'd be fucking right on that. Violet had been mine from the moment I laid eyes on her. Nothing could've changed that.

"You want me out of this charter?" I asked him seriously.

It made sense. I was a recent patch. Didn't have the same roots here that Swiss did.

"No fuckin' way," Hansen's eyes flared with surprise. "You're family."

Those simple words hit me somewhere deep.

"We're a fucked-up family," he continued, "and sometimes families fight." He shrugged. "Let's not draw blood at a kid's birthday party, though. Have a beer. Lock it down. There will be plenty of time for the truth later." He gave me a slap on the back. "No one is gonna make you leave this charter, brother. Not even him." He nodded to Swiss.

Then he walked away, to be with his woman.

I waited for mine, a weight off my shoulders but that lingering sense of dread not entirely gone.

VIOLET

"How am I going to tell Swiss?" I asked Mom, taking the mascara wand she handed me.

We were in her and Swiss's bathroom, both of us reapplying our makeup. The stone counters and double sinks were beautiful, the tones similar to Mom's restaurant, leaning toward a desert vibe, neutrals and rough textures.

The counters were littered with beauty products, perfumes. It was clean but not painstakingly organized like her other bathroom had been.

Although this was only the beginning of what I guessed was going to be a very long, complicated and possibly violent journey, I felt much lighter.

I'd cried for what seemed like hours.

But no one had sent a search party, and Swiss would definitely come looking for his wife if she was out of his sight for too long.

Elden would look for me too. I knew that. No matter where I walked in this world, he'd be beside me. Or not far behind.

"You're not going to tell him anything," my mother said firmly, looking at me in the mirror. "Nor is Elden, though you're probably going to have to convince him on that because he'll surely have some ideas about having a 'man to man' talk with my husband." She rolled her eyes. "The only reason I know he's not doing it right now is because it's a child's birthday party, and even though Declan is going to grow up to be a badass, one is a little young to witness a gunfight."

I felt the blood leave my face. "Do you think Swiss will really hurt him?"

"He'll want to," she squeezed my arm. "These men are wonderful and unlike any other, but they are also *men* at the end of the day. And when it comes to those they care about, those they think it's their job to protect, they tend to err on the side of violence because they seem to think that solves everything." She rolled her eyes again. "It's probably not going to be pretty," she sighed. "And it's probably going to take Swiss some time. He may be reactive and overly dramatic, but he is also a romantic." She winked. "He loves you and just wants you to be happy."

I put the mascara down, relieved.

"Plus, when he finds out you're pregnant, he's not going to kill or maim the father of his grandchild," she added with another wink.

That really did not make me feel better.

"Ready?" she asked.

I looked at myself in the mirror. My eyes were still red, my face a little blotchy, but I felt different, stronger, less alone. I hadn't realized what a toll it had taken on me, keeping all of that inside, keeping my mother on the outside.

"Ready," I told her.

We walked back into the party together.

"We need the candles, Countess!" Swiss yelled from outside, proving that we'd chosen the right time to finish our conversation. "And the cake."

Mom shook her head, smiling with her whole face. Her whole soul. She took a moment to kiss the side of my head.

"Are you going to be okay?" she asked quietly.

I looked out to the party. "Yeah," I replied.

She gave me one more look before walking toward the kitchen. I went outside, intending on eating since I was suddenly ravenous without all that toxic truth taking up space.

He was on me the second I stopped at the large table of food.

"You okay, baby?" Elden murmured, coming to stand beside me at a distance that was much closer than he'd ever risked.

I glanced around. Mom was in the kitchen preparing the cake, Swiss in there with her and Declan. All of his focus was on them. Everyone else was distracted with their own children or wives.

"I'm fine," I told him, taking a carrot from the table and nibbling on it. I searched the table that was overflowing with all kinds of snacks. "I'd love a glass of wine," I groaned, staring longingly at the ice bucket.

Elden chuckled.

Chuckled.

Like we didn't have my stepfather's reaction to my pregnancy right before us. Like we didn't have my pregnancy and the life of our child right ahead of us.

Like he didn't have a care in the world. Though that was vaguely worrying, I could not help but marvel at what Elden looked like when he chuckled. How he held himself. It was no longer as if the world was on his shoulders. There was something freer about him. And that was because of me. Of us.

"You're really happy about this." I leaned forward, closer to him than I should've been, brushing up against the edges of his cut.

Elden looked down at me. "I'm really fuckin' happy about this, baby."

The air buzzed with electricity. I drifted off somewhere different. Somewhere ours. I was about to go up on my tiptoes, clutch on to his cut and kiss him in front of everyone.

"Cake!" Swiss's voice boomed from the kitchen and tore the moment apart.

I scuttled back. Elden's lips clamped together.

I gave him one last look before moving to the kitchen where everyone had gathered for the cake. Elden stood behind me. Much too close. His hands found the hem of my dress. Crept up it until his palm was flat on the skin of my ass. It stayed there the entire time we sang my brother happy birthday.

Because, it seemed, Elden was done hiding things.

We weren't just playing with fire now. It had been set and was readying to blow with the direction of the wind.

It remained to be seen if it would burn everything to the ground.

CHAPTER
Eighteen

"YOU'RE NOT PUSHING ME AWAY," I pointed out as we laid in his bed. I'd gone back to the club, slipping out with Elden after Declan had shoved his face in the cake.

We'd gone straight to his room where Elden had torn my sundress off me and spent a long time making me forget about everything but our bodies moving together.

Then I washed my face, complaining about the poor options I had in regard to skincare and brushed my teeth with him standing beside me. It felt surreal to be standing at a sink with Elden, wearing his tee, pregnant with his baby, brushing my teeth. It also felt right.

But a small voice was telling me to run. Telling me that something was going to happen to rip apart this fantasy.

I tried my best to quiet that voice as we climbed into bed, and he immediately yanked me to his chest.

It was probably much too risky for us to be sleeping together at the club. My mother knew, yes. Swiss did not. And he was apt to notice that I was not at his home in my bedroom.

Sure, I'd been at the club plenty during my visits. Partying, hanging out with my friends here. Sleeping with Elden. Or more accurately, slipping off to fuck in his room when everyone was too drunk to notice.

But I'd never slept over.

Elden held me tighter to his chest after I spoke. "Why in the fuck would I be pushing you away?"

"My mom's little speech today." I toyed with the comforter. "Everything she said about the club, brotherhood."

Elden stiffened for just a moment, then he moved so he was on top of me, bracing himself on the bed so he was hovering.

He trailed a finger down my cheek. "Not anything I haven't thought a million times over since the beginning."

"I guess," I sighed. "But was it different hearing it out loud, knowing there's no escape from that now? Not knowing what will happen with the club?"

"Nope," he continued caressing my face. "Swiss is my brother," he agreed. "And yeah, if I'd just fucked you, treated you like some club girl and nothing else, he'd be entitled to put a bullet in my brain."

My stomach dropped at the mere thought.

"But," he continued, "I knew that if I was going to touch you, it was never going to be a fuck. Knew that from the very beginning. And now you're carrying my baby. Now you're my woman." His finger went to my lips just as I parted them to argue. "And I know that you've got a lot of ideas about what that means. And fuck, maybe those ideas are right for your generation. Or with a different man. In a different club. But to me, it means something. And my words aren't meant to make you feel smaller, make you feel like you're not your own. You're just mine too. And, baby, before you talk about equality, I'm yours too."

Although I did want to argue, I couldn't. Not really.

"I don't know what I want yet," I admitted. "With us."

"Don't recall asking you to make any decisions," he leaned down to place a soft kiss against my lips. "But I'll tell you one thing, I'm gonna be sleeping next to my woman. However the fuck we work that out, I'll be doing it. And I'm not sneaking around. I'll talk to Swiss first thing tomorrow."

All of those squishy feelings disappeared, replaced with panic. "You should let me do it," I said quickly. "Or my mom. He's not going to hurt either of us."

Elden's brows furrowed. "Not gonna hide behind you or your mother, Violet. And I've already disrespected him enough by not going to him the second I knew you were it. Gonna do the respectable thing. The honorable thing."

"When did you know I was yours?" I asked. That was not the portion of the conversation I should've been latching on to. I should've been trying to convince Elden to abandon his stupid bro code and just let the women handle it. But I knew that would be fighting a losing battle.

"The second you asked me to kiss you on the rooftop."

Before I could even process what was happening, tears were spilling down my cheeks.

He wiped them away as they escaped without my consent.

"It's the hormones," I blubbered.

"Baby, you didn't shed a single tear, not one since you had your life turned upside down almost two years ago," Elden said gently, not knowing about the breakdown in the closet. "And crying doesn't make you weak."

I scowled at him. "Well how come I've never seen you cry?"

"Watch *Up* with me, I'll cry on command," he smiled down at me.

I gasped. "I don't even know where to start with that... you willingly watched an animated movie to begin with or *that's* what makes you cry."

His eyes twinkled. "Well, you've got a lifetime to discover that, and more."

"A lifetime?" my breathing quickened.

His expression turned serious. "Violet, I would not have taken you raw, would not have fucked you, if I didn't intend on being the only man doin' that for the rest of your life."

More tears wet my cheeks.

Today had been a lot. A whole lot. Elden was just verbalizing what I already knew in my heart to be true. Despite that, despite what my mother said today, despite everything, it still terrified me.

Which I guessed was the point. If you weren't afraid, you weren't living.

"Since I found out the truth about my father, I've felt a sense of guilt because of what my mother lived through to give me what I had," I whispered, staring at Elden even though I itched to turn my gaze away from him. "On a wider scale, I have so much more than the generations of women who came before me. To give myself the title of 'Old Lady' and nothing else does a disservice to everything I thought embodied my character my whole life."

I took in a ragged breath, looking to the ceiling.

"But…" I forced myself to meet the eyes of the man I loved. "I don't give a fuck about being extraordinary. I just want to be yours."

Elden's lips landed on mine. I kissed him hungrily.

"You're mine, and I'm yours," he promised.

And he spent the rest of the night proving that.

We woke up together the next morning. I did not sneak out. But Elden had. I woke up to his lips on my forehead and the smell of coffee. He was dressed and holding two cups of coffee from Julian's.

"Okay, I'm officially glad you impregnated me," I mumbled, still half asleep.

Elden gifted me with a dazzling grin as I sat up, handing me the coffee cup.

"And he smiles," I added, cradling the cup and letting its warmth seep into my bones. But the majority of the warmth filling me wasn't from the coffee. It was all because of Elden's smile. It would take some getting used to, seeing him like this. It was utterly wonderful, but I couldn't help feeling tense, waiting for the other shoe to drop.

"You're happy," I pointed out.

"You're in my bed," Elden kissed my forehead. "And you are pregnant with my baby."

"And that's all it takes to make you happy?"

His eyes were glittery and stormy at the same time. "No, it's *everything* I need to make me happy."

My stomach did a flip. Which definitely had to do with what he said… and maybe a little bit to do with morning sickness.

"If you're happy then maybe I can convince you to reconsider your plans for the day," I said after taking a sip and placing my cup on the side table while my stomach decided whether it was going to expel it or absorb it.

"You mean my plans for eating you for breakfast then fucking you after that?" Elden moved the comforter back to expose my bare legs and how his tee had ridden up past my waist.

Elden spread my legs apart, his hands creeping up the inside of my thighs.

"Okay, I'd really like that," I murmured, my eyes already rolling to the back of my head. "If you promise not to talk to Swiss today," I added while I still had coherent thought.

Elden's hands stopped moving.

I scowled at him.

"You're not changing my mind on that, Violet."

My scowl turned into a pout.

His mouth turned up. "That's not gonna work either."

"Why can't we just enjoy a day together that's… normal?" I whined.

"Because things aren't normal with us. And whatever will pass for normal can only happen once we're not keepin' this a secret from the club and from your stepfather." His lips were a thin line. "This is real now, Violet."

I sat up farther in bed, thinking his plans for the morning may not be happening due to the turn of the conversation.

"I know it's real, Elden," I groused, snatching my coffee.

He frowned at me over his own. "This being real means me having a difficult conversation and maybe a fistfight with Swiss."

"A fistfight?" I gasped, almost choking on my coffee.

Elden shrugged. "A minor bullet wound, worst case scenario."

"Explain to me a *minor* bullet wound," I demanded, rather alarmed at the prospect. When I started thinking about the blood, Elden having a hole in him from a bullet, my stomach lurched, and I tried to climb off the bed.

He stopped me, gripping my hips. "Where are you going?"

"I'm going to throw up," I informed him sweetly while glowering at him. "Or would you like me to do it in your lap?"

Elden did not let me go like I wanted. Instead, he carried me to the bathroom.

My stomach turned as he set me down, but I managed to control it for the time being. "Leave," I ordered weakly.

"Not goin' anywhere." He folded his arms.

I was going to argue with him, but my stomach didn't let that happen. Therefore, I threw up in front of Elden as he held my hair off my face, rubbed my back and made soothing noises.

It might've been romantic if not for all of the vomit.

"You're not supposed to be around for that," I informed him after I washed my face and brushed my teeth, feeling a little more human, though my stomach had not entirely settled.

"Newsflash, baby, I'm gonna be here for this entire pregnancy and then some," he replied, eyeing me with worry.

I pulled my hair up into a messy bun. Even though I'd just thrown up and didn't have any of my skincare here to do a proper routine, I looked… good. My skin was clear, my cheeks flushed, my eyes were glowing to an almost bright violet. They got more vibrant when I was really happy.

My eyes met Elden's in the mirror. "And then some?" I repeated, turning around.

His hands settled on my hips. He nodded, kissing my nose.

It was impossibly sweet and an act of affection that was unfamiliar with us, and gave me butterflies that had nothing to do with morning sickness.

I was going to prod him as to what exactly that meant, if it was the declaration of forever that it sounded like. Last night had been suspended from reality. Yes, there were all of the 'I'm yours' promises, but what did that really mean? Marriage? A house? Matching tattoos? There were many questions I needed to ask.

But there was a commotion coming from the common room, meaning no time for questions.

For the commotion to filter all the way back here, it must've been something intense.

Elden was on guard in a second, the sweet man who'd kissed my nose nowhere to be found. Instead, it was my biker, badass baby daddy who was now holding a gun.

I'd seen Elden's gun before. He wore it in a holster underneath his cut. We'd even had sex while he was still wearing it, which I'm pretty sure wasn't safe at all, and turned me on way too much for someone who was passionate about gun control.

I'd never seen Elden holding a gun, preparing to use it, though. "Stay here, lock the door," he ordered.

"I fucking mean it," he clipped out when I opened my mouth to argue with him. Then he was out the door.

Though I probably should've listened to Elden due to the criminal nature of the Sons of Templar and the various threats they could be facing at any given moment, all I could think about was the 'minor bullet wound' comment.

I shoved on my sundress from yesterday and poked my head

out of the door. There were no sounds of fists thumping against fists or even gunshots.

But I saw something that did reassure me that Elden was not going to get shot. At least not yet.

I rushed forward to see him standing in the corner of the room, his arms crossed and his gun nowhere to be seen.

She obviously hadn't seen him because she was arguing with Colby.

"I will ask for the fourth time, who are you?" Colby demanded. He had his hands on his hips, facing off against the 5'5" spitfire in bright pink Valentino platforms.

Sariah blew the hair from her face before pushing her bright pink sunglasses to the top of her head. "I'm Sariah Cardoso. Who the fuck are you?"

Colby stared at her a few seconds before his lips spread from ear to ear. "I'm the man you've been waiting for."

I swallowed a chuckle as Sariah arched her brows and purposefully looked Colby up and down. "Honey, I don't wait for any man. I don't even pause for one. I'm here for my girl, who has gotten impregnated by one of you." Her eyes found mine. "Her!" she yelled, pointing to me. "That's who I'm looking for. My bestie who got knocked up by her biker."

Elden's turbulent eyes found mine, somehow he'd not been able to use his badass biker spidey senses to note my presence until that moment. To be fair, Sariah in her pink platforms, pink leather pants and a cropped bustier yelling at Colby was a sight to behold.

"I told you to stay the fuck in the room," Elden bit out from across the room. He was charging forward, probably to growl at me some more. But Sariah was closer and more determined.

She pulled me into a tight hug.

"Careful, you're gonna squeeze the baby out of me," I joked, happy for her embrace.

I'd missed my friend. I had only been able to send her a quick text last night about the pregnancy to which she'd replied with a bunch of emojis and curse words even I hadn't heard of.

She had been surprisingly quiet for the rest of the night, which made sense because she had been making the trek here.

She let me go, still keeping hold of my upper arms. Elden was hovering close by. "Chill, dude, she doesn't swing that way," she muttered, eyes flitting to him for a moment. "Plus, you've already impregnated her, it's too late for anyone else," she added with a wink.

Colby, who by the grace of God was the only person in the common area right now, gaped at me.

"You're *really* pregnant?" he asked. I hadn't had a moment alone with him since yesterday.

I tugged on my ear, looking from Sariah to Elden to him. "It seems so."

I was pretty sure there were rules about when to announce pregnancies, and I knew a lot of women kept it secret until the twelfth week because of all of the risks in the first trimester. But none of that mattered anymore. Now that it had been announced here at the club, I knew it wouldn't stay secret for long.

"Oh, shit, I didn't ruin the announcement, did I?" Sariah winced. "What do bikers do to announce pregnancies? Shoot guns in the air?"

I smiled at her. "You have to remember that this is an *unplanned* pregnancy. I'm not sure the protocol is the same." Though I didn't know if you could consider it unplanned when both parties stopped using protection and had crazy amounts of sex.

I was still coming to terms with I had, on some level—on multiple levels—wanted to get pregnant.

"No one knew," I told Sariah. "Well, except you. And Elden. And now Colby. And my mom."

Sariah's eyes bugged out. "How did your mom take it?"

"She was shocked at first," I sighed. "Mostly because she didn't even know we were…" I trailed off, looking to Elden.

"Fucking?" Sariah offered.

I swallowed a chuckle. "Yeah, that. But she's supportive. I don't think Swiss will take it as calmly, though."

Nausea coiled through me as I looked to Elden again.

"Parents will be parents," she shrugged. "Oh, shit, that's going to be you!" Her hands covered her mouth. "You're going to be a *parent* in like eight months."

The nausea increased, making me wonder if I needed to start heading toward the bathroom again. "Don't remind me," I groaned, suddenly overcome with worry.

I had been focused on not freaking about the actual pregnancy, and not on the fact that it would indeed result in a child in eight months.

I would be a *mother* in eight months.

"Okay, she looks like she might faint or vomit or something," Sariah exclaimed, letting go of me. "And, honey, I love you, but this is Valentino," she gestured to her outfit.

Elden took advantage of Sariah's retreat to make his approach, putting an arm around me. "You good, baby?" he asked sweetly.

I didn't get to answer that question because all hell broke loose.

CHAPTER
Nineteen

ELDEN WAS NO LONGER in front of me. No longer touching me. When the door crashed open and the angry man barreled through it, Elden created as much distance between me and him as possible. Colby moved quickly too, grabbing on to Sariah's arm and dragging her out of the line of fire.

A low ringing had erupted in my ears the second the door smashed against the wall, and my stepfather entered the room, gun pointed at Elden.

A *gun* pointed at him.

My mother had rushed in behind him, grabbing on to me as we both watched in horror.

Hansen and Jagger entered after them, either having come from the garage area or having arrived at the same moment. They'd obviously seen Swiss storming across the parking lot holding a gun and hauling ass.

But when he strode across the living room and held it to Elden's head, they didn't do anything.

No one did anything.

I didn't know what I expected everyone else here to do… something, like, I don't know, tackle Swiss. Everyone just watched.

"I should blow your brains out right here, right now." Swiss sounded nothing like the stepfather I had come to know and love.

My stomach dropped at the sincerity in Swiss's tone. The lack of humanity.

Elden didn't say anything. Didn't do anything. I knew he had a gun because he had just been holding it to protect me from unknown intruders only a few minutes ago.

But him pulling a gun on Swiss would probably mean one of them would get shot. I didn't want *anyone* to get shot.

"There was a time in my life when I might not have fought you," Elden finally spoke, his voice even. "A time when I might've just let what happens happen. When I didn't care if I lived or died. Because I didn't have anything to live for."

My mom clutched on to me when I started shaking from the force of my tears, remembering what he told me in the café. My sorrow for Elden and my terror that Swiss might actually do something mingled together.

"Now I've got something to live for." Elden's eyes were no longer on Swiss but on me. "I've got everything to live for."

My heart was beating in my throat.

"Not gonna argue with you that this got fucked-up," he said to Swiss, still looking at me. "That I made some bad fucking choices in the midst of this. But you're never gonna get me to wish away what I did. 'Cause I wouldn't be standin' right here."

Still, he stared at me, despite the gun being pointed in his face.

It was sweet. Impossibly sweet. But sweet wasn't going to penetrate Swiss's fury right now. I couldn't be sure that anything would penetrate Swiss right now. So, I didn't think. I just acted. Even though he wasn't good at macho man declarations in the face of death, Elden was everything to me too.

My mother only let me go because she wasn't expecting me to rush forward and stand between Elden and Swiss.

"Violet," Elden growled the second I stepped in front of him, grabbing my shoulders. "Get the fuck behind me."

I stepped out of his grasp.

"No," I hissed, eyes on Swiss who had lowered the gun the second I stepped in front of it. "You're not going to point a gun at him," I snapped. "You are not going to threaten to kill him. You are not going to lay a hand on him."

"You need to move aside right now, Violet," Swiss said in a tone that cooled my blood. "This has nothing to do with you."

I'd never heard him speak like that before. He didn't sound like the man who doted on my mother, who cooed at my brother.

He sounded like a cold-blooded killer.

"Violet, get the fuck behind me," Elden seethed from behind me.

But I didn't move.

"I'm not moving." I widened my stance, arms folded. "This has *everything* to do with me. And I swear to everything I hold dear in this world, including the man behind me, if you hurt him, I will never speak to you again. I will never stay under the same roof as you again. You will not meet this child." My hand went to my flat stomach. "The one I intend on having, by the way."

There was a venom in my voice I didn't recognize, but there was also a promise there. I was willing to do it. To break up my family, to cause my mother pain and suffering if Swiss made the choice first.

And I also knew that he'd rather cut off his own hand than hurt my mother in any way. Even in this almost primal state he seemed to be in.

Silence rang out in the club, and everyone was on tenterhooks, waiting with bated breath. But I wasn't looking at anyone else. I was only looking at Swiss.

His eyes went from me to the man who had now yanked me to his side, tugging at me until he was slightly in front of me. That pissed me off, but it still meant that Swiss wasn't going to discharge his weapon with me so close.

Swiss's eyebrow twitched with fury.

My mother walked toward him and gingerly took the gun from his hand. I was finally able to pull in a full breath of air when he let her. She handed it wordlessly to Hansen.

The tension in the room did not abate even a little, though. Because Swiss was not done.

"You're getting married," Swiss growled.

Both my mother and I gaped at him.

Elden was still in an alpha stare-off.

"You've got to be fucking *kidding* me," I shrieked, not breaking their stares from one another.

"I'm not fucking kidding," Swiss grated out.

I waited for Elden to come to my aid, but again, he was busy with the aforementioned stare-off.

Which was fine; I didn't need anyone to come to my aid.

"You remember *my mom*, right?" I addressed Swiss.

That finally made him break the alpha stare-off. He glanced at my mother, who was still gaping at him, and his eyes softened, but even the crazy love he had for my mother wasn't enough to fully penetrate his alpha fury.

"I'm familiar with her," he grunted.

"Since you're married and in love in a way that I wouldn't have believed unless I witnessed it, I imagine she's told you about her history."

Although his eyes remained fixed on Elden, Swiss's hardened expression softened a bit more. Not completely yet, though, so I pressed on.

"You're doing the nonverbal thing, but I assume you have retained the ability to hear sounds." I leaned forward, glaring, rage shaping my words into pointed, dangerous things. "So, I'll remind you of what happened when my mother got pregnant and was then forced to marry the man who impregnated her."

Swiss froze, and Elden exhaled loudly.

"He wouldn't lay a hand on you," Swiss sneered.

"No," I agreed. "Not unless I wanted him too," I added wickedly, causing Swiss to curse.

Elden rubbed his temples.

"And I did," I continued. "*Want* him to touch me. Which is how I ended up pregnant. Just in case you missed that one health class. And I do… want him." My cheeks flamed. I hadn't intended to go so far, but my fury was paving the way. "But I don't want to marry him." I didn't look at Elden because I didn't want to see disappointment or relief in his expression. I didn't know which one I wanted. All I knew was, in theory, I was very against marriage. I had been before I knew about my father and after.

Marriage did not start off as some wholesome, sweet thing. It never was wholesome or sweet, it just had a great PR team. Marriage was about forcing alliances between families, women used as cattle in transactions that had nothing to do with what they wanted. Because history didn't care much about what women wanted.

I forced myself back to the present. Where I was currently furious at my stepfather for thinking we'd time-traveled back a couple of hundred years.

"I don't want to marry him because my stepfather is *forcing* me to do so," I hissed at him. "The stepfather who is supposed to be all about living life on the fringes of society, about abandoning social norms like forcing a woman to get married because she had the gall to engage in unprotected sex."

"You tell him, girlfriend," Sariah chanted from her spot beside Colby. He was still gripping her arm. She was smiling.

Interesting.

Though I didn't know everything about my best friend, I could be certain that she hadn't witnessed something like this before. But she didn't look shocked or traumatized. The bitch was smiling…

There wasn't time for wonder at that because I wasn't done telling Swiss off.

"We should not have kept this from you for so long," I admitted. "But *I* was the one who wanted to keep it quiet." I pointed to my own chest as I continued to glare. "Although I'm sure you like to think you're pretty special, and I would tend to agree with you when you're not waving a gun at my man and threatening to kill him." My eyes narrowed on Swiss. "Right now, you're not being special. Or kind or funny or anything like the man I know you are. You're acting the *exact* way I thought you would. Like I don't have a mind of my own. Like I don't deserve to choose who I want to be with."

"How about someone who's not almost two decades older than you?" Swiss snarled.

"It's too late for you to argue about whether or not he's age appropriate," I rolled my eyes. "But even if it wasn't, I'm an adult. I'm going to make my own decisions, and I just buried a father who liked to control me and my mother."

Swiss was the one who flinched now. It was a low blow, and maybe he didn't deserve it. But then I remembered the feeling of seeing a gun pointed to Elden's head.

"So, you better make some choices." My voice was no longer loud and passionate. I was tired. Already. And I knew this battle had just begun. "You need to realize that you can pound your chest, wave your weapon and make declarations of violence. But those actions have consequences. And your word is not law. I'm pretty sure this whole fucking club was founded because of your mutual distaste of laws. You may have been founded in a time when women didn't have a voice, didn't have much of a role beyond procreation and pleasure, but it is not that time now." I put my hands on my hips. "I fucking *dare* you to try and tell me what I should do with my life now."

Swiss appraised me for a long time. It hurt, much more than I let on, to see that coldness in his gaze, that disappointment. I hated that although I might've been talking some big talk, I felt very small and vulnerable.

At least I had a good poker face.

Mom was watching me with glassy eyes. I knew she was torn between me and Swiss, trying to gauge who needed her most in that moment. I hated that this was hurting her, that she was in the middle of this conflict. But it wasn't me who chose to turn it into a conflict.

Swiss didn't say anything more. He just stared at me for a beat longer, glared at Elden then stomped out of the room.

Mom looked at me helplessly. "He'll come around, sweetheart."

I rubbed my hands up and down my arms, giving her a weak smile. "You should probably go with him."

Her lip was trapped between her teeth, obviously torn between going to make sure her husband didn't burn anything down and comforting her pregnant, unwed daughter.

"Mom, I'm fine," I lied. "Please go with him so he doesn't do anything stupid."

She nodded, blowing me a kiss before quickly chasing after her husband.

There was a very long, very loaded silence that followed.

"It's official, I *love* it here!" Sariah cheered with glee.

I didn't have the opportunity to respond to her or respond to anyone for that matter because Elden grabbed my arm and dragged me down the hall.

I didn't fight him because I knew doing so would be pointless. He was mad. I expected him to be mad. I'd just stood in front of him and made a whole speech in front of him, a speech for him. For us.

So yes, I expected him to be pissed.

I did not expect him to slam the door to his room closed then sweep everything off his dresser to send it crashing to the ground.

I jumped, my back pressed against the door. I wasn't scared, exactly. But it was unnerving, very unnerving to see him like that. Completely out of control.

"I told you to *stay in this fucking room*!" he roared, turning back to face me.

He was shaking. Literally shaking with rage. I'd never seen him like that. He'd never yelled at me. Not once. He'd gotten pissed. He'd done the growling and glowering thing. He'd manhandled me. But he'd never yelled like that. Never turned into the man standing in front of me.

"It was Sariah," I said quietly, not moving from my spot against the door. "I knew it was Sariah."

"You only knew it was her because you *left this fucking room*," he spat out. He wasn't yelling anymore. Or smashing things. But this was somehow worse.

"It was fine," I argued with him.

Elden stood in the middle of the room, his hands fisted at his sides. "It was not fine, Violet. Because you stepped in front of a gun for me." His voice shook.

"Swiss lowered the gun the second I stepped in front of it."

That was not the right thing to say.

"My *pregnant woman*, instead of staying the fuck in this room like I told her to, instead of believing me when I said I was going to handle it, *stepped in front of a gun*."

It was all too much. All of these men yelling, pointing weapons, smashing things, telling me what I could and couldn't do. Thinking that protecting me meant taking away my agency, locking me in rooms.

"Yes, I stepped in front of a gun for *you*!" I screamed. "I stepped in front of a gun for you because you were calmly standing there, declaring your love for me like you were saying goodbye to me." I stepped forward so I was right in his face. "I am not letting you say goodbye to me. I am not letting you take a bullet for me. I am not doing this alone." I was screaming so loud now that my throat ached. "You are with me. I'm not a girl, I'm a *woman*. One who is not going to cower in a room while you might be in danger. I am not going to stand back and watch as someone waves a gun in front of your face. I am not an instrument in your story, that you save. I will save you. Whenever I need to, as much as I can, so I do not have to live life alone."

My chest was heaving at this point, and there were black spots dancing in my vision from how loud I was yelling. I didn't feel at all like myself. I wasn't myself. Screaming at people wasn't really my thing.

But in for a penny, in for a pound.

"You want to smash things?" I asked, not registering that Elden was no longer scary broody, he was just plain broody.

"Fine, we'll both smash things!" I yelled, looking for something and focusing on the lamp, picking it up and throwing it across the room. Well, I tried to. It was still attached to the wall, so it landed on the bed disappointingly. So, I pushed the nightstand itself over.

That crashed satisfyingly to the ground. Unfortunately, it took my coffee with it.

"There," I declared, breathing heavily. "Now we've both smashed things." I stepped forward, glaring at him. "Don't *ever* yell at me like that again," I whispered. My voice was much shakier than I intended it to be, and all broodiness left Elden's face. But it was too late. "Don't you *ever* think that because you're angry you get to scream at me and smash things," I added, tears streaming down my face. I wiped them away angrily.

Elden stepped forward, face stricken.

I held my hand up. "Don't come near me."

Elden stopped in his tracks. "Violet," he murmured brokenly. His voice was full of apology. But it was too late.

I slammed the door closed when I left the room.

Sariah was waiting at the end of the hall looking concerned.

"I was waiting to see if the yelling and the smashing continued and I needed to come in to save you," she explained. "I was also prepared for the yelling and smashing to stop and the makeup sex to commence." She winced, looking at my face which was likely blotchy and tearstained.

She then scowled at the door. "Do I need to kill him?" she offered hopefully. "I know you just totally told off your stepdad for attempting to do that, but that was for him forgetting women got the vote and the right to make their own decisions quite some time ago." Her gaze was hard at the door. "My offer comes from a place of womanly rage at a man for yelling at my pregnant bestie."

"I need to get far away from here," I said quietly, my throat sore from yelling, and I was also afraid that if I spoke any louder, I was going to burst into tears.

Sariah nodded, linking her arm in mine. "Let's get the fuck out of here, then."

We ended up in the next town over at a kitschy diner that made great malts and greasy eggs that I did not throw up in the bathroom, which I counted as a win.

My phone had been on the ill-fated nightstand, so no one could call me or track it, as I assumed Elden tried doing.

Sariah did not talk about the yelling match, which I was thankful about because I was not ready to talk about it.

I knew it came from somewhere unrelated to the events of today. It was triggered by them, sure. But it had been a fear response. One that had to do with my father. And I really, *really* did not want to unpack all of that right now.

Sariah, the angel that she was, kept me distracted.

"Okay, so I've been keeping up with the news in Garnett, because I'm officially enchanted by the way that town works," Sariah said, sucking on her own milkshake.

"It seems to be glossed over by capitalist America, no big box stores, just family-owned businesses on Main Street. No gross developments like chain hotels or whatever, even though there's a seriously fancy celebrity retreat not far away and *really* good yoga studios," she waggled her eyebrows. "Then there's this *thing* at the center of the town. An outlaw motorcycle club that has endured throughout the years, without getting broken up by law enforcement even though they are definitely breaking a dozen laws, not to mention the laws of nature… How can that many hot guys exist in one place?"

She was really on a roll now, eyes bright with excitement.

"The club's history itself is fascinating," she continued, speaking enthusiastically. "Someone should write a book about it. Not just the history but the love stories. From what you've told me, they could make movies… Netflix would eat that shit up." She tried sucking on the milkshake, but there was none left, so she frowned at the glass.

"Anyway, that's not even what I'm talking about. I'm talking about how there have been three murders so far in the area."

I startled at the direction the conversation had taken.

I knew about the murders in the area. They'd been the talk of the town. The men in the club had been more protective over their wives than normal. Elden had told me not to walk anywhere alone late at night. Though I fucking hated it, that little survival tactic had been drilled into me long before these killings started.

Don't walk home alone late at night.

Don't run with earbuds in.

Never take the same route.

Don't leave your drink alone.

Be careful how you say no to a man.

Be careful how you break up with a man.

The list of how we avoided getting raped and murdered was endless.

When in reality there should be one item on one list for men.

Don't rape and murder women.

Apparently, that was much too difficult, and men couldn't be expected to follow that singular rule, so women had to change everything about their behavior and routines.

"Now, considering that there is an outlaw club operating in the area, the crime rate around here is actually pretty low," Sariah continued. "Apart from the big massacre that apparently happened a few Christmases ago," her lips curled downward. "That was *dark*." She held out her coffee mug to the passing waitress, thanking her.

I gratefully accepted a refill too, thinking fondly of the coffee that had gone flying with the nightstand that made diner coffee seem like the dirty water it really was.

"Anyway, the women in question aren't actually from your town," Sariah continued. "They were all found outside town limits. Naked. Posed. And stabbed at least fifty times." "Thank you," she addressed the waitress who had gone a little pale at Sariah's mention of dead bodies.

"Anyway," she focused back on me. "They were all sex workers. Who, unfortunately, are commonly victims of serial killers, and the police don't treat their lives with the reverence they deserve." She shook her head in anger.

I agreed with her on that one.

"We should start a podcast about it," Sariah suggested thrumming her hands together.

It did not surprise me that Sariah knew all the details of these murders. She was a child of this generation, and we were all obsessed with serial killers. Well, not *we* because I did not share that same fascination. I had nightmares every time she made me watch those true crime shows with her.

It did surprise me, however, that she was proposing this at all, especially right now, considering everything going on.

"We are not starting a podcast," I told her.

She pouted at me. "Why not?"

"Because everyone and their dog has a podcast these days," I pointed out the obvious. There were a lot of other reasons too, like us being in college, me being pregnant and having just split my family in two.

"No, every toxic white guy has a podcast," she argued. "They've ruined the medium for everyone."

She wasn't entirely wrong, although I still loved podcasts when I had the time to listen to them.

"No one, not even the cops, have caught on yet," Sariah whined. "Partly because they're still a part of a patriarchal institution that looks down on sex workers and also because all of the cops around here seem to be idiots. Except for the new sheriff in Garnett who is actually quite well regarded, but it seems like he's more focused on the Sons of Templar."

I stared at her. "He's focused on the Sons of Templar," I repeated, suddenly worried.

She nodded, sipping her coffee. "I wouldn't worry," she waved her free hand at me dismissively. "They don't have anything that isn't like a decade old."

My stomach twisted. "How do you know what they do and don't have?" I asked her carefully.

She looked sheepish.

"Sariah…"

"Ollie might've hacked into their system," she confessed, hiding behind her cup.

"You made Ollie hack into a law enforcement system?" I yelled at her.

"She offered."

"She did not offer," I countered.

"Well, I may have asked her," she grimaced. "But she was more than happy to do it."

I rubbed my temples. Here I was, thinking that Sariah was getting better when really she was convincing our roommate to commit federal crimes.

"I think we should investigate at the very least," Sariah continued, inspecting her nails.

"Is that why you came here?" I asked her. "Because you want to start a podcast?"

She looked shocked and offended. "No, I came here because my best friend is knocked up, and I figured she needed moral support." Her features smoothed and her lips relaxed as she reached across the table to squeeze my hand. "The serial killer thing is just like... a bonus."

"Women are dead, Sariah," I scowled.

Her expression was somber. "I know. And I can't change that. But maybe we can make enough noise to make sure that they take this serious enough, and no more women die."

Her eyes shone with passion, with desperation. My heart hurt for her.

"How long are you staying for?" I changed the subject.

Her eyes lit up even more. "Until we go back to school?" she asked hopefully. "As long as your mom and Swiss don't mind me staying." She looked out the window, probably thinking about this morning's scene. "I could always bunk at the clubhouse," she said thoughtfully, a wicked and familiar glint in her eye.

"Mom and Swiss would be happy to have you," I replied quickly. The last thing Sariah needed was to be tangled up with an alpha badass right now.

"You'll be a good buffer," I decided.

"You're not going to be staying at the club?" she asked tentatively.

I toyed with my straw, even though my milkshake was long gone. I thought about the way Elden had yelled at me. Then the horror on his face once he'd realized what he'd done.

I wondered if my father wore that same horrified expression after the first time he hit my mother.

It was cruel of me to be comparing the two. Especially considering Elden had a gun pointed to his head in the moments before that outburst, but I couldn't help it. I couldn't trust my feelings right now. My heart.

"I don't know," I sighed.

Sariah stared at me for a long time. "He's not your father, Violet," she said softly.

I fought against the burn in my throat that came with her words, and even though it was my first instinct to tell her I knew that, I couldn't get the words out.

"Sometimes men yell," she shrugged. "Because they don't know how to properly express their emotions. Because they're really just toddlers. Because they're scared. And I will say, I don't know that man very well, but he stood in front of a gun declaring how much he loved you."

My heart rattled at the mere memory.

"It is still not okay for him to yell at you like he did, though," she added, eyes brimming with passion. "And he owes you an apology centered around a nice purse or multiple orgasms," she winked. "He's not your father," she squeezed my hand.

I nodded, hearing her words. Knowing that they were technically true, but my heart couldn't trust them.

Couldn't trust him.

Because even though my father was buried, I didn't know when he'd stop haunting me.

If he'd ever stop haunting me.

CHAPTER
Twenty

I WAS nervous walking through the door of Mom and Swiss's house. I hated that. That I almost felt the way I used to feel, walking into my old house in Carver Springs. Tense... holding my breath for something I didn't even completely understand.

It wasn't until I walked into the little house my mom lived in before moving here that it became clear that I'd never been in a *home* before. I grieved and celebrated that. It sucked that I didn't get that growing up, but it would've sucked a whole lot more if my mother had never found the strength to leave, had never been able to create what she did.

I had to be thankful for that. For her protecting me from the truth for as long as she did.

"You're back!" Mom yelled, pouncing on me the second the front door closed behind us.

"I was worried sick," she said into my hair. "Everyone was. You left your phone at the club. I'm so sorry, sweetie," she said, squeezing my upper arms. "I knew that there was never going to be a good way for that news to come out, and I really thought if I caught him when he was soft and agreeable, he wouldn't go all…" she trailed off.

"Crazy homicidal biker?" Sariah offered cheerfully from behind me.

Mom nodded, not at all surprised to see that my best friend had traveled to Garnett to be here for me. "Yeah, but I should've known better," she sighed. "I really do apologize that that was your first impression of the club, honey," she told Sariah. "We are a little bit crazy but not usually brandishing a deadly weapon kind of crazy."

Sariah shrugged. "You've got absolutely nothing to apologize for. I was worried that Violet was exaggerating about the club, and it turns out she was downplaying it," she giggled.

Mom's concerned eyes moved back to me. "Are you okay?" she asked, looking me over.

"Mom, I'm fine," I reassured her. "I'm annoyed at all of the people with an XY chromosome and a Sons of Templar cut within a fifty-mile radius, but other than that, I'm good."

"I'm not exactly thrilled with them either," Mom's brows pinched together. "But no one was expecting the news that you're not only pregnant but in love… Especially since you had been very adamant about avoiding both of those things."

"Are you disappointed in me?" I asked, peering up at her from below my lashes.

"Of course, I'm not." Her face fell. "No. I'm shocked. I'm worried in a way that a mother worries. I'm trying to recalibrate. I'm also trying to compute that I'm going to be a grandmother *and* the mother of a toddler." She scrunched up her nose. "But I'm not disappointed. No way, no how."

"Okay." I exhaled a relieved breath.

"Now," Mom clapped her hands together. "Swiss is away brooding somewhere, and if he has any sense he'll only come back here with chocolate and apologies. So, let's have a girls' night."

A small person came running in and attached himself to Sariah's ankle.

"As long as you don't mind one boy crashing the party," my mother amended.

Sariah picked him up, blowing a raspberry on his stomach as he squealed in delight.

"He can always crash the party," I said, looking to my little brother while trying to process that he would have a little playmate in eight months.

Instead of thinking too hard about that, I focused on my baby brother and our girls' night. Or at least, I did my best.

Sariah and my mother had a lot of fun that night. My mother cooked up a storm, dancing around the kitchen, trying to overcompensate for the events of the morning, I guessed.

Also, because her and Sariah could drink wine. They had two bottles. The bitches.

I was sipping on seltzer water, both hating and loving seeing my best friend and my mother getting along so wildly.

Mom had already started talking about building an addition onto the house for the baby, as if it were obvious that the baby and I would live there. I didn't have the energy to dispute that because I didn't even know where we were going to live.

Elden and Swiss were topics we avoided.

I retired to my bedroom earlier than either of them, tired, overwhelmed and confused. Both of them understood me well enough to know I needed that.

Or at least I *thought* I needed that.

I took a long shower. Did an elaborate skincare routine. Put on washed cotton PJs. Brushed my hair exactly one hundred times. Curled into fresh sheets with my latest spicy fantasy read.

It was the recipe for a comforting night, a cure all for the ills of this world, disappearing into another one where the woman was the hero, and the male character was written by a woman.

It should've been.

Except I reread the same page about fifty times. My mind was running over the events of the day. The way Elden had looked at me, utterly devastated, disgusted in himself.

The things he'd said to Swiss and everyone else in the common room at the club.

The way Swiss had looked at him. The unfiltered hatred in that gaze.

Then I stopped thinking of the past and started wondering about the future. What did that look like? Was I going to join the ranks of Old Ladies? Their lives seemed so wonderful... So unique, so outside of what was expected.

But that would mean abandoning the dreams I had for myself.

My hand was on my stomach the entire time I ruminated on this, working myself further into a spiral.

There was a knock at the door, and I looked up to see Swiss standing there hesitantly, holding a plate.

"I brought cookies," he held them up as if they were a white flag.

"You may enter," I replied, putting the book down.

His boots thumped as he entered the room I had made my own since they moved in. I had my own patio, my own bathroom complete with a tub, and the floor to ceiling bookshelves in a nook by the window were bursting with books.

Nothing from our house in Carver Springs had come here. All of that was tainted.

I watched Swiss as he gingerly handed me the plate of cookies.

"I'm sorry," he said, sitting down on the end of my bed. "I was an over the top, protective asshole."

I tilted my head as I nibbled on a cookie. "Did my mom tell you to say that?"

The corners of his mouth turned up. "No, but that was one of the many things she called me when she told me off."

My mom told Swiss off. That didn't surprise me. She never

hesitated to snap at him for being too protective, too alpha. They spent almost her entire pregnancy arguing over whether or not she could work at the restaurant.

Mom won all of those arguments.

I'd never seen my mother tell my father off. She hadn't dared argue with him.

Mom was safe enough, comfortable enough to have a voice, raise it if she wished.

We both were. I'd yelled plenty at this man earlier today, in front of his brothers, his president. Many men, lesser men, would not come in here looking sheepish or carrying cookies.

But the Sons of Templar men were an anomaly. Alphas. Possessive. Deadly. Soft. Kind. Loving. Feminists in their own, warped way.

Swiss let out a long sigh. "I know you don't have exactly have fond feelings toward the inner workings of the club and the things we consider sacred."

I didn't reply because I didn't need to. I'd made my feelings rather clear earlier.

"When I met your mom, I knew she was mine," he continued. "The second I laid eyes on her. And I need to make something clear… I don't mean she was mine to own. She was mine to earn. To treasure. Protect. And again, I know you've got feelings about whether or not women need to be protected," he pointed out, telling me he'd heard me when I'd yelled at him. "And fuck, maybe we are all just cavemen," he showed me his palms. "But not because we don't respect you. But because we do. Because we all understand what kind of woman it takes to live this life, to love us, fucked-up as we are. And maybe we're a little intense about it."

"A little?" I repeated.

"A fuck of a lot," he sighed again. "But that's 'cause life has taken a lot from all of us. We're all just waiting, prepared for it to take another thing." He sucked in a deep breath. "I consider you my daughter, if not in blood, in everything else that matters. Your future, your health, your happiness, it's something that I consider my job to ensure. It's any father's job to want that for their little girl."

Though his words punctured me somewhere soft and vulnerable, I opened my mouth to correct some of them.

"And you're not a little girl," he added before I could speak. "You're a young woman. One who is more than strong enough to stand up for herself, for others, to yell and swear and pretty much do anything else she puts her mind to," his eyes twinkled. "You're a woman who knows what she wants and takes it. I'm very proud of that, even if it had nothin' to do with me and everythin' to do with your mother."

He studied me, rubbing at his chin. "I'm excited to be a grandfather," he said finally. "Thought I'd like to be a little older," he shrugged. "Thought I'd be walking you down the aisle before that happened. Thought you'd give me some gray hairs before you settled down, if you ever did."

I grinned at his bald head.

"I feel betrayed," he continued in a more serious tone. "Not by you, but by a man I consider a brother. And I get that you're no one's property, that you made choices on your own. Not asking you to understand or even respect how things work here, but I'm telling you I'm an old dog. I'm trying my best to learn new tricks, but I can't promise I'm not gonna bare my teeth, draw some blood along the way."

I leaned toward him, giving him a pointed glare. "You're not to draw his blood."

"Can promise not to use any weapons," he offered. "But, honey, I'm gonna have to at least punch him in order to move forward. We don't really do cocktails and long conversations. We fight shit out."

"You know that's fucking insane," I threw my hands up.

He nodded. "Maybe. But that's the world you've got yourself into. You're smart enough to understand that."

"Maybe," I chewed on the inside of my cheek. "But I'm not going to like it."

He grinned and leaned toward me, kissing my head. "Maybe this next generation will be a little more peaceful."

A crash and a shriek of delight sounded from somewhere in the house.

We both looked in the direction where my baby brother was likely smashing something for the joy it brought him.

"Or maybe not," he countered with a wink, standing and walking out of the room.

"Swiss," I called when he was almost gone.

"Yeah, baby doll?" he asked, turning.

"Please don't hate him," I requested quietly.

He looked down at his boots, jaw set. "Don't hate him, Violet. Just love you a fuck of a lot."

"I love you too," I whispered, my throat thick with tears.

He smiled at me and closed the door, leaving me with my thoughts.

Swiss was not my last visitor that night.

I was halfway through the plate of cookies and still on the same page of my book when the door to my patio quietly opened and closed.

The dark shape entering my room did not scare me.

I'd been hoping he'd come, even though I hadn't made peace with him yet. Even though I hadn't found a way to bury my father and his influence properly.

He didn't come to me right away. He stood there, half illuminated by my lamp, half in shadow, staring.

Even now, after everything, I was still uncomfortable under his gaze. Not in a bad way. In the way that I was reminded that no one had ever looked at me like Elden did. No one saw me like he did.

I was frozen in place as he stared then eventually crossed the distance between us to sit on my bed.

"You're brave to break into the house of the man who pointed a gun at your head today," I commented, unable to think of anything else to say.

Though it was the truth. Swiss had promised he wasn't going to kill Elden, but that promise was fresh, raw.

Elden did not respond to that. He kept staring at me with that tortured devastation on his face. "I'm sorry," he finally said, trailing the back of his knuckles down my face.

I waited for more. For the 'but'. Nothing came.

"You're sorry," I eventually questioned, puncturing the silence that had felt like it would suffocate me.

"I'm *very* sorry," he repeated, his tone serious.

I swallowed my smile. Even though today was heavy, very heavy indeed, it was quite something seeing Elden look so sincere and apologetic. But there was something else too.

"You're not adding any amendments?" I asked him.

A crease formed between his brows. "The point of an apology is to not add amendments."

"I received two apologies today," I informed him. "From two different men."

Elden's gaze remained intense but stony now. "You deserve two different apologies from two different men."

I swallowed hard. "I've never been apologized to by a man who was important to me before," I said in a small voice. "I know for a fact that my father never uttered the words 'I'm sorry' to me. Even though he definitely did things worth apologizing for, and that's not counting all the things he did to my mother."

The words burned like acid.

Elden's expression was tight, his back ramrod straight and his eyes squinting with anger. "Hate that you haven't experienced what it's like to be loved by a real man. Real men apologize, Violet. Without amendments, without excuses. And although he did indeed hold a gun to my head earlier today, I'm glad as fuck that for the rest of your life, you will have a father who is unafraid to apologize to you when he fucks up. Ready to go to battle for you and then back down when you battle him right back."

He smiled sadly, his hand moving down to my stomach.

The stomach that skipped at his featherlight touch, his reverent gaze.

"And if we have a girl, we're gonna have one who isn't afraid to go to battle with her father if he steps a foot out of line." His eyes blazed with intensity. "I'm gonna do everything in my power to ensure I don't step a foot out of line in our daughter's eyes. And if I do, I'm gonna show her what a real man does, how they apologize. And, Violet, I'm gonna try really fucking hard to fix what your father broke." His hand cradled my jaw. "For as long as I live, I never want you to look at me the way you did today."

My breath hitched.

He wiped a tear that had escaped the corner of my eye. "I'm not good at this," he admitted. "The second I became a free man, I swore that I would always be in control. So I'd never feel the way I did while locked up in there. But with you, I have no control. None. Don't want to control you because you're wild, beautiful, brave, infuriating and perfect the way you are. So, I can't promise I'm not gonna get pissed at things I shouldn't get pissed at. Can't promise I'm not gonna spend the rest of my life wanting to protect you. But I can promise you that I will never fucking hurt you. You are safe with me, Violet."

He let the words sink in for a moment, or maybe he was waiting for me to say something.

I'd lost the ability to form words.

"I know it's just words," he continued. "But I'm gonna prove that to you, Violet. That you're safe."

"I know I am," I whispered. My hand covered his on top of my stomach. "I know we both are."

We lingered for a long time before Elden tore his gaze from me.

His eyes landed first on the cookies then on the book I'd long abandoned.

He slipped his hand away to pick up the book and skim through it.

I watched his mouth and eyebrows twitch as he likely arrived at particularly spicy scenes in the book.

His cheeks were even flushed by the time he set the book back down.

Elden's cheeks were flushed.

"*This* is what you've been reading without me?" he asked in a low rumble.

I swallowed my smile, my own cheeks warm. "I enjoy magic, dragons and smut," I shrugged. "Don't try to shame me for that."

"I would never shame you for that," Elden replied, voice gravelly. "You read this for as long as you want. When you're finished, I'll fuck you better than any book hero can."

I cocked my hip. "Is that a promise?"

"I'll put it in my vows if you want," he replied.

There it was. Cold water on the moment.

Elden must've seen my face fall, softly adding, "Not gonna rush you. I understand your thoughts on marriage. Respect them. But I hope one day I can convince you to be my wife. Can prove that marrying me doesn't have to look like anything you've ever seen. Doesn't have to be something that holds you back. But for now..." He scooped me up and out of the bed.

I let out a squeal, not expecting that.

"We need to get the fuck out of this house," Elden groaned. "Because I need to fuck you. And that will not be happening under this roof."

I agreed with him on all of that.

The topic of marriage was not revisited that night. Or the one after that. But it hovered like a shadow, following me around, making me feel cold no matter how bright the New Mexico sun shined.

CHAPTER
Twenty-One

ELDEN and I did not have to wait long for another argument.

I had a shift at Oliver's the next day.

Which was what I told him when I woke up, asking for a ride back to Mom and Swiss's in order to get changed.

First, he'd pulled me back into bed and fucked me.

I hadn't argued about that.

Then he'd said we needed to get my clothes, skincare and 'smutty books' from my mom and Swiss's and move them to his room at the clubhouse.

I hadn't argued about that either.

As much as I loved the atmosphere at Mom and Swiss's, as much as I loved the space my mother had created, it didn't fit me. Not now that Elden was a part of me. Which he was. There was no denying that. There was a lot to work out. A lot. But that was not something that would ever change.

The argument started at Oliver's. We went there after we picked up something for me to wear for the day. I settled on tight black jeans—may as well enjoy them while I could—and a cropped black tee with the leather jacket Swiss got me for my birthday.

Elden did not come into my mom and Swiss's house. He sat on the bike, looking like sex and sin.

Swiss stood in the kitchen, glaring in the direction of the rumbling bike. He did not go out onto the driveway to challenge Elden to a duel, so I called that a win.

"Thank God you're here!" Julian shouted at me the second we walked through the door. "Get your ass to the coffee machine."

I was about to do what Julian so politely asked when Elden grasped my waist and pulled me to him.

It felt exceptionally strange, him touching me like this in public. Good strange. Or it would've been had Elden not been glowering at me.

"It's okay, honey," I reassured him. "He's really sweet, and he's Australian… That's just his way. I know you're under the impression that you're the only man who can order me around, but he actually *can* order me around because he's paying me. If you start paying me… No, that wouldn't work because that would move to an ethical gray area." I shook my head. "Anyway, he doesn't mean any harm."

"I know he doesn't mean harm," Elden bit out. "I want to know *what* he means."

I tilted my head in confusion. "He means he wants me to get my ass to the coffee machine," I clarified, even though he'd made that pretty clear. I gestured to the long line of people waiting for coffee. "Or they might start getting violent."

People took their coffee very seriously here. Which you could only understand once you tasted what real coffee was meant to taste like.

"You are not working," Elden replied through his teeth.

I frowned at him. "Uh, yeah, I am."

"You're pregnant."

I blew a strand of hair from my eyes. "I'm aware."

"Your morning sickness is getting worse." There was no denying the concern in Elden's tone.

My stomach lurched as if on cue. "Of that I am also aware."

"You're not standing on your feet all day when you're pregnant and sick."

"I am working because I made a commitment to Julian, because I enjoy it and because there are millions of pregnant women at this very moment, managing to stand all day and exist in general," I refuted.

"Violet," Elden warned.

"Elden," I warned right back.

We had a very long stare off.

Elden was probably used to winning those kinds of stare offs because he was a badass, irritable, dangerous guy, and any regular person would not just break the stare off but likely go off running.

I was not a regular person. Not since I met Elden.

"I could stand here all day," I informed him.

"You bloody can't stand there all day," Julian chimed in.

"I can't promise the coffee deprived customers won't drag you out," I told Elden, ignoring Julian for the time being.

Elden's eyes had a hard glint, but he let out a very frustrated sigh.

I smiled wide in triumph. I might've even done a little dance if not for the morning sickness and the alpha male yanking me in for a publicly inappropriate kiss.

Julian whistled.

Or I think he did. I was in a vortex. On an alternate plane where only we existed.

"I'll be here to pick you up at three," Elden murmured against my lips.

"I'm scheduled to work till five," I argued.

"I'll be here at three." Elden's jaw was granite.

I swallowed my grin. "Okay."

Elden gave me one more hard look, kissed my nose then dragged me—lovingly—toward the counter.

The previously hostile customers parted for Elden. They were coffee deprived, not insane.

"She is not to lift anything heavy," Elden barked at Julian.

Julian, to his credit, did not even bat an eyelash at the hostile biker barking orders at him in his place of business.

"Ten-four, big boy," he saluted.

Elden narrowed his eyes. "She gets regular breaks. And make sure she eats something."

"*She* is standing right here," I smacked Elden's arm. "*She* can also speak for herself, and by golly, she can feed herself."

Elden looked sideways at me. "Did you just say 'by golly?'"

I jutted my chin up. "I thought something from your generation might sink in better."

He shook his head, chuckling.

Though I was currently irritated with him, I couldn't help but revel in the chuckle.

Elden gave me a firm kiss, closed mouth. "See you at three, baby."

My irritation melted to nothing. "Yeah," I murmured back.

He held on to me for a moment longer, staring at me like there wasn't a line of people behind us. Like he had all the time in the world just to look at me.

Then finally, he walked off. I, along with the entire café, watched him. The difference between me and everyone else in the café was that I was entitled to stare dreamily after him because he was mine.

"Violet!" Julian snapped me out of my trance. "Stop with the lovey eyes, and make some fuckin' coffee!"

THREE DAYS LATER

ELDEN

When everyone sat down, the air was tense. Very fucking tense. Swiss and I had not been in the same room since he pulled his piece on me.

Violet said he apologized to her for that, which was all that mattered to me. He didn't owe me an apology. I sure as shit owed him one. But I didn't think he'd be amenable to anything I had to say at that point.

Yes, he'd promised Violet he wouldn't kill me, and he'd kept that promise. No need to make him reevaluate that.

Not yet, at least.

Plus, there were a lot of ways not to kill someone and make them want to die, and Swiss was an expert in such things.

"We're designed for conflict," Hansen said as his eyes skimmed over the men sitting at the table. "Bred for it. It's going to be a part of this club and a part of our lives till we meet the reaper." His gaze found me then Swiss. "But I will not have it tear this club apart from the inside out." His voice raised an octave, hardening. "That's how charters get destroyed. That's how people die. If you don't believe your brother has your back, you slip. I'm not burying another friend." His thumped his chest. "I'm not telling an Old Lady her man died 'cause he was too fuckin' stubborn to squash a beef. So this is gonna end."

His chair screeched as he stood up.

"You two." He pointed to me and Swiss. "Outside. Now."

I stood immediately.

Swiss remained seated. "I'm not gonna fight him." There was no denying the bite in his tone.

"You sure as shit aren't gonna open your heart to him over Cosmos," Hansen's expression contorted into one he didn't often wear. One of authority that he rarely had to wield with us. "Up. Now."

Swiss considered it for a split second then stood.

"Weapons on the table," Hansen ordered.

I put my piece and the knife at my belt on the table. Swiss did the same, slower than me, though.

Colby clapped me on the shoulder as we made our way outside. "Your Old Lady's gonna be pissed about this."

My step stuttered. Though I'd considered Violet mine for years now, no one had ever called her my Old Lady out loud. She wouldn't like the term, despite the importance of it. She definitely didn't like the term 'wife' either, if the way the blood drained from her face when I mentioned it meant anything.

She was skittish about commitment. Rightfully so. If only her father wasn't dead so I could kill him with my bare hands.

I had to keep reminding myself that titles didn't mean shit. She was mine. With or without a ring or a piece of paper.

But fuck if I didn't want her wearing my ring, walking down an aisle to meet me. To be mine in the eyes of the law, something I hadn't respected in a long time.

Swiss and I shrugged off our cuts, him giving his to Hades, me giving mine to Colby.

We circled each other, neither of us moving toward the other.

"I'm gonna be in your life forever," I informed him. "Because I'm gonna be in *her* life forever."

He locked his jaw. "Don't remind me."

Swiss was my friend. My brother. He was a good man. So, it fucked with me to have him stare at me like he'd be happy to see me bleeding out on the pavement.

"I'll take care of her," I vowed. "I love her."

Swiss continued to glower at me. "You hurt her, you let any hurt come to her, I'll forget some promises I made."

I raised my chin in confirmation.

"Okay, let's do this," I said, loosening my shoulders. He was entitled to land the first punch. I'd betrayed him after all.

Swiss didn't hesitate, his fist connecting with my face.

He did not hold back.

VIOLET

Elden came to pick me up from my shift, as always. I was not alone in the café for even a second, and despite my shift ending before it got dark and my ability to park right across the street, Elden would not hear of me driving to and from. No one had caught the serial killer Sariah still believed we needed to start a podcast about, even though she'd already gone back to Providence.

I'd tried to dissuade her, but she was not a woman to be dissuaded.

I had a bad feeling about it. But maybe that was because finally, for the first time in a while, there were no secrets, conflicts or tragedies in my life, and I was uncomfortable, so I was trying to create them.

Not that a serial killer wasn't a definite source of conflict and terror, it totally was. And someone really should've been investigating to make sure those women weren't forgotten, but I just didn't think we should be dragging ourselves into that. Not when we'd achieved a somewhat tentative peace.

I should've known better than to think my life was free of conflict when I was involved with the Sons of Templar.

Elden sauntered into the café like usual.

All eyes turned to him, as usual.

Including mine.

My heart did that little flutter like it always did when I saw him.

Except he looked a bit different than he did when he'd dropped me off this morning. I hung up my apron and rounded the counter, arriving in front of it at the same time as him.

He didn't hesitate to greet me the same way he did every day, yanking our bodies flush together and kissing me in a way that wasn't fit for public consumption.

As he always did, Julian called out, "Get a room before all my customers think they can do that in here!"

He was always smiling when he said it, and he had not seemed at all surprised about Elden and I being together or me being pregnant.

Nothing much surprised Julian.

Because I was not yet immune to Elden and his badass powers, I kissed him back without commenting on the change in his appearance.

But I managed to pull back enough to inspect his face up close.

"You have a black eye," I glared at the bruise.

"It's not black yet, a little red maybe," he shrugged.

"You have a cut on your cheek," I sucked my teeth.

"A scratch," Elden corrected.

"What happened?" I demanded, putting my hands on my hips.

"We're not gonna talk about it here."

I rooted myself to my spot. "We are going to talk right here, right now."

He considered me, as if he were assessing how serious I was. "This needed to happen."

"You and my stepfather?" I deduced.

He nodded.

"Men!" I threw up my hands. "Are you all like this?" I looked to Julian.

"We're definitely not all like *that*." He motioned to Elden.

I tried not to smile.

Elden's fingers went to my chin, gently turning me to face him.

"Like it or not, this is the first step to things getting close to sorted between us."

"I don't like it," I muttered.

Elden flashed me his teeth.

"Not fair," I whined. "You can't just smile at me and win every argument."

Elden chuckled.

"Now he *chuckles*!" I groaned. "I'm powerless against you."

"Ditto, baby," he murmured against my mouth.

"Out of here!" Julian demanded. "Before you get pregnant all over again."

It was my turn to chuckle as we did what Julian asked.

And although it was biologically impossible, when we made it back to the club, Elden did his best to get me pregnant all over again.

I went back to school because even though I was questioning what I really wanted out of my future, I knew I didn't want to drop out. I wanted to close this chapter, whatever that meant.

Elden came with me.

Not something I'd expected.

"You have a life here," I'd argued when he started packing his bag the day before I was scheduled to leave.

"I have a life *here*," he countered, placing his hand on my stomach. "Here," he whispered, love shining in his eyes.

My heart skipped about a million beats as it did when he got all soft and romantic.

"What are you going to do every day?" I asked. "I don't think there are many pastimes for biker badasses on campus."

"Rhode Island charter needs an extra hand," he explained. "I'll keep myself busy."

I chewed on my lip. Although I had a pretty wild imagination, I had yet to ask what Elden actually did on a day-to-day basis. I knew that he worked part-time in the garage. I knew that because he'd come back to our room wearing coveralls, rolled back halfway to show off his incredible torso, grease on his cheek. I'd all but pounced on him every time.

I also knew the club owned a bar, did a lot of charity drives. But they weren't called 'outlaws' because it sounded cool. Although it really did.

"Ask me," Elden said.

I stared at him.

"Ask me what the club does," he clarified. "Know you want to. Know it's probably been driving you crazy."

It had been. But I'd been doing *really* well with not thinking about it. Mainly because I had a lot of other things on my mind the past two years. "I don't know if I want to know," I admitted. "I mean, secrets were the foundation of the first eighteen years of my life, so I certainly don't want more of them. But I know the things you do are in direct opposition to a lot of the things I believe."

"Like what?"

"Well, you're involved in a club that blatantly excludes women for a start."

Elden's eyes lit up. "You've made your feelings about that known since the moment you arrived here."

"And I won't give up on the crusade to let women patch in," I informed him. "Especially if we have a daughter."

Elden's hand went to my stomach, as it tended to do a lot these days. "I expect nothing less."

I stared into the eyes of the man I loved. The father of my baby. "What is the club involved in?" I whispered.

"We run guns," he answered without hesitation. "On occasion, we provide protection. Don't kill for hire. Have legitimate businesses too. Garage earns enough. As does the bar. But majority of the club's capital comes from—"

"Running guns," I finished for him.

He nodded.

"I'm for gun control," I informed him.

"I'm aware," he replied evenly.

"I've protested about it."

"I'm also aware."

I scratched my cheek. "Does the club have any plans to… I don't know, go legit or whatever?" I knew there were plenty of motorcycle clubs around the country that didn't break the law. The term one percenter existed for a reason. The other 99 percent of motorcyclists were law abiding citizens, according to the American Motorcyclist Association.

Elden's lips flattened into a thin line. "Not that I know of."

I regarded him. "Can't you make that happen?"

"Above my pay grade, baby," he shook his head, stroking my jaw.

I considered this. The club ran guns. It shouldn't have been a surprise. They were an outlaw motorcycle club. The outlaw part communicated the fact that they lived outside the law. They had really nice appliances, they had top shelf booze, an impressive compound, fancy motorcycles, and each member who owned a house owned a really kickass house.

They earned good money from their various criminal and noncriminal enterprises.

Those enterprises were also responsible for almost the entire club getting murdered one Christmas.

An icy chill slithered over my skin.

I clutched at Elden's cut. "You're not allowed to die."

His eyes crinkled at the corners, gaze turning hard. "I don't plan on it, Violet."

"Of course, you don't *plan* on it," I frowned. "But you're involved in things that put you in danger on a daily basis. I know you're tough and strong and badass, but as far as I know, you're not bulletproof. And you run guns. Which contain bullets. Which likely pisses off rival people who are in possession of guns. With bullets."

"Take a breath, baby," Elden pressed the palm of his hand against my cheek.

I scowled at him, though I had been ready to rant much longer without breathing and might've passed out.

"And you're breaking the law," I added once said breath was had.

"Aware of that," he murmured.

"You're breaking the law, and the new sheriff is intent on bringing down the Sons of Templar," I babbled. "He wants to put you in prison again. You don't like small places. I'm not going to let you go to prison again."

A vein pulsated in his forehead. "How do you know the new sheriff is targeting the club?"

"Ollie hacked the department's computers," I replied, too deep in my spiral to worry about the change in Elden's tone.

I was not too deep to see his reaction to my words, though. His body stiffened, and he got all broody and dangerous once more, looking at me through heavy lids.

"Ollie, your roommate hacked into police computers?" he repeated.

Now I worried about his tone. But it was much too late.

I pursed my lips.

"You better fuckin' answer me, Violet."

I let out a dramatic sigh. "Yes, Ollie hacked the computers. No, it was not my idea. I didn't even know about it. Sariah wanted to… research the town," I shrugged. I figured it wouldn't be the best idea to tell him about the podcast she was still determined to start.

"I should've fuckin' known it was Sariah," he grumbled.

"You better not be making insinuations about my best friend," I narrowed my gaze on him.

"I'm not makin' insinuations," he scoffed. "Your best friend is fuckin' insane."

"Don't you dare talk about her like that," I bristled, ready to go to battle for my friend.

Elden blew out a long breath. "Not sayin' she's insane in a bad way," he gripped the back of his neck. "Every bitch in this fuckin' club is insane. It's why their men love them like they do. Keeps us on our toes. It's why Colby can't keep his fuckin' eyes off your best friend."

I perked up. "*Colby* can't keep his eyes off Sariah?"

Elden looked at me like I was an idiot. "It's pretty fuckin' obvious. How have you not noticed?"

I rolled my eyes. "I don't know. Maybe because a lot of my life is spent throwing up these days."

He ran his hand through his hair. "How did we go from talkin' about the club to this?"

"You're with me… I can migrate from topic to topic with ease, so keep up, or get left behind."

Elden's face softened. "No way you're leavin' me behind, baby."

My insides melted.

"And I'm never leavin' you," he promised, stroking my face.

My previously melted insides twisted as we made our way back to the original conversation.

"You can't promise that," I whispered.

He searched my face. "This gonna cause a problem between us, Violet? What the club does?"

I didn't answer him right away, though I wanted to tell him that nothing would ever and could never cause a problem between us. My heart wanted to say that, but my head, my ethics, my morals weren't so sure. Coming upon my mother being involved in a motorcycle club had been quite the shock, coupled with the truth about my father. Then there was the unplanned pregnancy and existential crisis… My focus had been on other things.

And yes, it was exciting, dangerous and wonderful to see the way the Sons of Templar lived their lives. I'd been caught up in that and in my feelings for Elden for quite some time. I'd been focused on what would happen when the club found out about us, how that would affect my family.

I had not been focused on what it meant for me, what being in love with someone who broke the law on a daily basis meant for my future.

Elden would leave the club... If I asked him. Fuck, he offered to do that before he even got me pregnant.

I searched Elden's eyes, the aquamarine glaciers flecked with navy. I had misgivings, about guns, violence and the patriarchal structure on which the club was built. But those things could not supersede the love, the family, the fierce loyalty they felt for one another. Those things could not supersede what the club had given Elden, my mom… me.

"No," I said finally. "It's not going to cause a problem."

Elden's body sagged in relief, then he leaned in to kiss me.

I held my finger between us. "But that doesn't mean I'm going to stay quiet about the things I don't like."

He smirked. "Wouldn't expect anything less." Then he grabbed my wrist, pulled me in and kissed the ever-loving hell out of me.

CHAPTER Twenty-Two

IT WASN'T AS MUCH of an adjustment having a man in our household as I thought it might be. Actually, it was safe to say that everyone liked Elden living in the house. He was handy with spiders, tight jars, getting things off high shelves, and he was a fucking great cook.

He cooked for us all.

Almost every night. Except the nights he was out on 'club business' and came home late.

Elden cooked for us because he was very concerned about me getting all the nutrients required to grow a healthy baby. And because dinner was the only meal I could keep down.

My morning sickness was one of the *many* things he asked our doctor about at our first checkup. She'd reassured him that it was normal. I was normal. We'd heard the baby's heartbeat. Elden had gone still and misty-eyed.

I'd sobbed because of the misty eyes and the pregnancy hormones. They were a bitch.

I was tired all the time. School was killing me. I fell asleep at my desk many nights, but I always woke up in my bed. With

Elden. Because he carried me there the second my head hit the book, maybe even before. I didn't have solid evidence of this, but he was always sitting in the armchair in our room, staring at me over whatever book he was reading, as if waiting to catch me.

We didn't exactly have a routine, but we had a… life. Our separate lives had intermingled to become one. We were a… *couple.* Although we weren't using labels. I didn't want labels. Just thinking about them made my stomach spin in a way that had nothing to do with morning sickness and everything to do with my dearly departed father.

My mother called constantly, asking how I was feeling, what I was craving. I made the mistake of telling her I was craving jalapeno potato chips, then a whole box of them was at our front door the next day.

Swiss spoke during those calls too. He asked about how I was feeling, how I was sleeping, and told me he would threaten my professors with bodily injury if they tried to work me too hard.

He did not mention Elden.

So, the fistfight was not some magical cure for man feuds, it seemed.

"Okay, is it bad that I just used my vibrator for like… thirty minutes after my hot boyfriend came and fucked me?" Sariah asked, slumping down on the sofa beside us.

I had been at class all day and had planned on going straight to work after, but Elden had ordered me onto the sofa for at least one hour of rest. I'd argued solely because he ordered me to do so, but then I'd relented because I was actually very tired.

And then Sariah slumped down and asked about the vibrator.

I was used to those kinds of questions. I probably wouldn't have even registered it as unusual if we didn't have a large, older, muscled biker living in a household of four girls. One, to his credit, who didn't even raise his brow at Sariah or her question.

"It's not bad at all, not on your end, at least," I told her sincerely, happy that she was talking about sex openly and having sex again. She still got shadows behind her eyes sometimes, and I knew she was thinking of what happened to her, but those shadows passed quicker these days.

Despite what Elden had said about Colby, she had not mentioned the man or hinted that she had any kind of feelings for him. But her suddenly having a boyfriend when she'd previously been very against monogamy was suspect.

"I have a boyfriend. One who is hot, edgy, talented, plays a musical instrument and believes wholeheartedly in women's rights, LGBT rights, civil rights… pretty much any rights that don't pertain to rich, old, straight white men." She winced, her eyes rushed to Elden as if she only just realized he was there. "Sorry, dude."

At that, Elden's brow raised a tad. "No apology necessary," he replied. "I'm on your team, in your club, part of your collective… whatever won't get me kicked out of here."

I swallowed my smile at Elden exposing his neck to my tiny spitfire of a roommate, something I didn't think even the baddest of the outlaws had been able to get him to do.

Sariah nodded as if that was good enough for her. "Actually, a man's perspective might be quite valuable here." She turned so her full attention was on Elden. "Okay, so as I said, I couldn't have written myself a more amazing boyfriend. And *technically*, he does all of the right things in the bedroom, you know? He's obviously spent a lot of time learning the female anatomy, and most of the time, he lasts a decent amount of time." She screwed up her nose. "Okay, the majority of the time he lasts about five minutes. Which is honestly fine because I last about five minutes too, at least sometimes." She reached forward to the glass I had just set down on the coffee table.

After she took a sip, she made duck lips. "There's no booze in this," she complained.

I stared at her then at my stomach. It was still pretty flat. "I'm pregnant."

"Oh, and it's frowned upon to drink while pregnant," she teased.

"In some circles, I gather," I replied dryly, grinning at Elden.

Sariah got up and went to the fridge, taking out a bottle of wine, a glass clanging as she took it out of the cupboard.

It turned out she'd taken out two glasses when she set them on the coffee table, pulling the cork out with her teeth.

"Uh, babe, I'm serious about the no drinking thing," I informed her.

"I know you are," she sighed, pouring. "This isn't for you, it's for him." She motioned to Elden.

I pursed my lips to hide my grin. "Sweetie, does Elden strike you as the kind of man who enjoys a buttery Chardonnay?"

Her eyes trailed over Elden. "Don't stereotype him like that," she chastised. "He could love it but be imprisoned by conventional standards of masculinity that judge him for indulging in what has been categorized as a female-only drink."

"That is impressive, and thank you for standing up for me, but I don't like white wine," Elden told her with dancing eyes.

It was something of a delight watching him… unfurl like this, watching him speak in complete sentences and not brood as much.

I couldn't hide my chuckle.

"Tough shit." Sariah glared, holding out the glass. "My ride or die bitch cannot drink for me, and as the man who is responsible for this current condition," she waved her hand at my stomach, "you have to take one for the team and drink with me."

There was a challenge in her eyes as she dared him to deny her.

After a brief standoff, Elden took the wine.

I smirked once more.

"Okay, so, Elden, as a man, would you be mad if you found out Violet used a vibrator after having sex with you?" she asked, completely serious.

"She doesn't," he replied, looking at me in a way that made my ears feel warm.

"How do you know she doesn't?" Sariah asked. "You could think you're satisfying her, but really you're not."

Elden's face was blank as his eyes fastened on me. "Am I satisfying you, baby?"

My toes curled, working really hard to keep my hormones under control with Elden staring at me like that. Suddenly I wasn't so tired.

"Okay, I get it. You're a sex god, and my best friend is *very* satisfied," she moaned in exaggeration.

"He's a boy," Elden pointed out, going back to Sariah's subject. "Whatever he knows about the female anatomy doesn't mean shit. He obviously isn't a man."

She exhaled loudly, looking down into her wine glass.

"Maybe you could introduce the vibrator when he's there." I offered my friend a better solution than 'he obviously isn't a man.' Elden was not well versed in giving dating advice.

Sariah sighed. "I guess."

"Or you could get rid of him and find a man," Elden suggested.

I shot him a withering look.

His eyes sparkled, as they did those days.

"Or I could get drunk on Chardonnay and avoid all my problems," Sariah smiled.

I smiled back. "Sounds like a solid plan to me."

Elden, the trooper that he was, stayed up with Sariah and me, watching *Gilmore Girls* while pretending he wasn't getting his badass card revoked for doing such things. Then again, that badass card was tattooed into his very being; nothing could take it away.

"Sariah has no filter," I told him as I was rubbing oil on my stomach. There wasn't a swell, not yet at least. But there was something. I could feel it. A fullness, despite the fact I was almost constantly puking my guts out. My body was no longer my own. I was growing a human being. Growing something that would change my life forever. My feelings were a mix between wonder at the power of my body to be creating—I felt powerful, feminine, it felt right—yet there were also times I felt removed from my body, unable to fathom that I was pregnant with an outlaw biker's child before I graduated college. I'd be celebrating my twenty-first birthday… pregnant.

"I noticed," Elden replied as he took the oil and began rubbing my feet.

Again, there was something infinitely and carnally powerful about my biker—baby daddy?—rubbing my feet and just generally worshiping me.

"She's my best friend," I continued.

Elden looked up from my feet. "Know that too, baby."

"I want you to like her," I said, biting my lip.

"I do like her."

I raised a brow.

"Look at me like that all you like," he murmured. "It's true."

My brow did not lower. "You *like* living here?" I waved at the room. It was large with enough room for a plush armchair by the bay window where I had a small bookshelf that now housed a bunch of Elden's books. He read there often. Most of them were baby books these days.

Not that he read them for long. Whenever I walked into the room, saw him holding a book, with his reading glasses on… my pregnancy hormones went wild.

There was a closet that was large enough for both of our clothes, only because his clothes consisted of a handful of tees, Henleys, jeans and motorcycle boots.

My desk was nestled on one wall, cluttered with textbooks, a computer and some bottles of perfume.

It was cozy, it felt nice… wonderful actually. But it was a room in a shared house in a college town. Not permanent or suitable to raise a baby.

Nor was his room at the club, the place we'd been living before we came here. I'd spoken to my professors, who had been pretty fricking understand—so understanding I worried that Elden somehow got to them—about me structuring the finishing of my degree around my pregnancy. There was even a suggestion that I finish school online. With my Summer school classes and credits I'd accumulated in high school, I could at least get my undergraduate degree and go from there. You could do anything online these days. I hadn't told Elden about that yet because I didn't know how I felt about it.

As much as I didn't feel right in the college atmosphere, I loved this house, loved living with my friends. If I completed my degree in Garnett, the decisions I'd been avoiding—like where we were going to live, what exactly we were to each other and what I was going to do with the rest of my life—would become unavoidable.

"I do actually," Elden answered the question I'd forgotten I'd asked because I was lost in my own head. "I like it because you're here. I like seeing the way you live your life. Like being a part of it."

"You've always been a part of my life," I admitted. "Ever since that night on the roof." I considered that night. The one that seemed to have occurred decades ago.

Elden was staring at me with his forehead wrinkled.

"Where do you want to live?" he asked after staring at me like that for a few moments.

"What do you mean?"

"When you graduate. You have goals for yourself, dreams. Big ones." He glanced to where I had all my work splayed out on the bed. "And you're fuckin' talented. You could be designing museums, winning awards. You shouldn't be wasting away in some town in the middle of the desert."

That was when I got it. He was worried. About dragging me

down. There I'd been, stuck in my own head, worrying about labels, about admitting what I really wanted when it was in direct conflict with what I thought I wanted, and he was ruminating on *that*.

"I know that, after your bachelor's, you were planning on studying for three more years," he continued. "Rhode Island charter would be happy to have me if that were the case. We'll find somewhere close to campus—"

I sat up, silencing him with my finger on his lips. "You've been thinking about all of that?"

"Of course, I have." He grasped my wrist and kissed my hand.

"And you would move… to a new state, a new club, a new house. For me." My hand went to my stomach. "For us."

He gave me a look that I guessed was meant to communicate that he'd do anything for me.

Which he would. He'd move here for me. Move to a new club. Uproot his life.

I digested all of this, looking around the room that had been mine yet was now both of ours. The life that was mine, now ours. "I wasn't planning on meeting you," I informed him. "And when I did, I wasn't planning on falling in love with you, even though I had *a lot* of fantasies about you."

Elden's eyes dilated. "We're gonna be talkin' about those later."

His words went straight to my core. "We will," I promised, already having trouble finding my train of thought.

I found his icy gaze again. "Before you, before I left for France, my life was about plans. Since I was a baby, my life had been planned out for me. The school. The Ivy League college. The further study after. A fancy job. When the time is right, a fancy man. A McMansion, preferably in a Stepford town similar to how I grew up."

I drew in a deep breath, wishing it would alleviate the chill that raced down my spine at the memories.

"I don't want any of those plans anymore," I admitted. "I don't want to stay here to study more after my bachelor's degree… not when I've got a baby. *We've* got a baby. I don't want to be half a country away from my mother. From my family. Your family. I want us to live in a little cottage in Garnett. I want the desert. Want our baby growing up with its uncle, who I'm thinking we're going to have to refer to as his or her cousin so it doesn't get too weird." I chewed on my nail, thinking about that. Mom was right… our lives were pretty *Jerry Springer*.

"What I really want is… to have no plans," I continued. "I want a home with you. Want to wait for life to happen with you. I want the future to figure itself out."

Elden stared at me for a long time, his eyes crinkled in the corners. "Yeah, I want that too."

I scratched my head. "My professors said they could make it work with me finishing most of my classes remotely," I told him. "Everything is online these days."

Elden didn't say anything; he didn't look surprised either. Shit, I wouldn't be surprised if he had talked to my professors.

"I think… I want to go back to Garnett," I announced. "Be close to my family, not waddling around campus."

"You think?" Elden repeated.

"I know," I stated firmly. "I want us to go home."

His whole expression softened. Elden would've gone anywhere with me, I knew that. And he wouldn't have resented whatever choice I made because that was him. But he'd wanted Garnett.

I beamed at him. "It's settled Now, I would like to discuss those fantasies I mentioned." My eyelashes fluttered.

Then we proceeded to do that.

All night.

The second I finished classes before the winter break, Elden and I went back to Garnett. I'd missed it. He missed it… even though things were still likely to be tense between him and Swiss. A weight lifted off my shoulders the moment I'd made the decision to move back.

Of course, another weight, a new weight, took its place. Concern over where we were going to live, what my day to day would look like with a newborn baby and a… baby daddy at twenty-one years old.

Sariah promised she would be there as soon as she finished with classes. She was now allowed to use the coffee machine at Oliver's. She didn't seem in any rush to get a 'real' job, and it appeared her parents were happy to continue financing her life even though she hadn't seen or talked about them in all the time I'd known her.

My mother was happy with Sariah living with her and Swiss for as long as she needed, but Sariah had already been looking at rentals in the area for her to stay in while she was here.

Mom also told me during one of our phone calls that the nursery was already being set up at their place.

She sounded excited, happy. And it broke my heart to delicately remind her that Elden and I were a package deal right now, so it would not be in our best interests, or in the interest of the structural integrity of the house, for him and Swiss to be under the same roof.

My mom had understood, but I could tell she was hurt. Not because of the Elden and Swiss thing. Because it was clear that although she was my mom and my friend and I needed her greatly, we were entering a different phase in our relationship. One where *I* became a mom. I would be someone's *mom* when I still called my own asking for advice on the best way to clean my cashmere, if my rash was caused by stress or if I was actually dying, and how to get red wine stains off the sofa.

It felt odd. I definitely didn't have that illusive 'Mom knowledge' about anything and everything. I still thought I was going to die if I ate hummus that had been expired for a week.

"What are we doing here?" I asked, confused, as we got off the bike at Mom and Swiss's old cottage in Garnett.

I was also confused about my car being in the driveway. The last time I'd used it, I'd parked it at the clubhouse. Not that I used it often. Whenever we went anywhere, it was on the back of Elden's bike. And I didn't go many places alone these days. Everyone was still on high alert with the murders that hadn't yet been solved. As expected, Sariah had been following them very closely.

I'd assumed that we were going to the clubhouse since that was where we'd been living before. I'd liked living at the clubhouse. Liked living at the clubhouse with Elden. Liked the parties and the midnight taco runs that he did because I was pregnant, and which Colby and Lucas weaseled their way in on because they loved tacos.

I liked the warmth there.

My birthday was tomorrow. Twenty-one. It didn't feel like the milestone it should've. Sure, I was old enough to legally drink, but I'd been drinking long before that, and I couldn't even drink if I wanted to. All thresholds to adulthood had been crossed.

Well, except marriage. Elden hadn't mentioned it again since that night at Mom and Swiss's.

"We're living here," Elden gestured toward the house.

I looked from him to the cottage.

I had a scary sense of déjá vu, remembering pulling up here for the first time after a long flight, only knowing that my mom and dad were getting a divorce. I'd thought that my world was shattering because a boy had hit me. My father had been alive. He was problematic, but I still loved him.

I'd been pregnant and didn't know it.

Now I was a college student, had a boyfriend—it felt weird calling Elden that, but that was the only label I used out of necessity—and was pregnant again. This time with a baby that was much wanted.

"We're living here?" I repeated, staring at the wild garden which had held on through the winter, the charming façade, the walkway, the desert all around, the closest houses specks in the distance.

I loved this house. Had fantasized about us living in something similar to this.

"Not havin' you living at a clubhouse while you're pregnant, much less with a newborn," Elden said, hand on my stomach. "We need a home."

My heart stuttered. My foundation cracked a tiny bit.

A home.

Something so simple yet complicated at the same time.

Something so wonderful yet terrifying at the same time.

"If you don't want to live here, we can find something else," Elden said, judging my silence as disappointment.

"No!" I replied much louder than I'd intended. I looked at him. "No," I repeated, looking into his eyes. "I want this."

He leaned in to kiss my head. "Good."

I let out a squeal as he lifted me into his arms and strode down the walkway.

"What are you doing?"

He shifted me in his arms so he could open the door. "Carrying you over the threshold."

I frowned. "That's only for brides." The mere thought of that made my skin itch.

"Maybe I just wanted you in my arms," he snickered.

I couldn't argue with that.

I looked around once he set me on my feet in the middle of the living room. Most of the furniture that Mom had when she lived here remained, apart from the velvet sofa she'd loved. In its place was a cozy looking, white slip-covered sofa and two new, vintage looking armchairs. There was also a new addition… an entire wall of bookshelves and a drawing desk.

"Your mom chose the sofa and chairs," Elden explained. "Bookcases were my idea, for all your dragon and magic smut."

His hand moved up the side of my body to caress my very sensitive nipples, and I let out a little moan of pleasure.

Elden loved my fantasy novels. He routinely took me shopping for new ones. Book boyfriends didn't threaten him one bit. Likely because he was like one come to life.

"I figured you'd want to put your stamp on it," he continued, voice thick with desire. "We can get whatever you want."

"What I want," I breathed, looking up at him. "Is for you to fuck me."

His eyes flared, and I was in his arms again. My legs wrapped around his waist.

"Oh, I've been planning on doin' that from the second we pulled up," he growled against my mouth, setting me down by the sofa.

He whirled me around so I was facedown, my arms resting on the edge of the sofa.

I shivered as his hand snaked down my back and around, undoing my jeans before making quick work of taking them and my boots off.

I was exposed to him in a second, already wild and ravenous for him.

His calloused hand ran along the skin of my ass then around to my pussy, cupping me where I was already wet for him. My knees shook as he coated his finger with me.

"Yeah, my bad girl is ready for me," he rasped, using his feet to kick my legs out wider, to press me farther down so I was more exposed to him.

Elden grasped my hips, pressing against my entrance.

"Can finally fuck you when and where I want," he murmured, teasing me with his cock. "I can finally make you scream." He fisted my hair in his hand, pulling it slightly. "Hold the fuck on, baby."

I did as he asked and held the fuck on. Then he plunged into me with beautiful brutality.

And he did make me scream.

CHAPTER Twenty-Three

"YOUR MOM IS ARRIVING in about an hour, so we should probably get dressed," Elden said.

We were naked on the sofa. In the middle of the day. In our house.

It felt wild, weird and wonderful all at once.

"My mom is arriving?" I asked lazily, coming back down to earth.

"You're going shopping." Elden drew circles on my shoulder.

"For what?" I asked, repositioning myself so I could look at him.

He shrugged. "Whatever the fuck it is women shop for when they're decorating a new house."

I grinned, forcing myself up even though I could've stayed there for hours. "Well, then we could be gone for hours. Especially since there's a lot of baby stuff to buy."

We both got dressed, then Elden got his wallet from the pocket of his jeans, handing me a card.

I frowned down at it. "What's this?"

"For shopping," Elden jostled the card.

"I have a card for shopping," I informed him. "My mom also

has a card that she will fight me to use, especially if it is anything baby related."

"Take the card, Violet," Elden demanded.

I finished buttoning my shirt. "I don't need your card."

His expression darkened. "Yes, you fuckin' do. You're shopping for our home, our baby. And I'm not lettin' you or your mother pay for it."

"Because you have to take over the financial responsibility of the house?" I glowered at him, not restraining the warning in my tone.

He did not get the warning in my tone. "Yep." He turned to head toward the kitchen as if the discussion was over.

"You've got to be fucking kidding me," I snapped, getting ready to go to battle on this.

Elden stopped walking, turning to me with a calm, level gaze. "Besides my bike, I haven't had anything to my name in decades. Despite what I did to them, my parents left everything to me," he widened his stance. "It was all mine when I got out of prison. Didn't want it. They left it to their son… I wasn't him."

My heart quieted, the fury in my veins dissipating completely.

"Haven't touched it in years," he continued. "I probably should've donated it or some shit." He shrugged. "Held on to the thought I might meet a woman who made me feel like the man my parents would be proud to see. Granted, they wouldn't be proud to see me wearin' a patch in an outlaw motorcycle club."

His tone was solemn, his gaze heavy. The words tore at my soul.

"But," he stepped forward, "they'd be proud to see the woman I found. The woman that I'm nowhere near worthy of but will fight for every day." He cupped my stomach. "They'd be proud that they're getting a grandchild. And they'd sure as fuck want their money to go toward building a home, a life for my woman and child."

I fought against the lump in my throat.

"So you gonna take the fuckin' card?" Elden asked.

I nodded, taking it.

"Good," he murmured, kissing my head then stepping back so I could slip the card into my purse.

"The bed," he pointed to the master bedroom, "it's new. Your mother picked it."

"Okay?" I questioned why he was telling me the bed was new. It was an abrupt change in subject. I guessed Elden didn't want to linger in the past for long. I understood that. If only I could escape mine sticking to my shadow.

"Because the last bed…" he trailed off.

"My mom and stepfather used it," I deduced, feeling kind of icky yet also amused.

He nodded. "We don't have to use that room if you don't want to."

I rolled my eyes. "Oh my god, we're using the room."

"We can sleep somewhere else, while we wait."

"First, I don't want to sleep somewhere else, I love it here," I told him sincerely. "And secondly, what are we waiting for?"

"For you to design our house," Elden said.

I went back on one foot, that's how hard his words hit me.

"Excuse m-me?" I stuttered.

"Bought us some land," he said as if it were no big deal. "We sign the papers next week. It was supposed to be a surprise for your birthday, not an actual present, though. Sariah would skin me alive if I didn't spoil you with one of her *many* suggestions."

I might've smiled at that if it weren't for the current circumstances. "You bought us land?" I repeated.

Elden nodded. "Quite a bit of it, in fact. No one around for miles. Plenty of space. You can design whatever you want. For us."

My heart slammed against my rib cage; panic rose up my throat.

"You bought land for us, for me to design us a house," I clarified, my voice sounding like it was coming from faraway.

Elden's posture changed as he registered my reaction, his shoulders straightening.

"Violet," he stepped forward.

"You know, I'm just going to meet my mom at her house," I said quickly, snatching my purse.

Elden blinked, stopping in place. "Violet," he repeated, softer this time.

I couldn't deal with it. The softness. My perfect, rugged, dangerous biker soft for me, doing things that people just didn't do in real life.

"I have to go!" My voice cracked at the end.

I expected him to fight. That was kind of his thing. He got all possessive and intense when I got in my own head.

Except he didn't. Fight.

He kept the distance between us, although his expression made it clear it was difficult for him to do so.

"Okay," he said.

I didn't take the time to register how out of character that was for him, what he was giving me. I just needed to escape.

So I did.

"Violet," Mom greeted me in surprise when she opened the door. "I was just on my way to pick you up."

"Mom," I cried.

Instantly, her smile melted from her face, her eyes creasing with concern, and she took me into her arms without hesitation.

"Sweetie," she murmured. "What is it? Is it the baby?" Her tone was tinged with panic now.

"No, the baby is fine." I pulled back from the hug.

"What did he do?" Swiss demanded, appearing from somewhere in the house. "If he hurt you—"

"He didn't hurt me!" I yelled.

Swiss jumped back, obviously not expecting me to yell at him. And I did sound a bit manic, to be sure.

"He is *never* going to hurt me," I snapped at him. "So you can stand down. I get that you love me, that you want to make sure I'm happy and keep the threat of death and dismemberment over his head to ensure he keeps me that way. But newsflash, buddy, he doesn't need the threat of death or dismemberment to treat me well. He treats me well. He cooks me dinner. He carries me to bed when I fall asleep at my desk. He rubs my feet. He buys me land in the desert and tells me he wants me to *design our house*!"

Swiss slowly backed away once it became apparent that I had not been harmed in any way by Elden and he could not dismember him, realizing that I was hysterical for other reasons that were not easily fixed by violence.

"I'll just be… finding all the potato chips we have in the house," he muttered before scurrying.

"She doesn't like potato chips anymore," Mom called after him. "It's pork skins!"

But Swiss was already gone.

"I'm not craving pork skins," I hiccupped. "It's green apples. But they have to be a certain kind of green. A fresh kind. And crunchy. And cold. Elden spends like *fifteen minutes* in the produce section looking for the perfect apples. Because he's perfect. Yes, he's a biker, and he's too old for me—according to you, not me—yes, he's ornery with a tortured past and wants to protect me from things I don't need protecting from. But I love him, and he loves me and we're going to have a little girl—"

Mom let out a little scream. "A girl!"

I nodded. "We just found out."

My breakdown stalled for a second so I could recall the memory at the doctor's. We'd chosen to have the genetic blood tests—which thankfully all came up clear—and which also told us what we were having.

"Are you disappointed?" I asked Elden as we walked out of the

doctor's office, me clutching the new ultrasound picture where the baby actually looked like a baby now, not just some tadpole.

Elden hadn't said much of anything since we found out.

"Disappointed?" He'd stopped walking, his voice strange.

"Yes," I said in a timid voice. "That it's not a boy you can craft into a badass and teach to shoot and ride and kill a man thirty different ways." I looked down at the picture in my hands.

Elden grasped my chin, tilting it upward so I met his eyes. They were glassy with emotion.

"First off, our daughter is going to be her own kind of badass who can shoot, ride and kill a man thirty different ways."

I smiled, though I was pretty sure it wasn't a joke.

"Second," he said, softer now. "Seeing our baby, hearing her heartbeat, finding out she's healthy… One of the best moments of my life." He stroked my face. "Just tryin' to figure out how the fuck I got the whole world and how I'm gonna protect it. Treasure it."

"Why didn't you call me?" my mother demanded, hurtling me back into the present.

"Because, Mom, I was amping up for this breakdown," I groaned, the beautiful memory making my throat burn hotter.

She sobered. "Right."

"He loves me and bought us land and wants to marry me and give me a life I couldn't have even fantasized about, but… I'm scared." I searched her face, hating what I was about to say. "I don't trust myself. Don't trust it. Because what if…"

"What if he turns out to be some kind of monster like the one that you never knew your father was?" My mother vocalized the thought that I'd been trying to push away for so long.

The thought that Elden did not deserve. But one I couldn't get rid of.

I nodded, my vision blurry from tears. "He did that to me. And he didn't care. He didn't love me, and I'm so mad at myself for not seeing that. I'm so mad at him," I swatted the tears from my cheeks.

"I can't ever forgive him for what he did to you, Mom. But I can't stay mad at a ghost. It'll eat me alive."

Mom stroked my face. "Oh, sweet girl. You don't have to forgive him for what he did to me. You have to forgive yourself for still loving him despite knowing what he did. Even if the rest of you hates him. You can't change the fact that you love your father. You have to find a way to get right with that."

I chewed on the inside of my lip.

"I have pork skins and chips!" Swiss appeared once more, holding both bags with triumph.

I smiled weakly at him.

"Come on." Mom tugged me toward the kitchen. "I'll make you some tea."

I shook my head rapidly. "I need to go."

She nodded in understanding. "Of course, honey." She kissed my head. "We'll go shopping another time. You make things right with Elden."

I smiled, said my goodbyes and didn't correct her. It wasn't a lie… I did have to go. Just not back to Elden. To the airport.

It was a weird, happy accident that the house was empty.

Mom had sold it when I told her it held no sentimental value to me. The proceeds went toward charities helping women affected by domestic violence.

It was a good thing.

Apparently, the house itself was haunted in some way since the new owners barely lived in it for over a year before they sold it again.

The alarm wasn't activated.

Another stroke of luck.

Colby had taught me how to pick a lock, among other things I hadn't thought I'd ever have practical use for.

Fate was maybe on my side again.

My footsteps echoed against the marble floor. I remembered sliding across them in socks, delighting in the fun the cold, expensive floors gave me.

My father had caught me and held me by the arm, chastising me for being so childish. I could've hurt myself. Shouldn't I be reading? Or playing with dolls?

The air smelled stale. No one had opened the windows or burned expensive candles in a long while.

It had always smelled of my mother's cooking, my father's cologne, a vague edge of disinfectant because my mother was always cleaning.

The ceilings were high, the entryway with its ostentatious stairway was always grim, uninviting to me despite my mother and grandmother's tasteful decorating skills.

I walked through the house like a ghost, struggling to find a happy memory that wasn't tainted by hindsight.

I wanted to wish away those happy memories. The ones where my father sat up with me until midnight studying for a test or how he tried all different combinations to get the perfect volcanic eruption for my science project.

Except I couldn't wish away those things. Couldn't turn my father into an irredeemable villain. That's what I figured out, sitting on the floor of my childhood bedroom.

My father had been a father during my childhood. That was separate from the kind of husband he was. However fucked-up that was, it was true. Now that I knew what kind of husband he was, I couldn't revise my entire history to make it so he was a terrible father.

Nor could I use that information to jeopardize my own future.

I loved my father.

I hated my father.

Both of those things could be true at the same time.

Elden was nothing like him. I didn't need to hold my breath

every time things got better between us, every time he proved how different he was. I was afraid of getting too comfortable, too busy bracing for the blow that would tear it all apart. I had imposter syndrome in my own relationship. I didn't feel like I deserved it because I loved my father. How could I deserve happiness when I couldn't entirely hate the person who withheld it from my mother for so long?

"When you said you needed some space, I didn't think you meant hundreds of miles," Elden said dryly.

I let out a little cry of surprise. Having been so deep in my thoughts, I not only hadn't heard his boots on the floor, but I had not seen him enter the room.

"You're here," I breathed in relief.

I hadn't been running from Elden. Not even a little. I'd been trying to find a way to move forward with him.

Elden sat on the floor, dragging me to straddle him. I let him do it because I needed him. His touch. His presence. His scent.

"I've been here, the whole time," he murmured, pressing his lips against mine. "Told you, I'm always gonna keep up."

"How did you know I was here?" Though I was hungry for more of him, there were questions that needed to be asked. "And how did you get here so fast?"

I'd driven straight to the airport and was able to get on a flight leaving within the hour. Then I'd rented a car at the airport and driven straight here.

I realized, only just now, in Elden's lap, that I was fucking exhausted. I had been running on adrenaline and was now safe to crash.

Not quite yet, though.

"Swiss called me," Elden said, stroking my hair.

That perked me up. "*Swiss* called you?"

He nodded. "Was worried about you, wanted to make sure you got home okay." His eyes hardened ever so slightly. "Obviously, I didn't realize this was the home you were going to without tellin' me. Luckily, I do track your phone, and I drive faster than you." He grasped my chin. "We're gonna be talking about you not knowing I was tailing you the entire way to the airport and all the way here," he grumbled.

I gaped at him. "You were on the same plane as me?"

He nodded.

"How in the fuck did I not notice?"

Elden's mouth ticked up. "Don't know, baby. Probably because you were deep in your own head. Which is why I'm not fuckin' furious with you." He kissed me again. "Don't ever take off like that again."

"I won't," I promised without hesitation, filled with shame for taking off on him when he was being perfect. And right after he'd been vulnerable with me about his parents. I was such an asshole.

My chin trembled, tears escaping the corners of my eyes.

Elden wiped them away immediately.

"I'm s-sorry," I stuttered. "I-I needed to do this."

"I know," he murmured.

"But I-I d-didn't consider your feelings," I sobbed. "I was being selfish and bratty and just mean, and I'm fucked-up. I mean, I know you knew that from the start, but maybe I'm even more fucked-up than I thought. And it's too late for you to back out because you already put a baby in me." I was spiraling now.

Elden's hands fastened around my neck. "Violet," he said firmly, his voice the anchor I needed to find my way back.

"The one and only time I even thought about backing out was when you asked me to kiss you on the rooftop," he said, eyes blazing.

"But we weren't even us then."

His lips landed on mine. "Weren't we?"

That only made me sob harder. Which was fine since I had a man who wasn't afraid of my tears, my demons, my imperfections.

"You ready to go home now?" he asked.

I looked around the room.

"Yeah," I said quietly.

I was definitely ready to go home.

Elden and I arrived back from Carver Springs renewed.

Or at least, *I* was renewed. It wasn't Elden who had needed to face his demons, make peace with them. It was I who needed to linger in hell for a minute so I could enjoy our version of heaven. It was I who needed to learn that heaven and hell were both the same place, viewed through a different lens.

An important chapter of my life was closed. I was done with letting my dead father sabotage my happiness. I was sure that there would be shit that came up, that I'd be fucked-up forever. But I was okay with that. I had Elden. I could let myself sink into the life I was going to have with him.

Fear remained, as I figured it always would with this new, unplanned, uncertain life ahead of me. But I wouldn't let that fear dictate my happiness.

The second we got back, after visiting Mom and Swiss and quelling their worries—Elden and Swiss even managed to be in the same room and share a beer—I went straight to the computer at our cottage, designing our forever home.

It got dark without me noticing, and Elden practically had to drag me to bed.

Well, he didn't have to *drag* me since I was still a living, breathing, pregnant woman who was ruled by chemistry and hormones, and was indescribably obsessed with her man.

Even though I was incredibly busy and unable to slam a tequila shot, Mom threw a birthday party for me at the restaurant. The whole club was there. The food was amazing, I was spoiled with gifts. Though nothing compared to the first edition, signed hardcovers of my favorite fantasy series that Elden had somehow managed to get. They were incredibly scarce and worth a lot of money. He would not tell me how he got them, and I wouldn't be surprised if he threatened some poor book collector into parting with them.

Sariah arrived in Garnett not long after we did, to have a belated birthday celebration for me—where she drank for three: me, her and the baby—to go shopping, to celebrate Christmas at the club—which she loved—and to move herself into a little apartment she was renting above Oliver's on Main Street.

She still had another semester at college, and paying rent on another apartment in a town she wasn't living in full time didn't make sense to me, but she'd waved it off, mentioning that the rent was nothing.

Nothing to her, apparently.

She also said there was nothing going on with her and Colby, even though they were constantly bickering and glaring at each other. Glares with definite sexual undertones. She refused to talk about it, therefore, I didn't talk about it.

She had other things to talk about, though. This became apparent as we drank coffee at our cottage—ours, *mine and Elden's…*It was still wild to think that—having a quiet morning since Elden was at the club, and neither of us had shifts at Oliver's. I knew my time there was limited, the further along I got. Elden was getting increasingly protective as time went on. It didn't piss me off as much as it should've. In fact, it didn't piss me off at all.

I liked feeling protected, nurtured in that way. Loved that he loved me and the changes I was going through while growing our daughter. There was not a moment I felt insecure or alone.

"There was another murder while we were gone," Sariah informed me, putting her mug down.

"Another murder?" I shivered at the thought of it. Maybe that's what the meeting at the club was about. Maybe that's what all the overprotective stuff was about. Elden and I hadn't talked about the murders, and it wasn't like it was exactly the club's job to be investigating.

"Only the next town over this time," Sariah nodded. "She was our age. Home from college. She was working at a strip club to pay her way."

Blood pounded in my ears.

Sariah nodded at what I guessed was my horrified expression. "Definitely a serial killer. And fucking no one is reporting about it. The only reason I know is that Ollie's monitoring the police stations in the area." She shook her head. "Someone has to do something."

I sighed. "Someone does have to do something," I agreed. "And not just when some girl with a rich family or the right photo for a news piece gets hurt."

Sariah drained her coffee mug, standing. "Let's go, then."

I frowned at her. "Where are we going?"

She put her hand on her hip. "We're going to do something. Because like you said, no one else will until some pretty rich girl gets hurt. And who knows how many other women he will go through before the police get their heads out of their asses or the media decides someone is worth reporting on."

I thought about it. It was wildly irresponsible to get involved in something like that. But letting the police do their job didn't seem to be working out, especially if Sariah was right, and our local sheriff only cared about bringing down the club.

"Elden will be mad." I grimaced.

She smiled. "I know. Won't it be great?"

"Sariah," I groaned. "Things are peaceful between us now."

She rolled her eyes. "Snore. Plus, we both know it's worth the make-up sex. And I'm not going to put you in any danger. I never would. We're just going to put some fire under some asses. Unless you're already a boring old soccer mom, then fine…" she trailed off, inspecting her nails.

The bitch knew how to get to me. "Fine," I huffed, standing up. "But Elden can't know."

"I promise," she rubbed her hands together. "We'll be as quiet as church mice."

We had been planning on going in there to ask some questions. Innocent questions. We certainly hadn't planned on getting into any trouble.

But Sariah was there. I was there. We got a little angry.

Trouble happened.

CHAPTER Twenty-Four

THE POLICE STATION itself was small, well maintained, quiet. Which made sense. The town of Garnett wasn't exactly wild with crime.

I'd not so much as been pulled over for a speeding ticket. And I did speed. A lot. Elden yelled at me about it all the time.

I ignored him all the time.

The lobby of the station itself was the same as the outside, clean, quiet. There was one officer behind some plexiglass who looked up when we walked in. He did not look back down at whatever he was doing. His tongue was practically wagging as we approached.

Which made sense. I mean, I guessed I looked okay. My jeans were tight and showed off my mid-section in the crop top I was wearing. I planned on wearing jeans as much as possible and showing off my flat stomach as much as possible before it stopped being flat and my jeans stopped fitting. As it was, they were pretty fucking tight right now. My tits were also almost double the size, which Elden loved. My stomach was mostly flat but there was a definite swell. Especially after I had a big lunch. I'd only just started feeling well enough to eat lunch, though.

It was likely Sariah who had the officer's tongue wagging. She was wearing tailored, pinstriped pants and a matching vest without anything underneath. Her hair was piled on top of her head, she was wearing square framed glasses and bright red lipstick. In other words, she'd gone full Erin Brockovich.

"Can I help you?" the officer asked enthusiastically. He wasn't much older than us, wore thick glasses and his nose had been broken one too many times. He worked it, though, in a nerdy Owen Wilson kind of way.

Sariah beamed, leaning on the counter in front of the plexiglass so her considerable cleavage was on display. "I sure hope so," she drawled, fluttering her lashes.

"Oh my god," I muttered from behind her, grinning.

Her head whipped around, and she mouthed, "Fuck off," before returning her attention to the desk jockey.

"I'm here because I'm a journalist," she continued.

I snorted at that.

She flipped me the bird behind her back.

"And I'm investigating the murders that have been happening in the area over the past few months."

"Murders?" the officer repeated.

Sariah's megawatt smile dimmed. "There have been four young women brutally murdered within fifty miles of this town in the past eight months."

He scratched his head. "Well, that's not our jurisdiction."

"Not your jurisdiction?" she parroted. "So, you don't have to know about them, then, as an officer of the law?"

"We are aware of the situation and monitoring it," a deep, smooth voice commented from my left.

Both Sariah and I had not noticed the police officer in our periphery who had obviously heard the gist of the conversation.

The man in question was in a uniform that was pressed immaculately and showed off his lean muscles. He was tall, maybe Elden's age though his hair was styled slick, and he was clean shaven, showing off a tan, square jaw. He had brown eyes that were so dark they were almost black.

"And who might you be?" Sariah asked.

"I'm Elijah Turner, the sheriff," he introduced himself.

This was the sheriff.

He seemed too young.

And I'd been picturing a straight-laced, Tommy Lee Jones type, who was intent on bringing down the big, bad criminals.

I disliked him already despite his friendly smile and relaxed demeanor. He was trying to bring down the club. Trying and failing, but still. His main goal was to ruin the family that my mother had only just found.

Put Elden back behind bars.

My nails sank into the inside of my palms.

"Perfect, just the man we wanted to see," Sariah purred, turning her full attention to the sheriff, obviously not full of burning hatred like I was.

"About the murders," he deduced.

"Yes," she replied.

"And you're…" he looked between us, "journalists?"

Sariah nodded enthusiastically.

"Forgive me for saying so, ladies, but you look a little young." A bit of a Southern drawl peeked out from his deep, masculine tone.

"The four young women brutally murdered were probably a little young for that too," I shot back.

Sariah turned her head to me, giving me a subtle thumbs-up.

The sheriff gave me his full attention. His gaze was not hostile. Not quite, but it was measured.

"As I said, we're monitoring the situation," he repeated calmly.

I cocked my head. "And does *monitoring the situation* actually mean something, or is that some kind of political bullshit to cover up the fact that you don't actually care about women being murdered because you're too busy trying to bring down a club of people who have done literally nothing to you?"

His gaze was no longer even. "I don't know where you're getting your information, but the Sons of Templar are not a club, they're a gang. A criminal organization that brings crime and unsavory characters to this town." His voice was colder now but remained that same, even level.

"Unsavory characters?" I scoffed. "Where did you escape from? A '60s sitcom? Which I guess makes sense since you seem to me like a small-minded asshole with his head up his ass and his mind on whatever awards you think you'll get from arresting the Sons of Templar instead of, I don't know, protecting and serving like you're paid to do." I stepped forward. "And just remember, you're paid by the taxpayers of this town who just happen to include every member of the Sons of Templar."

"You should leave now," he said mildly.

"I'm exercising my right of free fucking speech," I countered.

"You're getting very close to disturbing the peace."

"Oh, far be it for me to disturb your peaceful day when there's a man out there murdering women!" I exclaimed.

He looked at Sariah now. "You should get your friend to calm down and out of this station before I'm forced to take action."

Sariah put her hand on her hip. "I don't have to get my friend to do anything since she is in her right mind, and as she said, exercising her right of free speech, otherwise known as calling out an asshole. I know I don't know you that well, and it could be considered a stretch to label you as that before getting to know you, but I'm working off a pretty solid hunch." She smiled not so sweetly.

He looked between the two of us, sighing. "I'm gonna have to ask you both to leave right now."

Sariah tilted her head in question. "And on what grounds? Highlighting the ineptitude of the local sheriff is merely us doing our civic duty," she pointed out. "And again, you have yet to make any worthwhile comment about the serial killer who's prowling this area."

"And you've yet to prove what news organization you're from," he returned, eyes focused on Sariah. Though he was pretty pissed—with his hands on his hips and his spine steel, his eyes kept dropping toward her lips—it was also clear that he found her attractive. He was a male with a pulse after all.

"I'm from an organization that's very interested in the survival of any woman under forty in a hundred-mile radius," she told him.

"We appreciate your concern but not the hostility," he replied.

"Oh, pardon me, sir. You want us to be more agreeable, soft spoken, delicate?" My voice rose as I moved forward.

"I would like you to remember that you're speaking to an officer of the law," he stated in that frustratingly mild tone.

My gaze raked up and down his body. "I don't know, I think I was pretty apt in calling you an asshole," I hissed.

His hand went to his hip not so casually. "You keep goin', missy, I'll be forced to take action," he warned.

I stopped just inches in front of him, meeting his stare. "Be my fucking guest, *champ*. See what happens. I'm sure some of the nation's foremost news organizations would love to hear about a jumped-up sheriff wanting to make a name for himself, not only ignoring a serial killer but then arresting two innocent, young women who simply want justice for a misunderstood group who have done nothing but good for this town."

His stare turned chilly. "I don't do well with threats."

I hoped my own gaze matched his. "Good thing I'm not threatening you, I'm literally informing you of what I plan on doing if you don't leave the fucking Sons of Templar alone and start investigating these murders."

My fury had taken on a mind of its own; my fingers twitched with the urge to rip his badge off his chest.

"Violet," a voice barked.

I jumped, turning to see Elden standing behind me, Colby beside Sariah. Neither of them were smiling.

Sariah was beaming, obviously amused.

"Outside now," Elden pointed to the front door.

"They're with you?" the sheriff asked, his tone no longer even vaguely friendly.

I turned around, beaming at him. "Why yes, we are. I'm carrying the child of this here man." I rubbed my stomach. "Brewing up another wicked criminal."

"You need to get them out of here right now," the sheriff said, speaking to Elden.

Elden wasn't looking at me. "Your wish is our command, sheriff." His own tone was full of venom I hadn't heard before. "Violet…"

I sighed, giving the sheriff one more glower before turning on my heel and walking out the door.

"What the fuck do you think you were doing?" Elden seethed, grabbing me by the upper arm. The grip itself was tight, but carefully so. He wasn't treating me like a delicate flower now that I was pregnant, but he was much more controlled when touching me, that was for sure.

"There's a serial killer near this town," Sariah jumped in. Her eyes were locked on with Colby who was scowling at her in a way that confused me because usually, this was the kind of thing Colby enjoyed. Us yelling at the sheriff. Investigating murders. His facial expression informed me that he definitely was not enjoying this.

"We were simply asking the sheriff why he wasn't taking the murders seriously," I told Elden.

"And getting material for our podcast," Sariah offered, unhelpfully.

I spun around and glared at her. Elden stopped walking. "What podcast?"

"We don't have a podcast," I told Sariah.

"Not *yet*," she corrected, not understanding what my wide eyes were communicating.

"Let me get this straight," Colby said. "You think there's a serial killer here—"

"There is," Sariah interrupted.

Colby's jaw ticked. "And you think the most logical thing is to go poking around places you fucking shouldn't in order to what… catch him?"

Sariah shrugged. "Looks like we're going to have to since the police aren't doing shit."

Colby put his head in his hands.

Elden gripped me harder.

"You are not catching a serial killer," Elden ground out.

"So you agree that it *is* a serial killer," Sariah exclaimed triumphantly.

"That's not the point of this, babe," I said, wincing.

"Whatever," she rolled her eyes.

"Get on the bike, Violet," Elden ordered.

I looked at the bikes, then at Elden. He was not amused. Not even a little. In fact, he was *really* pissed off.

Though I did want to argue about the manhandling, the over-the-top moroseness and the ordering of me around, I didn't think this was the right time to argue with him.

"It was fun while it lasted," I sighed, looking at Sariah with a 'what can you do' shrug.

She grinned. "I wish I'd recorded you dressing him down. Lost opportunity," she sighed.

"You're getting on the bike too," Colby addressed Sariah, still not smiling.

Sariah's eyes bugged out, and she put her hand on her hip. "You have ventured into a parallel universe, bless your soul," she cooed sweetly. Then her eyes narrowed. "Oh, wait, actually no, there is no universe where you can order me around. There is no way in *fuck* I'm getting on that fucking bike."

Colby's jaw worked, and I really wanted to settle in to watch the duel, but Elden was too busy directing me to the bike.

"Hey!" I argued.

"We're not stayin' here a moment fuckin' longer," he hissed in my ear. "Get. On. The. Bike." His tone told me there was no point in arguing.

So, I got on the bike.

The good thing about the bike was that you couldn't have a conversation during the ride. Elden's body was taut the entire time, the ride doing nothing to calm him. He waited until we'd gotten off and into the door of the house before he started speaking.

"You're pregnant," he seethed the second the door had closed behind us.

"Thanks for the reminder," I replied smarmily, folding my arms over my chest. "As if the radiating heartburn and constant morning sickness weren't enough clues."

Apparently, he did not find that funny, pacing the small living room. "You're pregnant and you think that investigating a fucking serial killer is what you should be doing?"

"I'm not investigating. Sariah is doing most of it. I'm just along for the ride."

I quickly learned that that was not the best thing to say.

Elden stopped pacing, and he looked like his head might just explode. "You're fucking kidding me, right?" he asked quietly, his tone a complete contradiction to the fury in his eyes.

I pursed my lips, not answering because it was most definitely a rhetorical question.

"I'm very mindful of the conversation we had the day Swiss found out about us."

My throat constricted underneath his powerful glare.

Elden wasn't done. He didn't stop glowering. "I'm very aware of the promises I made you. But you're making it really fucking hard to keep them when you are not only provoking someone who is trying to find a way to hurt the club at the same time as trying to get close to whomever is butchering women."

He was wound so tight he was shaking.

"Tell me, Violet, how am I supposed to think about anything, do anything else but worry about you when you're doin' shit like that?" There was no longer any fury in his tone. Just naked fear.

"You want to hold assholes to account for their bullshit," he continued in a soft tone. "I understand you want to bring about action, change and justice." He stroked my face. "Hearing even the tail end of you going toe to toe with that fuck for the club made me proud as fuck that you're my woman." He placed his hand on the swell of my stomach. "Not asking you to change who you are. But I'm asking you to be mindful of the reality that you're carrying my whole world around. That you're fucking irreplaceable. That I wouldn't function if any harm came to you."

My eyes watered. I had been impulsive. And I had been operating like it was still just me. But it wasn't.

Elden clasped the sides of my neck. "Will you promise me that you won't try and go all vigilante justice on this? At least not without me by your side?"

"I promise," I whispered.

Unfortunately, Sariah had not made the same promise.

"I'm going to date him," Sariah declared.

"Date who?" I asked, frowning at the very disturbing image in my baby book. I was lying in our bed, Sariah helping herself to clothes from my closet that no longer fit.

"The sheriff." She pulled her hair off the nape of her neck.

I put the book down.

"Please tell me you're joking."

Sariah did not look like she was joking. "Look, it's the best way to get some info on what exactly is going on. Plus, he's hot," she shrugged.

"Sariah, he is literally looking for ways to bring my family down," I reminded her.

Her brows furrowed. "Yes, I *know* that. Which is why I plan on breaking his heart so completely he'll quit his job and go farm yaks or something."

"You have not thought this through," I groaned.

"I have not," she agreed cheerfully.

"Colby will be pissed," I added.

She scowled. "I don't give a fuck what Colby thinks."

"What is going on with you two, anyway?" I asked, abandoning my book. It only scared the shit out of me anyway.

"Nothing," she snapped. "Absolutely nothing is going on."

"I don't believe you."

"Believe what you want," she huffed. "Nothing is going on. And I get that you're pregnant, and you can't really go undercover trying to catch a serial killer, but my womb is empty, and my heart is full of fury at men who think they can go around murdering women or men who don't think they need to do anything about it." She winked at me. "Don't wait up."

I made her text me routinely throughout the night, deciding it was not the best time to tell Elden about Sariah's plan. Though I didn't keep secrets from my man, I also didn't want him to have an aneurysm.

Plus, I'd chosen to have a possessive alpha biker in my life. Sariah hadn't. And as much as I was worried about my friend, she was a force of nature… Nothing was going to stop her.

Which was why I was relieved when she texted me later that night informing me that she hadn't had any luck.

I hoped that was the end of it.

TWO WEEKS LATER

We were at the club. Arguing.

Our age difference very rarely became an issue between us except on things pertaining to my pregnancy. Then again, I was pretty sure that it was not an age difference thing, I was pretty sure it was an over-the-top alpha male thing.

"It's not happenin'," Elden spat.

I put my hands on my hips. "It sure as fuck is. Home births provide a calmer atmosphere to bring a baby into."

His glare was withering. "Calm until something goes wrong and you're not in a hospital."

"Nothing's going to go wrong," I informed him, shooting a withering glare of my own.

We were having this conversation in the common room. Lucas and Colby were sitting at the bar with beers dangling from their hands, watching us like it was a very entertaining show.

"You know, I also read about Lotus births," Colby offered with a grin.

"First of all, shut the fuck up," Elden barked. "And how in the *fuck* do you know what a Lotus birth is?"

"How do *you* know what a Lotus birth is?" I addressed Elden.

"I read the baby books," he seethed. "The ones written by medical professionals who *operate out of hospitals*."

"This country is one of the worst in the developed world for infant mortality," I fired back.

"And you think giving birth at home is going to improve that statistic?" Elden's eyes might've been wider than I'd ever seen them.

Swiss walked into the common room while we were having this conversation. I expected him to walk right out upon seeing Elden, or to ignore him, but he didn't. He came to join our little conversation.

Though I hated that Swiss was still not Team Elden, I was

thankful for their little feud at this moment since I'd get some reinforcement.

Elden ran his hand through his hair in frustration. "You need to talk some sense into her," he turned to tell Swiss.

Swiss looked at me. "You need to listen to Elden."

I gaped at the two of them. "Since when are you allies?"

"Since you decided you wanted to give birth without a medical professional present," Swiss replied matter-of-factly.

"I will have a doula," I argued.

"And she probably got her medical degree from fucking Hogwarts," Elden muttered.

"First off, Hogwarts doesn't offer medical degrees," I glared at him. "That's further study. And don't you turn your nose up at a very important profession."

"Not turnin' my nose up at the profession," Elden folded his strong arms in front of him. "In fact, you can have her there, at the hospital if that's what you want. You can have a whole army of them. I don't give a fuck. As long as my baby is born in a hospital."

"*Your* baby?" I squawked.

"Think I had an equal hand in creating it," he returned, not missing a beat.

"This is gonna be good," Colby whispered loudly.

I ignored that.

"Oh, wow, you had an orgasm," I applauded. "Someone get this guy a medal. Or should we erect a statue in your honor for doing the single thing required of you to create life." I started to pace. "It's almost as if it's *you* who had to suffer through five months of morning sickness that wasn't morning sickness at all, really just a constant hangover. And then there are the hormones that make you seriously wonder if you're going to give birth to your child in a state penitentiary after you've been convicted of murdering your overprotective, insane baby daddy and your equally overprotective, equally insane stepfather," I ranted, pointing at each of them. "It also must be *you* who spent the first trimester worrying yourself sick that you might lose the baby that wasn't planned but was most definitely wanted," I continued, pacing once more. "And then, once that part was over with, it must've been *you* thinking you had to literally push a baby out of a very narrow place and thinking about the ripping."

"I don't think I need to be here for the conversation about the ripping," Swiss muttered, making his way over to the bar with Lucas and Colby.

"Coward!" I called to his back before my eyes darted back to Elden. "For bikers who I assume kill and maim people on the regular, you seem positively faint at the thought of a perineal tear."

Elden was looking at me in a very peculiar way. Not exactly pissed off, though there was a shadow of that. Yet there was also a shadow of amusement and warmth.

"We do not kill and maim on the regular," he replied. "Only very rarely."

I stopped pacing, looking him directly in the eye. "I'm having the doula."

"In a hospital."

I scowled at him. He did not blink at the scowl.

We might have continued this for much longer had Swiss not interrupted.

"We've got cops," he announced, looking at the security screens showing all the entrances to the club.

Both Lucas and Colby quickly lost their amused expressions and their beers.

"We got anything in here we need to worry about?" Elden asked.

They both shook their heads.

"I'll call Hansen, tell him to steer clear and give our friendly neighborhood lawyer a call," Lucas said, phone to his ear.

Elden nodded. "Good. We need Violet outta here." His voice

was calm, purposeful, empty. As was his expression. But he held me tight enough to hurt.

Swiss's jaw clicked. "Don't have time. They don't have shit on us. Won't find shit. We'll be good." My stepfather looked at me. "Stay close to Elden."

Elden's arm tightened around me, then he kissed my temple. "It's going to be okay," he promised.

Just then, the door crashed open. Actually crashed open. I jumped, and Elden moved me behind him.

None of the men looked worried, so I did my best not to be, even though my heart was thundering all the way up in my throat, and I was seriously thinking I was going to vomit all over my shoes.

"You know, you could've knocked," Swiss pointed out casually. "But at least now we'll get to bill you for a brand-new door."

The sheriff, along with a bunch of other uniforms, walked in, guns drawn. Though the sheriff was the only one who looked like he really wanted to be there.

His handsome face was pinched with distaste. "On the floor, all of you. Now."

"You mind telling us what this unlawful entry is about?" Swiss asked again, tone still casual, though his posture was rigid, like Elden's. "You don't have to tell us, but it sure does help us with the billable hours. Our lawyer is expensive as fuck but worth it. She'll have us owning the station by the time she's done with you." There was an edge to his tone now.

The sheriff directed a cold stare in his direction. "We have a warrant," he informed Swiss. "Now on the ground."

"Happy to comply with an officer of the law," Colby said with a massive 'fuck you' grin.

Elden kissed me on the temple again, eyes blazing with fury as he complied with the sheriff's order.

Hatred and fury seethed through my veins seeing Elden, Swiss and my friends lying on the floor, the sheriff smiling in satisfaction at them doing that.

His eyes found mine. "You too," he pointed to the ground.

"Excuse me?" I asked, venom in my tone.

His hand went to the gun on his hip, resting it there. "I said everyone on the floor, which includes you, young lady."

I scowled at him. "Bite me."

His scowl intensified. "Officers, assist this young woman to her rightful position," he nodded to the ground, speaking to the two uniformed officers beside him.

The men in question did not move right away, both of them looking uncertain. They did not look happy to be here in general. They were likely residents of the town who had been here longer than the sheriff, likely did not have the same career aspirations and were likely—rightfully—attached to their arms. Which would probably get ripped off if they tried to force me to the ground.

"She's six months fuckin' pregnant," Elden hissed, standing quickly so that he was in front of me.

"She's going to get on the ground if she doesn't want to get arrested," the sheriff repeated in a clipped tone.

When Elden stepped forward, I grasped on to the back of his cut in an effort to stop him from attacking an officer of the law who was armed and looking for a reason to lock him up or hurt him.

"You make my *pregnant woman* get on the fuckin' floor, I'll end you," Elden promised, his tone low.

"Careful, brother," Swiss warned from his place on the floor.

Boots thumped against the floor until the sheriff was toe to toe with Elden.

"On. The. Floor." The sheriff's voice was eerily quiet. "Both of you."

I grasped Elden's cut tighter. "It's one thing for you to come in here and misuse your authority for some fucked-up search. You can get away with that. For a time. But you manhandle an innocent pregnant woman, *my* innocent pregnant woman, you can't explain that shit away," Elden replied just as softly, in a way that was equally menacing.

The air was thick with tension. I did manage to hold in my vomit, which I counted as a win. But that was likely because I was too terrified.

"I'll take my chances," the sheriff finally said.

Things happened rather quickly after that.

All I remembered was the sheriff reaching around, presumably trying to grab me. Maybe I imagined that. And the rest.

But what I saw, with crystal clarity, was Elden, in handcuffs, being taken away from me.

CHAPTER *Twenty-Five*

HOURS LATER, the entire club was back. The police were long gone. They got what they wanted after all.

The club's lawyer was at the station. She had been at the station for hours. Elden had been at the station *for hours*. They wouldn't let me go see him. Something about my blood pressure. Or my safety. I didn't know what. All I knew was that they weren't letting me go to the station. So I was there. At the club. While Elden was locked up.

"Please sit down, sweetie." My mom's expression was pinched with worry. She had arrived not long after they took Elden away. She had been trying, and failing, to calm me down ever since.

"Elden doesn't like tight spaces," I told her as I began pacing. "He doesn't like losing control. Being locked in somewhere. And that fucking piece of shit, cockhole, *cunt* locked him up."

Though this situation was not worth smiling about, not even a little, it seemed my cursing amused the peanut gallery consisting of Colby, Javier, Lucas and Sariah.

Sariah arrived shortly after my mother. She hadn't attempted to calm me down because she likely took one look at me and knew I wasn't going to calm down, so she then situated herself at the bar with the boys. She pointedly ignored Colby. Something I noted with detachment.

"Don't use that word, sweetie," Mom said under her breath.

I stopped pacing to look at her. "I am a woman. I am allowed to use that word however and whenever I wish. And right now, I wish to call out the sheriff for being a *cunt*."

More snickers came from the peanut gallery, even Hades, who was sitting with his wife, had a twitch to his lip. It could've been an involuntary tic.

"I'm going down there," I decided for the four hundredth time. "I'm not standing here doing nothing."

Macy got up before my mother did. "You aren't doing nothing," she told me, a hand on my bicep. "You're here, calling people cunts. Growing bones. Eyes. Ears. You're growing his baby. You're keeping it safe. And going down there in the state you're in jeopardizes that very important job."

Her words penetrated, but barely. She squeezed my arm.

"Yes, okay," I murmured.

"Good," she smiled at me.

"Does it gross anyone else out the way she just explained that Vi is growing fucking eyes and ears inside her body at this very moment?" Colby asked the room.

I whirled on him. "It's the miracle of life, you donkey fucker," I hissed. "Treat me like the goddess I am, or you'll be eternally sorry."

He pursed his lips in a way that told me he was fighting a smile. He held up his hands in surrender, eyes gravitating to the door. "Thank fuck," he muttered. "I think she might've murdered someone soon." He was talking to the door, not me.

I spun around, seeing a large form. He was wearing a cut. He had a chocolate goatee peppered with silver. His eyes were ice blue. It was my biker.

I didn't hesitate to sprint toward him and launch myself into his arms.

He caught me without effort, my arms and legs wrapping around him.

I inhaled deeply, reveling in his scent, in the hardness of his muscles, the buttery leather of his cut, the firmness of his arms around me.

"Did anyone hurt you?" I grasped on to his neck, inspecting his face. Devastatingly handsome, as always. "I'll fucking kill them if they hurt you. I'll burn that station to the ground."

Someone, likely Lucas or Colby, chuckled in the background.

Elden stroked my face. "No one hurt me, baby," he murmured. "I'm assuming you've been freaking out."

"No, I haven't."

"I was afraid for my life," Colby called out.

Elden's forehead wrinkled. "You feeling okay?" he asked, worry in both his tone and in his eyes. "The baby?"

I sighed. "The baby is fine. I'm fine. Again, *I'm* not the one who was locked up without cause. We're suing." I turned to Hansen. "We can sue, right? I'll sue them all."

Hansen smiled. "We've got our best lawyer on it." He looked to Elden. "You good?"

Elden lifted his chin, his arms tightening around me. "I'm good."

"Was gonna call church, but I think we can do that tomorrow, since your Old Lady doesn't look like she's gonna detach any time soon," Hansen smirked.

I tightened my limbs in response.

Elden smiled.

Smiled. After being locked up, he was smiling and not looking traumatized at all.

"We need to go home," Elden murmured, looking at me.

"Yes," I agreed, my voice breathy. "You've been locked up for so long."

His eyes flared, and he didn't say goodbye to anyone, just walked us out of the clubhouse with me still wrapped around him.

It was late.

Or very early.

Whatever it was, all that I cared about was that we were in our little cottage in the desert, in our bed.

Naked.

Elden had indeed fucked me like he'd just got out of prison, which technically was true.

"Are you sure you're okay?" Elden asked in a concerned tone while drawing circles on the swell of my stomach. "You were worked up. We need to get your blood pressure checked."

I pursed my lips. "You didn't seem too worried about my blood pressure or me getting worked up a few moments ago."

My body vibrated with his chuckle.

"And also, I should be asking *you* if you're okay," I added, a lot less teasing in my tone. "Are you okay? I can't imagine what that brought up for you." I fisted the blanket. "I will kill that fucking sheriff."

Elden turned my face toward him. "Baby, please let the club deal with the fucking sheriff. I really don't need my baby born incarcerated."

"Not funny," I sneered. "Plus, they'd never trace it back to me, not with Sariah's help."

"Neither you nor Sariah is getting involved," he grumbled.

I wet my lips. Sariah was definitely already involved, but it was best not to tell him that.

"Seriously," I changed the subject back to him. "Are you okay?"

"Baby, I'm fine," he said firmly. "He was gonna put his hands on you. My pregnant woman." His tone grew colder. "And I saw red, the same way I saw red that night."

The night at the bar. I knew that's what he was talking about.

"Figured I was gonna lose control like then. That I was gonna kill him," he blew out a sharp exhale. "And even the fancy lawyer the club has wouldn't be able to get me out of it."

My blood chilled at the mere thought of it.

His hand fastened on my chin, his soft lips landing on mine. "Except I could hold it together. Because I held on to you. Our baby. I'm not leavin' either of you, Violet."

My body warmed at the vow.

"Promise?" I whispered.

"I promise."

Though I didn't sleep easily that night, I held on to that promise tightly, Elden's arms around me, reminding me he was here. We were safe.

For the time being.

I assumed things with the sheriff were done because there weren't more raids on the club. And Elden's charges were also dropped. Because they were bullshit.

Sariah had gone back to school. She never said anything else about the sheriff, which meant her dating attempt hadn't been successful. I was attending classes online while designing our house. *Our fricking house*. Of course, since I technically wasn't a qualified architect, we were working with a firm that was somewhat impressed and had already offered me a junior position once I graduated. And had the baby.

The firm was well regarded. I liked them. I liked the prospect of working there. Everything was falling into place in a scary way.

Although I had yet to have a mental breakdown and fly back to Carver Springs again, I still had moments of complete fear over just how well everything was falling into place. I'd jerk awake in the middle of the night from some nightmare or another, and Elden would be there. His arms would be tight around me, he'd murmur something comforting, kiss me. His hand would be on my stomach. Then he'd make quiet, reverent love to me.

That's what he did those days... made love.

Not that it wasn't amazing. It was totally fucking amazing. But he became more tentative as I got more pregnant. He was more careful with me. Tender.

It was an adjustment. I liked tender. Loved it. But I was also working him back toward grasping my hair, ripping my panties off and bending me over the sofa.

It was those thoughts, along with if I wanted to go with arches in our living room or if it would be more streamlined to have sharper edges, that were going through my mind as I crossed the parking lot and walked into the clubhouse.

The clubhouse was quiet. It made sense. Everyone was at Hansen and Macy's for a pool party. I was supposed to be there, but I'd left brownies in the kitchen. Mom made them for the clubhouse. They were like crack to most people. To a pregnant woman, they were something else entirely. I'd had all the best intentions with this pregnancy. To eat only natural, whole foods. The processed crap Americans ate on a daily basis was full of crap that would kill us, give us diabetes, cancer and all sorts of other things.

I knew all of that.

But my baby did not. She wanted pork skins. Burgers and fries. Brownies. And as hard as I tried to fight her, she won. I told Elden it didn't bode well for us, if our daughter was already winning fights in the womb. He'd smiled and kissed the side of my head.

Nothing bothered him lately. Sure, there was the undertone of the murders and the sheriff who wanted to destroy everything, but even that didn't seem to cause ripples in the calm waters we'd entered.

There was an odd smell in the kitchen, and not like that time when Lucas had tried to make paella. It was bitter. Coppery.

Granted, my sense of smell was magnified right then. I could no longer stand having bananas in the house. Something about the smell turned my stomach. Also, no one could write with permanent markers anywhere around me. The thought of it alone made my nose wrinkle.

My phone buzzed as the smell became stronger the closer I got to the pantry.

"Baby," Elden greeted. "Where the fuck are you?" There was worry in his voice, like there always was these days when we weren't together. He also sounded anxious. Swiss was definitely at the pool party, and the tension between them remained. Even though they had been somewhat of a team during the raid, things reverted back to their tense holding pattern straight afterward.

Mom's fury toward Elden had cooled entirely. She wasn't good at holding grudges anymore, she was entirely too cheerful. Plus, despite her misgivings about me being pregnant so young and her being a grandmother to a child who was less than two years younger than her son, she was happy. Excited.

"I'm at the club, getting brownies," I said, pointing out the obvious. The pantry door was slightly open. "I swear, if some biker has already eaten them all, we're going to engage in a blood feud."

"A blood feud?" Elden repeated, obviously amused.

"This is serious," I snapped. "As my… baby daddy, you must promise to engage in battle with whomever ate the brownies."

We still had not nailed down what we were to each other. No labels. I was already terrified enough that I was having a baby so young, that I was fitting into all those clichés I'd been certain I was going to stay away from. Even worse, they felt comfortable to me. I *liked* them.

There was a pause where I imagined Elden was swallowing a chuckle. I also imagined he was struggling with the 'baby daddy' comment. He was not worried about clichés, about ancient, patriarchal structures. He just wanted me to be his.

And I wanted that too. Yet here I was, fighting against it, pregnant with his baby.

"Okay, baby, I swear I will engage in battle with whomever ate the brownies," he agreed solemnly.

I searched for the light in the walk-in pantry, flicking it… nothing happened.

"Hang on," I told Elden. "Apparently, badass bikers can't replace lightbulbs… Or mop the floor," I added as I stepped in something sticky while I was turning on the flashlight on my phone.

Elden replied, I was sure he did. But I didn't hear anything after the shrill howl entered my ears as the flashlight illuminated the narrow space in the pantry.

Maybe I screamed, though I think I let out more of a shocked whimper. I really hoped I didn't scream, it was far too cliché, and I hated when they always made the woman scream in movies.

"Violet," Elden sounded urgent, his voice instantly changing, that warm teasing completely gone. So, I must've let out some kind of sound to trigger his alarm.

My hand shook but didn't move from where it was illuminating the body of one of the club girls. Jenna, I think her name was. We'd spoken a couple of times, she was sweet. She loved fantasy books too. Her little brother was going to Harvard. She was really proud of him.

And now she was lying in the pantry, covered in blood. It was everywhere, splattered on the walls. I was standing in it.

"Violet," Elden repeated, louder now.

"J-Jenna's dead," I stuttered, my breath catching in my chest. The world swayed as I tried to blink the image away. It didn't seem real. Couldn't be real. There was so much blood. Too much. It seemed like an over eager extra on a horror movie set had gone overboard with the ketchup.

It couldn't be real because that would mean I was standing there looking at the brutalized, dead body of a girl who had a brother in Harvard and liked to read books about magic.

"She, someone stabbed her," I continued whispering, unable to look away. "Like a lot. Her eyes are open." I stared at them. They were hazy. Empty.

"Violet, get out of there right now," Elden demanded with a tinge of panic in his voice.

People spoke in the background of the phone. I didn't hear what they said.

"That means she's dead, right?" I asked. "Maybe she isn't, maybe she's just… in shock."

I wished desperately for that to be true, even though the blood, the gruesome state of her body meant she was definitely dead. My brain could not accept that I was staring at a dead person. One who I'd seen alive, happy, smiling yesterday.

"I need to check for a pulse," I muttered more to myself than Elden.

"You need to get the fuck out of there right now," Elden barked, no longer calm at all.

Just as I knelt down, in her blood, I noticed distantly that there was a creak.

I froze.

The creak was the sound of a footstep against the floor. Somewhere. Not far.

"Someone's still here," I whispered in alarm. My heart thumped in my ears. My hand went to Jenna's neck, even though my stomach protested as it did so. She was still warm. But there was no pulse. I was no forensic investigator, but I could deduce that she had been murdered recently. If I hadn't stopped off at the gas station to pee, I likely would've happened upon the attack. Maybe I could've stopped it. Or maybe I'd be lying next to Jenna.

"He's still here," I whispered, quieter this time, fumbling for the flashlight on my phone that could be seen through the pantry door.

"I'm coming to you, Violet," Elden said as I heard the roar of a bike. "We're coming."

That would've been comforting except I knew that Hansen and Macy's place was ten minutes away. And that was being generous.

I heard another creak. Closer now.

I placed one hand protectively on my stomach. I was cold with terror. I crouched down farther, wanting to make myself as small as possible, as if that would help. What I needed was a weapon. But this pantry was full of snacks and nothing else.

How in the fuck did a biker compound not have a secret cache of guns and weapons in every corner?

I froze as my keychain clanged with my movement. I had a weapon dangling off it. Yes, it was bright pink and couldn't mortally wound anyone, but it was something.

There was another creak. My eyes were glued to the sliver of the kitchen that was visible through my vantage point… the spot between the island and the entrance to the kitchen from the hallway that led to the common area.

I stared at it like my life depended on it, which it did. There was a flutter in my belly.

Our lives depended on it.

I could still hear the low rumble of Elden's bike through my phone, and he must've switched to the Bluetooth system I'd set up for him because his voice was clear from the phone. I remember joking with him about him being so old, he couldn't even figure out how to set up Bluetooth. He'd just smiled at me and kissed my head.

That felt like a million years ago.

"Baby, I need you to talk to me," he ordered. I could tell he was fighting for control.

Elden was scared.

My eyes didn't move from the spot in the kitchen. "I have to put the phone down," I whispered as low as I could. Even that felt too loud in the eerily silent clubhouse.

"Baby, don't you leave me," Elden growled, voice low to match my energy.

I didn't want to. I wanted to cradle the phone to my ear, let him tell me everything was going to be okay, to wait for him to save me, but I knew it wouldn't work that way.

I had to save myself. Both of us.

My hand shook as I reached blindly upward, placing the phone on a flat surface as I fumbled with my keys.

The entire time, my eyes had been on that corner of the kitchen, endlessly imagining seeing the legs of the man responsible for this. I'd been imagining it because that was how my mind worked, having seen scenes like this countless times in the movie marathons I'd had with Sariah.

But I wasn't expecting it to really happen. I'd removed it from reality. My mind was fractured at this point, faced with things I knew happened in real life but only on documentaries set years in the past.

But what was happening was occurring right then, in the present. To me.

And the second I saw the motorcycle boot land on the kitchen tile, it became starkly clear...

He was here, and I was alone.

CHAPTER
Twenty-Six

IT WAS ONLY a moment before all of the lights turned off, and the only light came from the dying sun shining through the small window on the other side of the kitchen. Everything else was shadows, varying shades of black.

My keys were too loud as I scrambled for my taser. The footsteps grew quicker, less hesitant. He knew I was there.

I was literally cornered, in a fucking pantry, with no escape. I moved on instinct, knowing that if I stayed where I was, Elden and my stepfather would be finding two bodies instead of one.

That wasn't going to happen.

I slipped in blood as I pushed off from where I was crouched down, darting out the door just as the footsteps became a roar.

I smelled him. As I brushed past the warmth of his body. He reeked of sweat. Of blood.

I was still jostling my keys as he reached for me. My goal was the hall, toward the door leading to the parking lot. There was more light there, I'd be able to see him. I'd have a better chance.

But I didn't get there.

He grabbed me, yanking me back with a firm grip.

I let out a strangled scream, struggling like a banshee,

unwilling to let him get his arms around me. I somehow knew that if he could get his arms around me, I was dead.

We were dead.

I'd never been more scared in my life. Never had I felt so hopeless, so aware of how easy it was for a man to overpower a woman. Never had I felt like such a victim.

No.

I wouldn't be a victim.

Couldn't.

I thought of my mom.

My baby brother.

My stepfather.

And finally, Elden. I focused on those piercing eyes of his. The ones that lit up for me. That had welled up when he saw our baby's heartbeat. That had promised me whatever kind of future I wanted. That had promised me forever no matter how hard I tried to fight against it.

I would not let him find me like that.

Finally, I found a good grip on the taser, and I reached out wildly, ripping myself from his grip the same moment I pressed down. There was a loud buzz then a grunt of pain. I kicked out blindly with my legs, finding impact and earning me another grunt of pain.

I didn't hesitate to run then, crying out as I misjudged the distance between the island and the walkway, my side jamming against it.

Pain and panic mingled as I cradled my stomach, burning with worry over the precious thing I was growing in there.

I didn't let myself think, didn't let the pain penetrate. Sticky with blood, my feet slapped against the floor as I ran. I made it to the common room just as I heard his loud footfalls behind me. It was dark and shadowy in there too; all I could make out were shapes. The blinds were pulled. They had been open when I walked in.

He'd prepared. He'd heard me come in from the start, maybe. Had been planning for this.

I ached to hear the rumble of motorcycles, the sign that I wasn't facing him alone. But there was nothing but my ragged breathing, the horrific rhythm of our footfalls. I was halfway toward the door when he grabbed me, yanking me back by the hair.

I let out another cry of pain as I landed against his chest. I tried to take in details. He was taller than me. Bigger too. Stronger.

He reeked of blood. Something else too. A cologne that was bitter and cheap and vaguely familiar.

My body exploded with panic and terror as he held me tightly to him.

"Let go of me, you piece of shit," I snarled, slamming my foot down on his. He was wearing boots, so the impact sent pain splintering from my heel. There was a shooting, burning pain in my shoulder too. I ignored this and lifted my elbow, just as Sariah and I had been taught in our self-defense course. There was a satisfying crunch as my elbow made impact with his nose. He stumbled back, loosening his grip, and I took advantage of that by pulling myself out of his grasp and sprinting toward the door.

I'd gained a few seconds, but the sound of him coming after me, his breath hot on my neck, told me I hadn't done enough.

I heard the sound of motorcycles the second I found purchase on the door. I didn't hesitate to open it, letting the light in.

And that was then I did something stupid. I didn't run blindly into the parking lot. I turned around, knowing that he was already running from the sound, knowing he didn't have time to kill me and escape from the bikers who would rip him limb from limb.

I knew that I needed to find something, anything that would give me a clue to his identity, give us the chance to avenge Jenna and the girls before her.

But all I saw was the flash of his black hoodie with an insignia on it I couldn't decipher. He'd rounded the corner to the kitchen, toward the back door before I had a proper chance to look.

The clamor of the motorcycles was deafening now, and I blinked rapidly, my eyes adjusting to the light as the bikes pulled in with a dizzying, worrisome speed. My vision was blurry, unable to make out anything but the shapes until Elden threw his bike down on the concrete and raced toward me.

A lot of things would haunt me in the days, weeks and months after that. But the sheer terror on his face was something I could never shake.

I didn't realize at the time that I was covered in blood, not realizing just how much of Jenna's blood I'd coated myself in.

"Violet," Elden breathed my name like a prayer once he made it to me.

Swiss wasn't far behind him. "Jesus," my stepfather uttered in a low, devastated voice.

"I'm okay," I reassured them both quickly, my voice foreign, flat.

Elden's eyes were wide and horrified as he took me in, his hands finding my stomach.

I let out a little yelp of pain when his hand landed on the spot I'd hit on the counter.

Both him and my stepfather froze at my yelp of pain. Or at least, I thought that was why.

Both Elden and Swiss were staring in horror over my shoulder. I began to twist to see what the big deal was, but Elden's hands found my neck, the grip tight enough to still me.

"Don't move, Violet," he murmured, dusting his thumb against the bottom of my jaw.

"Hansen!" my stepfather hollered, nowhere near as calm and collected as Elden.

Hansen appeared in front of me as did the rest of the club.

They were all staring at me in varying degrees of horror, which really didn't do well for the calm I was desperately trying to hold on to.

"He ran. Out the back," I told Hades and Jagger, both of whom had guns drawn and disappeared inside along with everyone but Colby, Hansen and Elden.

"Baby, I need you to stay calm," Elden told me, his voice gentle, careful.

"You know when you tell someone to stay calm it has the exact opposite effect," I retorted. "Especially when you're looking at me like that." I was holding on to my irritation, but it was slippery, and spots danced in my vision. My fingers and toes were numb.

Hansen's eyes were on me but he spoke to Elden. "Need you to let her go," he told him evenly. I liked Hansen's tone. It was even calmer than Elden's. Comforting. He'd been a medic in the Army, I was pretty sure. He was used to stressful situations, at staying even-tempered. Also, it probably helped that I wasn't his woman and pregnant with his baby; he could be slightly more removed from the situation.

Elden's jaw flexed at Hansen's request. He didn't want to let me go. Which I understood because I didn't want him to let me go. I had the overwhelming feeling that something terrible was rushing toward me. Like that scene in *Deep Impact* when Téa Leoni and her dad were standing at the shore after the asteroid hit, and the ocean receded in preparation for the huge tsunami to come in.

Yeah, I felt just like that.

And Elden was the only thing keeping the wave at bay.

"I'm fine," I reassured Hansen in a shaky voice. "I just bumped my hip on the counter."

Elden's hand went to my stomach, the touch featherlight but enough to warrant a little kick. Our daughter had always loved her father's touch.

His body visibly relaxed, but his expression told me he was still wired.

"See?" I said, glancing to Swiss. "She's fine." My hand covered Elden's. The movement made my shoulder burn a little, but I made sure not to show that. "We're fine."

Swiss looked from Hansen to me to Elden. "Who the fuck is

going to tell her?" he asked, his voice strained, eyes clouded with concern.

Colby was startlingly pale.

"Honey, you've got a knife in your shoulder," Hansen told me calmly, without any of the barely restrained anger and panic radiating from the rest of the men.

I tilted my head, considering his words. "I've got a *knife* in my shoulder?"

He nodded matter-of-factly, like we were discussing the weather. Like a knife in the shoulder was no big deal. Which I guessed, to him, was true. He'd been on battlefields. He'd seen much worse. I'd worry when he looked worried.

Swiss, Elden and Colby only looked like they did because they were seriously overprotective. It was no big deal. Surely, they'd seen worse, being outlaw bikers and such. They were just worried because I was a girl, and they were expecting me to freak out. I straightened my posture. I would not freak out. In fact, I would prove just how much tougher we were than men. It was my duty. For the sisterhood.

"Okay," I said calmly. "But I can't feel it."

"You're in shock," Hansen informed me, moving around my body to inspect the area which I assumed had a knife protruding from it. The knife that had likely been used to kill Jenna. That had ended her life.

My vision swam for a moment on that thought.

"Don't touch it!" I shouted quickly. "I mean, it's got his fingerprints on it, won't it? The killer?" I looked at Elden. His gaze was steely, cold and intense on me. "I mean, maybe he was wearing gloves. But maybe he wasn't. And we can't take that chance. Plus, it's not really even bothering me," I lied.

Now that I knew it was there, the burning in my shoulder was getting more intense by the second, and spots danced in my vision quicker. My stomach heaved, and I forced myself to swallow down the bile creeping up my throat.

The ground swayed.

Elden grabbed on to my hip, the opposite one from the one I'd hit.

"We need to get her to a fucking hospital now," he seethed.

Hansen nodded. "Can you walk, honey?" he asked me in that gloriously calm voice of his. He wasn't panicking. Neither was I.

"You're like a flight attendant," I blurted.

He blinked, and Swiss and Caleb exchanged worried glances.

"Did you hit your head, baby?" Elden asked, carefully brushing the hair from my face, looking at my forehead for a bruise or a cut, I assumed.

"No," I huffed out. "I mean, when there's turbulence, if the flight attendants are still handing out drinks, smiling and laughing, you know that it's all good. You're not going to plummet to your death in a ball of fire." I nodded to Hansen, wincing at the pain that radiated from my shoulder. "He's the flight attendant," I said around the pain. "He's calm. Which means I'm good. Therefore, you all," I motioned to Elden, Swiss and Colby, "need to stop with the masculine fury and worry because it's *freaking me out.*"

Hansen smiled. No one else did.

"Hospital, now," Elden ground out.

"Can you walk, Violet?" Hansen asked, nodding to the van that had pulled up in front of us. I guessed we weren't waiting for an ambulance. I was glad about that. The reality of being put in an ambulance would've made the situation much too real.

Not that the dead body, the blood, the struggle with a serial killer and a knife in the shoulder wasn't real. But it felt faraway. Maybe Hansen was right... I was in shock.

"Sure, I can walk," I said with more confidence than I felt. It was only a handful of steps away.

"She can't fuckin' walk," Elden snapped. "I'll carry her."

"Can't risk the knife moving," Hansen informed him. "If she can walk, it's better."

Elden stared at his president for what felt like a mighty long time, as if he were measuring his words before he finally gave in.

Elden moved to the left side of me. The burning was coming from the right.

"Lean on me, baby," he murmured, kissing my hair.

"I'm fine," I argued, walking forward.

The world shifted when I did, so I was thankful for Elden's solid form next to me. Both Swiss and Colby were watching helplessly as Hansen climbed into the van first, holding out his hand to steady me as I climbed inside. Elden was right beside me, and I clamped my teeth together so I didn't cry out in pain with the effort it took to get myself in the seat.

Elden was beside me in an instant.

He kissed my temple. "Good work, baby." He looked to Swiss who had climbed into the driver's seat. "Get to the hospital. Now."

There was definitely a ride to the hospital. Definitely hard jaws and glowering looks of concern. Surely. But I was removed from it all as if I had floated away, even though Elden's hands were on me.

Even his firm, loving presence wasn't enough.

The wave came and washed everything away.

ELDEN

She was sleeping.

They'd removed the knife, and by the grace of some higher power, it hadn't done any permanent damage, nothing that required surgery.

The baby was fine too. There was a large and angry bruise where she'd bumped her hip, but nothing internal. A strong heartbeat. Both of them.

All good news.

She'd make a full recovery.

Physically.

The door opened and closed. I didn't look up to see who it was.

I kept my eyes on Violet. They'd cleaned all the blood off her. She looked paler, smaller than normal in that bed.

My eyes flickered to the monitor every now and then, first hers, then the baby's. Then they went back to her chest, the rise and fall, finishing on her face. It had been my routine for hours.

Kate had been here, on the other side of the bed, clutching her daughter's hand, forcing smiles and jokes, hiding her horror as only a parent could.

She left only because Violet urged her to. Because she had a baby boy at home. It had been tense since it was clear Kate did not want to let her firstborn out of her sight.

"Elden's here," Violet had argued. She was tired. Crashing. You could see it. Hear it. It had been a miracle that she'd been alert and together for as long as she had. Except for when her eyes had gone blank and glossy somewhere between the club and the hospital. That had been the scariest moment of my fucking life.

But she came back to me.

She was a fucking miracle.

"He's not going to let me out of his sight, right, handsome?" she'd asked me with a teasing grin. My gut clenched.

"Right, baby," I kissed her hand.

Kate looked at me uncertainly. With the same uncertain edge that had been there since she found out I impregnated her daughter.

But now there was something else. Trust. She might not like what I was to Violet, but she understood how it worked in this club. What we did for the women we loved. She knew come hell or high water, her daughter was safe with me. Even though I'd fucking failed them both with Violet in this hospital bed.

So, she left, promising to be back the second she bathed and put her son to bed.

Violet had crashed not long after that, holding it together only for her mother's sake, not wanting her to worry.

Boots thumped against the ground as Swiss sat beside me.

He'd been here beside his wife too, then he'd been at the club, trying to figure out who the fuck did this.

The piece of shit sheriff didn't help. He was treating the fucking club like suspects. Apparently, he'd tried to come in here to interview Violet. Swiss had made sure that didn't happen. I couldn't be within five feet of the man. I might've ripped his head off.

He didn't speak as soon as he sat down beside me.

"She's going to be okay, brother," he said finally, clapping me on the shoulder.

It was only the second time he'd called me brother since he'd found out Violet was carrying my baby. There was no violence in his tone now. No undertone that communicated he would kill me if he could.

I might've felt relief if the situation were different. If my woman wasn't in a hospital bed with a fucking stab wound and trauma that would live in her bones.

"I can't stop thinking about pulling into that parking lot," I said, not taking my eyes off her. "Seeing her standing there, covered in blood. Covered in it." I shuddered. "Can't stop hearin' her crying out in pain on the other side of the phone, hearing her fighting him off."

My stomach turned at the memory that wasn't a memory. I could hear it right now, clear as day. Could feel the bike underneath me, willing it to go faster when I knew I was already too late to save her. Knowing that she was completely fucking alone. Pregnant with my baby, and it could all be taken away from me.

"Gonna be marryin' her," I said, still staring at Violet.

I took a breath, a long one, finding enough control to convince myself that if I took my eyes off her for a moment, she'd still be there, her chest would still rise and fall, and the heartbeat monitors would stay steady.

Not much would get me to look away from her at that point,

but this was important to me and I was going to do it right… Well, as right as I could given the current circumstances.

My eyes found Swiss's. They were hard with worry, but not with the borderline hatred he'd been directing at me since the news came out. Rightly so. I deserved it.

"Know this isn't what Kate wanted for her," I continued. "Know that this is not what you want for her. Know I did it in a fucked-up way. But I love her."

The steady beeping of the monitors kept me calm. Or as calm as I could be.

"I'll give her the life she deserves," I told him. "Wherever that takes me. Even if I have to abandon the cut, I'll do it. For her." The thought wasn't as terrifying as I thought it might be. The club, the cut, had quickly become a part of me when I had nothing else.

Now I had something else.

I had two heartbeats that I'd do anything for.

Swiss looked at me. I hoped he wouldn't challenge me on this. Not because I wasn't up for it, because Violet didn't need that shit.

"Thought, very seriously, about burying you in the desert, up to your neck and letting the sun, the coyotes or the ants get you," Swiss said coolly.

I nodded once, knowing that was not hyperbole. He was a sick fuck and would do anything for those he loved.

"Thought of about a hundred other ways to end you," he said conversationally. His eyes shifted to Violet. "I knew Kate was mine the second I saw her. And when I heard her talk about Violet, knew she was mine too. Knew it was my job to do what her father didn't. Couldn't. Love her. Protect her. Make sure anyone in this world who thought about fucking with her wouldn't be breathing for long."

His eyes found mine again.

"Not crazy about the way this started," he grumbled. "But having the time to figure it out, see what you'd do for her, the love you feel for her... The other bullshit falls away."

His eyes trekked to Violet again, as if he too needed to remind himself that she was there, breathing, heart beating.

"I realize now that I wouldn't want anyone who wasn't wearin' a Sons of Templar cut to be lookin' out for her," he murmured. "Granted, I wanted it to happen a little later in her life and earlier in yours." He grinned. "But who the fuck am I to talk about what's appropriate. What's normal. You make her happy, keep her safe. I don't give a fuck about the rest." He squeezed my shoulder. "You break her heart, I'll carve out yours and feed it to you."

"Wouldn't have it any other way," I replied.

We both looked at her. "I was the easy one, you know," he gestured to the tiny body lying in the bed.

"She's gonna be the challenge, with all of her progressive ideas on marriage and patriarchy."

I wanted to smile. But it was impossible when my woman was lying in a hospital bed with stitches in her shoulder and a bruise next to the place my daughter was growing.

"Oh, I know," I said.

"You're up for the challenge, then?"

"Oh, fuck yeah." I looked at him once more. "You gonna walk her down the aisle?"

"You get her there, I'll walk her down the aisle," he promised.

And there it was, one hurdle crossed. I could feel it, the chasm between us being closed.

But Swiss was right… he was not going to be the difficult one. The small, pregnant woman in the hospital bed would be it. The one who had just fought off a serial killer then walked calmly to the van when she found out she had a knife protruding from her shoulder.

Yes, she was a miracle.

And she'd be my wife.

Even if it took forever to convince her.

CHAPTER *Twenty-Seven*

VIOLET

ELDEN WAS SITTING in the chair next to my bed when I woke up. That didn't surprise me. It wouldn't have surprised me if I'd been in a coma for three months. He would've been at my side the entire time.

He jerked the second my eyes opened. The *second.* He was watching me with a concentrated intensity that likely would've woken me up if he had those kinds of powers. I hadn't ruled out that possibility.

"Hi," I rasped.

Elden rushed to grab the pitcher of water beside my bed, pouring it into a glass—glass, not a plastic cup, which meant my mother or Freya had been here—and gave it to me.

I took it thankfully, my throat burning and dry.

Elden watched me, his eyes full of cerulean fire.

I handed him back the glass and took stock of my body. My shoulder burned dully, my entire body felt tight, tense, achy, as if I'd done a really intense workout the day before. It made sense, my fight or flight response had been triggered, and I'd done both. My hand went to my stomach, comforted to know that the doctors had found a steady heartbeat.

On cue, our little girl wiggled beneath my palm.

"I'm fine," I told Elden, though I knew that wouldn't make much of a difference to him right now.

He didn't respond, just continued with the intense stare thing.

I sighed, pushing myself up, or trying to. Elden was at my side in a moment, lifting me up to a sitting position with care.

His lips landed on my head, and he stayed there for a moment, breathing me in before he sat back in the chair that was as close to my bed as humanly possible.

"We need to get married," he said.

I rubbed my eyes, staring at him and waiting for the punchline. None came. He was Elden, serious, intense, somber.

I didn't reply because what did someone say to their baby daddy who informed them they were getting married—informed, didn't ask—after they woke up in a hospital bed after having an altercation with a serial killer?

"You're gonna argue with me on that," he murmured.

"Yes," I sighed. "When I've gotten my bearings, we are going to argue about the marriage we both refused when my stepfather tried to force it on us. When I told you that a baby is not a reason to get married, and that I loathed the institution of it because all it does is make women the property of men."

Elden just looked at me. He didn't smile, face completely devoid of emotion. The corner of his lip didn't even turn up in that kind of smile he had. He just stared, his eyes twinkling ever so slightly. But there were also plenty of shadows in them. Surrounding him. He was haunted, already by what happened. It hurt me to see it, but it didn't stop me from being pissed.

"If this is you without your bearings, I'm gonna need to prepare," he commented dryly.

I scowled at him, but before I could launch into another

diatribe, he moved forward, grasping my hands in his and lifting them up to his mouth, kissing them lovingly.

My readiness to argue drained out of me.

"I've never been more scared in my life," he whispered, eyes searing into me. "Hearing you cry out like that, hearing you fight off that fuck and knowing I wouldn't get there in time." He shuddered. No, *shuddered* was not the right word for it. Something cracked in the core of him, like a massive earthquake, destroying everything. And this was just an aftershock.

"I'm okay," I told him in a whisper, trying to fight back tears at seeing my strong man unraveling before my eyes.

He was still grasping my hands, like they were his only lifeboat in the middle of a storm.

"I wasn't there," his nostrils flared. "I should've fuckin' been there."

"How could you have known that a serial killer would be lying in wait when I was innocently getting brownies?"

The joke didn't land.

"This isn't your fault," I told him firmly. "And you *were* there. You *were* with me. You helped me fight."

Elden shook his head, lips still at my hands. "No, you fought for yourself. For me." His hands went to my stomach. "For us."

My eyes filled with tears that I fought not to let fall.

"Did someone call Jenna's family?" I asked weakly.

Elden blinked at the change in subject.

Jenna. The girl whose smile I couldn't remember now because she was coated in blood. All I could recall were those barren eyes that saw nothing.

Elden squeezed my hand. "Yeah, baby. Hansen did. Macy was with them when they arrived."

I nodded once, still fighting against tears. "Will you find him?"

Elden's gaze instantaneously filled with bloodlust. "Oh, yes. We're gonna fuckin' find him and pull him apart, piece by piece."

The promise in his tone ran over my skin, cold but also comforting.

I wanted revenge. Wanted the person who could do that to women suffer in a way that the judicial system was not capable of delivering.

"Good," I whispered. I searched his face, the man I loved. The father of my baby. The man who had been there since that night on the roof. Who had traveled to another country to punish someone for putting their hands on me. Who called me when it rained. Who was mine even when he wasn't.

My ideas on marriage were a knee-jerk reaction, informed by my own past more than anything else.

I knew that the marriages within this club did not even resemble the contract or the prison I'd been convinced matrimony was. Knew it was because these men wanted the world to know in every conceivable way that they were taken. Owned. It was not the men who owned the women, it was the other way around. Even if, upon first glance, their unions looked like some bullshit patriarchal structure, I'd come to understand that this club was one of the most progressive organizations in the country.

"Okay," I said.

He stiffened. "Okay?"

"We'll get married."

His expression shifted. All of that fury melted in an instant. Something akin to… joy took its place.

I cursed myself for fighting it this long when this was what I got. This was what I could give Elden.

Joy.

"We're not doing it in this hospital, though," I added, envisioning him running through the halls to find someone to marry us. He had that alpha urgency about him.

His mouth ticked upward. "Wouldn't dream of it," he murmured. "Want to do it before the baby's born, though."

"Of course," I rolled my eyes. "You couldn't wait until I'm not a whale and won't have pictures of me with five chins and giant ankles in our house for the rest of our life."

His eyes darkened, but only slightly. "First off, you're the most stunning creature I've ever seen carrying my baby. Not gonna listen to you talk about yourself like that."

I pursed my lips against my smile. Elden had made it clear, very clear, that the changes my body was going through were very attractive to him.

"Second," he continued. "We don't have to have a big ceremony; we can do the courthouse thing and wait for whenever you want to have the big wedding. What's important to me is that you're my wife."

"Fine," I sighed, holding his gaze.

His beard parted, presenting me with a dazzling grin. "That's a story to tell our daughter. What did your mother say when I proposed? Fine."

"Well, considering the start of the proposal was her father ordering her mother to marry him after being attacked by a serial killer, it tracks."

His expression faltered.

I reached out to brush his beard. "We'll find a more PG story," I promised.

He didn't look convinced as he nodded.

We didn't have time to say anything else, though, since that was when the doctor came in.

And unsurprisingly, Elden transitioned into a scary, protective biker, peppering him with every question under the sun.

I had no end of visitors, even though I was due to be discharged the next day. Me being in the hospital was merely a precaution, and I had the option of being discharged sooner, an option Elden would not even consider.

I didn't even try to fight about that since I knew I wouldn't win. If it were just me, I would've had more to say. But it was not just me. Our baby had a shock, but despite slightly high blood pressure, she was fine. Even though I felt profound relief over that, I was also filled with a fierce protectiveness, a visceral fear that I hadn't felt before all of this started.

This was my baby. Our baby. Our future. A precious, priceless thing that was so vulnerable. That some fucking asshole tried to take from us.

Sariah, who had dropped everything to get here, was also alternating between fury, false cheer and planning mode.

The first time Elden left me alone, presumably to have some meeting about vengeance somewhere in the hospital—no way was he leaving the premises—he left me alone with Sariah. My mom was getting food and coffee, and the rest of the Old Ladies were getting the house ready for my homecoming. I had no idea what that really meant, but I was too tired to ask.

Tired and a bunch of other things.

"I feel like I failed," I admitted to Sariah while she was fussing with the flowers in my room.

She spun around, frowning at me. "What did you just say?"

I toyed with the blanket on the bed. It was cashmere. While I was having my first shower—with Elden, because he wouldn't dream of me showering alone, lest I slip or linger outside of his watchful eye for too long—Sariah had replaced the bedding. Freya brought in silk pajamas and a twelve-step skincare routine. Macy had arranged a stack of books at my bedside.

Mom brought a never-ending supply of brownies and other baked goods.

Caroline set up a laptop, connecting it to the internet so it was constantly playing *Gilmore Girls*.

The Sons of Templar had done what they did best, like the forces of nature they were.

I couldn't help but feel inadequate.

"I should've done something more." I played the events over again, thinking if I'd done something different, Jagger and Hades might've been able to catch him.

"Babe, you fought off a serial killer," Sariah reminded me. "You did it while pregnant, with his knife protruding from your *fucking shoulder*. You're better than any dumb, two-dimensional horror movie heroine. If I hear you talking shit about what more you could've done, when you did the absolute most, I will bitch-slap you, even if you're pregnant and in the hospital." I could tell that she was trying very hard to keep her voice light. To keep the fear and worry out of it.

Everyone was.

Everyone was shocked in a way that surprised me for a club of men and women who were, unfortunately, accustomed to violence and death. I supposed a lot of it was what they'd invited in... Part of the life they'd agreed to when they put on the cut. Or formed a union with a man wearing one.

But this was something different.

This was the horrors of the outside world coming in. This violence was not retribution for something the club did. This was a senseless evil that permeated everything and shook even the baddest of badasses. I saw it with my own eyes. I only wish I saw more.

The sheriff had come in not long after I woke up, only because I heard Swiss arguing with him in the hall, and I'd convinced Elden that I wanted to speak to him.

Elden was not happy about that. Elden was not happy about anything right now. Sure, he was trying to force smiles, keep his gaze light and unworried on my account, but I saw the concern in his eyes, the terror that had yet to recede.

When the sheriff came in, Elden was a statue at my side.

To his credit, at least the sheriff managed to look sheepish, staring down at me in the hospital bed.

"Are you ready to take this seriously now?" I asked him, not bothering to hide the irritation from my voice.

He nodded tightly. "I assure you, we're doing everything we can to catch this monster, and we appreciate you working with us. Tell me everything you remember."

The problem was, I couldn't remember much. I didn't hold anything back when I spoke to the sheriff. I mentioned the motorcycle boots, the detail causing Elden to stiffen, the detail that had the sheriff's hand stutter as he wrote down my statement.

He'd given Swiss and Elden a careful look then, but he was smart enough not to say anything.

I knew what they were all thinking, though. That there was a possibility this was someone in the club.

I didn't believe that.

But I couldn't rule it out either. My details were that he wore motorcycle boots, was taller and stronger than me, wore shitty cologne and a sweatshirt with an insignia on it I didn't recognize.

Nothing much for anyone to go on.

Regardless, the sheriff took my statement and assured me they were working overtime on it.

"Does that mean you're not wasting your time on the club and working to make sure you're actually protecting and serving the community?" I asked sweetly.

Swiss, who had been hard-faced during the interview grinned. Elden did not.

Nor did the sheriff.

"I'll be doing everything I can," he replied. "If you remember anything else, please let us know."

"You'll be the first person I call," I lied.

His eyebrow twitched, but he didn't say anything else, just nodded and walked out.

"Promise me you're not going to get involved with this anymore," I said to Sariah.

She blew out a raspberry. "Babe, I'm staring at you in a fucking hospital bed after he tried to kill you. How can I not get more involved?"

My heart hammered at the thought of my brave, feisty, impulsive friend doing anything for me. "Because I need you as my baby's godmother and my maid of honor."

Her eyes widened. "Way to bury the fucking lede!" she shrieked. "You're getting married?"

I nodded. "It seems Elden is no longer willing to take no for an answer, and I'm no longer willing to refuse him."

"About fucking time," she beamed at me. "Now, I love that you're independent and fighting the system and all that jazz," she waved her hand, "but you and Elden are something else, babe. And you procreating is really helping out humanity because your babies will be gorgeous badasses." She looked at my stomach. "You could be growing the first female president in there."

"There is definitely going to be a female president before then," I told her. "Fuck, *you* could be the next female president."

"I would rock that shit," Sariah agreed, tapping a finger to her lips. "But I'd never pass the background check." Her eyes narrowed. "Plus, we're getting off topic. Wedding... When, where, and most importantly, do I get to choose my own dress?"

I grinned and let Sariah go off on a wedding planning tangent, unable to shake my dread, my certainty, that this was not over.

ELDEN

We were holding church in the hospital chapel. Something I might've found ironic and amusing had my pregnant woman not been lying in a hospital bed.

The only reason I was leaving her was because we had two Prospects at her door and Sariah inside with her.

Even if anyone did manage to get past two armed Prospects, they stood no chance with my woman's best friend. I knew a couple of patched members who were equally scared to death of the woman and infatuated with her.

Javier was one of them. It should've relieved me that he was no longer brave enough to look or speak to Violet, but something about the fuck still rubbed me the wrong way.

"What do we have?" I barked the second the door to the chapel closed.

Despite knowing logically that Violet was safe, I could barely stand not being able to see her, not being able to use the image of her clean, breathing, beautiful and unharmed to chase away the one of her covered in blood. If I couldn't hear her voice, then I couldn't drown out the sound of her fighting against a fucking serial killer.

Everyone's faces were grim. This had rocked everyone.

Jenna had been new but well liked.

Lucas was hit hardest, he had taken a liking to her. But everyone was shaken.

This had nothing to do with the club. This was something different. Something wrong and evil that had made its way into our world, had touched our women.

"He must've had a vehicle somewhere close," Jagger said, face stormy. "We didn't even get a glimpse of him when we made chase."

"He also overrode the club's security," Colby shared. "Cameras, gates, everything."

That was no mean feat. The security was done in tandem with Greenstone and Wire from the Amber chapter. That shit was top-notch and rivaled some of the most high-tech government shit.

"So, he knew our security and was familiar with the layout of the club," Hansen rapped his knuckles against the pew. The fucker looked troubled. Deeply fucking troubled.

The club and everyone involved was his responsibility. He was taking this hard. Blaming himself.

"Must've been inside at least once," Hades said. "Also knew

that no one would be there. Had to have been watching Jenna for some time to know she was going to be there alone."

"She shouldn't have been there alone in the first place," Lucas grumbled, obviously full of blame.

"This isn't your fault," Hansen clapped him on the shoulder. "She should've been safe at the club. We are taking care of all of her funeral costs and her brother's tuition at Harvard." He looked around. "This is top priority over everything else," he announced. "We don't have a shipment to run for a few weeks. We'll spare who we can for that, but our main focus is nailing this fuck, getting all the information we can."

"Sariah has been lookin' into him when I explicitly forbade her from doin' it. I'll get what she's got," Colby said.

Swiss grinned. "You've got some shit to learn if you think that woman is gonna do anything but the exact opposite when you try and forbid her to do shit."

Colby did not grin back at him.

"Get whatever she has. Wire is going over all police reports as we speak," Hansen told us.

How that fuck actually survived was anyone's guess. He was on call for half the clubs in the country and could hack into anything.

"Violet's old roommate… Ollie, she's been lookin' into shit too. Seems to be a college version of Wire," I said.

Hansen nodded. "Okay, I want all the club girls followed everywhere. Want new security at the club and eyes open."

Even though he didn't have a gavel to hit, everyone took that as their cue to go.

Hansen eyed both Swiss and I, so we lingered, knowing he had shit to say.

He only spoke once the door shut, leaving just the three of us. Though I was itching to get back to my woman, I managed to lock my shit down.

"Worries me that whoever this was knew the club so intimately," he muttered.

He was vocalizing what we'd all been thinking.

"You think it's someone wearin' a patch?" Swiss asked, cracking his knuckles.

A muscle in Hansen's jaw twitched. "I hope to fuck it's not," he replied. "But we can't rule it out. I trust each of the men in this club with my life. Wouldn't have given them patches otherwise. But no fuckin' way I'm taking any chances."

Swiss nodded, I tightened my fists. The thought that it could be a brother left me itching to cause mayhem. There were men I knew for a fact couldn't do this. Men with Old Ladies, children. But the ones without that, fuck… who knew.

"If it is a patch, they're fucking excellent at hiding what they are," I growled.

Everyone wearing a patch went through a year of prospecting. Before they even prospected, they had extensive background checks. That's how Hansen knew about my past.

It was not unique for a brother to have a record. Fuck, it was practically a requirement, along with a fucked-up past. That's what made men seek out this life.

Unfortunately, that also could be a recipe for a piece of shit who liked to kill and torture women.

"Wire is going over everyone's shit again, with a fine-toothed comb," Hansen sighed. "But that fucker is busy as it is. There's a lot to wade through. This piece of shit covers his tracks well, hasn't left so much as a scrap of evidence at any crime scene. It's not gonna happen quickly, so we need to be on guard."

Both Swiss and I nodded. I imagined he was going to have a similar conversation with the men we all knew had nothing to do with this. Problem was, prior to what happened, if you'd asked me which man in the club could be capable of this, I wouldn't have been able to point to a single one. Sure, I didn't like every single brother, but I trusted each of them with my life.

We were all silent for a moment, considering what the reality of a brother betraying us would look like.

"Onto something a little more cheerful," Swiss clapped his hands together, breaking the silence. "You convince Violet to marry you yet?"

It was hard to remember that my brother no longer wanted to kill me.

"It just so happens I have," I replied.

He grinned, clapping me on the shoulder. "Impressive. I would've put money on it taking you at least another week."

Hansen smiled too. "We needed something to celebrate. The bad comes whether we want it to or not. The good we need to celebrate."

I nodded, thinking of my woman in that hospital bed. The woman who would be my wife.

I tried to focus on that instead of the man who tried to kill her still walking this earth.

He wouldn't be for long.

CHAPTER
Twenty-Eight

VIOLET

MOM and I were out shopping.

We were not alone.

Colby was with us.

Not because he wanted to be shopping for dresses that didn't scream 'shotgun wedding,' but because I did not go anywhere alone anymore.

Elden was with me as often as possible, which was almost constantly—this was the first time he'd let me out of his sight for a prolonged period of time since I'd gotten out of the hospital.

He'd been… intense, to say the least. But I'd needed that. As much as I liked to consider myself strong and capable, I had PTSD from seeing a mutilated dead body then fighting for my life afterward.

There were nightmares. Flashbacks. Panic attacks.

But Elden was there for every single one. He was my calming, strong presence. My port in the storm. He chased off the most severe effects. And I had become somewhat insatiable since we got out of the hospital, desperate to feel alive again.

The most enjoyable way to feel alive was to be fucked by him.

Fucked.

I didn't need gentle. Which I'd communicated to him as he undressed me in our bedroom.

"Please," I murmured, his lips against mine.

His hand at my breast stalled. "I don't want to hurt you, Violet," he sighed. My shoulder was healed, the nasty bruise at my side remained, though it barely hurt anymore.

"I need you to hurt me," I implored, desperate. "I need you to mark my body. To give me something else to focus on. I need you."

His eyes warred, fighting against his instincts. He wanted to protect me, make sure no further harm came to me. But I knew his baser instincts needed this too. That he was just as hungry for this as I was.

For a second, I was transported back to the roof of the clubhouse, watching him decide whether he was going to kiss me or not, whether he was going to bring us right here, to this moment.

Then, he thrust me firmly back into the present, flipping me so my hands landed on our bed, my ass in the air.

My hands fisted the sheets, my body ripe with anticipation as Elden's hand had trailed down my spine, hooking into the lace of my underwear and tearing them off.

"You're my bad little girl still, aren't you?" he rasped in my ear, spreading my legs with his feet.

"Always," I promised. "Always yours."

He grasped a handful of my hair, yanking me back so my neck was exposed to him, and my scalp burned with delicious agony.

Our eyes met. His blazed as the control he'd been clutching to lately slipped out of his grasp.

"Violet," he warned, voice thick.

"Fuck me, Elden," I ordered.

His eyes flared, and then he thrust in. Brutal. Fabulous. He didn't stop until the world fell away, and we were the only people left on the planet.

"What about this?" Mom asked.

I jerked back into the present, looking at the light pink, lace dress she was holding up.

My cheeks flamed.

It was completely inappropriate to be thinking about that as I shopped for my wedding dress with my mother, but I couldn't help it. Elden did that to me. I wore marks on my thighs, my ass as evidence that I was alive, loved, cherished and that that fucker didn't win.

They still hadn't found him, something that I knew haunted every man in the club. The sheriff was still investigating, whatever the fuck that meant.

Sariah, luckily, had been too preoccupied with planning things for the wedding next week to be doing anything that would get her on either the sheriff or the killer's radar.

My wedding, which would be taking place during the eighth month of my pregnancy while I also somehow managed to finish my degree.

Both Mom and Elden had tried to convince me to contact my professors after I got out of the hospital. As far as excuses went, being attacked by a serial killer while pregnant was a pretty good one to get me out of my final assignments. But I fought them. Because if I didn't have assignments to finish, then I would've had a bunch of free time to think about everything.

Thinking was bad.

Which was why I threw myself into schoolwork and into putting the finishing touches on our house. We were breaking ground the day after the wedding.

Elden had taken me out there the day I got discharged from the hospital.

It was perfect. Everything I could've imagined. It wasn't far from Mom and Swiss's place, closer to the mountains than them, the sky and desert endless around us. I could envision exactly where everything would go. Where we'd have our greenhouse—I planned to grow as much of our own food as possible—where the pool would go, my studio, a large garage.

I could see our entire life there.

But right now, I was looking at dresses.

"It's pretty," I said, fingering the lace.

"See, it's pretty! Perfect!" Colby exclaimed. "Buy it. Then we're done."

I chuckled at my friend. He had been a good sport during the first hour, even offering helpful suggestions. But his patience had worn thin after the tenth dress, and he was slowly losing the will to live.

"Even if this is the one, which I'm not convinced it is, we're not done," I informed him. "We still have to find shoes, which will be extra challenging since my feet have ballooned to what must be three times their normal size."

"Why can't I be fighting rivals somewhere, seconds away from death?" Colby groaned.

Mom and I both grinned. "Your feet are not three times their normal size," Mom argued.

I sighed, looking down at them. I may have been exaggerating, but they felt like it. My stamina for shopping had greatly decreased, especially since every dress I tried on was wrong.

We weren't doing a courthouse wedding. I didn't want that. I wanted to celebrate with my family and friends, make it a big event. My grandparents were coming. My brilliant, loving, unflappable grandparents had taken in stride that their granddaughter was not only pregnant but marrying a man much older than her in the same outlaw motorcycle club as the man my mom married.

My grandmother was already shopping for our nursery and for her great-granddaughter.

Since it was going to be a real wedding, I wanted something specific. I didn't want a traditional wedding dress. I did not want it to look like a shotgun wedding. Which was impossible since I was eight months pregnant. Sure, my slight frame hadn't blown up that much, and every woman in the club had told me how lucky I was, how good I looked, but I was sure they were only saying it to make me feel better.

My tits were huge. My stomach wasn't *huge,* but it was approaching that. Not that I wanted to hide it in a dress, but I didn't want it looking like maternity bride.

For the millionth time, I wished Sariah was here. Not that my mom wasn't wonderful… she was. But Sariah had a kind of magic when it came to fashion. She'd find exactly what I wanted even when I didn't know exactly what I wanted. Something elegant, classy, sexy and not over the top. Something that complimented my bump but didn't highlight it.

"I think we need to call it," I sighed, wondering what could be so important that my best friend couldn't help me shop for a dress a week before the fucking wedding.

Time was quickly running out. Even if Macy told me she could alter whatever we got in plenty of time. At this rate, I'd be walking down the aisle in sweatpants.

Not that there would be an aisle. We were having something at Mom and Swiss's. Which suited me just fine. As long as we had family, the desert, and most importantly, Elden, I didn't much care.

Mom glanced at her phone. "Okay," she chirped, putting the dress back.

It was odd since she'd been intense about us searching every store for something 'perfect'.

"Thank the fucking lord," Colby muttered.

I shot him a glare.

"We're never going to find anything," I whined to my mother.

She put her arm around me. "I promise, we will."

Though I didn't think my mother would flat out lie to me, I thought she would also omit some things so she didn't have to face the wrath of a bride who was eight months pregnant.

"How about we get a pretzel, huh?" she suggested warmly.

I pouted. "I don't want a pretzel. I just want to go home."

And I kept pouting and sulking the entire drive home, munching on a pretzel. Not exactly mature of me, but I was at the mercy of hormonal mood swings. And despite my reluctance to get married, I actually *wanted* to be Elden's wife, very much. I may not have ever been the girl who fantasized about her wedding, but I did want it to be *something special*. And I wanted to look like a goddess.

Heaven knew my groom was going to look handsome as all hell no matter what.

The bastard.

Men should be the ones who got pregnant.

Then again, if they were, the species would be extinct within a generation.

I was much too deep in my thoughts to take notice of where we were going until we pulled up at Mom and Swiss's instead of our place.

"What are we doing here?" I asked as Sariah skipped out of the front door.

Skipped. As if the bitch hadn't just stood me up on our ill-fated shopping trip.

She opened the door to the car. "What is going on?" I demanded.

She only grinned wider at the irritation in my face. "Be revealed, soon, it will," she said in her best Yoda impression.

I rolled my eyes but let her pull me out of the car, knowing fighting Sariah was futile.

There was soft music playing in the house, and all of the Old Ladies were in the kitchen.

"What is going on?" I repeated.

All of the women smiled. Each of them was dressed to the nines, their hair and makeup done.

I recognized Marilyn, Freya's best friend, situated at the dining table, a plethora of beauty products laid out in front of her.

"Sit," Sariah demanded.

I frowned at her. "Not until you tell me what's going on."

Her eyes danced with happiness. That was how I noticed that my friend was all dolled up too. Her clothes were casual… as casual as Sariah got, that is. But her chocolate locks were wound in braids, flowers scattered through them. Her makeup was subtle, light pink blush glowing on her cheeks and long eyelashes that had to be fake but looked natural.

"You're getting married today, duh!"

That did not help. "I can't be married today," I snapped. "I don't have a dress."

"You have a best friend who should be getting her bachelor's degree in style and fashion instead of psychology," she shook her head. "What, you think I'd let you get a dress off the fucking rack from a department store?" She shuddered then pointed to the chair. "Sit your ass down. Let Marilyn make you more radiant. We will bring you non-alcoholic champagne, which I think should be illegal, but your over-the-top fiancé would likely scalp me or something if I dared to give you a sip of champagne, even the French stuff." She rolled her eyes. "And I really like my hair today, so…" She pointed to the chair.

I looked at the women then to my mother. "You knew about this?" I gaped at her.

She grinned. "Well, you knew about my surprise wedding, so it's only fair."

Shit. I had nothing to say to that.

Nor could I argue with Sariah, so I sat my ass in the chair.

"Sariah," I breathed.

"I know." She beamed.

"*Sariah,*" I repeated.

"I *know*!" She jumped up and down.

We were in my mother's closet.

I was wearing the wedding dress that she'd found me. Normally, even a best friend buying you your wedding dress would be out of the question. But I was the only person who had Sariah as a best friend.

And she was magic.

The dress fit me like a glove. I had no idea how, unless she'd measured me in my sleep or something, which I wouldn't put past her.

It was a light violet, so light that it was almost beige, but not quite. It somehow didn't wash me out and complimented my alabaster skin perfectly, which in and of itself was utter sorcery. The bodice was a 'v' that constrained my new boobs to perfection, off the shoulder sleeves displaying my collarbone and the necklace my mom had gotten me for my nineteenth birthday.

It had a silk lining and tulle that flowed down my body like butter. The sleeves themselves cascaded down the dress, flowing into the small train behind me. The fabric flowed over my bump like a waterfall, somehow not making me look like a cream puff but instead…

"A goddess," I whispered to myself.

Sariah stroked my hair. It was done similar to hers with intricate braids and wildflowers woven through it. "Took the words right out of my mouth," she whispered.

My makeup was light, blush high on my cheeks, neutral eyeshadow and lashes that made my eyes glow almost purple.

"Thank you," I told her, meeting her eyes in the mirror.

She was in her dress now. A burnt beige silk, also off the shoulder, it hugged her every curve and dipped way low at the back.

"Thank you for the dress. For choosing to be a part of that house share back in Providence. I don't know what I'd do if I hadn't met you," my voice broke.

"You sure as shit wouldn't look this good on your wedding day," she joked before wiping my tears away. "No crying," she murmured. "Marilyn will yell at us both."

I smiled weakly.

"You're my family, babe," Sariah said quietly. "It is me who would be fucking lost if I hadn't met you that day." She squeezed my hand. "I'm honored to stand beside you as you wed your biker." She winked. "Gives me more material for the novel I'll be writing about you all."

I laughed at my friend.

"Oh my god you're an angel!" my mother declared, walking into the room.

She was also wearing something Sariah had sourced. Hers was a deep purple, almost black, a striking contrast against her skin and the silk skimming over her curves.

"Well, I don't know about an angel since I don't think they get pregnant out of wedlock, but something close," I teased.

My mom's eyes glittered with tears.

"No crying!" Sariah demanded, her eyes suspiciously wet. "We need to keep ourselves perfect for the drive."

"The drive?" I questioned. "We're not having it here?" I'd assumed we were since this was the original venue for the wedding I knew about.

Sariah shook her head. "Fuck no, we aren't."

ELDEN

"You nervous?" Swiss asked.

We were watching the dust fly up from the approaching cars.

"No fuckin' way," I replied, keeping my eyes glued for my bride.

If you'd told me three years ago that I'd be standing there, with Swiss as my best man, waiting to marry the woman carrying my baby, I would've... Well, the cliché is overused, but it gets the point across.

I hadn't let myself imagine any kind of future where I was

happy. One where I was alive was the best it was going to get. I'd made my peace with that.

Until Violet.

"Happy for you," Swiss said in a voice that was no longer teasing. "Truly, there's no one I'd rather have for a son-in-law."

Hades, who was standing next to him, snorted out a chuckle. Fucking *Hades*.

"You're not gonna be starting with that shit." I punched him playfully in the arm.

Swiss's lips were spread in a wide grin. "Oh, yes, I am, *son*."

"Fuck, I might've preferred it when you wanted to kill me."

"Well, I'd love to stay here and chat, but I'm needed." Swiss squeezed my shoulder once more before jogging down the aisle to meet the cars.

As expected, the women got out first. Music was playing from somewhere. But everything fell away when she got out of the car, when Swiss took her by the arm and walked her down the aisle.

Violet.

The ground shifted underneath my feet. No one else moved or seemed alarmed so I knew that they didn't feel it. Like my whole fucking world had rocked upon seeing such a creature walk down the aisle toward me.

Mine.

That fucking angel was *mine.*

She glowed with happiness, tears shining in her eyes as she clutched on to Swiss. It was only through sheer force of will that I remained standing, that I didn't fall to my knees watching her walk toward me.

"She's beautiful, man," Hades leaned in to say into my ear.

Even Hades, the baddest motherfucker to walk the earth was affected. I noted that with detachment. All of my attention was on her, my fists at my sides, anxious to yank her out of Swiss's arms and into mine.

They stopped in front of us.

Violet was beaming. She was the fucking sun itself.

She leaned in to kiss her stepfather on the cheek before leaping into my arms.

She fucking leapt into my arms. It was only because she was my whole fucking world that I got my bearings enough to catch her, my arms tight, reveling in her warmth, in her scent, the feel of our daughter between us.

I lifted her up, content to hold her forever.

But I was also mindful of the fact that I wanted her as my wife. So slowly, I set her down on her feet.

"You're the most exquisite thing I've ever seen," I whispered.

She reached up to wipe the tears from my face. Ones I wasn't ashamed of in the fucking slightest. "You too," she whispered back.

Someone cleared his throat. My head turned to Hansen, and I realized we might've been standing there staring at each other for some time.

"Wanna get married now?" he asked with a grin.

My arms tightened around Violet, and I opened my mouth to speak, but she beat me to it.

"Fuck yes, we are."

There were chuckles all around at the most perfect woman to walk the earth cursing like that.

I kept hold of her while I made her mine forever.

CHAPTER
Twenty-Nine

VIOLET

I WAS NOT the girl who imagined her wedding in great detail. I had not given it a thought. No scrapbooks or Pinterest pages. None of my many fantasies included a wedding.

But if I had spent my life dreaming up my perfect day, it would've been today.

Somehow, Sariah had managed to erect an oasis in the desert on the land our home was being built on.

Complete with a huge, portable trailer that included bathrooms. Actual bathrooms.

Mismatched antique rugs formed the aisle, long benches on either side with lanterns and large vases of dried flowers flanking them.

To the right were long tables fully set up for what I guessed was our reception. One table with two comfortable armchairs that I assumed were for Elden and myself.

I took all of this in when I got out of the car, in absolute, complete shock.

Swiss's eyes were shining as he took my arm. "You look gorgeous, Violet," he said, voice thick with emotion.

I might've said something to him... I was sure I did, but my eyes found the arch at the end of the aisle. Or rather the man standing at the end of the aisle, wearing black slacks and a shirt underneath his cut. The man who I might've sprinted to if Swiss's arm hadn't been linked with mine. The man who looked at me like I was his everything. Who cried when he saw me walking toward him.

The ceremony passed in a blur. All I remembered, all that mattered was that Elden's hands were on me the entire time, and I said, "I do."

There were cheers all around, and to Sariah's dismay, no gunshots. There was incredible food. There was laughter and toasts, even my grandparents were here, surprising us with news of the vacation home they'd bought and were going to be at by the time I gave birth.

Elden's hand on my thigh during dinner moved higher and higher until it got to the point where it was either let him take me into the desert to fuck me—which I would've totally done—or take me home.

Elden, obviously slightly more sensible than me, took me home. The party in the desert was likely to rage on to the wee hours by the looks of it.

We said our goodbyes to our family, and barely made it home before ripping each other's clothes off.

My lovely wedding dress was in a pile by the front door.

I likely should've gone to retrieve it to hang it with the reverence it deserved. But I no longer had use of my limbs, and I was tangled up in my bed with my husband.

My fucking *husband.*

I was a *wife*.

Soon to be a *mother*.

Those thoughts no longer filled me with unease or dread. They wrapped around me, settled into a place deep inside.

We hadn't spoken in a long time. What else was there to say?

"Didn't believe in a higher power," Elden eventually murmured, cutting through the silence. "But I have to since all the sins I've committed, the lives I've taken and ruined… I still get you." He stroked my face. "It's impossible. But fuck, am I grateful for whatever it is that gave you to me. Every single year, every single minute I spent locked up, I'd do it over again in a heartbeat. So I could be right here."

My breath hitched when his hand landed on my belly.

"You have to stop saying things like that," I hiccupped. "There's only so much a pregnant woman can take in a day. Getting married to her impossibly hot baby daddy in an impossibly perfect scenario with all of her friends and family in addition to all those orgasms… I'm at my limit."

Elden chuckled and kissed my nose. "Well, hold on, baby, I'm about to take you to new limits." He then spread my legs, cupping me between them.

My eyes rolled to the back of my head, unsure if I could take anymore. But as it happened, I could.

You would've thought that was it.

That was our happily ever after.

The perfect dress. Perfect wedding. Perfect wedding night.

All wrapped up in a tidy bow.

But things didn't work that way.

They never did.

TWO WEEKS LATER

It was an accident that I happened upon them meeting.

I'd been shopping, and I wanted to show Kiera the cute outfit I got for the baby. Of course, I hadn't been shopping alone. There was still a serial killer on the loose, and I was due to have a baby soon, so I barely went to the bathroom alone. Freya and Hades had been with me, which itself was amusing. It should've been against some law of physics for a man like Hades to be in a baby store.

But he managed to cross the threshold. And he also had opinions on things. You could've knocked me over with a feather. His opinions were fucking spot on too. Then again, he had a super stylish wife and a baby girl, so some of it had obviously rubbed off on him.

They had come inside the club and gone straight to the room he kept there—since they had a babysitter, were no longer babysitting me and had been giving each other looks all afternoon—and I went to find Elden. His bike was there, so I knew he was. I also wanted to convince Elden to take me back to the cottage for an afternoon quickie.

Although it wouldn't take much convincing, and it definitely wouldn't be a quickie.

Elden tended to give me anything I wanted these days, and sex wasn't just something *I* wanted, it was most definitely something he wanted too. I worried that I was becoming unattractive to him with the swollen ankles, the stretch marks, veiny boobs and the huge belly. But no. If anything, our sex life had become more intense. Especially since the wedding.

Which, considering our sex life prior, was kind of insane.

My sex drive was almost out of control. Anything and everything turned me on. As expected, Elden had an opinion on that. He thought that I was dealing with my trauma by ignoring it and wanting to feel alive by having all the sex.

Which I had told him was a pretty healthy way of dealing with trauma since I wasn't on coke or anything.

He hadn't seemed that reassured.

He and everyone around me was worried. Waiting. For me to break down, I guessed. Which kind of made sense. I'd seen a dead body and been in a tousle with a serial killer. That kind of constituted a breakdown.

I was determined not to break down.

And apart from the nightmares, I was… okay. I was okay because Elden was there when I jerked awake from those nightmares. I was okay because our baby was healthy. Because I'd finished with classes. Because we had our little home. Because we'd broken ground on our house. Because Sariah was back and was even making noises about buying something instead of staying in her rental.

She was planning on building some kind of hotel spa just outside of town.

The Sons of Templar were the ones who killed all development and growth that haunted the town's borders so that it never turned into a capitalist nightmare.

They'd chased off billionaires, celebrities, all sorts of developers. But I knew they would be no match for Sariah.

Despite the business opportunities, the town's charm and its residents, I knew that Colby had a bit to do with her plans. Even though she wouldn't admit it. Even though they were at each other's throats whenever they were in the same room.

Especially because they were at each other's throats. Their chemistry was undeniable.

So yes, there were many things making me happy.

My due date was only a week away. It was incredibly odd for Elden to let me be without him since at my last checkup, the doctor said the baby was already in position, so I could go into labor any day now.

Granted, I was with Hades and Freya, and less than fifteen minutes away from him, but it was still unusual.

"How do we know he has her?" Elden's voice filtered from the open door across the common area.

I stopped in my tracks, redirecting my path, needles of dread pricking me upon hearing the tone of Elden's voice.

"We don't," Jagger sighed. "But we know that her car, along

with her purse and phone, was just sitting on the side of the road. Bitch does not go anywhere without her purse or phone."

All blood had drained from my body by the time I got to the door that had been left ajar.

"We have to tell Violet," Colby's strained, anxious voice filtered out.

"No way in fuck," Elden replied.

"She knows her better than anyone else," Jagger argued. "She may know something that could give us a chance. Give her a chance."

"We're not telling Violet shit," Elden barked. "Not until we know for sure."

"Too late," I informed him, pushing the door open, staring at the table full of very serious and worried looking bikers whose heads had all swiveled in my direction.

Rapidly, Elden stood, stalking toward me. I held up my hand to stop his approach.

Instead, I focused on Hansen at the head of the table. My flight attendant.

Except he did not look calm, in control. His features were tight. His hand was fisted on top of the table.

This was not just turbulence. The plane was going down.

I swayed on my feet.

There was a screech as a bunch of men prepared to come to my aid.

But naturally, Elden was much quicker than anyone else, his arms around me.

I scowled at him but needed his arms because I wasn't completely sure I wasn't going to fall over.

"What's going on?" I demanded.

"Why don't we get you to sit down?" Elden tried to guide me toward the nearest chair.

My eyes found his. "I don't want to sit down. I want someone to tell me what's going on."

"Sariah is missing," Hansen told me, his tone tight but controlled.

I forgot how to breathe. "Missing?"

He bobbed his head. "We can't be sure, but we think he took her."

He.

By *he* Hansen meant the killer who had been butchering young women and had almost killed me.

My brain struggled to process this information.

Elden's arms tightened around me.

"But this serial killer has a specific victim profile," I argued. "Sex workers from a troubled background. Sariah is a college student from a wealthy background."

Colby's face was a mask of fury. "No, she's not," he grumbled. I'd never seen him look so serious, so angry, so worried.

No, I had seen him look like that before. The day I'd escaped covered in blood with a knife protruding from my shoulder.

"What are you talking about? I go to college with her," I argued. "She is one of the most well-liked students on campus. By the faculty and students."

"Yeah, but she pays for her tuition, her fancy shit, her entire lifestyle by working webcams." Colby's voice was colder than I'd ever heard it.

Nothing of my easygoing, cheeky friend remained. This was a cold-blooded outlaw. A chill passed through me at the sight… along with what he had said.

I looked from him to Elden who was holding me in a vice-like grip.

"What?" I whispered.

Elden rubbed my arms. "We only just found out. We've got a hacker in the Amber charter who informed us."

I saw his lips moving and heard the words, but they were coming through a vacuum.

"And you found out that she, her parents…"

"They live in a small town in Utah," Elden said somberly. "They live paycheck to paycheck."

I gulped at the information.

"So, she makes her money, all of her money from her webcams," Colby said. "From what we can gather, she doesn't actually go on any dates with clients. But I doubt he's strict on that facet of his victim profile."

Victim profile

Sariah was a *victim*.

Again.

After she'd finally healed from the last time a man tried to make her into a victim because of what he thought he could take from her.

My breathing was rapid and shallow, my throat was bone dry, making it impossible to swallow. I squeezed my eyes shut through that and the burning pain at the base of my spine.

"You need to calm down," Elden murmured against my ear.

My jaw dropped. "Let's forget that saying that sentence to a woman, in any circumstance, is an act of war, let alone saying it to a pregnant woman," I informed him as evenly as I could muster. "But it is straight up insanity saying it to a pregnant woman whose best friend has just been taken by a *serial killer*!" Now I was screaming.

"And you are almost nine months pregnant," he hissed, obviously hanging on by a thread.

I should've given him some compassion since he was likely traveling back to the place where he thought I was going to die at the hands of this killer. But I was almost nine months pregnant, hormonal, and worried about my best friend who I had just discovered I didn't really know at all.

"Yes, Elden, I'm pregnant," I gripped my eyes between my thumb and forefinger. "Vikings fought while pregnant, women in countries that don't have maternity leave and don't have any other options work through labor. I think I can handle getting a little pissed off and worried."

Elden had finally released me, so I was now pacing up and down the long table that I'd never actually seen up close before. This room, referred to as 'church' was somewhat of a mystery to everyone who didn't wear a Sons of Templar cut.

It wasn't anything special. A long table with chairs arranged around it. No sigils to betray any kind of devil worship or witchcraft that might have been able to explain the sheer hot guy to normal guy ratio around here.

"What do we know?" I huffed out.

Elden was watching me with worry etched in his features, but I focused on the table, my eyes running over the men. Almost everyone was there except Hades who was in the back with Freya, Swiss who I knew was at home with Mom and Declan. And Javier —I had no clue where he was.

"We found her car less than an hour ago," Lucas offered, glancing to Elden who was staring daggers at him. "As we said, all of her shit was there." He paused, eyes darting to Elden again. "Sign of a struggle."

The world swayed again, and again, Elden's arms went around me. I didn't look at him, and I ignored the lance of pain at the base of my spine.

"What about the police?" I demanded.

Colby scoffed, his hands fisted in front of him. "Can't declare someone missing unless it's been twenty-four hours, fuckin' piece of shit sheriff's orders. Even though the fucker isn't even there." He slammed his fists down on the table.

I jumped at the violence.

"Local uniforms are loyal to us," Jagger spoke up, looking at me. "There's no love lost between them and the new sheriff." His mouth tightened. "They're doin' everything they can, but we've probably got more resources and manpower at this point.

I nodded, trying to fight against the panic constricting my throat.

"We're going to find her," Elden told me, moving me to face him, clutching my upper arms.

I looked into his eyes, the ones I trusted without question. But even my strong, brave, badass husband could not make promises like that.

But I just nodded again because there was nothing else to do. These men would do everything in their power to find her. I knew that. And Sariah would fight like a banshee. I knew that.

I also knew that even that might not be enough.

Elden's gaze scrambled around my face. "Baby, you sure you're okay? You're pale as fuck."

My spine burned. "Yes, considering what I just found out, I'm pale," I snapped back.

He scrutinized me for a moment longer, brows pinched, but he finally nodded.

"Swiss and your mom are on the way," Hansen announced, putting his phone down. "Got our best hacker on this, got all hands on deck here… we'll get her."

I clamped my teeth together against the pain, hoping that Elden would think I was just concerned.

"I think I need to… use the bathroom," I said, not entirely lying considering the pressure I felt in that general area.

Elden's eyes flared once more. "I'll come with you."

I tilted my head at him. "Thanks for the offer, but I think I can remember how to use the bathroom on my own." Although, if this baby stayed in much longer, I would be needing help getting up off the seat.

His brows stayed knitted, and the pressure on my arms remained for a few moments before he let me go.

I sagged in relief as he laid a firm closed-mouth kiss on my lips and let me walk to the bathroom.

Except I didn't go to the bathrooms directly off the common

room, though they were more convenient, and the walk down the hall almost killed me. I went to the bathroom in Elden's room—the bathroom that had various skincare and makeup products neatly lined up on the counter—and sat on the toilet where I let out a stifled moan as a contraction speared my womb in half.

Or at least that's what it felt like.

It took everything I had to get up, touch up the mascara that had smudged over my face from the tears I'd let out, and make myself somewhat presentable.

Elden was right... I did look a lot paler than normal, my eyes strained with discomfort.

I laid my hands on my considerable bump. "Not yet, baby girl," I whispered. "We have to get your aunt Sariah first."

As if she could hear me, my daughter stopped trying to claw her way out of my womb. For the moment, at least.

Long enough for me to walk into the bedroom and prepare myself to face Elden and his eagle eyes.

"Get it together," I whispered to myself. Sariah was going through God knew what right then. I could handle getting through a couple of contractions.

Just then, something wet trailed down my legs. It didn't come in a huge surge like in the movies, but it was enough to make it very clear that I was in labor.

"Fuck," I muttered, searching for a towel to hide the evidence.

Luckily, I had a decent supply of clothes in here for when we utilized the room.

A knock sounded on the open door. "Hey, Elden wanted me to come in to check on you since he's currently yelling at the sheriff, and—holy fuck!" Colby walked into the room, staring at me then staring at the small but not unnoticeable puddle on the floor.

"Your water just broke." He gaped at the ground and then me.

"No, it didn't," I hissed, looking at the door then rushing to shut it. It was uncomfortable and painful to move so quickly, but I managed it.

Colby looked from me to the floor. "I understand that pregnant women don't have complete control over their bladders, but I know you didn't just piss yourself." His expression sobered. "You've been in pain since the second you walked in. Now your water broke. I'm gonna tell Elden."

I clutched his wrist in a death grip. "You will do no such thing."

He winced. "Fuck, loosen up, Violet. I need this hand."

"You need to promise me you won't tell Elden or Swiss about this." I did not let go of his wrist or loosen the grip.

His eyes grew to saucers. "Let's forget for a second that they will both straight up kill me, and not figuratively, I mean bullet to the head if they knew I knew you were in labor without telling them," he said, voice tight with pain. "If we forget that, we'll just skip over to the fact that whether or not I tell them, eventually, you're gonna have to push a baby out, and they're gonna get hip to what's going on."

"First, labor lasts hours," I squeezed my eyes shut against the pain. "Maybe even longer than a day. But they aren't going to be thinking about that. They'll get themselves in a tizzy then focus on me." My voice shook. "I don't need any focus on me right now. I need all of their focus to go toward finding my best friend. I'm not having this baby until we do."

Colby gave me a strained smile. "Although you are definitely more versed than me in women's anatomy, I'm pretty sure that's not how it works. You don't get to choose when and where you give birth."

I narrowed my eyes on him. "I can if my best friend's life depends on it."

He just looked at me, obviously not convinced.

"I know she means a lot to you too," I whispered. "I know you're worried and scared. And I want you to channel that worry and fear into finding her," I ordered.

I watched Colby battle with his obvious concern about me, his alliance to Elden and Swiss, his friendship with me, and then his very real fears about Sariah's fate.

"Okay," he conceded, releasing a long exhale.

My entire body relaxed. Or at least it would've had a contraction not just threatened to break my spine.

"Can you let go of my hand now?" he asked. "I'm in a lot of pain."

"*You're* in a lot of pain?" I gaped at him. "*A girl* is holding your hand. I have a child preparing to exit my body, and my body is literally pushing her downward and splitting my hips in two to accommodate that," I hissed. "You're fine."

I gave his hand an extra squeeze before letting it go.

He shook it out, wincing as he did.

I rolled my eyes.

"Go," I shooed. "Go and exact vengeance or investigate or shake down informants while I change."

Colby lingered at the open door. "We're going to find her," he vowed.

My eyes watered. "I know."

Though, like when Elden promised me, I didn't fully believe it.

CHAPTER *Thirty*

I SHOULD'VE GOT A FUCKING medal or an Oscar for my performance over the next couple of hours. My contractions were still relatively far apart, and Colby kept looking my way with panic in his eyes every time I so much as breathed heavily. I had to glare at him to get him to look away. That little snitch did not have the stomach for this shit.

Luckily, the clubhouse was a hive of activity, and I was able to white knuckle my way through most of my contractions without anyone raising a brow. And every time Elden came close to me and looked too hard, I ordered him back to whatever he was doing to save my friend.

It worked every time except this time, when he refused to move, and my body tightened with an oncoming contraction. I struggled to find something else to distract him and my mother, who had been watching me much too closely too.

"Violet," Elden said, hand on my stomach. "You're going to tell me what's goin' on right now."

Shit.

"Javier's not here," I blurted.

His expression moved from concern to confusion.

"What?"

"Javier." I was struggling to speak clearly. "He's not here, and he hasn't been here since we found out Sariah disappeared."

There was a beat of silence over the whole room.

"Holy fuck," Colby muttered.

"He brands women," Elden said slowly.

I wrinkled my nose, thinking of the way that he'd come on to me countless times. He'd always given me the creeps, but I'd thought he was just strange.

"Fuck," Hansen grumbled, putting his phone to his ear. "Wire, I need you to do a deeper dive on Javier right now. Check into every fucking corner."

"He was right under our fucking nose," Lucas seethed.

There was a bunch of manly rage and mutterings after that. Even Elden jumped in, saying what, I didn't know. But it did not give me enough grace to fight my way through another contraction unnoticed.

I really fucking hoped they found him soon because I knew I didn't have time. *We* didn't have time.

"We still don't have shit on him," Hansen sighed, hanging up the phone and pinching the bridge of his nose. "Doesn't have any alternate property rented or owned, his fucking cellphone isn't pinging, and…"

He stopped speaking, staring at the door. Everyone else did too.

Javier waved at the group. "What'd I miss?"

"Where the fuck have you been?" Elden recovered first, standing from where he'd been sitting on the sofa next to me.

I had been forced to sit, even though it was uncomfortable, and walking made things feel less like I was giving birth to a hot poker.

Javier looked uncertainly at everyone who was glaring at him.

"Why is everyone staring at me like I'm a serial killer?" he joked.

"Surprisingly astute," Caroline commented, tilting her head to survey him.

"Where the fuck have you been?" Hansen demanded.

Javier's cheeks flushed. "I have brunch with my mom on Sundays," he shrugged. "Then we watch *Real Housewives*."

Everyone just stared at him.

"Why the fuck don't you have your phone on you?" Hansen asked.

"Mom makes me turn it off," Javier responded. He looked around the room again. "Seriously, what is going on? You guys are freaking me out."

"Killer took Sariah," Colby clipped out, folding his arms and glaring at Javier.

Javier, to his credit, looked sufficiently shocked. "Holy fuck," he muttered. "Do we have any idea who this fuck is?"

No one answered.

"Jesus fucking Christ," he muttered. Then he looked upward. "Sorry, Lord." He glared around the room again. "You seriously thought I was the serial killer? That blows, man."

"You brand women," Colby stated, obviously still not convinced.

Javier scratched at his five o'clock shadow. "Yeah, but as far as I know, in this club, having certain sexual proclivities doesn't mean you're a fucking serial killer," he hissed.

"He's got a good point," my mom muttered from beside me, looking at Swiss.

I would've been a mix between amused and grossed out if I wasn't battling with my body and silently yelling at my daughter for trying to rush out so soon.

There was no way I could remain seated. I needed to walk around. And Elden was still staring at Javier, so he couldn't stop me from moving. I not so subtly pushed myself off the sofa, waddling around it so I could pace.

Despite Elden's concentration, his eyes rushed in my direction the second I started moving.

"Dude, I'm not a serial killer!" Javier exclaimed, looking at Colby who was still glaring at him.

There might've been more of an interrogation and definitely an alpha stare off if I hadn't let out an involuntary groan of pain as I moved wrong, and my womb tried to kill me.

All eyes, unfortunately, went to me.

Javier looked relieved to have the attention off him. "I can't *believe* you thought I was a serial killer," he muttered to no one in particular.

Elden, of course, had rushed to me and was now holding me up. Although I was mad at his overprotectiveness, I was thankful for him stopping me from falling to the ground.

"Violet?" he demanded, his voice full of concern.

"I'm fine," I replied weakly, trying to smile.

Elden was not convinced by my smile.

"Oh, for fuck's sake. I can't take it anymore, and you are going to explode at this point," Colby yelled, pacing. "She's in labor," he told Elden, pointing at me.

Elden's eyes went wide.

"You're in labor?" Elden asked so quickly, it sounded like one jumbled word.

"Barely," I replied through a painful breath.

"What did Colby just say?" Swiss demanded, joining the huddle.

"Nothing," I said at the same time Elden yelled, "she's in fucking labor!"

"We have to get you to a hospital," Swiss said, eyes tinted with panic.

"I am not going anywhere," I declared firmly, standing my ground and glaring at both men.

"You fucking are if I have to drag you kicking and screaming," Elden refuted, already trying to move me toward the door.

I planted my feet and leveled my gaze on him. "I promise you, I will never forgive you for that," I told him. "I'm not bringing our child into a world where her godmother is being held captive by a serial killer. You can keep arguing with me, or you can make sure that does not happen."

"It's not as simple as just squeezing your legs together, hon," my mom said mollifyingly, joining the fray. "At some point, this baby is going to come whether you want it to or not."

"And by that point, Sariah will be here," I informed her.

"She's gone crazy," Swiss muttered.

"Get the club doctor here, right now," Elden called out to the room at large. It wasn't clear who exactly he was talking to because his eyes were on me.

He was very mad. And also very worried.

"I'm not going to let anything happen to her," I told him soothingly.

"You're not going to let anything happen to you either," he replied. "And I promise, Violet, if there is a chance, even a small fucking chance I could lose either of you, I will drag you to the hospital kicking and screaming. I will live with you bein' mad at me for the rest of time because you'll be alive to be mad. That's fine with me."

I nodded. Despite what my stepfather said, I wasn't insane. I would not put our daughter or myself in any undue danger.

But I was also determined. This baby could not come into a world that didn't include Sariah.

It just couldn't.

I had been relocated to Elden's room, which I was thankful for since the lovely doctor arrived and had indeed had her head all up in my vagina, and I didn't think the club at large needed to see that.

Elden was positioned with his back against the headboard, and I was leaning mostly on his body. He was holding my hand, not complaining no matter how hard I squeezed it, and generally looking like he was on the edge of freaking out.

My ever calm, ever controlled, port in the storm was close to freaking out. Then again, he wasn't in control of the situation. He was not a medical professional, and I'd refused to let him take me to the hospital. He could sit here and let me squeeze his hand… Essentially, he was helpless. Elden was not good at being helpless.

My mom was sitting in a chair next to me, wiping a cold towel on my face every now and then, giving me water and looking much calmer than all the males in the vicinity. I'd banned all the other men who weren't out following leads, so it was just Swiss pacing at the door, murmuring into his phone.

"I'm sorry," I said to Elden.

"What the fuck are you sorry for?"

"For making you worry and not making this easy." I gestured to the room.

Elden let out what sounded like a snort. "Newsflash, baby, never thought you bringing a baby into this world would be easy. Fuck, it kills me that it's hurtin' you so much."

"It's not that bad," I lied.

Elden stroked my forehead. "You're fuckin' amazin'," he murmured. "But we're going to the hospital in five minutes."

I pinched my lips closed to hold back the curse words dangling off the tip of my tongue. I wanted to argue with him, but I knew I couldn't. My contractions were close together now, the pressure getting more and more intense. Something instinctual inside of me told me it was almost time. Whether or not I wanted it to, a baby was coming into the world.

As I was thinking that, Swiss entered the room, his face grim.

My entire body tensed, and I squeezed Elden's hand tighter, bracing for his words.

"We have her," Swiss said, phone at his ear, looking at me.

I sagged against Elden. "And she's okay?"

He hummed in confirmation.

"Okay," I whispered, needing more information but unable to demand it at the moment. There were other pressing matters. "*Now* we can go to the hospital."

At that moment, a contraction hurtled through my body, and I panted through the pain, proud that I didn't scream at the top of my lungs.

"I don't think we'll make it to the hospital," Sarah, the doctor, informed us, replacing the sheet that was covering my modesty.

"What?" Elden gasped from behind me.

"I can make it," I protested, my voice pinched with pain. "I'll just… hold her in."

Sarah smiled with warmth, placing her hand on my thigh. "Unfortunately, it doesn't work that way. She's already crowning. I promise, you've done most of the hard work already. You can do this."

The room suddenly seemed much smaller, and my lungs were unable to produce air. "I can't have the baby here," I moaned. I looked up to Elden desperately. "I know I talked about doing a home birth, but that was under different circumstances. There was calming music playing, essential oils. I'd researched a tub you could get. And even then, I'd secretly known I wanted to go to the hospital," I babbled, impressed I was able to string all of those sentences together while I was in complete agony.

Elden, to his credit, did not look like he was barely holding it together anymore. He looked much more like my fully capable, utterly badass husband who could and would save me from anything.

"You can do this here and now." He squeezed my hand. "I'm here. I'm not going anywhere." He kissed my nose. "We're going to meet our daughter, baby."

I smiled at him, the thought of that cutting through the worst of the pain. For just a moment, at least.

"You can do this," he repeated.

I nodded, finding strength in his eyes, his presence, his firm body behind me.

"Okay, I can do this," I told Sarah confidently.

"Let's have a baby," she replied, smiling.

My mom squeezed my hand.

And things went well. For about five minutes. Then I realized why women did this in hospitals, where they gave you drugs. I really fucking needed drugs.

"I can't do it," I cried, shaking my head, tears streaming down my face, squeezing my eyes shut.

"Yes, you can," Elden replied calmly.

"I can't!" I screamed. "And if you were trying to push a human out of you, you wouldn't either." I stared into his infuriatingly captivating fucking eyes. "I cannot do this!" My eyes squeezed shut once more, and I let out a sound that was more animal than human.

"Bitch, you better fucking do this. If I just escaped that sick fuck, then you can give birth to a tiny baby."

My eyes snapped open and found Sariah. She was standing in the doorway, leaning heavily on Colby, and looked paler than I'd ever seen her, but she was alive.

"You're here," I rasped.

She smiled weakly. "It takes a lot more than a deranged serial killer to get me down. "Now please don't embarrass the cause by bitching out at this moment," she joked, clutching Colby's arm. "Let's have this baby."

I stared at my best friend. Then my mom, then... finally... my husband.

I found the strength.

Only five minutes later, Willow Sariah Donovan came into the world.

I cradled her against my chest, exhausted, overwhelmed and overcome. My eyes found Elden's. They were bursting with wonder as he delicately laid his lips on our daughter's head.

"Kiss me," he whispered. "I need to feel my whole world."

Epilogue

TWO YEARS LATER

ELDEN

I WOKE UP ALONE.

My eyes found the skylight directly above our bed, staring at the smattering of stars above me.

It was late, at least for us since we had a daughter who woke up ready to attack the world at exactly 5:30.

Though she was wild, willful, stubborn and extraordinary like her mother, she, like her father, liked structure. Order.

She also slept through the night, peacefully. So peacefully, Violet had ordered some fucking sock that monitored her breathing and heart rate. Which was a fucking waste of money since Violet had been up every hour on the hour checking to make sure she was still alive the first six months.

Violet was an amazing fucking mother. I thought I'd seen everything she was already, but seeing her with our child was something else.

I'd been right when I'd thought it would take a lifetime to know her entirely. She was patient. She handled the sleepless nights, the crying, the colic like she was made for it. I was in awe of her. She oversaw all of the construction on the house she designed for us.

The house she designed for me with vaulted ceilings, large archways and more windows than walls. Everything was open. Because she didn't want me to feel trapped. I knew there was no way to tell her that living in a home with my wife and daughter… I was never fucking trapped.

Though Violet no longer got up to check on Willow every hour, she was up for different reasons.

I threw back the covers, noting that Artemis's bed was empty too. She was always with Violet or Willow. She considered it her job to protect and adore them. She merely tolerated me because I fed her and took her on morning runs.

The doors off our bedroom were open, the balmy desert breeze moving the curtains.

Violet was standing at the edge of the patio wearing my tee, her perfect ass peeking out from underneath as she folded her arms.

Hunger sparked within me, seeing that alabaster skin in the moonlight. My wife had always been beautiful. Fucking perfect. But while she was in college, stewing on shit, suffering from her father's sins, her frame had shrunk. She hadn't been eating.

Even during the first months she was pregnant with Willow she barely gained a pound because she couldn't eat.

Now that she had all the curves her body was designed for, wearing evidence of creating our daughter, my need for her had grown fucking tenfold. I was like a horny fucking teenager whenever she was around, thankful that our daughter napped in the afternoon and slept through anything.

Artemis, the black lab that Violet had surprised me with for my birthday, was sitting beside her dutifully, scouring the desert too.

I didn't hesitate to slip my hand underneath the tee Violet was wearing, pulling her back to my front and cupping her perfect breast.

She let out a contented sigh, sinking into me.

I nuzzled her neck, inhaling the delicious scent that was my wife. That drove me crazy to this day and would until the day I died.

"You're getting too good at getting out of bed without me noticin'," I grumbled, annoyed at myself for not noticing my wife leave.

She leaned her head back against my shoulder. "I didn't want to wake you," she said. "You know that you're the one Willow wants in the morning anyway."

I grinned, thinking of it. Willow adored her mother with everything she was, but the mornings were ours. As soon as Violet stopped breastfeeding, I let her sleep, taking Willow with me into the kitchen, sitting there with her, sipping coffee and watching the sun rise. We'd go on long walks with Artemis in tow, dutifully protecting her sister because she didn't seem to trust me to do it.

The quiet. The desert. The sun rising. My daughter's warmth, smell, the noises she made in delight as she discovered something new about the world, they were like nothing on this earth. I hadn't known such peace existed. Especially when we got home to my wife either wearing my tee or a nightgown, holding two coffees, smiling sleepily at us.

"Don't give a fuck," I told Violet. "You're not getting up, shakin' off nightmares, standing here in the middle of the night alone." I tweaked her nipple, and she let out a moan I felt in my dick.

The need to take her was almost impossible to control.

Almost.

"She's gone again," Violet whispered.

I moved my hands down her sides, slowly turning her to face me. "She'll come back. She always does."

Violet let out a long sigh. "I'm worried about her."

Everyone was worried about Sariah.

She had survived what most people wouldn't at the hands of that piece of shit.

The fucking sheriff.

Yeah, no one had been expecting that.

No one had thought he'd be smart enough to bury his fucking craziness down that deep. Separate it so completely from his outward persona.

It was Ollie, Violet and Sariah's old roommate, who had found it out. Figured out a twisted and well buried trail that led to what he was.

A fucked-up piece of shit with an equally fucked-up past.

His mother had been a club girl.

Long fucking ago.

Attached to a different club, not the Sons. One that didn't treat women with respect. One that used them up whenever and however they wanted until they were done with them then threw them away like trash.

Apparently, the young sheriff had been old enough to remember that. Remember the cigarette burns in his dear mother's skin. Her bruises, her broken bones. The drug habit that they hooked her on.

Little Elijah—or Beau was his birth name—acquired a healthy hatred for motorcycle clubs in general and toward 'loose women' who reminded him of the mother he loved and hated in equal measures.

He had been watching the club for some time, had been making plans.

He told us all of this after we caught him. He stayed alive for a good long while, each of us taking our time with him.

Our new sheriff, one of his former deputies, was a local and more than willing to work with us and declare the perpetrator as 'missing.'

We caused him pain. Made him bleed. Made him wish he was

dead long before we killed him. But that wouldn't heal anything. Wouldn't change shit.

Sariah, to her credit, was one tough bitch. She shouldn't have even been able to stand when she was there for the birth of our daughter. The fuck had cut her up good. She was bleeding out, standing there. Had done it quietly, without a fucking word while Violet gave birth.

She'd almost fucking died in the hospital. Something she forbade every single patch to tell Violet. Something everyone had agreed to do because they didn't want to face her wrath.

She wouldn't tell anyone, not even Violet, what he did to her in those hours he had her. But whatever that sick fuck did was enough to cause damage. Damage that birthed a darkness in her that hadn't been there before.

I knew she and Violet had spoken about what Sariah'd kept from her. Knew that Violet didn't give a fuck about how her best friend got her money; all she cared about was that her best friend was breathing.

She moved to Garnett permanently. Colby barely left her side. At first, she fought it. Then she did her best to ignore him. She was there for Willow. For my wife.

Until she wasn't.

Until one day she left with a note and a promise she'd be back.

No one knew where she went, and not for lack of trying. The bitch was fucking smart and evaded even Wire. I suspected she had help from her hacker friend.

Wanted to be mad at her for putting my wife through all of this worry, but I couldn't. Not with the devil she had on her heels.

"She's gonna come back," I repeated, clutching Violet's neck, looking into her troubled eyes. "As much as I know you want to do something for her, you can't, baby," I said as softly as I could. "She's tough. Toughest person I know. Including every man who wears a patch."

That was not a fucking lie. The club would agree with me on that one.

"She's runnin' from shit. Maybe chasin' shit," I continued, stroking her bottom lip. "But she's not alone. Not with Colby making it his mission to tear this country apart looking for her."

Violet smiled weakly. Colby had a one-track mind when it came to Sariah. No matter what she did or said to push him away, he stayed fast.

"We've got another Sons of Templar courtship on our hands," she muttered.

"This one is likely to be the most explosive of them all," I replied, laying my lips against hers. "We can't do anything now," I murmured, reveling in the taste of her. "But we do have about two hours before our daughter wakes up. I'm thinking I'm gonna bend you over the patio furniture so you scream into the desert."

Violet's dazzling eyes flared with desire, her body stiffening with need.

Artemis seemed to sense things were changing, and she trotted back into the bedroom.

I grinned, taking my wife by the hips and lifting my tee to expose her bare, sexy ass.

She opened for me, submitted to me, and eventually, screamed for me.

Hours later, I left her sleeping soundly in bed and found Artemis sitting by Willow's door, waiting for us to begin our day.

Not for the first time, I thanked fucking whatever controlled this world that I kissed Violet on that rooftop all those years ago.

Then I opened the door, my daughter already standing in her crib, staring at me with her mother's eyes, showing me my whole fucking world. Showing me that even villains got a happy ever after.

Acknowledgments

I was so so overwhelmed with the response I got for Wretched Love. Seriously. It made my heart so very happy. I have been having the best time writing this 'new' series, introducing you to new characters while keeping our old friends in the picture.

Everyone has been waiting for this book. I got messages daily asking about Violet & Elden … and I LOVED it. It means so much you were all so invested in their story. I was so invested in their story. I thought about them day and night, constantly.

This book has been a labor of love. I've never spent so much time combing through a book, going back, reworking, tweaking, changing things as I have this one. I wanted it to be absolutely perfect.

I wanted to do Violet and Elden justice.

And not to toot my own horn, but I think I might've done that. But it took a long time. Hours and hours on the computer. A couple of mini breakdowns. Tears. Coffee. Wine. Chocolate. Sleepless nights.

And it was all worth it.

I would not have done it without the people around me. This list is long, and could honestly be MUCH longer. I'm that lucky.

Taylor. My husband. The man who comes home with flowers, with treats, who treats me gently and kindly when I'm slowly unraveling. My biggest cheerleader. My best friend. My soul mate. I'm endlessly glad fate brought me to you.

Mum. You always pick up the phone. You listen to me cry, vent and talk a million miles a minute after many, many coffees. You tell me to buy the purse. You were the one who introduced me to reading. Who told me I could be whoever or whatever I wanted.

Dad. You're not here to read this but so much of who I am is thanks to you. My expensive taste comes from you. My stubborness. You taught me to do everything a man could do and to do it better. I love you. Not a day goes by that I don't miss you.

Jessica Gadziala. Yet another beautiful soul who gives me advice, who lets me vent, who gives me a safe space. You are supremely talented and a wonderful friend and author.

Amo Jones. My ride or die. I love you endlessly. We are soul sisters.

Cat Imb. Your light is so bright, your heart is so big and your talent is endless. Thank you for creating covers that make me want to write a book worthy of them. Thank you for being my friend. I adore you.

Annette. You handle my crazy always. I would be so fricking lost without you. I'm so grateful to have you as my friend.

Kim. Yet another badass woman who handles my crazy. Who edits these words tirelessly and is so dedicated to make this story the best it can be. Thank you for all of your hard work.

Ginny. Thank you so much for always being there. For loving my characters as much as I do. For telling me what I need to hear. You are the best.

My girls. Harriet, Polly & Emma. You're half a world away but distance means nothing. You've all gotten me through some of the hardest times of my life and I'm so so lucky to have you as friends, as sisters.

And last but not least, **you, the reader**. Without you, dear reader, I would not be here. I would not be creating stories as a job. Thank you for making my dreams come true.

About the Author

ANNE MALCOM has been an avid reader since before she can remember, her mother responsible for her love of reading. It started with magical journeys into the world of Hogwarts and Middle Earth, then as she grew up her reading tastes grew with her. Her love of reading doesn't discriminate, she reads across many genres. She can't get enough romance, especially when some possessive alpha males throw their weight around.

One day, in a reading slump, Cade and Gwen's story came to her and started taking up space in her head until she put their story into words. Now that she has started, it doesn't look like she's going to stop anytime soon, with many more characters demanding their story be told as well.

Raised in small town New Zealand, Anne had a truly special childhood, growing up in one of the most beautiful countries in the world. She has backpacked across Europe, ridden camels in the Sahara and eaten her way through Italy, loving every moment.

Now, she's living her own happy ever after in the USA with her brilliant husband and their two dogs.

Want to get in touch with Anne? She loves to hear from her readers.

You can email her: annemalcomauthor@hotmail.com

Or join her reader group on Facebook.

Also by Anne Malcom

THE SONS OF TEMPLAR

Making the Cut

Firestorm

Outside the Lines (Hansen & Macy)

Out of the Ashes

Beyond the Horizon

Dauntless

Battles of the Broken

Hollow Hearts

Deadline to Damnation (Jagger & Caroline)

Scars of Yesterday

Three Kinds of Trouble (Hades & Freya)

UNQUIET MIND

Echoes of Silence

Skeletons of Us

Broken Shelves

Mistake's Melody

Censored Soul

GREENSTONE SECURITY

Still Waters

Shield

The Problem With Peace

Chaos Remains

Resonance of Stars

THE VEIN CHRONICLES

Fatal Harmony

Deathless

Faults in Fate

Eternity's Awakening

Buried Destiny

RETIRED SINNERS

Splinters of You

THE KLUTCH DUET

Lies That Sinners Tell

Truths That Saints Believe

STANDALONES

Birds of Paradise

Doyenne

Midnight Sommelier

Hush - co-written

What Grows Dies Here

A Thousand Cuts

Printed in Great Britain
by Amazon

86972605R00253